AF255984

DIVISION

SOUL SEER CHRONICLES, BOOK 3

S.J. CAIRNS

Black Thumb
Publishing

Copyright © 2023 by S.J. Cairns

All rights reserved. No part of this book may be reproduced in any form on by an electric or mechanical means, including information storage and retrieval systems, without permission in writing from the publisher, except by a reviewer who may quote brief passages in a review.

This is a work of fiction. Names, characters, places, and incidents either are the product of the author's imagination or are used fictitiously. Any resemblance to actual persons, living or dead, events, or locales is entirely coincidental.

Cover design by Getcovers
Logo created by S.J. Cairns
Logo image by CNuisin depositphotos.com ID 265803116
Tree vector by clairev depositphotos.com ID 3040518

ISBN 978-1-7782426-6-3 (Ebook)
ISBN 978-1-7782426-7-0 (Paperback)
ISBN 978-1-7782426-8-7 (Hardcover)

Previous editions printed 2018

Black Thumb Publishing
Ontario, Canada
www.sjcairns.com

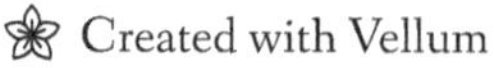 Created with Vellum

ACKNOWLEDGMENTS

This series has been many years in the making. Along the way, I learned more than I could digest and more than I could share with others. If you're reading this, understand I have had a small army of loyal supporters who gave an appropriate kick to the arse when needed, kept all egos in check, reminded me I have passion and talent when confidence was in low supply, and were a digital shoulder to lean on when life gave a sucker punch that drained my will to get behind a keyboard. My writing group—The Quillies—bursts with love and understanding for the trials accompanying an undertaking such as writing a novel. Thank you for refusing to let your support end on the page.

For my readers, you've stuck it out so far, thank you for taking on Sophie's journey. I hope not to disappoint.

To Mom

For being the one to instill a love of reading, for lending me books even when you didn't know it, and for being the first one to read, review, and edit my words when they were still embarrassing and unfit for human consumption. My passion for words would never exist without you. For giving me life and giving me purpose, I owe you a debt I could never repay.

1

RESTORED

Mesmerized by the restored Ballard Family Estate, I stood in the threshold. High, molded ceilings with an opulent chandelier throwing confetti-coloured sunbeams down onto sturdy furniture, wallpapered walls, and dark wood flooring. The estate greeted me with its ancestral power, blooming in my chest like an over-exuberant hug. Contentment rolled through my limbs. My great-aunt Olive's home was hers again and, one day, may be passed to me.

"Move your ass, lass. This bitch is heavy!" Serena shouldered me out of the way and dropped a floral suitcase inside the entrance. I murmured a reflexive apology to my cousin, which went ignored as she grabbed a smaller bag from Olive.

After spending decades in the mental institution—now The Royal City Wellness Centre—as well as a short time in my shitty apartment, Olive was moving back in and set to resume her place as heir of the Ballard Family Estate. My great-aunt stopped inside the threshold with a sigh, placing a hand on her chest. The power-laden welcome brought a sheen of emotion to the woman's dark eyes.

She squeezed my arm and smiled. "Let's bring everything upstairs. Leave Joshua on the table, Firefly."

I was growing used to my new nickname, even without an explanation of where it came from. Remembering that "Joshua" was the potted ivy clutched to my chest took more of a memory stretch.

With another suitcase and stack of hatboxes in the hands of my boyfriend, Caine, and dutiful best friend, Kim, we all followed Olive up the wide staircase to her room. I left Joshua next to a picture of a smiling young woman with short curls waving in the wind of a sunny day, knowing Olive would move him somewhere with better light.

Left and to the end of the hall was the master bedroom. I set Olive's stuff down with a thud as I wheezed a little from the trek upstairs. I hopped up onto the high bed and collapsed onto a freshly laundered duvet, surrounded in the light scent of freesia. Tracing the angelic cherub and devilish counterpart governing the top corners, I remembered the first time I saw the hand-carved piece. A scramble of conflict, Olive had called it. The scene seamlessly intertwined both the whimsical and barbaric elements of a carefree time when Magics frolicked in the trees and the Witchburners tortured innocent families.

A young couple was alone amongst the trees, oblivious to the horrors unfolding close by. They reminded me of a past life version of Donovan and I in a faraway time that somehow felt too close.

Light pressure touched my back. I pulled away from the headboard and the memories it evoked. Caine removed his hand from my back, his smile disappearing in response to whatever my face portrayed. I wasn't about to explain what monopolized my thoughts. I strived for honesty, so we faced this any time something about Donovan grazed my mind. Since Donovan was in our Coven and shared my past life, one he saw whenever he touched me, it happened too often. My guilt became a hippo-sized jerkface, laughing at Caine, as I wouldn't talk about him unless I had to. Caine always knew when the guy was on my mind.

"When are Lewis and Priscilla coming by?" Asking Olive was the only distraction I could think of. It was lame and the hitch in Caine's eyebrow told me he saw through it.

"Soon." Olive looked around at her stuff as if unsure of where to start and then gave up. "Re-establishing the Ballard Family Coven is goal number one. It's about time we put the Ballards back in power."

"Hell yeah, sister!" Serena held a hand high. Olive looked at it a moment before giving a hearty high five. "And—" Serena pointed at me "—I'm gonna be in it! I don't care what anyone says. If Kim can be all glowy with her Kitchen Witch powers, then I'll get there too."

"Hell yeah, sister!" Kim parroted Serena, catching a high five over my head from Serena.

"You'll get no argument from me. Give me a moment and then we'll head up to the attic to work on that." Olive disappeared into the en-suite bathroom and Kim and Serena chatted about being a Kitchen Witch. Serena had many questions Kim was always intent on answering in full.

Caine positioned himself between me and the others, looking down at my face. "You okay?"

"Winded worse than a two-pack-a-day smoker, but I'm good."

He nodded once, his grey eyes narrowed.

"Onward and upward, my lovelies!" Olive burst back into the room and headed into the hall.

I took the opportunity to escape Caine's assessing gaze, both of us following my great-aunt to the attic access door.

At Olive's request, Caine opened the only door that didn't require a turn of the knob. He pulled out the top corners of the doorframe attached to a steel rod embedded in the wall, twisting each clockwise, and then pushed them back in. After a barrage of loud clicks and clanks, the door slid into the wall pocket, stopped by the decorative doorknob against the jamb.

Olive pushed in the button on the old light switch in the green-washed room and sat behind the 1860's sewing machine. She spun the wood-covered metal handle in different directions like a combination lock until the shelving unit popped away from the wall to reveal a wrought iron staircase leading up to the attic—our place of solitude.

The first time I entered this room, my brain threatened to check out. The room spans the length of the entire building and contains tree-trunk thick rafters overhead a space stocked with magical items for most anything ever needed. The welcoming sensation from the estate doused the rush of suffocating heat, saving me the embarrassment of fainting and bouncing my skull off the plank wood floors.

Olive put a record on the Victrola. Soothing music filled the attic, projected from the large gold horn. She then sat at the beaten desk to work on her "contribution to the lineage" by creating a catalogue of all the items within the attic.

Serena was drawn to the amulets and stones—all similar to the white gold sapphire ring I bought her in Diluculo. Not only had the ring itself been beautiful and unique, but Serena was ecstatic she could say it was bought in a one-of-a-kind place. Of course, she couldn't tell anyone about the Creation where I got it—since Diluculo was a Magic-made world on the other side of the veil used to celebrate the use of our power in peace—but the secret made the ring worth bragging about.

Attracted to less flash, Kim had her nose in reference books. I wasn't sure what Caine was doing but caught him watching me as I looked at vials of random ingredients I had no use for. Acting casual so he would find something else to focus on was difficult and made things more awkward.

In the two weeks since Aunt Lacey and the Elders' gruesome murders, Caine and I interacted at a distance. I didn't think it was all on me. He killed his father in the same battle. That's enough to mind-fuck anyone, but he seemed more concerned with me than himself. I understood his brand of avoidance but watching from a distance was still watching. I needed him to give me more than physical space, but I didn't have it in me to insist on it.

I realized I was holding a nude, tarnished brass fertility statue, and quickly shelved it and went to talk to Olive to escape my own thoughts.

"Take a look-see, Firefly." Olive flipped pages to the beginning of a large tome and then spun it my way. "Here." She pointed at a page and slid over loose paper and a pen. "Copy and memorize." The yellowed page was titled "Soul Colours" and beneath was a list of colours with meanings next to them.

"You know what the colours mean?" My tone sounded accusatory. I suppose it was.

Olive nodded and leaned forward in her seat. "Someone got the genius idea to categorize abilities with the emanating colours of Magics." She pointed down the page. "Caine's blue colouring marks him as a Controller—Magics responsible for controlling the actions of others as with his Persuasion ability. Effective and useful once mastered."

Scary was another way to describe it, but I trusted him not to use it on me without reason. "How come you never showed me this?"

Olive switched the thick black record to another female singer whose voice was softer than the last. "You've been distracted since your return, Firefly."

A gentle way to say she knew I was on the brink of losing my shit. Apparently, I wasn't as good at hiding fragile emotions as I used to be.

She held my hand, making it worse. "The world will mourn Elsa's loss longer than she lived." The heartfelt comment spoke of another name Aunt Lacey went by, forcing me to nod and seek more evasive tactics.

"What colour are we?" I was curious since Soul Seers can't see their own soul glow.

Olive gave me a small smile. "Green." She pointed at the upside-down word on the discoloured page. "All us Seers are." The tome also listed Psychics and any others that see in any form in the same category.

Light footsteps came from the metal staircase. Olive wasn't alarmed. She focused on the papers in front of her as Uncle Lewis and Aunt Priscilla entered the attic. Lewis had an underlying hint of Seer green beneath the bright white of his soul glow. Both meant so much more now that I knew the meaning behind what I was looking at.

"Hello everyone!" Lewis bellowed.

Priscilla's greeting was less exuberant but high-pitched. She had her perm reset, this time the curls looser, shaving five years off her age.

Everyone exchanged hellos, all formally introduced at the recent family reunion, then returned to whatever originally captured their interest.

I caught a glimpse of Caine on a wooden chair, elbows on his knees, dark hair falling in his face, reading a book. He welcomed the new guests without a speck of happiness in his grey eyes. I was the cause but couldn't find it in me to comfort him.

"Whatcha doing, Sophie?" Lewis clasped a heavy hand on my shoulder.

I forced a smile. "Learning about soul colours."

Lewis peered at the old pages. "Well, close the brothel doors." He took the tome as Priscilla made her way around the desk. "Would've been nice to have a manual when I was starting out." He chuckled. "I had to figure them out as I went."

Olive put down her pen. "Why didn't you look for yourself? It's been here all along."

"You forget how I was back then, sis." He handed the tome back to me and fixed his black dress pants being pulled down by his stomach. "I loved the power, but studying?" His expression twisted. "Damn near killed me to sit and read. Once I found out about the power, I wanted to learn it all by experiencing it firsthand. Bucking tradition and figuring out the magical world by trial and error." He laughed again. "Of course, a colour scheme would've given me a heads up on picking a fight or walking away. Plus, no one was allowed here. I didn't need Elizabeth breathing down my neck. No one wanted her as an enemy after what she did to you."

Olive exhaled and shook her head.

The thought of Lewis physically fighting anyone was beyond ridiculous until the family reunion. He was more the tongue-whipped debate kind of fighter. Though, there were a lot of years between now and my doughy great-uncle's youth. Without the Ballard Coven, I imagined many things changed for him when Olive was institutionalized. Especially when dealing with my grandmother.

"Uh, Priscilla dear? Do you want to get the food trays? I'm sure everyone could use some lunch."

"Of course, darling, I know I'm hungry." She turned. "Kim, would you mind assisting me with the punch?"

"Sure," Kim answered with a clenched smile, looking to me in question.

I returned Kim's smile and then looked at Lewis and Priscilla. Something about the exchange sounded rehearsed.

"Caine?" Priscilla used the same tone to call him and I understood what this was. "I'm afraid I'll need some strong arms to carry the trays while I get the glasses."

He tossed the book onto the chair and followed, giving a last sweep of his sharp grey eyes in my direction before the three of them disappeared down the staircase.

I stopped Lewis before he could speak. "Next time, ask for some family privacy. They'd understand."

"I don't know what you mean."

"Really?" Serena's sarcasm was thick. "You should get into acting."

"I'll keep that in mind." He clasped his hands in front of him. "While we happen to be alone—"

"Oh, brother." Olive shook her head.

Lewis continued as if oblivious. "I assume, Serena, you are serious about joining the family coven."

"No need to question my commitment, big guy."

"Perfect. The four of us, plus Priscilla, now officially make up constituents of the new Ballard Family Coven." His cheeks reddened with his excitement as Serena bopped on the balls of her feet in her flip-flops, hands fisted as if she might thrust them into the air in a *Breakfast Club*-style celebration.

"What about Caine?" Lewis rose his eyebrows in question.

"To join? Oh, umm."

"No?"

"No. I mean....he probably would." I squirmed beneath their stares.

They knew nothing about our complex situation, but no way was I repeating the fact I couldn't have sex with my boyfriend because my past life lover would feel it. The thought of the restriction made my thighs clench. And the sex problem only nuzzled the nipple of greater issues. An emotional, and now physical, connection bound me to Donovan and clouded everything since entering Diluculo a couple of weeks ago. I second-guessed every evoked feeling every moment of every day and it was sinking me in a constant emotionless void as I attempted to appease both Donovan and Caine. Not hard to see all three of us were losing out.

"Bet you're glad I got 'em to leave." Lewis joked. But I was and responded with a side-eyed glare of gratitude.

"What now?" Serena interrupted Lewis's laughter.

He shifted his weight, chuckling harder at Serena's enthusiasm, while Olive answered. "I guess we should discuss recruitment strategies. How and who."

I raised a finger. "Gloria and Iris were members back in the day."

Lewis clucked his tongue. "I spoke with Gloria. She's unwilling to join."

"Really?" Olive crossed her arms.

Lewis nodded. "Thinks she's too old for a young woman's power."

"And Iris?" Serena sat on the edge of the desk.

"Didn't think asking was worth my time. They're a package deal, those sisters."

We went over a short list of hopefuls, ones with soul glows at the family reunion. No one had an issue with the prospects until I suggested Mason, my eight-year-old cousin. "He's young but already glows brighter than most."

"I'd want to know." Serena's tone held a hint of anger. "We should have known."

Olive put her hand on Serena's shoulder. "None of us should be born into our world Blind, yet we are. We cannot recruit Mason without his parents' approval. Dwayne also holds magic, as he glows a reasonable amount. As he's Mason's father, he will be approached first."

Minus Mason, we were on the same page. While we discussed the possibility of calling a meeting with the hopefuls and dealing with them all at once, including demonstrations to back up our claims, Priscilla, Caine, and Kim re-entered the attic. Priscilla conversed loudly and walked with unneeded force as her sandaled heels slapped the iron steps to announce their presence.

"I don't care about being on catering duty so you guys can hammer out Coven details—" Caine held out a tray "—but the plastic is cutting my arms."

Serena laughed, though Caine didn't.

We cleared the desk so he could put them down. Another smaller one fit the rest of a lunch I tasted but wasn't hungry for.

The sounds of laughter filled the attic late into the night. Serena chucked objects around the room for Caine to catch. Not with his hands. This task was a test of his telekinetic prowess. The noise of their excitement grew when Caine managed to succeed in catching possible priceless items mid-flight or apologies when he failed. My nose was in the pages of the Ballard Family Tome. I wanted to cram everything I could into my brain, especially intrigued by the origin story of the Ballard family's power.

A woman stumbled onto an incapacitated man in a wheat field near her home. While she attempted to care for his wounds, she watched them slowly heal on their own as he lay unconscious. She was astonished and afraid of what he might be but stayed to watch over him.

Another man materialized in the field, appearing from nothing, maintaining his role as a friend of the fallen man. She saw past his gentlemanly manner to the lie in his words and distrusted his intentions. She placed her body between the fallen man and this new man as he tried to sway her protests. She held strong and stubborn. The injured man awoke and killed the new man in a swift motion without leaving his position behind her. He thanked her for her courage, revealed himself as a Sorcerer, and offered a fitting reward for her bravery by turning her intuition into the physical ability to see what lay in the heart of her enemies.

While helping her adjust to his gift, they fell in love. A chance meeting changed the future of an entire family.

The family took such a loving and prideful gift and traded it for selfishness and revenge. What a fucking embarrassment.

Maybe the story was a bunch of bull. Why take the time to document the story itself, but leave out the juicy details like the names of the woman and the Sorcerer? No mention of the time period, town, or country either, though it was a long time ago, even before it was written down, judging by the discoloured pages and fading ink. All the same, I thought it an interesting concept for a Magic to give another power without it coming from blood or practice or gifted to a new Elder like I had been told.

After absorbing the story, I found myself suspicious it was written by some crackpot relative with a romantic imagination. While interesting, I had other things I needed to learn—things that could help me now, which certainly didn't include a possible ancestor or her possible Magic husband. I wasn't much for romance these days and focused on copying the soul colours and corresponding abilities to add them to the grimoire Kim bought me as an Initiation gift. If I wanted to be useful with more than an accidental discharge of power, then I needed to study this shit with as much vigour as I did for my psychology degree. Which has received zero attention in the past two weeks. Concentration was clearly in short supply.

Pushing aside my potential academic failure and shutting down depressing thoughts from two weeks ago, I looked up to see Priscilla, Olive, and Lewis bent over a stack of papers. But it was the former who caught my eye. I noticed the earthy, brownish tone that glowed beneath her lightened soul. I didn't realize her glow was more than the everyday, positive ability as the colour was so muted.

"What do you read?" I interrupted them in mid-conversation. "Your soul colour. This lists you as a Reader. So, what do you read?"

Lewis gave a hearty laugh and tugged on his wife's sleeve. "I told her she had a unique gift, but she always claimed I was exaggerating." He drew out the word.

"And?" I fought against my impatience.

Priscilla mussed with her curls and rolled her eyes at her husband. "I know you told me, dear." She made a guarded smile. "Understand, Sophie—" she paused, "—I've always known what people want."

"What they want?"

She nodded. "Though, if you know people, you can gather the same assumptions, gift or not."

Lewis leaned toward his wife. "Except yours are never assumptions."

"Debatable." Priscilla waved him off. "I get a sense of what people want or need or even crave, only in that moment." She shrugged as if it were no big deal.

"Do you find it useful?" Olive asked.

"It came in handy when the kids were babies. I didn't have to guess if they were hungry or wanted to be held. I knew. As far as other people are concerned, just because I can tell what they want, I have no obligation to do anything about it. Dating as a teen was a hard lesson."

I had a fleeting moment of "ewww" and disguised this discomfort by retreating back to the tome. I was just too enthralled with learning something useful to remember to exercise my manners.

"I know you want answers, Firefly." Priscilla squeezed my forearm to gain my attention. "I don't mean to pry, but like yourself, it's not something I can turn on and off at my leisure and you're exuding such a deep need for answers. You already have some and they're drowning you in pain you think you can train yourself to forget."

I looked away to hide the impact while Priscilla perched on the edge of the desk in front of me.

"Knowing how answers would set your world straight, I want nothing more than to help you. To guide you through the journey in finding what you seek, but this journey isn't for me. Frankly, I don't envy your struggle."

Now I couldn't look anywhere but at Priscilla. I wanted her to stop talking while also wanting to know everything.

"You have so much to gain, Sophie. Know whatever choice you do make will come from a place of rationale that will find its niche in your heart." She patted my hand. "You have time, Firefly. Don't be so quick to make those choices or let others rush your hand. You're a young Witch. A Seedling that already shoulders too much burden. This can wait until things get straightened out."

I was taken aback. Most of what she said could have been learned by way of rumour, but again, not everyone knew my story. But the way it was delivered, the way Priscilla spoke the words seemed to touch on every jagged edge of my frayed nerves. She knew.

I felt pressure in my eyes and blinked a few times.

She had no solutions, no quick fix, no predictions, yet provided a sense of validation for me. Priscilla effectively muzzled me and then left me to sit in a fog of my thoughts until brushing them off like cookie crumbs was the only way to save face. Melting down in front of everyone wasn't an option, so I went back to the tome and read the family origin story again until the tension in my throat let go.

———

Olive was ecstatic to spend her first night alone in the estate, saying she felt safer within those walls than anywhere else her entire life, bar none. The strength of long-dead family members infused within every nook and cranny would watch over her and be all the protection she required. We weren't about to argue, but I couldn't tell if she spoke literally or figuratively.

As soon as I stepped a toe out of the estate, the sensation I had felt in my chest before disappeared. Not that it had been at its strongest the whole time, but I was aware of it, and its retreat was a devastating loss I had to force myself to walk away from. Olive was right. She was safe.

———

Caine drove the Infiniti down moonlight-bathed back roads on our way to St. Catharines. I watched as trees passed the window too slowly, then peeked at his speedometer. Fifty kilometers per hour—on the nose.

"You in a hurry?" Caine deadpanned.

"You channelling a granny with a gas pedal phobia?"

"Maybe." His gaze held straight out the windshield, hair falling into his grey eyes as the dashboard light dimly illuminated his strong features.

I sighed. "You don't want to go home."

"Naaaah. I love sleeping in a big, empty apartment. Sounds like a party to me."

No matter how clear the initial parameters were, we ended up here. Caine never wanted to leave my side—never wanted to be alone with himself more like—but although I enjoyed nights spent cuddled next to him, I also relished my space. With the parade of noise buzzing around my brain, I needed it.

"Look, I don't expect you to bounce the moment we get back.

Stay tonight. Tomorrow I've gotta deal with telling my mom about all this bullshit and I still have no idea how. I don't mean to be a festering dickscab, but you can't be around when I talk to her. I don't need her making you a target because she's got no one else to blame."

Caine nodded. I knew he wanted to support me, the argument probably dripping from his tongue as he licked his lips and kept it to himself, but I didn't want to hear it. He took my hand in his and kissed my knuckles before accelerating to his usual speed, the sound of the engine filling the conversational void for the remainder of the drive.

———

"'Kay, my shit is freaked." I paced from my kitchen to the living room and back for the hundredth time as Bosco's Pug tail uncurled and followed anxiously. Serena laughed. "This is not funny! I don't have words for this. What the fuck am I gonna say?"

"Relax your puckered taco, Soph. You know exactly what to say."

"Firefly, please sit." Olive chiming in grounded me for the moment. "You know your mother best. So, please, sit and enjoy the visit. You'll find the words."

"*Hrumph.* No, I won't," I whined worse than a pissy, middle-schooler and plopped onto the couch between my great-aunt and cousin. "My mom's not made for this. She'll never believe me. Or if she does, what if she can't accept it and gets all weird and bolts? Or uses it as an excuse to have you locked up again." Last thing Olive needed was being sent back to The Royal. "What then? Have Ranlyn chase her down and wipe her memory? Wait, is that a thing?" I asked Olive.

"Ultimate safety net. That's boss," Serena said.

"*Not happening.*" Ranlyn's voice sounded in my head.

My shoulders sagged. "Party pooper!"

"He's out there?" Serena asked. "I figured he'd be off searching for that evil dude who—"

"Apparently, he's back in time to jack it in my corn flakes." I cut her off, so I didn't have to hear her say what I knew she was going to say. Because we assumed Loring was still looking for me, Ranlyn was sticking close by. Not every day, but he knew my mom was coming by for "the conversation" and I thought it more likely he was present for support while creeping outside my door.

"Thanks for the chunky visual, Soph. Relax. If Aunt Lu can't accept you and her own family's truth, then she's not as cool a mom as you think. You had no prob writing Grandma Lizzie off."

"Grandma Lizzie deserved every bit of it, if only for insisting that we deserve to be demon chum for eternity, not to mention what she did to Olive."

"I get it, I get it." Serena sat back, bringing her opinions with her.

"Are you telling your mom?"

Serena's lips pursed.

"Exactly."

The phone rang. My stomach dropped. A "dead man walking" feeling washed over me and my thoughts ran wild. Did they use gas chambers still? Electric chairs? Yes, but in Canada?

"*Arizona, Missouri, Wyoming, and Oklahoma have gas chambers. No death penalty in Canada since nineteen seventy-six.*"

"*Not helping, dickcheese,*" I thought, knowing Ranlyn could read my mind.

"Someone's buzzing up from downstairs." Serena picked up the phone, pressed a button, and hung up.

"Is it my mom?"

"Were you expecting a strip o' gram? Is that why Ranlyn's here?" She smirked and went to the kitchen.

I took in a steadying breath, which did shit-fuck-all because, in my experience, yoga was bullshit propaganda to sell yoga pants for comfort and ass-gazing. My eyesight went fuzzy. I rushed to the bathroom. The chill of a cold cloth on my neck was about as helpful as bullshit yoga breathing.

A deep voice came from my living room. Did Caine show up after I told him not to? That scab-eating piece of shit.

I threw the wet cloth into the sink and raced out into the living room with a mouthful of choice words. When I got there, I found a man I've never met sitting on my couch. Everyone looked at me like I might pull a gun.

"Sophie-doll." My mom stood with the man who now extended his hand. I didn't hear anything else she said. When I realized he was waiting for a return to his nervous greeting, I blinked into my role and reciprocated with a handshake. Water squished between our palms.

"Wow." He laughed. His smile rounded his cheeks and creased his dark eyes as he twisted our hands awkwardly. "I'm excited to meet you, too, but you didn't have to forgo the toilet paper to rush out here."

"Brian!" My mom scolded him.

"Shit, sorry." I wiped my hands on my jean shorts, pleasantly taken aback by his sense of humour.

"Sophie Olivia, really? Your mouth."

My mother's mothering went ignored as I grabbed a dishtowel and handed it to Brian, hoping it was halfway clean.

"At least Lu doesn't reserve that tone for me." He smiled again, passed the dish towel back, and sat next to my mom, who looked mildly pissy at our colluding banter.

As far from my mom's type as Brian was in his golf shirt and slacks, he managed to be down-to-Earth and a better fit than the greasy engine polishers she's dated since my dad.

I should have told her this was an invitation for "the talk" and not another get-together, but I never guessed she would show up with an investor who had an inherit sense of adventure with no children or ex-wives.

The happy couple stayed an hour. When Brian visited the bathroom before they left, my mom asked if I was okay.

"Yeah."

"Liar, liar pants on fire."

"Shut it, Ranlyn."

"Do you not like him?" Mom asked.

"Oh, yeah. No, he's great, mom. Truly. You bagged a winner." I added a smirk to sell it.

"Was there something else?"

"Ah, we just need to talk, so yeah. Let me know when you're good to do that." My positive tone was rice paper thin.

Mom gave a light gasp. "Was that what this was? Are you pregnant?"

"What? No! Ewww."

"Well, I don't know. You sound so serious. Is it school?"

"No, Mom. No spawn and school is fine. It can wait when you have a free day."

The bathroom door opened, Brain headed our way.

"I'm sorry, dolly. You're sure?"

"Yup. No big."

Brian looked between us and we flashed him a nothing-to-see-here smile, mine hinged on shaky patience for them to leave. A hug and a handshake devoid of bathroom humour and they were on their way. I collapsed on the couch, my face in my hands.

Olive landed a consoling hand on my back. "Don't worry, Firefly. Maybe it's a good thing."

"And maybe Aunt Lu would be happier if you were pregnant with a two-headed goat."

"At this point, I would rather a two-headed goat baby."

"Watch out for hooves."

"Again, not helping, dickcheese."

2

SOCIAL CALL

Donovan

"Y ou can't say that!" Kim screeched so high my balls flinched—and not in a good way.

I started down the basement stairs knowing she would follow. "Yes. I can. And who catapulted your ass into the number one seat?"

"We need to keep things unchanged from the way Aunt Lacey did them. She didn't say, 'Here take over the Sect I've run forever and by the way go ahead and denounce the existence of Jesus Christ'."

The loud crinkle behind me was the fistful of agendas for the coven meeting. She was so obsessed with ensuring our first meeting was flawless she forgot she had been to a meeting before. One offhand comment about the remote possibility that Jesus Christ never existed, man, mortal, or divine—in jest—and she turns into a fiery ball of raging bitch. A deep-seated drive to irritate her was ugly and too easy to resist, but mention of who should be leading the meeting tonight shifted my clamped-down anger over the line.

I spun around on the stairs and glared up at her. "Are you seriously going to bring her up now? Or pretend I wasn't face-to-face with her when she gave her last wishes?"

She crossed her arms. "The Mother Coven allows individuals to retain their own belief system or lack of. Aunt Lacey never forced anyone into any belief, nor did she insult the ones she disagreed with."

"Do you forget I've been in the Mother Coven years longer than you and was raised within one my entire life?"

"Obviously not, but the Sorrels—"

"A Tainted coven is still a coven. Works as a dysfunctional family, lives for the power, strives for their goals, and finds a way to keep everyone happy. I know what's expected of me. Of us. Watching the Sect crumble knowing it was the opposite of her plan—" I couldn't say her name "—is not an option. Neither is turning it into an example of my father's life's work. I don't give a shit about much, but I give a shit about this Sect, and no cheat sheets or manual is going to tell me how it's done."

Her eyes dipped to the papers in her hands. She tightened her grip on them and set her jaw.

Things would work as they always did. At least I showed up sober and ready to roll. If that didn't make her feel better about my intentions, nothing would.

"Lovers' quarrel?" Caine came around the corner and down the stairs, Bosco pushing in front of him and bounding down the steps. I scooped him up before he could get past me. Caine bypassed Kim and I. Sophie came down behind him looking about as happy at Caine's impulsive need to antagonize me the second we shared breathing space as I was.

"I don't remember fighting," I said to Sophie and ruffled Bosco's fur.

Her dark eyes narrowed, the tilt to her head displaying her aggravation.

"She's not your lover." Caine's hard stare wasn't as intimidating as he probably thought.

I grinned. "Neither are you."

We all knew it to be true and I could spit unicorns I was so happy about it. While things began lusty, the connection Sophie and I had rendered sex for her and Caine impossible. Since I felt everything she did it meant no nookie for me either, but I got off on knowing it was getting to Caine. I was betting he couldn't hold out for long.

"Sword fight later." Kim pushed by us and headed towards the closet. "The Coveners will be here soon and I'm not putting up with either of your dick play."

Sophie's smile was worth being put in my place.

The kitchen counters were covered with potluck dinner containers and Louise's treats. The house filled up with Coveners and laughter for the first time in weeks. Not that any of them were there to see me. I stood aside and watched as Rachel and Deidra arrived, hand-in-hand, both with a hug for Sophie before heading outside to play with Bosco. She took it with a smile while her insides cringed, wearing sunglasses that hid more than the Covene

r's soul glows. Not with any brand of hate as they were among a few worth hanging out with. I wasn't sure where her discomfort stemmed and not knowing was forcing a hyper-vigilance unknown to me. Every blip of emotion meant something but wasn't enough to paint a picture. She wasn't enjoying the people she normally did, wasn't enjoying the crowd, wasn't enjoying much of anything, but you couldn't tell on the outside. Faking it so well was an art and not one crafted with any amount of pleasure.

I tried to spare a smile or two, but the Coveners didn't meet my eyes long enough to register my attempts. Fuck it. I headed for the basement.

The party moved downstairs, leaving the mood of celebration on the main floor. Now people forced themselves to look at me through a cast of tears and failing strength. It was the burial ceremony all over again. Except then, I was steeped in whisky and had Sophie to cling to.

Everyone found a comfortable spot in a large circle as per usual, looking at their leaders, who were far from the usual. Kim looked down at her notes. I gave an incredulous laugh and took lead. "We can never replace her," I began, as this aligned with Kim's notes and what had her close to breaking down. "This Sect has been around far longer than I've been alive. Appareo and Paian—" I used the selected Coven names for Louise and Henry— "have been members since their inception into the craft in the sixties." The pair seated on the couch grinned and nodded. "Neither myself nor Kim wish to make changes that would upset the tradition or balance or whatever." I looked at Sophie and found her expression blank. Listening, but not fully present. "She chose us to continue the Sect, so that's what we're doing, whether you agree with it or not." My personality leaked with impatience the longer I talked. Sophie's stern internal reaction had me reeling it back.

"What I mean to say is we want everyone to get something out of this." I looked at Kim, forcing her to find her voice.

"We understand not everyone's comfortable with offering up ideas or complaints, but please bring things forward as they come up. You can also privately call or email."

"That means both of us." By the looks of everyone, they would rather snort shoelaces than come to me with anything, but leaving them to lean on Kim marked her as the stronger leader and I needed them to see me as her equal, even if her experience was appalling in comparison.

I expected a snarky glare from Denise and her minion bestie, but she looked apathetic at best. No one else took the opportunity to speak up. Good or bad, the Coveners knew where we stood.

"We have something for everyone." I nodded at Sophie. She and Caine were already versed on the next step. "Aunt Lacey—" Saying her name caused my voice to catch. I recovered and pushed through. "She wrote everyone a letter before we left for Diluculo." The

Coveners became restless. I spoke over them. "Her power was something none of us may ever live up to, let alone surpass. She, more than anyone, deserves to be walking an Earth she watched evolve, but before we left, her sight was blocked. She thought this meant something might happen to her and feared it meant her death."

I didn't want to speak anymore, pissed Kim dropped the ball and lost her nerve, leaving me to speak in the first place. Refusing to say more, I shut my mouth and waited as Sophie handed out the envelopes. The sounds of ripped paper and choked sobs had me retreating into a numb headspace where the basement and all this Coven Leader bullshit fell away like a scab. Escaping upstairs was the only way to keep from absorbing the room's heavy sorrow, and the bottle of whisky only contained memories of the last time I used it as a crutch.

Gut-wrenching emptiness took over by the time I returned to the basement. My feelings or Sophie's, I didn't know. Either way, the whisky barely smoothed the edges of loss.

"They need direction," Kim whispered.

"Who does?" Caine asked.

"Them." Kim's intense blue-greens glared around the room at the Coveners who finished their letters and moved to sharing with each other. "Without focus they'll get bored and leave."

"*Pfft.*" I took a gulp from my glass. "You think I'm about to stand around trying to remind you how it was when she was around? What'd you expect? Roller derby nights? Sitting in the circle holding hands and reminiscing about our former leader? Not doing it. I'll sacrifice a nut before listening to that horse shit."

"Everything's fine," Sophie said. "Look at them." Coveners were scattered amongst oversized furniture and in small groups taking or giving readings. "See. Totally normal."

"These things run themselves," Caine added.

"This has to be perfect." The snap in Kim's voice was pushing it. Sophie snapping back stopped me from doing so myself. Kim huffed and backed down.

"Kim, it's so perfect you could sit a level on its mole-encrusted nose. Now calm your perky tits before you freak people out. Denise smells blood like a blonde bull shark."

I laughed and took another pull of my drink.

When I lowered my glass, Sophie was standing in front of me. Her closeness made me swallow awkwardly loud.

"Really?"

"What?"

She crossed her arms and smirked. "What'cha drinkin'?"

I looked at my glass. "Not even halfway down the hatch and you feel it already? Lightweight."

"You're drinking?" Kim hissed and snatched the glass to smell the whisky thinly masked with cola.

I leaned closer to Sophie and mimicked her smirk. "Nark."

"Next time go for the rum stash and pour it a least half and half with a slice of lime."

Anger simmered from Kim and Caine, but I was focused on Sophie and her adorable need to put me in my place. "A little JD never hurt anyone."

"My thoughts exactly!"

It would have been dreamy if these words had come from the mouth of the dark-haired beauty in front of me, but as they were spoken, Sophie's smirking lips didn't budge. The harsh voice laced with mischievousness came from behind me. The owner was a willowy young woman with black hair and purple streaks pulled back in a ponytail with 1950s volume. Clad in tight black jeans and leather jacket, she approached us with swagger, putting herself between me and Sophie.

"Gonna pour a girl a drink or is this shindig self-serve?"

Black-lined green eyes focused on me. Sophie stood to the side, the strain of whatever soul glow she was seeing ached in my eyes, they already exhausted from the bright souls of the Coveners as she insisted on taking her sunglasses off.

"Joelly?" Fuck no.

She grabbed the drink from Kim's hand, raised a finger, chugged it like water, and then handed the glass back to her. "Thanks, Red."

Kim muttered a reflexive, "You're welcome."

Joelly raised a sculpted and pierced left eyebrow. "Surprised?"

"Maybe you two should talk upstairs?" Sophie's gaze was on the Coveners who looked paranoid about who crashed their meeting. Considering not all of them wanted the world to know about their involvement in a Sect, this was a huge security breach. Just fucking perfect.

"And why's that?" Joelly stared Sophie straight in the eyes in subdued confrontation, made possible by them being the same height.

Before Sophie's simmering anger boiled over, I grabbed the scruff of Joelly's jacket with a strained, "Let's go," to bring the conversation upstairs, away from prying ears.

Joelly spun from my grasp with blurred speed and grabbed my wrist. Painful images were forced in front of my eyes and a surge of ice ran through my veins. Sophie was unable to share in the visions but wasn't immune to the cold injection and the piggy-packing emotions—ones of fury, agony, and so much despair.

A swift yank got her off me, made easier as Joelly let go and trained her curiosity on Sophie's simultaneous experience. Caine braced her shoulders to keep her from falling. The Coveners were now on their feet. Before they could react, I was dragging Joelly away. She complied, keeping her eyes on Sophie until we disappeared up the basement steps.

"Who's the chick?" Joelly's tongue grazed her glossed lips.

"Not up for your bullshit today."

"It's Sophie, isn't it?" She laughed, all cocky bitch when I refused to answer. "How do I know? Word gets around. Plus, the whole jaw clenching and nostril flaring thing is your basic tell." She laughed again and leaned against the kitchen island, pushing her chest out like an offering.

"You have one minute to explain yourself before I kick your skank ass out."

Instead of making her case, she straightened, closing the distance between us. I refused to flinch. Her fingertip grazed my chest, lightly at first, moving down my stomach, stopping at my belt buckle. She then played with the edge of it without skin contact. When she failed to rouse my libido, she snaked her dark-painted nails along my jean-covered thighs, pausing short of her primary target.

"She can feel me, can't she?" Joelly's voice rasped in my ear.

Granting her an inch of triumph was a win to a Magic like Joelly. The fact she was right about what Sophie felt was confirmed by the tense confusion thrumming across the connection.

"Hmmm." She raised her eyebrow, settling back on her booted heels, and seeking my expression for her win. "I doubt you've changed that much."

She abandoned the stare down and went to the fridge. I inhaled with control as not to be confused with a sigh. I was sick of her games, but she never showed up for a social call. She wanted something or wanted to rub something in my face. Joelly was a bad omen. One who insisted on leaning into the fridge with conscious effort to draw me into checking her out, the desperate need for an ego boost before giving up her motive for showing up.

Joelly was tall, athletically lean, and had a great rack she wanted the world to appreciate. But I knew what conniving brain that body held and was far beyond disillusioned with her charms.

She didn't find what she was looking for, again, and closed the door. "Where's the Jack?"

She searched the cupboards when I didn't answer.

"Why are you here?"

She continued her search. "Oh, you know. In the market for tacky mansions and heard your sugar mama bit the dust."

Point for Joelly. I still refused to react, even if I was picturing strangling her to death with her hair extensions.

"Gotcha, you slimy bastard." Joelly found a bottle under the sink and stood mid-swig, slamming the bottle down afterwards, then tilted it towards me. "Want some?"

"Not even a little."

She rolled her eyes, wrapped her fingers around the neck of the bottle in a phallic gesture, and then pressed it to her glossy lips for another swig. When the thud of the glass hit the counter again, she changed her tune.

"He's coming for her." The threat came out nonchalant. Only one man would be out for Sophie's blood, so I didn't ask who. "He will kill her."

"You crawled out of the sludge to tell me that? What are you, his new messenger pigeon? I wouldn't stand too close. His cling-ons have a habit of getting their skank-asses killed."

She made a throaty noise. "Skank? No more than you." I didn't comment. "Plus, I wouldn't hole up with that old dishrag in the most desperate of times, though I've heard rumours it might be worth it." She giggled. I wanted to gnaw the visual out of my memory. "Think of me as a tornado warning. Your little Soul Seer will be hunted and slaughtered." She dug out a chunk of potato from the salad in front of her followed by a whisky chaser, letting the threat linger. "That's basically it."

"And I'm supposed to believe you because we're such good ol' pals?"

"No, because we're family, asshat."

I moved from my foothold for the first time, leaning into the granite counter. "We are not family."

Joelly huffed and rolled her eyes again. She took another quick swig than screwed the top back on the bottle. "Call it whatever you like, consider yourself informed. I'm sure you'll warn Miss Seer downstairs for me." She headed for the door.

"Don't think so." I telekinetically held her in place, then twisted my wrist to spin her to face me.

"Now you're getting kinky." I knew her well enough to see a layer of fear beneath her sass.

"You expect to dump your rumours on my kitchen floor and leave?"

"Let me go before I carve your balls into tiny jack-o-lanterns."

"The only way you could know Sophie was a Soul Seer was if you were affiliated with Loring and his coven, or a part of mine, so obviously, I'm suspicious when you arrive during a coven meeting with info you shouldn't have." Joelly remained silent. "Loring coming after Sophie again? Easy, and expected, since his ego was spanked and dusted like his lackeys. Why are you really here?"

"You think Loring is the only heavy hitter in town? That he's the only one salivating at the chance to cripple your precious Mother Coven?"

"Who else?"

"I don't owe you a fucking thing."

"You'd have to be giving an ear to the ones you're so afraid of. Maybe they promised you something you'd never have otherwise. Perhaps had you justifying your actions to get whatever self-serving bullshit you tell yourself makes it all worth it."

"I'm not into that shit anymore."

"You must think Loring gave me brain damage. He'd have to for me to believe a load of bull that steamy. You're no different. Showing up on my doorstep, prancing around my house, and goading me after what went down in Diluculo is no coincidence and proves my point." I shook my head. "Same ol' you."

Her expression softened for the first time. She took on a lost puppy pout—one that I would euthanize if killing someone on my first coven night wasn't a shitty example of the leader I was supposed to be. Scars of a past only we knew were heavy in the air between us and made its mark.

"Get your Soul Seer bitch up here if you don't believe me. I'm sure she could let me in on a thing or two."

I let my telekinetic hold go. "You and I both know no matter what Sophie sees in your soul glow, it's not who you really are."

"Fine. Figure it out yourself. Don't say I didn't give you a heads-up." She moved for the door. I didn't stop her this time.

"Tell Loring I said hi."

"Go fuck yourself!"

Gravel kicked up against the house as her motorcycle revved and took off. Two minutes passed before I trusted she wasn't coming back.

A gulp of whisky didn't change the fact that Joelly showing up was a harbinger of something. Loring returning was no surprise, but so soon? And who was the other heavy hitter she alluded to? I hated Joelly for so much but using Sophie to get to me in whatever scheme she was playing was beyond shady. I hated admitting how well it worked, even if Joelly didn't know it.

Worry crossed the connection. Shit. Sophie.

I headed for the basement. All attention swung my way when I made it back to the group, probably waiting for an explanation as to who Joelly was. They would have to wait. "Break time. Get to the food before I feed it to Bosco."

They hesitated until Jared stood and slapped Blake's shoulder before heading towards the stairs. "Bet you all the brownies I can do more push-ups than you."

"Not a chance, dude."

"You don't get all the brownies," Deidra complained and followed them.

I'd have to thank Jared later. He may be a muscle head, but he was smarter than Blake and effectively got the group moving upstairs.

I motioned for Sophie to wait. Kim and Caine stayed as well.

"Who was she?" Kim asked once we were alone.

"Sorry," I said to Sophie instead of answering Kim.

The nod I received was nothing but an emotionless gesture, but her discomfort cramped in her diaphragm and echoed in mine. "So, who was your guest?"

"First, tell me what you saw."

"Well, she's a Magic, obviously. I don't think she was Tainted. Her soul glow was red."

"Red?" Kim said. "You've never mentioned seeing a red soul before."

"I never have."

"What does that stand for?" Caine asked.

"No idea. The list is upstairs in my purse. Want me to get it?"

"No need." I paused. "She's a sponge."

"A sponge?" Kim snort-laughed. "Frightening."

"Underestimating Joelly's threat risk will get you killed. She's not some lost little Seedling you can take out and commandeer whatever accessory goes best with your skin tone."

"Really? You're gonna get ethical on me?"

"Just pointing out your psychopathic tendencies. Which, by the way, are nothing compared to Joelly's."

"Is a sponge a real thing?" Caine asked Sophie. "Sounds made up."

Prick. Why's he even talking?

"That's the technical term?" Sophie's question stopped me from calling Caine a tool.

"Call it what you want—Sponge, Absorber, Photocopier."

"Because a photocopier is terrifying," Caine murmured.

"Why's a Sponge dangerous?" Sophie spoke over him, our mutual annoyance ricocheting between us.

I grit my teeth and left fantasies of murder for later. "Joelly consumes other's powers. I call her a Sponge because not even the strongest of Magics can stop her from taking a piece of them with her. The light soul you saw was only what she wanted you to see. There's no way she's un-Tainted. She can manipulate which powers show up, which don't, and throw away the ones she doesn't need anymore, which is probably how she got in the door 'cuz the warding spell should've prevented her from entering."

Kim gasped. "She's evil?"

"Evil bitch to the core, but Tainted? Can't tell. She absorbs gifts from good and evil Magics. The whole greed for power is too alluring and she's as selfish as they come."

"Means a lot coming from you." Kim was happy to take pot shots at me like Caine. I stopped myself from cursing Aunt Lacey for choosing us as co-Leaders.

"The cold feeling when she touched you. That's an effect of her power?" Sophie asked.

I nodded. "She absorbed some of my power. Not because she wants it, she can't handle Psychometry, she dumped it right away. She just wanted to remind me she could."

"Sooo, she could be good," Caine said.

Stopping myself from punching the guy every time he talked was getting more difficult. "She says she's out of the game, but she hasn't changed." I looked at Sophie. "As I'm sure you felt. She'll do anything for cash or power."

"Yeah. She comes on strong." The blush of Sophie's cheeks was divine, but I hated Joelly for being the cause.

"I don't get it," Kim said. "Why was she here? Scorned ex or something?"

"She wishes. No, she's kind of my sister."

"What?" Kim blurted as Caine and Sophie stared owl eyed at me. Sophie's shock was laced with relief. Confusing as well as heart-warming.

"Relax. She's adopted."

Kim's laugh battered the walls.

"But you were together." Sophie must not have realized this came across as accusatory until everyone looked at her. "Well, at one point anyway."

"I'm not airing our family history. It's not what you think. I've seen this act of hers before. Besides bogarting my booze, all she told me was that Loring was bent on killing you and some other big bad is on his heels."

"What?" Caine stepped towards me. "You go on about screwing

your sister and leave that special tidbit till the end? I could fucking strangle you."

"If Loring wanting revenge is a news flash to you, you're missing crucial brain cells."

"You don't think it's important to mention this sister-ex of yours knows about it?"

"It was a generalization, not 'watch yourself he's twenty minutes out'. Loring is no pacifist. Saving his pride is crucial. He won't quit."

"Your sister, or whatever she is, shows up with a warning and then bounces? I don't think so."

"Caine—" Sophie scolded him. The connection prevented me from lying, but it did nothing for Caine.

"I haven't seen Joelly in years. Besides her threat, and trying to coddle my dick, that's all she gave."

"Dude! Gross." Kim shared a disgusted expression with Caine. Both making me wish I insisted on talking with Sophie alone.

"She's not blood," Sophie said with a look of distaste. "Still gross, though." I rolled my eyes at her. "Though it explains the awkward sexual tension I felt."

"Like I said, it's not what you think. Incest or not, that's all she said. She wouldn't cop to being affiliated with Loring's flock or to contacts in his Coven, so—" I focused on Caine, "—believe me when I say, I'd rather end her than wear her as a codpiece."

3

FIGHTING THE WEDGE

We stayed behind to help Kim and Donovan clean up. Thankfully, the mansion came with a larger-than-normal sized dishwasher.

"I'm usually stuck on maid duty alone." Donovan packed away leftovers while I fought with the remains of Louise's marshmallow concoction Kim loved so much, now glued to plates and bowls.

"Guess we figured it was taken care of in some witchy way. You should've asked for help." I bent to add more small plates to the bottom rack of the dishwasher. An influx of desire tingled in my pelvis. I thought I had to pee until I turned in time to see Donovan look away. I didn't call him out, he knew he was caught.

"What's with the zombie act?" he asked a couple minutes later.

"I don't remember snacking on someone's spleen. Unless that's what's stuck to this plate." I left it in the sink to soak.

"Riot you are." His superficial laugh was devoid of dimples as he tied up a garbage bag and tossed it through the glass sliding doors to the backyard. He sat on an island stool as I started up the machine. "What filters to me through the connection is strong, when it happens. You can't be that good at compartmentalizing."

"Can't I be?" I wiped down the counter confused at whose shoe prints I was looking at and how they got there. Not to mention why.

"Do you hate it that much?" I turned to lean against the counter when I felt examining tugs across the connection as he sought clues to his own question.

"I don't hate it." Shitsnacks. The small sentence was devoid of emotion. "With everything that's happened, even you're pretty zombie-like. Minus the spleen eating and military panic."

He cracked a pitiful smile. "Can't deny that."

Silence dragged out until I said, "I didn't want to make things worse for you."

"For me? Come on, babe. I think we know it's the other way around. Things have changed— too much already—don't change that too. Besides, it could never be a negative knowing you're happy. I know how you feel about me and what conflict that creates. You don't have to pretend it doesn't exist. I get it."

My head was nodding but I was absent, too busy pushing aside the memory of the moment he grazed on, when I admitted to loving him and broke down in tears. Guilt was right. I wasn't supposed to feel that way and Caine didn't deserve someone who loved another man, even if they still loved him. It wasn't that I didn't want to be happy, I just wasn't.

"Sophie." Hearing my real name from his lips was enough to refocus my attention. "You're not okay."

With the deep concern across the connection like sour candy in my gut, I knew he wasn't about to let it go while I remained removed.

"I don't know what to say." While honest, it didn't mean I didn't understand myself. Opening the floodgates now was more than I assumed Donovan was prepared for and the exhaustion of unloading on someone only for them to stare and blink at you was beyond my ability to take right now.

"You don't have to talk to me, but I hope you're talking to someone. Serena, Kim, and yes, even Caine. Anyone. You were never Suzy Sunshine, but you weren't this cut off. I'm worried."

Before I could pull a response out of my ass, one to express some type of gratitude or a snarky remark about how he didn't know me when my emotional dissociation was at its peak, Caine and Kim entered the kitchen after finishing with the basement to see if I was ready to get going.

I couldn't leave fast enough.

———

"Come on, I'll drive you in."

Blocking the TV to get me motivated to serve others wasn't doing it. "Maybe drive some hot sauce-encrusted rebar through my temple instead. It'll hurt less than training a newbie on a Monday. Besides, Ranlyn's bringing me in during the switching of the guards. The big man's got a big man Elder meeting. Better he hear me whine about it and save your earballs."

"*Something to look forward to,*" I heard Ranlyn in my head.

"*Perks of the job, Jeeves,*" I countered, my thoughts unprotected.

"Drew probably figures training on a slow day lessens the chance of you chasing them away like the last one."

"Drew doesn't think with anything but his wallet or his dick. Sometimes they're the same thing, And the last new hire disaster was Kim's fault." Caine glowered. "What? It wasn't my fault she got witchy on some college brats and lined my pockets with tips like Robin Hood."

"Well, you're not coming home rich wearing that."

I gasped and looked at my shirt. "Are you making fun of Dean?"

"No, I'm making fun of all twenty Deans. Especially that one."

"You'd scream like a banshee too if a cat jumped at you when you have Ghost Sickness."

"I'll take your word for it."

I stood up from the couch. "If anything, people should be tossing dollar bills at me for wearing this. Dean would appreciate that."

"We're Canadian. We don't have dollar bills. You want them to chuck loonies at you?"

"Mhmm."

"Have fun then."

"I will." Chin high in a bout of childish defiance, I kept the tank on, but changed out of the sweatpants. When I came out of my bedroom with my hands busy pulling my hair into a high ponytail, clad in the multiple faces of Dean, Caine was shaking his head and cradling my non-judgemental furry friend.

Bosco would have a pet sitter while I was babysitting the newbie bartender. Excuses kept Caine close, his as well as mine, and his luxury apartment remained well guarded, yet mostly empty. We needed a way out of the habit of being attached, but I couldn't figure out the best way to do it while still unsure if it was what I wanted.

Music filtered through The Lush's speakers, something too hipster for my liking, but the college brats liked it and the regulars ignored it. Inside, the tables were empty as we opened in thirty minutes. Behind the bar was the back of who I assumed was the trainee—tall, fit, and with a precision hairdo I would attempt and utterly fail.

Eddie looked around the trainee's shoulder and sneered. "What are you wearing?"

The trainee turned to look at who he was insulting as I was flipping him the bird. I gasped and dropped my bird like it had been shot.

Joelly.

She raised her pierced eyebrow and crossed her arms, wearing the smuggest grin I'd ever seen.

"Good job, Sophie. Flipping off the new girl in less than twenty seconds of meeting her."

"I can handle worse," Joelly said.

"See, Eddie. She'll get used to it." My smile was so tight, I doubt I managed to look sane, but at least Eddie was too dense to read my gasp as familiarity with the new trainee whose soul glowed red and may or may not be an evil bitch.

Fuck. I have to call Donovan.

"*Do it,*" I heard in my head. "*I'd love to share a drink with my old pal, Donny-boy.*"

Wonderful. She can read minds.

Unneeded confirmation came in the form of her giggle ringing in my skull. Yup. Definitely evil. Fuck my life.

She took a step towards me and extended her hand. "Danielle Baker. Nice to meet you."

Shitbuckets. I looked at her hand like she was showing me a palm of worms.

"Cool. Be right back." I avoided her power-stealing touch and headed for the bathroom.

"Maybe change your shirt while you're in there!" Joelly called after me.

Fuck. Fuck. Fuck.

I took out Caine's phone I had for emergencies, since he was at my house with a landline, and dialed Kim.

"Red's roller derby."

"What? Kim?"

"Sophie? Sorry, didn't check the—"

"Doesn't matter, I need help."

"What's going on?"

"Joelly's here."

"Here where?"

"At The Lush. She's fucking working here under an alias and can read minds and I'm wearing my Dean shirt. Ugh! I need that mind-blocking herb."

She gasped. "You're wearing Dean in public. Why?"

"Hey! People should be throwing dollar bills at me for wearing this shirt!"

"What? We're Canadian."

"Kim, I need the stupid herb before Joelly rifles through my brain and finds out shit I don't need her knowing."

"I'm at work."

"Can your guard get it and give it to mine?"

"They're not delivery people."

"If she has access to my brain, she can see how to get into the estate's attic. Plus, who knows what other shit I've got rolling around in there for her to take advantage of."

"Oh shit."

"Yeah."

"'Kay, on it."

On it how quickly, was the question, but I didn't have time to ask before she hung up. I couldn't hang out in the bathroom all night, so I had to brave Joelly and do my best to keep my thoughts off things I didn't want her to know.

My mind immediately went to the estate's locking mechanism.

No! Fuck.

I shook my head.

"Come on, Sophie," I muttered. "Think about Bosco. Think about the gallbladder surgery you saw on TLC. Sing a song other than this donkey-shit The Lush's playing. Anything."

A knock on the door made me yelp.

"I'm taking this off your break time," Drew yelled through the door.

I pulled the door open to see the crease in my boss's forehead at maximum depth. I squared my shoulders and didn't blink when I said, "You will?" in a deadpan tone.

"Just get to work." He stormed off, his back sweat already leaking through his shirt as he lost all confidence in his threat.

I had the power to end him. Not in the end-of-life sense, though that too. He didn't know how much I would love to turn him to ash for all the sexist shit he tries to pull, but in the ruin-your-life-with-jail-time sense was more appropriate. He wasn't a fan of the type of sex he would get behind bars, as far as I knew.

Since I got cold easily, and the a/c was always high in the bar, I put on the zip-up sweater I brought but decided against zipping it partially closed since it squished one of Dean's heads into my cleavage and would garner more attention than showcasing the whole shirt.

Guess it was time to brave the enemy.

"Enemy?" I heard in my head again and froze before rounding the corner. *"So dramatic."*

I continued. When I headed behind the bar, Joelly was leaning against the lower counter as Eddie was telling a story of when he had to bounce a rowdy customer who threw a shoe at someone. Laying the groundwork for a date most likely. While Joelly smiled and nodded, she looked completely bored.

"He really thinks he's interesting, doesn't he?" She relayed telepathically without looking away from him.

"You have no idea." I assumed she could pick up the thought.

This reminded me of what else she could read and had me panicking for something to think about. If she were good at it, she would get through the tactic anyway. I was still a Seedling without the skills to protect myself.

Joelly glanced at me when I started inwardly belting the lyrics to "Black Velvet" by Alannah Myles then made efforts to refocus on Eddie. I couldn't keep my thoughts from slipping, so I tasked myself with busy work and went to organize the storeroom since Eddie looked content to do the training. Twenty minutes later, while bent down to a bottom shelf taking inventory, I heard a familiar voice in my head and headed to the bar to find Ranlyn seated with a tumbler of whisky in front of him. He downed the rest like a shot as I reached him.

"Another please," he asked. A small baggy with a powdered substance in it sat in the glass. "I'm spelled so she can't see me as myself. Only you can see me, and I'll shield your thoughts until the mixture kicks in."

Drew didn't like us drinking on the job, but he couldn't stop us from having water. I poured Ranlyn two fingers of whisky and turned my body so "Danielle" and Eddie couldn't see anything.

I poured water into a short glass and then dropped the entire baggy in after it. "Fishdicks."

"Relax. No one can see. Now, why's she here?"

"No fucking clue." I fished out the baggy with my fingers. "I can't shield my own thoughts. No way can I read hers."

"Neither can I."

"Perfect." I drank the water too fast and it splashed up my nose. I sprayed it out in a violent sneeze. When I could open my eyes after the coughing fit, Joelly and Eddie were looking at me. I gave them a thumbs-up as I tried to fake-smile.

"Watch your shirt," Eddie said in a quippy tone.

My thumbs up turned into the middle finger real fast.

"What *are* you wearing?" Ranlyn asked.

I glared at him. He covered a smirk by taking a sip from his glass.

Ranlyn didn't know anything more than I did about Joelly. She was a sort-of relative of Donovan's with possible ties to evil factions.

"You're an Elder now. Maybe she wants you."

"Then I'm happy she can't see me."

I one-shoulder shrugged. "We don't know that either. She could've stolen a Magics ability to see through shit like that."

"Or enhanced hearing."

"Shhhiiiitttt." I whispered. "I didn't even think about that."

He tilted his head as if to say, "I know," and took another pull of his drink.

"Hey Jasper," Eddie said to Ranlyn as he passed us on his way to the bathroom. Ranlyn raised his glass in response.

"Jasper?" I said. "You're spelled to look like Jasper the creeper regular who—" Ranlyn's eyes narrowed. "No fucking way. You are Jasper, aren't you?"

Ranlyn laughed.

"I can't believe you've spelled yourself and acted like a gruff old regular just to spy on me."

"Sometimes the best guardian is one the mark doesn't know is watching over them."

"Aww. My own creepy stalker."

"You're welcome. And if Joelly continues her employment beyond a night to annoy you, you'll see more of Jasper. She's connected to Loring somehow. We'll figure it out."

Donovan seemed certain of the same thing and I wasn't about to believe her showing up now was a coincidence.

"Think I got what it takes?" Joelly said, now standing at my shoulder.

I turned to face her. "Oh, yeah. I'm sure you'll manage to sling drinks without killing anyone."

She smiled. "You think I'm here to kill someone?"

"Are you?"

"A little blunt, you think?"

"Yes."

She laughed. I didn't. "Look it, Soul Seer." I huffed and looked around to ensure no one heard her. She continued without caring if they had. "If I wanted you dead—"

"What? I wouldn't have seen you coming? Real original."

"Oh no, I'd let you know. I'd make sure you knew it was me and I'd take my time. Just as Loring will."

"So, you are a Loring devotee."

"No. I'm a Joelly devotee. Which rhymes better, and I reap all the benefits."

"Hilarious. I'm already bored of this. What the fuck do you want?"

"I want a lot of things. Things I can't get from your lame-ass brain. Good job in hiding your thoughts. Though you have someone helping you." She looked around me at "Jasper". "Hello Elder Ranlyn. Congrats on the promotion. Rigorous hiring process?"

Ranlyn braced his hands on the bar top to stand and Joelly raised a hand and sat him back down without touching him.

Shit. Guess she was stronger than Ranlyn thought.

Ranlyn glanced to the side at the room. No one saw what was happening, but there were too many witnesses for him to retaliate, especially spelled to look like an old man who already stood out.

"A birdy told me you were wearing another man's face. Kind of obvious chatting up the only other Magic in here. I can feel the glamour from across the room."

"You want him to make a scene? He can. You know he can. So, you're not going to do anything crazier than flash your clit control."

"Nice. So much better than dick power."

"Waving whatever you have around in front of an Elder won't end well if you persist, and only proves Donovan right. That you're someone the Mother Coven can't trust and should be taken out before these petty annoyances become something worth taking you out for."

"Not my Elder. Plus, I'm just protecting myself. He's the one posturing like an overprotective daddy. Sick of men waging wars for you yet?"

"Blow me."

She laughed. "Relax yourself, Elder. I'm not going to kill your precious Soul Seer. She can remain the pride of the Coven, now that you've trapped her within your band of goodie goods before anyone else could get a hold of her."

She reminded me that Aunt Lacey had put Kim in my path to get me to join. I knew it wasn't what Joelly was making it out to be, but it still itched between my shoulders enough for Ranlyn to shake his head at me as if to dispel any second-guessing.

"Besides," she continued, "Donovan would track me to the ends of the earth and beyond to punish me for killing his true love." She looked at me. "You will regret ever knowing him. I promise you that."

"Right. So, I guess your plan is to hang around The Lush, keeping

an eye on me, and what? Work on your alcoholism?" Her smirk disappeared. "I hit a nerve?"

Her pierced brow twitched. "You think you know something
about me?"

"I know you can put 'em down as easily as Donovan. If you're
from the same family, I imagine you come with some of the same
horrifying traumas as he does."

Her jaw clenched. "He knows nothing about horror."

Eddie returned and ended any chance of continuing the conversation, leaving me with a brain bulging with curiosity.

"Get you another round?" Joelly asked Ranlyn, her pasted on
smile returned as if she pulled on a mask.

"I got it."

She nodded and went back to letting Eddie entertain her.

Ranlyn remained for my whole shift, leaving only to return
spelled to look like another creeper and switching to beer so it wasn't
suspicious, remaining at the bar so Joelly knew she was under
constant watch. I had to work the floor, but Ranlyn made sure not to
let Joelly out of his sight. She didn't attempt to talk to him again or to
antagonize me. Instead, she hung on Eddie's every word and served
the bar's patrons like she intended on showing up for a follow-up
shift. I didn't get it and not knowing what she wanted drove me
fucking crazy.

Instead of making Caine leave the apartment, or maybe because he
didn't want me out of his sight, Ranlyn drove me home. Joelly had
remained with Eddie to learn closing procedures, leaving me free to
go, but Ranlyn didn't trust she was working alone and insisted on
escorting me home.

Met with puppy kisses at the door courtesy of Bosco, Ranlyn
followed me into my apartment.

"Hey!" Caine yelled and surged for Ranlyn.

"Stop!" We protested, and Ranlyn removed the spell to change his appearance. I hadn't thought about it coming up as he made it so I could see through the glamour each time.

"What's going on?" Caine asked.

I was already dialling. Donovan picked up on the second ring. "Yo, dude. Guess what?"

"No clue, dudette. What's up? Clearly, you're not hurt, but you sound pumped. I was getting eddies of aggravation from you all night, but you were at work and that place is a crazy house. You need a new job."

"What? It's fine. Well, not fine, which is my point. Guess what?"

Donovan gave a stout laugh and I heard what sounded like ruffling sheets. Was he in bed? "How 'bout you just tell me before you sprain something."

"I got a new co-worker today. Name's Danielle Baker." I paused to see if the name roused a reaction.

"Okay." A fridge door opening sounded in the background. "I'm pretty sure Danielle Baker should get a new job too. No offense, but why would I give a shit about your work? Love to chat, phone sex would be a treat, but if it's not on the menu can you get to the point?"

"Fine. Danielle Baker is an alias. You know her as Joelly Sorrel. I'm assuming you share the same surname."

"What did she do?"

Fury surged through the thread of connection. The anger was so strong I had to sit down. "Holy shit. You nearly knocked me to my knees."

"Sophie, tell me what's going on. Now."

"Shit. Okay. Nothing too horrendous, I promise." I went over the whole thing, feeling like an asshole when retelling the dig about my alcoholism crack. We never did talk about his family or the nightmare we shared while still in Diluculo about his childhood abuse. After full explanation, his worry scaled down a few notches and my back muscles relaxed enough to sit comfortably.

"I doubt Joelly will stay around long. I don't think she's ever held down legit employment."

"Meh. It's not a difficult place to be, but the money won't keep her happy."

"She doesn't need it. Which is another indication she's up to something." He groaned in frustration. "Don't worry, babe. I'll figure it out. Thank Ranlyn for me. Hopefully he can keep a greater presence at the bar between his Elder duties."

"Already on it," Ranlyn said loud enough for Donovan to hear.

Guilt and determination filled me as silence stretched over the line. "This isn't your fault, Donovan. As far as I can tell, it's Loring's. Maybe her presence is as innocent as catching up with her sort-of-brother and she just happens to be unemployed." Donovan made another throaty sound of disbelief, this one reverberating through the phone. "Yeah, yeah. Still. Don't shoulder the blame just yet."

"I'll talk to her again. At least I know where to find her."

"You can't go to the bar."

"Who says I can't?"

"Me. The one with her ass on the line, plus the innocent drunk people between you and your asshole sibling."

"I fail to understand why you told me where to find Joelly if I can't hunt her down."

"Hunt her? Cool it, Boba Fett. I work there. Don't give her a chance to jeopardize that. As much as I'd love to lie around and read my days away, I like paying for the roof over my head more."

"Cool the theatrics. Shit. I can picture a future filled with you getting your way." I ignored the comment. "I'll find a way to deal with Joelly without bringing it to your doorstep."

"You better."

"I said I would."

"Fine."

"Was that everything?"

"Yes, it was. Let me know what happens."

"I definitely will."

Once I returned the phone to the charging dock, I kicked off my shoes and Bosco bounced from Caine's lap to mine.

"So, Joelly showed up at The Lush?" The edge in Caine's tone was unmistakable.

"I'll be outside for a bit and on a stool for your next shift."

"Thanks again, Ranlyn."

He nodded and left, locking the door behind him.

"Yeah." I refused to engage with his snaky tone. "I have no idea why, but she's using a fake name and cozying up to Eddie."

"Hmmm."

"You okay?" The connection may not be the same with Caine as it was with Donovan, but sitting only a cushion over, it didn't have to be. The angry vibes he was putting out were intense.

Caine shrugged. Since he wasn't willing to share, I wasn't about to baby it out of him.

"What about Chinese?" I asked.

He looked at me. "People?"

"Food, you freak. Chinese food. I'm starving." Since he was struggling to digest the issue anyways, we may as well digest real food while we're at it.

A half an hour later, a knock at the door brought Ranlyn with a bag in each hand. He paid and sent the delivery guy away—his treat—and then went back to guarding the hallway. Double score. Whatever he was sucking up for, I was happy to let him keep it up.

"How can you use those?" I asked as Caine lifted a chunk of beef with a pair of thin wooden chopsticks.

"You ever try?"

"Tried and failed." I remembered making the attempt at a restaurant with my dad and brothers a few years back. Most of my food ended up in my lap while Ben nearly shot his peas out his nose laughing.

"It's all about the technique." He pulled out the other set and scooted closer.

"You're going to teach me?" I laughed. "I've seen this trick at the bar. I already know how to rack the balls and bank a trick shot."

"Good. Then you can teach me." His side-eye came with a slanted smile. "Unless you're lying to get free drinks I don't have. Let's see how good a student you are."

Caine's beauty took me off guard. Since we returned from Diluculo, I hadn't seen him smile often, though expected no different considering all that happened. He smoothed his hair behind his ears and showed me the awkward positioning of my fingers, which threatened to cramp at any moment. He then added the chopsticks. He supervised as I attempted to nip a green pepper from my chicken lo mein noodles.

"Almost had the fucker that time." I tried again. Again, the pepper dropped. "Ugh, crust-ass!" I dropped one chopstick and stabbed the other into the mangled pepper and popped it into my mouth. "I'm a quitter."

Caine's smoky eyes became serious. "You know, just when I think Donovan's existence in your life has the power to drive a wedge between us, I watch you wrestle and lose to a pepper and I love you more. Far too much to let the wedge win."

I was taken aback by his sudden candor, frozen by the fact this was what lay in the depth of his tension after the call with Donovan.

He moved in to kiss me and met no resistance—only a pause to make sure the defiant pepper didn't get lodged in my throat. Our lips reconnected the moment it went down, then parted in submission to built-up desire from weeks of no contact. Our arms wrapped around each other, our hands searching the confines of each other's bodies, my mind caught in the feverish spiral. Self-control, raw and aching by the constant reining in of anything remotely sexual, was thrown out the window. It all then reeled back in when Donovan's panic drilled through me.

"Wait." I pushed at Caine's chest as his teeth scraped my throat.

"I know, I'm sorry." He braced his weight, hovering above me. In the passion of the moment we found ourselves lying out on the couch.

"It's fine. Don't move." I moved his hair behind his ear and kissed him again—a peck that didn't hold the passion of the last. "Fuck. I'm the worst dick tease."

"At least I know there's still something between us."

"I know this is messed up. No matter what I say, you're still left with blue balls and I'm short an underwear change and a viable solution."

Caine pecked me on the lips and pulled me up, along with himself, into a seated position. After taking the chance to fix our twisted clothes, he held me close, and smoothed my hair.

"If we don't allow sex to define our relationship, we can do this." He found a way to hold me tighter. "It's a new one for me, but I promised to be understanding. I'm doing my best."

"I know you are. I am, too."

Usually, I was the one encouraging him, but this time he found the right words to erase my doubt. I didn't know him before the accident, but in my imagination, all it took was a lash flutter and he would find himself nestled between the thighs of some more-than-willing partner screaming his name at high volume. While my porn-sullied imagination might be wild and uncreative, I bet I wasn't far off. I didn't know how to have an adult relationship without sex or unhealthy complication. Now I didn't have a choice but to find doses of intimacy in other forms.

Stuck in my head, while relaxed by Caine's words, I passed out, waking up as he pulled the duvet over me.

"The food."

"In the fridge. You can eat it for lunch tomorrow." He kissed my forehead and knelt beside the bed.

"Bosco?"

"Walked, fed, and snoring." I could hear him in his bed on the floor.

"Are you staying?" I felt for him in the dim light of the moon flooding in from the window and wrapped an arm over his shoulder.

"Course." He kissed me again. "I'm going to shower. Get changed out of Dean if you can."

"Mmmm, Dean."

He laughed, and I watched him disappear into the bathroom. In a sleepy blur, I searched for the feeling of Donovan along the connection, wondering if he was okay. Hesitant warmth filled my chest. Guilt for the hesitation was unavoidable, but his assurance was insistent. Balancing everyone's needs while setting mine on the back-burner was exhausting, but I allowed Caine's lingering love and Donovan's reassurance to lull me to sleep.

4

CAN'T FIGHT THE TRUTH

Washing my hair beneath the warmth of the shower stirred up the memory of waking up next to Caine and the feel of his chest rising and falling with each shallow breath as he remained asleep. The thought left me with a contentment that was both gratifying and terrifying. After last night's orgasm-less game of stop and go, I expected him to be pissed. I realized I was projecting my ex's expectations onto him and reminded myself how different they were, but even with Brock, there was never anyone between us. Not like with Donovan.

Before the guilt crept in, I shut off the water along with my emotions surrounding the men in my life and dressed to the hum of the microwave. Caine was up and hungry.

The smell of leftovers drifted down the hall. When I entered the kitchen, Caine said, "Want some?" with a smolder to his eyes.

"Getting fresh, are we?" I played it up as I pecked his lips for his cheekiness. His chest rumbled in a laugh as he lazily wrapped his arms around my waist then grabbed my ass. "Hey!" I slapped at him before he moved in to kiss me again.

His playful side was infectious. Things were always so serious.

Too serious. Despite being re-introduced to a world worth smiling for, events found a way to piss on all my happy moments. Life as a Magic was not a relaxing one. So far, it sucked major vag pimples and I didn't want to lose the ability for a little grab-assing to make me smile.

The microwave beeped. "You wake up hungry?" He still held me against him.

"Sure."

"Chopsticks?"

"After last night's escapades? Not a good idea. Apparently, they get you all revved up." Without creating inches between us, I fished a fork from the silverware drawer.

He lifted an eyebrow and removed the steaming food from the microwave. "Watching you wield a weapon is hot."

I made a throaty noise. "Chopsticks are a weapon? What kung fu do you do?"

"That pepper was terrified."

I narrowed my eyes and forked another green pepper, holding it like a wriggling victim and shoved it into my mouth.

"See, even a fork is part of your arsenal."

I giggled and took the plate to the couch without any complaints that I snaked his food.

The flirtatious conversation was enough to start the day off on a good note, and we both finished off the plates started the previous night before the elastic of our sexual tension nearly snapped and created a shitstorm.

"Do you work tonight?" He lifted my feet into his lap.

"Nope. Which is awesomesauce, 'cuz I'm not into dealing with Joelly's circle jerk and Ranlyn has better things to do. Probably not a circle jerk, but who knows what he's up to."

"Feel like meeting some new people?"

Nervousness floated beneath his words and had me suspicious. "Is this when you tell me you're a swinger? I don't think you're Ranlyn's type." He huffed, shook his head, and grabbed my foot, pretending to gnaw on my toes. I squealed and pulled my foot away. "I'm not into feet either, swing boy."

"Me either." He returned them to his lap. "Mind in the gutter much?"

"You started it." He didn't look sorry.

"I meant some of my people. Eli and Bernadine."

"Oh." I sat up. "You want me to meet them?"

"Obviously."

"No, I know, I guess. Have you told them about Daniel?"

His mouth did a puckered twist as he sat back into the cushions. "I was hoping you'd help me with that part. You're good at this stuff."

"What stuff?"

"People stuff."

"You sure you know me? 'Cuz I've never mediated a 'telling people their evil piece of shit brother is dead' conversation before. Especially when it's my fault."

He turned his body toward me. "What the hell are you talking about?" Voice low, his smoky eyes captured mine in an intense lock. "I'm sorry!"

Before I could think "What the fizz-bomb was that?" he turned away. I blinked until comprehension dawned. He unintentionally used his Persuasion on me, getting to the point where he held my will before noticing and letting go. I shook off the remnants of his momentary hostage takeover as the rush of magic buzzing in the air subsided. I didn't even see when he jumped to his feet, now pacing the living room with his hands knotted in his dark hair.

"It's fine."

"It's not fine." His voice came out a growl. "I wasn't trying to—"

"I know. That's why I said it's fine. I'm not a bitchy it's-fine-when-it's-not-fine kind of chick."

Another uncomfortable minute passed before he returned to the couch edge, sitting with his elbows on his knees. "Why would you say that?"

"I could tell it was an accident."

"Sophie!"

"What?"

I waited. If he was going to continue yelling, he could leave. I gave him a minute and hoped something explanatory popped out of his mouth.

"I killed my father." His tone was devoid of any emotion.

"I know, but you wouldn't have attacked him if he wasn't killing Donovan, which was killing me." The memory of me screaming for him to "do something" was fresh in my ears.

"My initial strike could be considered in your defence." He paused. "What came after? That was all me."

"He would've killed all of us to prove himself to Loring. You heard Aunt Lacey. It was an act of courage, not cowardice."

"Aunt Lacey didn't want me to carry around the guilt."

Seeing the shame in Caine's expression made me hate his prick father even more. "I saw what made up the soul of that man." He finally looked at me. "Daniel made his choice. You forget the night in Pario wasn't the first time he tried to kill you. He agreed you and your brother dying was a wise choice for the good of Loring's plan. He was an evil fuck and had no plans on being anything else." I interlaced our fingers. "I'm not sorry to say his life wasn't worth yours. He forced you to save us and I never said thank you. So, thank you, for saving my life as well as Donovan's. It says more about your character than taking out a man who was genetically your relative, but in every other way so far removed from family."

Squeezing my hand tight, he kissed my knuckles. "See? You're good at this."

I smiled. "I'll edit out the evil fuck part when I talk to your family." Talking people out of their funks was a bartender's curse, though I hoped to be more than a bandage and then ply someone with alcohol. I did know Caine was undeserving of his anguish, even if I understood the dark place it stemmed from. He had too much hell to face in too little time, but he was worthy of happiness.

Of course, after a conversation like that, I used the next hour to get ready. I called Kim while staring at my closet. "What do you wear to meet the family of the man who tried to slaughter you?"

———

"Did you tell them we were coming?" The blue-sided farmhouse was quiet from the outside. The soft ping of rain against the tin awning punctuated the ticking seconds while we waited.

"No, but they won't mind us dropping by." Looking around us wasn't materializing anyone, but that didn't stop him from doing it for the tenth time. "I should have come as soon as we got back from Diluculo."

The fact he didn't was unsurprising. I put out prayers to the Goddess, Peter Pan, The Seven Dwarfs, and to whoever managed to get *Sliders* un-cancelled, for them not to be home. I wasn't against meeting Caine's family, but dreaded the conversation to come like a bout of chlamydia. Shit. Hopefully they didn't hear me thinking about that. I wasn't sure how long the brain shield of Ranlyn's lasted. They probably heard me. Fuck. Great first impression.

The door behind the screen opened with a loud scuff, sending me into a mild panic they could actually hear me. A young woman's face lit up at the sight of Caine huddling beneath the awning and I exhaled in relief that her attention was on him and not me.

"Hey Cuz, back for more?" Her bright smile matched her sunny soul glow as she opened the screen and motioned him inside.

"At last count, I was schooling you."

"Can't school the teacher, Caine. I'm always light on lesson one." Her long, blonde ponytail swayed as she moved aside. "Oh," she squeaked as her hand reached for her chest, "didn't see you there."

"It's okay, his giraffe-like height comes in handy for sneaking into the movies. I'm Sophie."

The short blonde made a high-pitched giggle. "I'm Bridgette. Call me Jet." She shook my hand with a grip of a labourer, then crossed her arms and looked to Caine. "Nice manners, doofus. Never heard of ladies first?"

"Yeah, doofus." I jabbed an elbow into his side. "And here I thought you were a gentleman."

"One second in the door and you turn on me?"

I shrugged. "She is the teacher. I was always a bit of a brown-noser."

"I should have known," he muttered, then slipped off his white zip-up sweater and threw it at Jet, who reflexively caught it. "Where's your dad, teach?"

"In the basement trying to rummage up some chain." She held up his sweater. "You wanna take this or should I tear it up for rags?"

"I'll take it." A voice called from down the hall preceding the entrance of a woman who pushed her plaid button-down shirt sleeves to her elbows and then took the sweater. "Forget where the closet is, Jet?" She slid open the entry closet doors and hung-up Caine's sweater.

"Yup. Where am I? Must be at your place where you left your fighting skills, Caine."

"Enough, you two." The woman trained her hazel eyes on me. "You going to introduce me to your friend, Caine, or should I guess her name?"

Jet snorted. "He forgot his manners in his fancy car out there."

"Geez." He looked at me wide-eyed. "When did you get time to recruit them into your posse?"

"Had to snatch 'em up before you could fill their heads with stories." The banter eased my nerves.

"Right. Aunt Bernadine, I'd like you to meet Sophie. Sophie, this is my Aunt Bernadine. There. Introduction accomplished."

I shook my head. "So posh of you. Nice to meet you, Bernadine." I received another firm handshake.

"Please, call me Bernie. Great to finally meet you, Sophie."

"Caine said you helped him a lot. I know he really appreciates it."

"I'm sure he enjoyed the competition." Jet pinned him with a comedic-yet-menacing stare that Caine returned in kind.

"We were happy to give it." Bernie waved off. "I assume this was also fine with your Coven Leader. How is Elsa?"

Fried shit noodles.

Caine looked down at me, waiting.

"All yours." I refused to catch the hot potato.

"Oh no." Bernie's light brown hair fell into her face as she closed her eyes and dropped her chin.

"It's part of why we're here." Caine put his hand on the small of my back. I tried to gather some strength from his touch.

"Get your father." Jet disappeared down the hall, her heavy footsteps bounding down creaky wooden stairs. "Both of you sit." Bernie guided us to a flowered couch but wouldn't sit herself. "Can I get either of you something to drink?"

"To be honest," Caine said, "I'd really like to get this conversation over with before we get comfy." This did nothing to relax Bernie as she stood, lips pursed with crossed arms in wait for Jet and Eli to return. She looked towards the hallway as if she might fetch them herself if they didn't return in ten seconds.

A man I assumed was Eli entered before Jet. He rubbed his dirty hands with a rag. "Good to see you, Caine." He looked at me. "Hi there, you must be Sophie. Sorry, my hands are covered in a decade's worth of grime, but it's nice to meet you."

"You too," I said hoping not to add him to the list of Caine's family members who wanted me dead.

Eli sat on the lounger, still trying to make the dirty rag do more than it was capable of. "What's going on? Everything okay?"

"Guess it depends on who you ask," Caine said. Eli, Bernie, and Jet waited for him to continue. He inhaled before saying, "Aunt Lacey is dead."

I felt myself flinch, envisioning the moment her last breath escaped her vessel.

"No." Bernie sat with a slump on the thick arm of the lounger, hand to her throat. Eli's jaw slacked, stunned.

"So is Daniel," Caine added.

The bombshell hit Eli so hard he couldn't look at his nephew, his attention now on his hands. Bernie covered her mouth and laid a hand on her husband's shoulder.

"Be right back. Gonna wash my hands." Eli was out of the room before he finished.

I felt horrendous for Caine and Eli. When Caine looked at me with worry and questions in his stormy eyes, I said, "Give him a moment to process."

No one else spoke as Jet moved to her mother's side to console her, both trying to be strong. I wondered if Jet ever met her evil Uncle Daniel or if she was absorbing her parents' sadness. Could she have met Aunt Lacey? I wouldn't have thought so, but I wasn't about to ask.

Eli returned five excruciating minutes later and reclaimed his seat. "Start from the beginning," he said with newfound strength.

As requested, Caine started from the beginning—before venturing to Diluculo, including our binding and Aunt Lacey's blocked sight. No one enjoyed the gritty details of what Loring and Daniel did to Aunt Lacey and the other Elders, but Caine managed this and the stabbing of his father with dissociated accuracy.

"Loring made mention of Cole going to their Coven Master with his plans to take down the Elders. Do you know who their leader is?" Loring was a devil of a man. I couldn't imagine someone crueller.

"Cole had a part in this?" Bernie's voice rose with her confusion.

"Who's Cole?" Jet asked.

I hadn't noticed Caine kept his brother out of the explanation. I looked to him in apology before he filled in the blanks.

Eli and Caine had more in common than blood. Both had a brother who was either too weak or too greedy to consider that their acts would put their families in danger. Daniel attempted, on many occasions, to bring Eli into some seemingly innocuous proposals, then

Eli would survive by the skin of his teeth and would vow never to get involved with Daniel again.

"Do you know anything about what he was capable of?" Eli inquired. "Regarding his abilities, I mean," he corrected, as it was already clear Cole was capable of a lot more than Caine ever imagined.

"Loring never said, and he was the one doing all the talking."

"At least you got the bastard running. Good for you," Eli said to me after hearing of Loring's escape.

"He'll be back," I said with confidence that unsettled the others.

Jet sat on a love seat to our left. "Loring, I get. From what I heard he's no one to mess with. What I don't get, is how sharing a past life with someone makes you connected to them now. Especially to the point someone like Loring can take you both down. You sure he's not influencing you somehow? You're still new to this."

Caine shifted next to me.

"I can tell when he's lying as if it was a lie from my own mouth. Plus, I've seen a vision of us in that time together. There's no mistaking the connection. Like right now, I know he's in the shower because I can feel hot water hitting my back and arms."

"Whoa. That's fucked up."

"Yup. He'll be across the city, but I still get tipsy if he's drinking."

Jet laughed. "Better than free drinks."

"Except he drinks more than he should. Especially after all this. He was related to Aunt Lacey, so he's taking it pretty hard."

"How's he related?" Bernie asked.

"No idea, but she left everything to him, so I'm assuming she knew. He's a Sorrel, so I doubt it was through that family. I can't imagine the lineage being too fresh considering how old she is."

"He's a Sorrel?" When I nodded, Eli let out a booming laugh. "Guess it makes sense you two are buds, Caine. The Berisfords and Sorrels go way back. Fought in the trenches, though for the wrong side."

"We're not friends," Caine said.

I found it hard to take so bluntly.

"Ah," Bernie said. "I guess that confuses things."

"A little." I attempted to tread lightly.

"No nieces or nephews in the near future, eh?" Bernie said with a knowing smile.

It took Jet a moment to understand and Eli even longer. "Yikes," Jet finally said. "The ultimate cockblock."

Eli cleared his throat. "No one said life would be simple."

My cheeks burned. I was so embarrassed I hid my face in my hands. When Jet burst into laughter, I couldn't help but get pulled in with her. No one knew more than me how serious a matter it was but looking at our problem from the outside was bizarre as well as hilarious.

We had dropped so much on his family I felt guilty for knocking on the door and then sitting here laughing about anything. "Sorry to bring such shocking news."

"Can't fight the truth, can you?" Eli asked rhetorically, leaving us to nod in awkward agreement. Eli patted his wife's hand on his shoulder and then he took a deep breath. "I know I have work to get done. You two sticking around? I'm sure Jet wouldn't mind getting in some practice."

"Damn straight." Jet sprung to her feet. "No way you're putting me down again."

Caine didn't look too psyched to stay, but I smiled with encouragement thinking it might be good for him. He agreed, and Jet squealed with excitement.

We followed Eli and Jet through the rain out the back door to a big barn. The barn was hauntingly familiar, resembling the one we were corralled to in Pario. Anxiousness prevailed until we went through a small doorway next to closed garage doors. We moved into the large wooden building. The floors were cement, unlike the dirt of the one Loring made his arena. It was nowhere near the size of the one Aunt Lacey and the Elders lost their lives in but was similar enough to make my hands tremble.

Caine's fingers kneaded into my shoulders as I walked in before him and stopped, rooted to the spot as I surveyed the barn, keeping him outside in the rain. "You okay?" he asked as water fell onto his face from darkened tendrils.

"Yeah. Sorry." I looked back at the large space, Caine following my eyes.

"Wow."

"Yeah."

"You good?"

I nodded. "You?"

He nodded.

He gripped my hand for a moment before Eli called for him to help with the tractor.

Jet knew minor aspects of what was going on with it, but it was cryptic to me. I took a seat on a pile of wood pallets while Caine dove into the grit, giving Eli direct help in way of hands, arms, and elbows covered in grease. When he asked Jet to jump into the driver's seat and turn the engine over, nothing happened. They sighed and went back to work. I would have offered to help, but Caine was tall enough to reach parts with barely a stretch, and Eli seemed to enjoy the time spent working closely with his nephew who heartbreakingly resembled his dead brother, grey eyes and all.

Eli gave up on the tractor after thirty minutes of failed attempts. He thought he had the problem down but didn't have the parts to make the repair.

Jet popped out of the tractors seat onto the ground. "Practice?"

Eli closed the hood of the tractor with a slam and grabbed a rag from his pocket to wipe off his dirty hands. "All yours."

A wave of energy from Jet knocked Caine back as she roused her power into high gear in a split second. He caught himself before falling on his ass.

"Hey!" Caine reclaimed his footing and returned a hazardous burst of energy of his own. His attempt fell flat as Jet jumped off the tractor into the air and hovered, his magic hitting the barn wall and knocking down gardening equipment. "Let me wash up first."

Jet hovered above us, laughing hysterically as I stared up in awe.

"You're cleaning that up, Bridgette," Eli said. "Anything you break, you replace."

"It's not my fault his accuracy sucks." She slowly made her way to the ground.

"My accuracy is fine. You caught me off guard."

"Payments of being the teacher, darlin'." Eli winked at me as he exited the barn into the rain.

"Yeah, Teach. Beat'cha when I get back." A kiss to my forehead and Caine was running out into the rain after his uncle to wash up.

Jet sat back up on the tractor. "He's actually pretty good, considering how new he is to his power."

"You should see him in action."

"I can imagine." Jet laughed. "I was sore as hell the last time he was here."

I remembered how excited he was to tell me everything the moment my ear was available.

"Wanna spar?" Jet asked. "After the story in there it'd be nice to see how I measure up against someone who can disintegrate their enemies. Though pump the breaks when you get to that part."

"I'm actually more of a floundering wingbat than a pro, it was—"

Jet hit me with a wave of power that flung me backwards on the pallet, smacking the back of my skull into the wood.

Jet's laugh warbled in my stunned ears. "Come on, you're better than that."

My skull vibrated. Pain shot down my spine. I grunted as I tried to sit up amidst the spins. "Stop. I can't—"

Jet thought hitting me with another wave of power was better motivation than talking.

"Bridgette!" I rolled off the pallet, managing to get on all fours.

I lifted my hand out in front of me and stood slowly. "You don't get it."

Jet sent another wave. I dodged to the left and it hit the wall behind me with a jarring shake of the barn. "There you go. Missed you that time."

My breath was punchy. Not winded, pissed. "Donovan feels it every time you hit me."

"So?" She tossed another shot of power my way, this one taking out my knees, knocking me to the ground face first, chin bouncing off the cement and jarring my teeth together.

Not only was I angry, but so was Donovan. The heat of confusion, fear, and fury burned my ears. I needed to end this. I pushed to my feet and wiped my chin of blood. I rushed towards Jet. She jumped with intentions of flying away, but I snatched her foot before she got far enough above me. A yank had her hitting the ground and me sitting on her, pinning her wrists in my hands, and enacting my power so she could feel the buzzing threat of it against her skin.

"Whoa. Don't—"

"Donovan thinks someone's attacking me for real. He can't get to me and doesn't know where I am. Can you imagine how that feels?"

She struggled, but I revved my power a hint in warning until she settled. "Can't you have fun and then he'd know you weren't actually facing death?"

"You already hit me, more than once. His body would've been thrown like mine was. And when you're not expecting an ass-kicking, it's not fun, it just fucking hurts." I got up off her and backed away, ready on my feet in case she attacked again.

Jet wiped off her butt as she stood staring at me with harsh blue eyes. "You care way too much about this Donovan guy."

"You don't even know him," I snapped back, matching Jet's attitude.

Caine's hurried voice burst into the barn. "All right," he growled, shaking off the rain and handing me his cell. "I don't appreciate him calling to scream at me."

I took the phone and paced a few steps away. "Hey."

"Whatthefuck, babe?" Donovan yelled in a voice so hurried his words slurred.

"Caine's cousin was trying to get me to play with her." I turned my back to Caine and Jet's stares.

"I was driving. They're lucky I pulled over in time before causing a pile up!"

"I'll let her know."

"Is this the type of Berisford I should be worried about?"

"Nothing like that. They were practicing, and she wanted me to have fun. She didn't know what it would do."

"You're lying!"

"I know I'm lying, but I'm fine, so you can stop worrying. I promise, no more fighting. Okay?"

"Obviously, it's okay." Anger left his words. "I'm not trying to invade your life, babe, but I was freaking out."

"I know." I heard Jet huff, but when I looked at her, Caine was urging her to stay out of it. "I gotta go. I'll talk to you later."

"Okay, but just a tip, babe. Get your own cell. Ten-year-olds are more connected than you."

"Yeah, yeah. Later."

I gave Caine back his phone. "He didn't know any other way to get a hold of me."

"Did you give him my number?" He dropped the phone in his pocket. I shook my head. I didn't give him my number either, but it didn't stop him from calling me at home. "How'd he get it?"

"I don't know." I hated feeling like he was accusing me of something. I understood he was deflecting because he couldn't do anything about the connection and how much it got in the way, but it still made me want to punch something.

"Stalker much?" Jet muttered, earning her a sharp glare from Caine. She raised her hands, refraining from taking it further.

"I'm sorry, Jet," I managed. "I wasn't exaggerating when I talked about the connection. He was driving when you hit me, and though it wasn't hard, it was still dangerous. I didn't mean to snap or attack you, I just needed you to stop."

"You attacked her?" Caine asked.

"Hardly," Jet said. "I've been put down harder."

"Wait," Caine pointed at Jet. "She got you down?"

"Don't even. She could've disintegrated my hands."

Caine laughed. "She beat you."

"Shut up." Jet flashed a smile. "I don't know how you two deal with this every day."

"It's more difficult when someone's trying to beat me up."

"Yeah, I bet." Jet was back to her sunny self. "Fortunately, Stretch, you have no excuse and your hands couldn't tear a paper towel let alone turn me to ash." She slapped Caine's shoulder. He jumped as she zapped him with a hit of magic and then she was up in the air again as they got back to their sparring match.

5

SPOTTY RECEPTION

Being on the sidelines felt like being a spectator at an elite boxing match. Power reverberated off the walls of the barn—Donovan could feel the runoff—but the cousins were laughing. They never hit each other hard enough to inflict permanent damage, but more than I considered in the name of fun, especially once Jet learned I could heal. This gave her license to hit harder, no longer fearing minor bumps and bruises, or cracked ribs for that matter.

Both were heaving in exhaustion, covered in sweat, and done for the day. Caine stopped before we reached the barn's exit and gave me a deep kiss that made Jet fake-gag and leave us alone.

"That was fun," he said after we pulled away from each other.

I wasn't the least bit insulted he was referring to the mock battle and not my make-out skills. The fact that his clothes were soaked in sweat, grease, and splatters of blood turned out to invoke a surprising effect. Now that sex was off the table, my libido decided it wanted it that much more.

"I thought you couldn't do that," Jet teased while fixing her ponytail when we entered the kitchen. "Donovan will be pissed." We laughed, half-embarrassed as Bernie was present, cooking something that caused the kitchen windows to steam and drip to the sill.

"Yeah, well, Donovan can deal with a little reminder now and then." Caine plopped down into one of the kitchen chairs.

Bernie turned with tongs in hand, smile tight. "If you stay in the kitchen, you help."

We escaped to the living room.

Ten minutes later, a little boy walked through the door. "Hey, Andy Pandy."

"Hi, mama." He dropped his backpack as Jet wrapped him in a hug.

"Is that where your bag goes?" Jet looked at her son with raised brows. He missed the reminder because he was busy staring at me sitting on the couch next to Caine. Jet noticed. Her expression tensed. "That's Sophie, baby. Say hi."

Andy scooped up his bag and dragged it to his room without a word, Jet yelling after him to clean up for dinner. "Sure you don't want a litter?" I returned a superficial laugh but found the child's instant dislike for me off-putting.

Jet was called into the kitchen to help her mother set the table, leaving Caine and I alone. "Was he like that with you?"

He squeezed my hand. "He was shy at first. He's six, he'll warm up."

I didn't have much contact with children besides my youngest brother Ben, but figured Caine was right. Andy came back down the hallway, stopped, and stared at me again. I smiled at him, but this seemed to frighten him more, and he ran into the kitchen.

I looked at Caine. "He's warming up so quick I need oven mitts."

"Mhmm."

During dinner, things got weirder. We sat around the dining table set with matching white dishes and a lacy table cloth. Besides its occupants, the dinner was rather normal. Chicken and asparagus kabobs with mashed potatoes and peas with cut chunks of corn on the cob. During the entire dinner, Andy watched me.

This irked me on two levels. One, because I hated being stared at no matter who the eyeballs belonged to, and some spawn I didn't know was gawking at me like I was the incarnation of the boogeyman complete with oozing sores and bug-laced hair. Two, the little boy's soul colour glowed white, his undertones shining green indicating he was a Seer.

"Can I ask what he sees?" I asked Jet.

Mid-chew into another chunk of chicken and tearing it from the wooden stick, Jet covered her mouth and said, "What do you mean?"

"Andy's a Seer." I smiled at him and looked back at Jet. "I just wondered what he sees."

After a hard swallow, Jet's expression soured. "Are you done, baby?" He hadn't touched his plate, so he left the table, more akin to fleeing the scene. Wiping her mouth with a paper towel, then dropping her hands in her lap, Jet looked reluctant to answer. I felt like a douche for asking.

"You don't have to answer. I didn't mean to cross a line."

The family was burdened by something. Caine squeezed my knee beneath the table. I put mine atop his. It was moments like this I wished I didn't know as much as I did.

"We weren't sure," Jet said in a whisper before clearing her throat. Everyone dropped their silverware and listened as her blue eyes glistened with tears. "He's so young, but you have to understand, he doesn't mean to stare."

"Since my gift surfaced, I've been far too nosey. I don't usually scare children away. On a roll today." My humour made things more awkward instead of less.

Although she attempted to fight against it, Jet couldn't hide the sudden shake of her chin. "His father died almost two years ago." I squeezed Caine's hand harder. "It was an accident, but for a long time before it happened, Andy insisted he saw—" She had her hand up in front of her face as the tears fell, "spots or shadows. He was only four, but he would keep saying, "Daddy is dirty, or daddy has spots" and point to his neck. When Rob died, I had to identify his remains." She shifted in her chair. "His injuries were in the exact places Andy said there were spots."

"Oh, my god." Why would a child be subjected to such a power? To see his father's wounds, knowing something was wrong before it happened. What was a four-year-old expected to do with that type of macabre knowledge? "Was that the only time?"

Jet shook her head no.

"Did they all die?" Caine questioned through clenched teeth. Jet hesitated and then gave a tear-soaked nod.

Caine took a ragged intake of breath. "No."

"He wouldn't lie," Eli finally spoke.

"He has to be," Caine blurted.

"Caine—" I tried, but my voice faltered too low for him to hear.

"I wish he was," Jet said.

"It's okay."

"How could your death ever be okay?" His grey eyes were blazing steel.

"He was just staring, maybe that's not what he saw. Maybe he just thinks I'm weird." By the look on Andy's face, it was doubtful, but he hadn't said for sure what he saw. "Do you mind if I talk to him," I asked Jet. "I don't want to scare him, but I don't want him to feel guilty if something does happen to me."

Jet reluctantly agreed.

I was sorry for interrupting their dinner, but no one was eating, and Caine was barely speaking. He stayed at the table with his aunt and uncle while Jet and I went to Andy's room. A small square of carpet was painted with a winding track, all a kid needed to imagine a full out race instead of whatever horrors he's already seen. I hated to ruin his fun, if only I could bring myself not to have this conversation, but I felt he may need it. I know I did.

"Hey, Andy Pandy." Jet smiled from ear to ear as her eyes glistened. "Come sit with me." Jet took a seat on his captain's bed with race car bed sheets and pulled him onto her lap. He held onto the car, his eyes fixed on it. "Sophie wants to talk to you, okay? She's special, too, so you can tell her anything you want." Andy didn't answer, but Jet kissed the back of his head and looked to me to begin.

I sat cross-legged on the ground beside the bed. "Like your mama said, I'm special, too. My gift tells me you're an extra special boy." Andy continued to play with the wheels of the little car without acknowledging me. "I'm going to ask you a question, Andy, okay?" I touched his socked foot dangling in front of me, he looked at me with suspicion. "You don't have to answer, but no matter what you say, I pinky promise I won't be mad." I paused, waiting for some type of reaction.

"What's pinky promise?"

I smiled. This one was easy. "You take your pinky finger like this," I showed him by curling mine into a hook. He copied me, taking a moment to figure out how to keep it up without it closing with his other fingers. "And then, you say, 'pinky promise' and you do this." I crossed my pinky with his, afraid he would pull away. When he didn't, I knew he was good and listening. Jet smiled through spilt tears.

"Now this," I shook our connected pinkies between us, "means, that no matter what, I have to keep my promise. Got it?"

He nodded.

"Okay, now that we pinky promised, I need to know something." Andy waited for the question. "When you look at me, do you see the spots?" Andy looked back to the car in his hands. "Remember, buddy, you have my pinky promise I can't get mad. You can tell me if there is." I pretty much knew the answer, but I needed to know for sure.

Andy nodded.

I expected this, but it still hit me. A squeak on the floor outside the room told me Caine was out there listening. No x-ray vision needed to know it was him. I wasn't upset with his eavesdropping this time, though he did make an uncanny habit of it.

"See, I'm not mad." I smiled at him, touching his foot again so he would look at me. Behind him, Jet was, silently bawling. "Can you show me where?"

His eyes swept over my body. I sat straighter, so he could see me better. "All over," he summed up.

Footsteps in the hallway broke off in the opposite direction. Caine had heard enough. His scuffle attracted Andy's attention, but I brought it back to me. "It's okay, Andy."

Andy shook his head. "But now you'll go away like daddy and Mrs. Fisher." Jet's head fell back as she tried her best to breathe through her sobs.

I didn't know who Mrs. Fisher was, but obviously, she was someone else in his life he saw the spots and ended up losing. "Well, you know what, Andy, it's true. It might mean that I'll go away like your daddy and Mrs. Fisher." Andy's face crumbled, and Jet glared at me. "All this means is that you're special. It's not your fault that your daddy and Mrs. Fisher went away, and if I go away, that's not your fault either."

"But it happens after I see the spots."

"You see the spots, but you don't make the person with the spots go away. You just see it before it happens. Like a warning, that's all."

"But I told daddy and it didn't matter."

Jet couldn't stop the sob from escaping this time.

I spoke above her. "No one knew what the spots meant before. Now your mama and your grandparents understand. So, the next time you see the spots, you tell them, and they can let you know if it's okay to tell that person. Sometimes people don't want to know when they might go away." I looked at Jet. "Is that okay?" She nodded and wiped her eyes. The last thing anyone needed was him telling strangers they had spots and were 'going away' soon.

"See buddy, it's not your fault if someone goes away."

Andy's forehead creased as he tried to work it out. "Pinky promise?"

I giggled. "Pinky promise." We shook our pinkies to solidify my word.

He reminded me of my little cousin Mason. Mason was older but both boys needed a little push and I was happy to give it. "You think your grandma has some dessert out there?" I looked to Jet hoping it was true or would hitchhike if it meant finding some.

Jet nodded and sniffed. "Cookie dough ice cream. Go ahead and get a bowl." She put him on the ground and he ran from the room. We could hear his excited voice in the kitchen as he let Bernie know his mom said it was okay.

Jet and I got to our feet. She reached up to put her arms around me for a tight hug. "I'm so sorry."

"Me too." No one expected the visit to result in this, but I felt better knowing.

Jet joined her son with a bowl of ice cream, but Caine was nowhere in sight. Eli motioned his blond head to the back door, so I went out to find him.

Caine was in the barn leaning forward, hands against the tractor, like he was using it to keep himself from falling over. He was wet enough from the rain that he must have been standing beneath the open sky for a while before seeking shelter. The expression on his face mixed with his soaking hair and clothes, reminded me of his time in the park during his sleeping curse.

My shoes scuffed on the cement. He looked through his hair at me as I walked towards him. He took in a ragged breath and turned his back to wipe his eyes. The whites were already bloodshot and swelling, cheeks reddened and streaked where he had missed some of his tears. I stopped in front of him. I hated to see him upset, but this wasn't something I expected him to suck up.

"How can you be so cool about this?" His voice was laden with so much anger.

I shrugged. "It's different being on this side of things." A cop-out, yet the only thing that made me feel like crying was the fact that he was so upset.

"I feel like I'm going insane," he muttered, his trembling hands moved through his wet hair, slicking it back as his expression crumbled again, tears sprouting he couldn't contain. "Fuck!" He punched the tractor's bulbous fender with a dose of power. It dented and curved to his hand with the sound of crunching metal, making me jump.

"Call Donovan." He grappled his phone from his pocket and shoved it into my hands.

The pass off was fumbled. I managed to snatch it. "Why?"

"Because he won't let you. Call him right now."

"Caine—"

"Donovan won't let you accept this. Talk to him."

"I want to talk to you first before I have two raving men on my hands."

"Fine." He snatched the phone back.

While his fingers shakily found Donovan's number, he paced as he searched, leaving me with a dented fender and Donovan's anxiousness growing as he no doubt saw Caine's number on his phone after the emotions filtered between us since the moment I found out about the spots. Caine started talking at a feverish pace. I didn't listen. I knew what he would say and as the conversation hit on the vital points, Donovan's confusion, and then anger, flooded me. I tried to concentrate on the tractor, but his furious denial threatened to pull me under.

To keep myself from crumpling alongside him, I worked with the power his emotions were pushing to the surface and built on them, laying my hand flat on the tractor. With no clue what was wrong with the machinery, I attempted to visualize it as whole and in working order. When I heard the dent pop into place, I knew something worked. As my power subsided to the lower hum Donovan's evoked, I climbed into the tractor seat and turned the key, only slightly flinching when the beast roared to life.

"What are you doing?" Caine yelled above the engine.

I turned off the tractor, pleased at least one thing in front of me was fixable. Caine returned to his conversation and I was forced to wait for him to finish.

"We're meeting him and Kim at Aunt Lacey's." He stuck the phone back in his pocket. "Let's go."

I didn't appreciate the demand, even in a crisis. "Slow down, Caine," I managed as calmly as I could. Now that Donovan wasn't on the phone, he was at home freaking out and it buzzed through my veins so frenetically my vision blurred.

"No. You need to get in gear. Let's go."

Another demand.

"Caine, this is happening to me, so how about relax for two seconds before we jump into your car and, I don't know, get into an accident because you're too upset to concentrate on the road." Caine's nostrils flared like a raging bull. "Andy's gift didn't come with a timeframe or cause of death, unless you count 'all over' as scientific proof."

"I understand this is happening to you." Caine spoke slowly. "But it's me and it's Donovan who will be left if it happens. And, since we're not sure how close this connection is between you and him, it could be his end too. While you might not care about your life, you care about his. If that's what it takes to get you moving, use it, and let's go. I can't be here any longer."

When Andy revealed what he saw, it never occurred to me Donovan was in any danger. We considered it when Daniel made mincemeat of Donovan's face, but this time I thought it would be my fate and not his. I wondered if Andy looked at him if the spots would be all over him too.

I made a point to hug everyone before we left, a first and possibly last meeting in one visit. As Jet embraced me, her guilt was undeniable. No matter what I said, the emotion was true to her and would be as it was, so I didn't argue. She thanked me for helping her little boy by confirming his gift and trying to explain the role he played when the spots showed up.

"Andy will be okay," I whispered in her ear as we held each other.

"I hope you find a way out of this."

"Me too." I fronted a smile as big as I could manage. "Well, little man." I bent to speak to Andy. "Do I get a hug?" I thought Andy would forgo the option, but he grabbed hold of me like we were old friends.

"Are you coming back?"

I gave him a squeeze and then pulled back and looked him in the eyes. "I don't know, buddy, but remember what we talked about?" Andy nodded. "You gave me a heads up, so I can try and fix this. If I can come back, I promise, I'll come visit just to see you, okay?"

"Pinky promise?" He put out his pinky like I taught him.

"Pinky promise." I hooked my finger with his and gave it a firm shake to complete the pact. Caine opened the door for us to leave, but I wasn't done. I flexed to my feet and looked at Eli. "I fixed the tractor."

"How?" he asked with a single dubious laugh.

I shrugged. "My healing ability surpasses human anatomy. Usually in smaller doses, so I guess you were lucky."

"Yes, I am." He hugged me again. "Let's hope you find a way to use it so you can keep your promise to my grandson."

"Let's hope."

To Caine's relief, we made our way out to the car.

As soon as I was strapped into my seat, Caine whizzed out of the driveway and sped down the road, only stopping by my apartment to get Bosco. We didn't see a guard and one didn't come to our aid. We left the apartment to Caine's family's assuming one was with us, but undercover, yet again, one didn't communicate with us as we rushed out of the building on our way to Donovan's in Niagara-On-The-Lake.

6

TEARS DON'T SOLVE PROBLEMS

Donovan

Annoyed. Why is she annoyed? Cataloguing Sophie's emotions became a daily habit once the connection roared awake. Since Diluculo, she shut down as much as she could, making her difficult to read. After pointing it out to her, blips of something more surfaced, but always muddied by her avoidance. Now, she finds out she's going to die and she's annoyed? Annoyed at Caine? If so, what the fuck was he doing to her?

Nausea hit so hard, I braced my hands on the arms of the couch and slowly sat when I knew my stomach bile was staying put.

"What's the matter with you?" Kim asked.

I took in another steadying breathe, trying to settle Sophie's stomach remotely. "Caine's driving too fast."

"Jesus," Kim mumbled. "What are we going to do when she gets here?"

"Whatever it takes," I said, followed by, "Fuck," when another wave of nausea sliced me across my stomach. "If I wasn't desperate to get her here, I'd kick his fucking ass."

"Desperate?"

I blew out the breath I was holding, wishing Kim would disappear, knowing I could make her and equally knowing Sophie wouldn't want me too. Kim's comment went unanswered. That I used the word out loud was testament to the strength of Sophie's motion sickness. She can send a Tainted Magic scurrying, but can't handle being in a car? She was as beautiful as she was baffling.

An unconscious rocking had me wondering if Sophie was doing the same. Why were they taking so long? What if whatever was supposed to happen, happened on the way here? What if I never got to see her again? We were together in a past life, we could be again, but what if we didn't find each other? The thought had me pacing. My jaw clenched against the quiver of my chin. I fought to get it in check and real fucking quick.

Tears don't solve problems.

The asshole's voice accompanying the saying was a nail in my temple. Clear and chalked full of derision. The fight to push him and the memory of his rage-inducing life lessons away came easy. Usually. Sophie was right, she wasn't the only one fighting for an even keel to save the other additional pain. The fact was, she was one of few others who sacrificed themselves to protect me. It only made it harder to gain control, so I fled to the kitchen away from Kim's glare, my footsteps putting distance between myself and the deep-down shit that had no place in this situation.

"They're here," Kim called from the living room as I had a jug of orange juice halfway to my mouth. I abandoned the jug intending to run out to Sophie. I stopped myself in the doorway of the kitchen and forced myself to wait.

Seconds passed as anticipation of seeing her built.

The door opened, and Caine walked in, his thick eyebrows peaked in anger. A lingering glance filled with hatred swung my way until he stepped aside. Bosco shot through the door and ran and barked at Kim before jumping on her lap.

Finally, Sophie stepped through the door.

As soon as both of her feet touched the entryway tile, she stopped and looked up at me. The room and the people in it blurred into non-existence. All except for her. I ran and grabbed onto her, needing to know she was real and whole. She matched my grip, up on her toes, holding on as I was close to losing it. Saving me from tears was my ear touching her temple, setting my psychometry off. Us. In the forest. In each other's arms. Feelings of dread. Of love. Of understanding. Sophie pulled away and, with her separation, ended the vision mirroring the emotions of this moment.

I thread a strand of her hair between two fingers, lingering in the bubble of rare closeness. "You're not gonna die."

Her hands rested on my covered arms. "I might." The emotion I injected into the connection closed off as if she readied herself for the possibility of becoming overwhelmed and was refusing to let herself breakdown.

A noise in the kitchen reminded me we weren't alone. I was surprised she engaged in this moment with me while Caine and Kim were nearby. She may have buttoned up her fear surrounding death to save me from grief and, although displaying my desperation was a momentary weakness, I enjoyed every passing second.

"No. You won't."

Stretching this time with her was impossible. Caine not already butting in was a miracle. I exhaled and tucked the memory away for a time when I needed her, and she was too far to touch. We joined Kim and Caine in the kitchen, both standing in clear discomfort I was happy to ignore.

"He's sure?" Kim asked, watery-eyed, with Bosco on her lap at the kitchen table. "He's sure he saw spots?"

"Not just spots," Sophie answered with a tilt to her head. "He said I had them all over. Andy recognized them on his father before he died. And it happened with others, too."

"Little heavy for a six-year-old," Kim added, stroking Bosco's back.

"No kidding," Sophie mumbled with a hint of something she suppressed.

I wanted to hold her again. "If Loring was dead, or if maybe Joelly hadn't traipsed in here with a warning of someone else in the periphery, I wouldn't believe a Coven-less six-year-old's gift would be anything but pure bullshit created by the parents to feel special. But we can't ignore his track record."

"Sounds like a form of precognition," Kim said.

I nodded. "Seedlings within Covens learn quicker, but your family doesn't congregate with others, not even other Berisfords."

Of all the people Sophie fell for, he *had* to be a fucking Berisford.

"You can heal," Caine said to her, "that has to pull things in our advantage."

"No matter how strong a Magic is, they're not invulnerable." I never thought the Elders would be dead in my lifetime. "Evil finds its loopholes."

"I'm more concerned about you," Sophie said to me after the room took on a dark lull. Leave it to me to find a way to make the situation more depressing. "We don't know what my death could do to you. Just because I have to die, it doesn't mean you should, too."

"You're not gonna die!" My power flushed into action. I caged it as Caine's also rose to the occasion in warning. A pitiful warning, but one nonetheless.

"Donovan," Sophie said slowly. "Raising your voice doesn't change reality. We don't know what this is or what consequences you'll face because of it." She looked at me with soft dark eyes full of far more understanding than I deserved.

"Call your Aunt Olive," I deflected. "Have her go through anything relating to the kid's power and soul connections. Maybe the estate has something useful collecting dust somewhere. We can check Aunt Lacey's stock while we're here. There has to be something, even if it's the mother of all protection spells."

Caine reached for his phone and began dialling. Sophie argued about not wanting Olive to know, but I was grabbing a bottle of water and heading to the basement to the closet of Aunt Lacey's books before the discussion played out. I didn't need their play-by-play, I needed answers.

7

CAMP OUT?

Caine hovered until I told Olive everything. She didn't freak out. More like refused to believe it could be so and kicked into research mode. Probably the same as Donovan as he took off the moment he could.

"Stay put, Firefly. Aunt Lacey's home is as safe as they come, except for the estate. I don't want you driving out here until we know what we're dealing with. I can push back the restoration event until this is ironed out."

"Not a chance. You earned the right to party and show off the place. The way Jet made it sound, Andy saw spots on his father for a while before he died. We have no timeline to work with and I'm not hibernating until I croak. I'd rather you introduce the family to part of their history than worry about something you can't predict. Besides, if I do die soon, I'm partying first."

"Then I'll make it the hit of the century." Olive said a quick goodbye as if refusing to believe it would be her last.

When we joined the others in the basement, Kim was on the phone pacing and Donovan sat on the floor surrounded with books, skimming the one in his hand with intense focus.

"I doubt this is a case of random girl meets random car accident, Ranlyn," Kim said into the phone. "This has to be Loring."

Great. Now Ranlyn knew. I half-expected him to show up, but with his new Elder duties, he wasn't readily available anymore.

Bosco stepped over books and found his way to my lap as I sat on the floor, intent on helping Donovan research. Caine grabbed a volume as Bosco snuggled into me. "I don't think a spell's going to fix this."

"This one definitely won't, it's not even English." Caine tossed the book aside and grabbed another.

"Let me see," Donovan said with a hand out. I was now closer, so I handed it to him. He opened the book to a random page. "It's Italian."

"Do you understand it?"

"Yup." He added it to his to-be-read pile before returning to speed read the book in his hand.

Caine looked at me a moment and I shrugged. I never would have guessed he could speed read, let alone in different languages.

"It's insulting you're so surprised," Donovan said though his dimples showed he wasn't mad about it.

Kim was on the phone with Ranlyn—then the rest of the Elders—for over an hour, leaving it on speaker phone so we could all hear. She gave up taking notes when the content had nothing to do with the current issue. Hinapouri's fury at Loring's incessant need to break through her security protocols brought out the Maori warrior in her. She was as beautiful as she was lethal with no leads on Loring's location. Miklos yelled a slew of hatred for our enemy in a Hungarian accent so thick Kim couldn't understand. He was stuck on believing a mole had infiltrated the Coven, to which Hinapouri took great insult.

Much of the conversation was monopolized by them arguing. Veata spoke once when she told Kim to give her regards to me, even though I could hear them, and to let her know when she was actually needed. Finally, Ranlyn rallied them back to the issue at hand and they eagerly agreed to reach out to their contacts.

When Joelly was mentioned, Veata was intrigued and insisted on hearing anything we knew about her. Donovan opted out of giving a review, so Kim told them the little we knew.

By the time Kim hung up, she was exhausted, and wilted into the couch. "I curse the fucker who's trying to kill you and caused me to suffer an hour of my life I'll never get back. Holy shit."

I plopped down next to Kim and smoothed the picture perfect red hair touching my arm.

"Are you scared?" she asked me.

I gave it thought. "I think I should be."

"Then why aren't you?"

"I don't know. It's not that I don't believe Andy. I do. But somewhere between the shock of the spots and learning Donovan can read multiple languages—"

"He can?"

"Apparently. But between them, I reminded myself I don't believe in fate. If Loring shows up, we'll deal. Caine didn't have spots, so he survives. It would've been nice if you and Donovan were there to know for sure, but I doubt Jet will rent Andy out to check everyone possibly affected by this."

"Doubt it, but that kid has an amazing future ahead. Amazing or terrifying. Probably both."

"Agreed. Plus, we can all die at any point. I could have an allergic reaction to your shampoo and die sitting next to you."

Kim grabbed her hair and gasped. "Don't even pretend it's my fault you die. That's cruel."

I couldn't help but laugh. "Don't worry, your hair is too beautiful to be murderous."

"Damn right it is." She settled back into her spot. "Have you told your mom about the power yet?"

I groaned. "Shitkittens."

"Is that a no?"

Why hadn't I thought of my mom until now? Or Serena? If I do tell my mom about the power, would she blame our family bloodline for me dying in the case that I do? Time to debate these questions was scant when I didn't know how much time I had to work with.

Another groan was my final answer and Kim gave me a tight smile in understanding.

"So," Kim drew out the word and lowered her voice. "How about the far-too-happy-to-hold-you hello when you got here?"

"What? You upset I didn't hug you? Show me some sugar, sweet lips."

Kim swatted at my arm as I lifted them. "I'll get my hug when you're not making fun of me for it."

"Oh, my lovely. I only have arms for you." I put my arms out again. Arms that were swatted yet again.

"You and Donovan. You're delusional if you think we didn't see it. Caine tried to put on blinders, but not looking was impossible. Even for me. Trying to deflect with conversation was awkward as fuck. Clearly it wasn't a one-sided embrace and the poor guy had no hope of keeping the jealousy off his face."

I closed my eyes, let my head fall back into the couch cushion. "I know you guys saw it, but it gets complicated when high emotions are involved."

"I believe it, but when you and Donovan nearly threw down on the beach in Diluculo, you were so upset. Shit freaked and lit-on-fire upset. You were worried you'd hurt Caine if he saw and were guilty it happened. Today? Zero guilt."

I huffed. "I don't think I felt any guilt. Which isn't fair for Caine and I realize how twatish that sounds."

"Sometimes you do twatish things when you're consumed. This time, I'm guessing it was the fact you might die and take Donovan with you. Which explains your worry, but not what happened with you and Donovan. Don't tell me you're thinking it was anything more than his emotions overruling yours."

"Maybe. Maybe not."

"No, Soph. Believe me, you spend enough time with someone and you're bound to find one redeeming quality. You can't trust it."

"I can't trust anything. Not how I feel about myself, let alone Caine and how the persuasion stuff plays a part, which also means I can't trust how I feel about Donovan."

"I didn't mean Caine. Why stay with Caine if you're not sure?"

"Leaving Caine, in his eyes, would be choosing Donovan, even if I stay single. Hence the wait and see approach mixed with paralyzing doubt."

"So, you're going to lie to him instead? I'll back your play, but, I'll be honest, it's a bit of a dick move."

"I love Caine. I'm not sure how Donovan fits into my life with all this 'connection' stuff and, unfortunately, unless you're Hugh Hefner, it's frowned upon to be flanked by more than one person. I'm not getting into a crossing swords debate with them." I was joking, desperate for levity. "Either way, I'm not pushing the issue until we get past this spots thing. If I die, it won't matter. And, since I'd rather not die, our focus should be on douche-sprayer Loring, not some uninteresting version of The Bachelorette. No thanks." I pointed at Caine and Donovan across the room. "They need to concentrate on whatever this is so if something does happen to me, they won't blame each other. That's if Donovan's left alive for Caine to beat the shit out of."

"I guess. If not, you're stuck putting on your big girl panties and making a choice."

"Yeah, yeah. I've got them stowed away in my purse ready for action when the time comes."

"Hey," Donovan called over. "Might be a good idea to help save your own ass, Soul Seer." He sneered without a hint of a smile.

"Hmmm. That's a new one."

"Better than babe," Kim said mimicking Donovan before I pulled her up off the couch.

I missed our girl talk.

———

We scrounged up handfuls of protection spells scribbled onto lined pieces of loose paper, including herbal fusions, charmed amulets, and lists of ancient talismans, if only we could get our hands on them. None of it mattered. Not one was specific to our circumstances and I wasn't up for hiding dragon's blood or devil's dung in my bra forever. Especially since devil's dung's smell was described as 'revolting' and 'akin to sulphur'.

"You're doing whatever it takes, that's what you're doing," Donovan said when I told him as much. "Don't chick out on me now. I don't care if it's stinky, sticky, or slimy. If it works, it's worth it to smell like you're dead than to actually be dead."

"Then why aren't you doing it?" I challenged. "You could be the one dying and taking me down with you. I should be worried you're gonna wreck your car or piss off a redneck in some ditch-pig watering hole. We're assuming I'm the instigator here, when you're more of a liability than I am."

Donovan blinked. "Ditch-pig watering hole?"

"My theory is solid, and you know it. At every turn, I'm in as much danger because of you, as you are because of me, so whatever stinky herb or protection spell you're gonna Guinea pig me with, double it, 'cuz you're doing it too."

"Guinea pig you with?"

"Stop that!" I was beyond irritated. Clearly, since I made the watering hole comment, Donovan was too.

"Fine. You're right. So, what's your solution?"

"Isn't that the whole point of us doing all this?" Kim said with her own flare of annoyance.

"You're looking for protection from death." He looked to Kim with a sharp glare and then back at me with the same attitude. "Since you don't trust me to ensure your safety, then I'm going to have to seriously crimp my watering hole lifestyle."

"'Bout time," Kim said and earned a smile from me.

"Meaning?"

A hint of excitement danced across the connection and leaked into his eyes when he said, "Camp out?"

Caine tossed the book in his hand down. "You're such an insect."

I wasn't even sure I heard right.

Kim attempted to stifle her laugh and lost. "Who calls someone an insect?" I shot her a 'please don't add to this' glare, but Donovan joined in and Kim couldn't contain herself.

"I knew you were an opportunist," Caine said with a laugh that held no humour, "but this is weak."

"She needs a safety net, which means I need to be safe. And since she," Donovan pointed to me then drew out his next words, "thinks I live some wild and crazy lifestyle, apparently, I need to be leashed before I kill her."

"I didn't mean it like that and you know it."

"Well, it goes both ways," Donovan said. "You work around a bunch of drunk assholes hyped up on college pride and eight-balls. Not to mention my psychopath of a sister. So, there's no way you're going to work. And the only way you can confirm I'm being safe without strapping a baby monitor to my ass, and vice versa, is to be around each other. What better place then here, where we're protected?"

"You forget," Kim raised her finger, "Joelly strolled through the door like Queen Latifah. I bet Loring could tap dance over it and we'd think it was a problem with the plumbing until he chops our heads off."

"I didn't say it was perfect, but it's safer than your apartment on hooker alley."

Kim looked at me. "Then we'll all stay here together."

"I guess." I was grateful for her modification. "Loring is after all of us." Far from the best-case scenario, but there were plenty of rooms so Donovan and Caine wouldn't be in each other's face.

"Fine," Caine said. "You won't talk me into believing you don't have ulterior motives, but if she's here, I'm here."

"Sure, fine, sweetbeans." This would be super comfortable. "I can bartend anywhere if Drew won't work with me, but what about you?" I asked Kim.

Kim's sculpted brow arched. "Do you have the impression I work in retail because I'm a people pleaser and don't mind working my ass off folding the same shirt over and over because people suddenly forget how to fold after they try it on? I have bills to pay. Oh, and avoiding starvation would be nice. I don't have ancient family money to keep the sheriff from locking me out."

"You're my co-Sect Leader. Your needs will be covered. I'll cover both your expenses until you find something else or return to retail heaven."

"I'm sure Sophie can work out her own finances." Caine's tone was sharp. "I don't have ancient family money."

"But you still have family money."

He looked to me with surprise. I told Kim about the benefit money he got from people who didn't know it wasn't an accident that killed his brother and stuck him in a sleeping curse for almost four three years.

Donovan clapped his hands once. "All settled? Wonderful. Back to work."

"I'll call Ranlyn back and let him know we're hiding out like twitchy apocalypse preppers so he can make changes in the guard's schedule," Kim said. "I don't know if one was at the apartment earlier. Seemed quiet, even for an invisible guard."

"We thought so too," I said.

We didn't know all the guards, better that way so our thoughts couldn't give up potentially important information to the enemy without knowing it.

We had multiple people with skilled bloodlines and powerful connections on our side, yet few options for ensuring absolute safety. A part of me wondered if our panicked solution to bunk at Donovan's would be our ultimate downfall. Maybe Donovan would annoy

Caine so badly that he took him out himself. I didn't mention the theory out loud but focusing on research was difficult with it slithering in the back of my mind.

8

DO YOU SEE WHAT I SEE?

Those of us who didn't live at Donovan's needed stuff to get us through our camp out experiment. He argued a guard could pick everything up, but we would spend longer explaining where everything was. Plus, it was one stop. Caine had enough at my apartment to last him a week. Silver lining to his inability to put space between us.

Caine pulled into the front parking lot of our building. I stepped out of the Infiniti, sinking my flip-flopped foot into a puddle.

"Hey, do we know Miss Daisy Dukes over there?" Kim asked as I shook off my foot.

I turned to see where Kim motioned over her shoulder and saw a woman in sheared jeans and stretched-out tank over a bikini top hanging off her thin frame. She stood off the curb and onto the road. Since the area was known as 'Hooker Alley' I would have guessed she was a Sex Trade Worker, though she ignored a passing car.

"Don't recognize her from The Lush."

I normally would have gone about my business, but the fixed expression on her mousey face was unsettling. Besides being in desperate need of a shower, Daisy Dukes was content to stay put, so I smiled and kept moving. A man in his sixties sat on the plastic bench the building provided. His presence, however common place, was as sterile as Daisy Dukes'.

"Just packing to stay at Donovan's," I said out loud as I unlocked my door, hoping the hallway guard was paying attention. We couldn't see anyone and went on faith they hadn't abandoned their post.

Donovan's impatience for our return fogged my focus. I battled his nagging irritation by listing off what I needed aloud, moving between my dresser, the closet, and the bathroom too many times.

Kim poked her head in my door and made me yelp. "How the fuck did you pack so quickly?"

"I pre-plan outfits a week at a time."

I scoffed. "Of course you do."

"Make sure you have your ID. Health Card, passport, whatever, in case we need to run further than the next town."

"I don't have a passport." I pulled out a larger duffle bag from the floor of my closet.

Caine came in as he was closing the zipper on his backpack. "Mine's definitely expired."

"A coma patient can't get a passport? What's wrong with the world?" Kim said.

"Can you grab Bosco's stuff?" I asked Caine. I was taking too long, and Donovan's anxiousness was growing.

"You think this is a good idea?" Kim sat on the corner of my bed.

"No clue. Hopefully the Coven or Olive can pull a gift-giving rabbit out of their asses."

"I meant staying at Donovan's when there's something going on with you two."

"Kim! What the tits?"

"I was quiet."

"Not quiet enough. Shit."

She made a throaty nose. "Come on, Soph, it's Donovan. Sexy asshole you share a cosmic connection with."

"I love you like a newly acquired sister, but I'm about to cuff you like a sister I caught peeking at my diary." Kim rose her brows in a derisive look. "If you've got a spell tucked in your cleavage that'll tell me the one hundred percent right answers, I'll dive in head first for it. Then I won't have to play referee, because it's more likely Caine and Donovan will kill each other."

"Sorry. It's slightly entertaining in a reality show kind of way, but totally messed up. I want everyone to come out of this happy."

"Happy. Right. You don't have to be sorry. Find me a week's worth of suitable outfits and you're forgiven."

"Now that, I can do."

———

Ready for the most awkward sleepover of my life, I frowned in annoyance when Caine was stopped by a red light. Preoccupied by the thought that we might get into a car accident and inadvertently do Loring's job for him, I yelped when a car behind us honked their horn. In front of Caine's bumper stood a man in his mid-to-late thirties, average height and weight, blond hair peeking beneath a white Under Armour cap, and matching jogging pants. He stared through the windshield at us, making no attempts to move.

"You've got to be kidding me." Beeping his horn did nothing to deter the man and the car behind Caine revved his engine and played with nudging the Infiniti's bumper as we were stuck on a single lane, one-way road.

Kim pulled herself between the front seats. "I'm not imagining this, right? He's staring like Daisy Dukes and the old man outside our building."

The person behind Caine was now yelling outside his window.

"Go around him," I told Caine. The anticipation of the man lashing out was too tense for me to sit with.

"I'd have to hop the curb. This isn't exactly an all-terrain vehicle." Instead, he waved for the guy behind us to back up. They finally did, and Caine reversed as fast as he could.

Kim and I were spun backwards in our seats, watching the man become nothing but a white blur. At no point did he move.

Caine hardly stopped the rest of the way back to Donovan's. We hoped if we were pulled over, he could use his Persuasion to get us out of a ticket or maybe to forget us altogether. Rolling through stop signs, making illegal lane changes, and ignoring blaring horns fading behind us was worth it when we pulled into the safety of Donovan's driveway.

"I think Loring's got a tail on us," Donovan said as we walked in the door.

Kim dropped her bag on the kitchen floor with a clunk. "No fucking kidding."

"You want to clarify the bitch routine?"

"They're watching us too," I jumped in before Kim warped into overdrive. Our luggage lay abandoned while we filled Donovan in on Daisy Dukes, the old man, and Mr. Under Armour's staring problem.

Bosco whined at my ankles, staring up at me with pug-faced concern. I scooped him up, cradling him in my arms, as his chubby body sat rigidly in my grasp. He didn't enjoy the tension any more than anyone else.

"Makes sense," Donovan said. "I took Bosco for a walk around the block and came face-to-face with the same thing. A mailman stopped dead in front of me in the middle of the sidewalk. He didn't even speak when I called him out for being creepy."

"I've seen someone with a death-like stare when Caine persuades them," Kim said. "This wasn't anything like it."

"My Persuasion removes someone's will. Hypnosis and coercive mind control is out of the question."

"The mailman's will was intact." Donovan was certain. "He made a conscious action to stare at me, even when I'd went around him and turned the corner."

"Could they be devotees?" Kim asked. "You were close enough to the mailman to give him butterfly kisses and he only stares? I don't get it."

"It's not Loring's style," Donovan said, then asked me, "Did their souls glow?"

"Nope. It doesn't make sense. People who have scores to settle, don't stand and watch. They shit-talk and goad you into confrontation, and if they're not talking, they're flipping you off."

"What are you thinking?" Caine asked as I hopped up to sit on the counter.

"Possession?"

"Linda Blair, head spinning off my shoulders, possession?" Donovan asked.

Dog-tired of life bringing me to these conversations, I dropped my head back onto the white wooden cabinets with a thunk.

"You asked!"

I shot Donovan a weary please-work-with-me-not-against-me look. "I was thinking more like when Loring possessed my dad. Or the merchant in Diluculo."

"We were at different parts of the city and the woman and old man were staring at the same time," Caine said. "Could he be strong enough to possess more than one person simultaneously?"

"Doubt it," Donovan replied.

"Has anyone called with ideas?" Kim asked.

"No." Donovan's tone was clipped.

"I'll harass Ranlyn again." Kim pulled out her phone.

"And I'll call Drew," I said. "Be prepared for my unemployment."

"Fuck him," Donovan said.

"Eww."

"Not literally. Tell him you need personal time if you want to actually return to that shithole."

"That makes it sound like I'd rather be masturbating than work."

"And who wouldn't?" Donovan had a flash of dimples I didn't miss. "Leave of absence to take care of Olive. Whatever. Lie better."

I thought about it a moment and decided I liked it. The excuse held the positive spin of truth.

As the phone rang, I sat on the counter. "Why do you sit up there?" Donovan sneered with a hint of a smile.

"Shut up."

"Excuse me?" Drew barked into the phone.

"Not you!" I recovered and bounded off the counter, while Donovan's laughter filled the background. I slugged him in the chest, hid the fact I felt it too, and shot him the finger on my way to the living room.

Drew wasn't happy. Would I have a job after all this if I wanted it? If our hiding lasted longer than a month, I doubted it, but I bought myself some time.

Feeling lighter for getting that detail out of the way, I re-entered the kitchen where the guys stood decisively silent. I broke the quiet by telling them about my call.

"Answer your friggin' phone," Kim said and redialled. "It keeps hitting his machine."

"Leave a message," I said, "he'll call back." Ranlyn was a new Elder. With them adding this to his long list of new responsibilities, it wasn't surprising he was unavailable.

"It's not like it's life or death, or anything fancy like that." Kim relayed the 'staring incident' to the machine, then hung up. "What now?"

Low on options, we went back to the books, seeking a shred of viable defence. Chances were our search would result in dick-all, but it beat scratching our asses.

———

Surrounded by literature should be a dream for me. Though reading didn't happen as often with Caine around, and not at all since Diluculo. I hadn't even browsed the shelves at the estate. And now, story upon story of Magics living through horrific trials and how their gifts guided them to safety was all around us. Endless lists of spells and incantations scrolled on every page. Happiness, wealth, love, and even celebrity, depending on what you were willing to put on the line.

All this available to me and I still couldn't focus on a damn thing.

"Wanna share with the group?" My daydreaming was messing with Donovan's concentration.

I closed the unread book in my lap. "Actually, yeah. Um, did any of your—The letters from Aunt Lacey, did they include a premonition?"

"You read mine," Caine said. It was as much as Aunt Lacey had said in the barn at Pario, plus a bit on myself and a warning to find strength in himself in case he finds himself wanting. But no premonition.

"Nothing on either of yours?" I looked to Kim and Donovan.

"No, but apparently yours did," Kim said. "Spill."

"Obviously, the letters were written for Aunt Lacey to say goodbye in the event of her death. Mine did that too, even gave advice." I strayed from looking at the guys. "But one part said she had some type of premonition she assumed was for me."

"And?" Donovan deadpanned.

"Give me that paper and a pen."

"Why?" Kim asked as she passed along the eight-by-eleven lined sheet.

"You guys don't need to see the whole letter."

"Just tell us," Caine yelled after me as I took off upstairs.

I wrote down the premonition word for word. Keeping the letter in my purse kept Aunt Lacey close in a small way and I was happy I hadn't left it lying around somewhere.

By the time I got back downstairs, no one was reading.

I sat next to Kim on the couch while Caine and Donovan hovered. "I'm telling you, it doesn't make sense, but, whatever, here goes.

"*A sequence of events will begin without aid but must be left incomplete before Puppets are made of men. More lies in the black hearts of the pioneers of hate, bearing power of the Human Engineer.*

They use One on the edge of man and gods, untrustworthy, yet the only one to turn to. Bloodlines ignite in a place that holds memory, wisdom, and torture, all prevalent in discovering the truth behind the eyes. Enemies come in threes, the next, more evil then the last, yet all share the same goal. Childish interference will bring dark understanding. This meeting necessary for enlightenment to bring souls back from Death. Only he will know not all is lost, only he can pay the ancient cost. Death's brief visit. The Trees of Heaven bring answers but will lead to the presence of the Devil. See without colour, react without shame."

Donovan reached out his hand with clear intention and I passed him the paper.

Hurt clouded Caine's stormy eyes. I never showed him the letter, even after he shared his. "I focused on what I thought was more important. For all I knew, the rest foretold the shit from Pario and we already know how that hoedown went. The 'truth behind the eyes' part reminded me of the letter. Then the 'bloodlines ignite' part too. I figure Aunt Lacey's death was the beginning of the 'sequence of events' and not the end. Hence, time for show and tell. Macabre style."

"I get the eyes part. Those creepers on the street are memorable," Kim said, widening her own. "But why does 'bloodlines ignite' make sense?"

"Olive's reuniting the Ballard Family Coven and having a restoration party since the estate is now an old shiny penny. She wants to show it off to anyone who will show up, but mainly to show the family a piece of heritage most had no idea existed. Bloodlines ignite, right? I don't know. That's the only thing I could think of."

"We're definitely going to that party." Donovan's gaze never strayed from the page.

"I don't see how the estate could be a place of torture." Caine ignored Donovan's self-invitation.

"Me either," I said.

"Could it mean Diluculo?" Kim suggested. "Many bloodlines

were there, and it's connected to Pario which is definitely a place of torture."

I shrugged. "I have cryptic prophesies, not answers."

"It says there are three enemies, so this isn't all Loring." Donovan passed me the paper back. Kim reached out for it and it changed hands again.

"Loring's definitely one," Kim said as her eyes scanned the paper.

"What about Joelly?" Caine offered.

Donovan popped an eyebrow and nodded.

"And lucky contestant number three?" I sat forward, elbows to knees. "Denise wishes I'd fall into a ditch of napalm, but I don't get an I-want-to-kill-you vibe from her anymore."

"The jealous bitch might want to be you," Kim sneered, "but I doubt she'd go as far as to kill you, especially not after you landed her ass in the sand in Diluculo."

"Could be the person Joelly talked about," I said. "The big bad she mentioned?"

"I've known Joelly too long to trust anything she says, but it's possible."

"It's weird it uses Death like a name, capitalized, as if Death itself was coming." Kim tried to hand Caine the paper, but he waved it off. "Could Death be real, as in a living breathing entity? Because that would be the biggest bad there is."

We looked to Donovan. "This shit is way over my head, babe. I know evil, I don't know Death and I seriously doubt Joelly has a direct line to Death Incarnate either. That'd be a stretch. And if Death's a real person, it doesn't sound like whoever faces Death wins."

"It's okay," I told him.

His jaw flexed. "Stop saying that."

"At least it's brief," Kim chimed in. "See—" She leaned closer to me, her finger underlining the words. "'Only he will know that not all is lost, only he can pay the ancient cost, Death is brief'." Not quite a how-to-blueprint for dummies, but it left room for hope. "And apparently 'he' will know what will happen and pay whatever the 'ancient cost' is. Hopefully whoever 'he' is, he isn't Death."

"Why?" Caine asked.

Kim shrugged. "Because I'm assuming Death would be reluctant to *not* do his job. If 'he' is either you or Donovan, then that's one person working in Sophie's corner."

The logic made sense.

"I'm not putting money on it being anyone useful. Not with your luck." Donovan's expression twisted at the absurdity. "Cryptic as ever." He shook his head. "'Human Engineer'? 'Someone on the edge of man and gods'? I feel like we're in a Batman movie and the Riddler's having a good go at us from behind."

"Batman would definitely come in handy right now," Caine said with a slanted smile. I returned a full smile wishing Batman were here too, especially the George Clooney version, and laughed at the thought of Loring and George duking it out.

"Instead," Donovan said with sudden and harsh enunciation as annoyance railed across the connection, "we have two covens to get working on this. One of them is bound to know what this bullshit means. Call Ranlyn again. If he doesn't pick up, recite the letter verbatim. I'm getting a drink." With that, Donovan walked away.

"Did he just give us orders?" Kim asked.

"Apparently," Caine grumbled.

Jealousy overrode Donovan's senses, and all over Caine making me laugh. Petty. Especially since he claimed Caine making me happy could never be a bad thing. Observing or sensing the emotional result firsthand proved to be too much.

9

JUST PEOPLE DYING

anlyn didn't answer. Kim recited the premonition with a clipped tone, hoping the machine didn't cut her off like a dragging Oscar speech. For all we knew, he hadn't listened to her last message. I tried not to worry about the fact that he still hadn't responded to the first.

I called Olive to let her know about the premonition and to ask her one thing, "Could Death be a real person?"

"Old tales speak of Reapers. Soul collectors of the dead who decide where your unending eternity should be. My only assumption is this is what it's referring to."

"No hooded skeletons with six-foot scythes in their bony hands, eh?"

"Well—" Olive sighed into the receiver. "Though I apologize for bringing this up, Firefly, really, I do, you've been present for the deaths of a few of our kind. Was Death present as they passed?"

I didn't have to think hard. I may have been preoccupied by the bloodied and tortured body of Aunt Lacey or huddled in Donovan's arms as Caine killed his father, but no fucking way would I have missed anything remotely described as Death. The memory of Aunt Lacey's soul as it left her vessel flashed in front of my eyes. She left our world alone, in peace, and I didn't see her escorted to wherever she disappeared to.

"No." The word came out as a whispered curse.

"Oh, Firefly." Her voice dripped with compassion. "I would never say a glimpse into the future from such an extraordinary being as Aunt Lacey could ever be mistaken, but my heart prays this one is."

Even without it, Andy still came with his own version of verification. One way or another, I was destined to die.

"I know," I said. "What about this party? When is it?"

The line was silent a moment. "You're minimizing your demise and now deflecting. You don't spend most of your life institutionalized without picking up a few things. I won't push. Not yet. Not while you're seeking answers but be prepared for it at some point."

"Right. Education from within. Noted."

"Mhmm. Now, to engage in your transparent tactic, the party is set for Thursday night. I thought it may be inconvenient for some since it's during the week, but the catering company had a cancellation. It's all been worked out, so fingers crossed people stay until the hors d'oeuvres are gone."

"Don't worry, people will show if only to satisfy their curiosity and gorge on free food and booze. I know I'm curious to see who turns out." My grandmother would either show up and choke back her attempts at eternal damnation or refuse her invitation and have family questioning her absence. "I'm not working while we get this death/premonition thingy figured out. Keeping low and staying with Donovan in case either one of us is responsible for our end. I used taking care of you as an excuse to get a month's leave of absence. Karma may kick my ass, but fate and I aren't exactly on speaking terms."

"That's smart, Firefly, can't be too careful." She paused. "Is Caine staying with you and Donovan as well?"

"Yes." I strained to keep my semi-bothered tone under wraps. "Kim's staying here too."

"Okay, okay."

"It'll be fine."

"I'm sure it will be."

More simmered behind Olive's statement, all the warnings and advice was hanging off the end of her tongue, but she let it dangle there without making further comments on the arrangement.

———

"This is about you too, right?" Kim gestured toward the paper. She sat on the couch next to me and read over the line. "'See without colour, react without shame.' Like, a soul glow?"

"The colours don't make someone a twisted psychopath. The Magic with the colour does."

"Twisted psychos aside, obviously you see soul colours. So, either you'll actually be blinded, or you'll have to look past your preconceived notions of what the colour means and then react to whatever you have to do with no shame."

"At this point, I'd know better about how to handle bestiality."

"Eww. Remind me not to hit you up once you're a hotshot psychiatrist."

"That's okay. I'll have you fill out bogus testimonials anyway."

"Deal."

The cover of the old book I held in my lap left a waxy film on my fingers. Rubbing them together made it worse. "Is it a crime to clean old books, 'cuz—"

Anger was a furious slap so hard I gasped and shot to my feet. I burst into a road-runner sprint two steps at a time up the basement stairs and down the long hallway to the kitchen. Donovan stood in the backyard, hunched over with his back to me while his fury rocketed through my veins. My name was a whispered echo from somewhere behind me, but I was already through the glass sliding doors.

The door hit its bumpers, flying back at me, hitting my shoulder, and knocking me off-kilter.

"Tell me!" Donovan held Joelly on her knees with a white-knuckle grasp on her scarf, choking her.

"Donovan!" My scream did nothing. His grasp tightened. Her face contorted and changed colour as she gasped for air and scratched at the skin around her throat.

"Tell me what you know!" he snarled and bore down on her.

"I-I told 'guh—" Joelly managed before Donovan twisted the scarf tighter, the veins in her forehead popping, her mouth wide open, her tongue protruding and rigid.

"Tell me something worth your life. You give me nothing but your incessant bullshit!"

Bosco's whining came from behind me, Kim and Caine had caught up, and he squirmed in Kim's arms to get loose.

"Tell me!" Donovan screamed again, the run-off of fury coursing through the connection.

Joelly squeaked, then gurgled a strained choking noise. I rose above Donovan's anger, begging him to let me join in and force the truth out of Joelly, to break a few fingers and start in on her toenails. I grabbed the scarf and used Donovan's anger against him by letting it fuel my fight to get Joelly free.

We struggled back and forth. Donovan tried to buck me off as I refused to let go. Joelly clutched onto to my wrist. A flash of Joelly's thoughts filtered through her touch, coherent and unmistakable, yet too quick to visualize. Her refusal to talk went beyond the stubbornness to torture her sort-of brother. She was terrified. Terrified of the Puppeteer.

Before I could process anything from Joelly's thoughts, an ice-like injection shot through my wrist where she gripped my skin. I went stiff, my eyes rolled against the chill through my entire body.

"No!" Donovan shoved me onto the grass. Caine and Kim's worried faces appeared above me as I shuddered and blinked in confusion.

Caine turned to go after Donovan. Donovan let Joelly fall from his grip and sprung to defend himself. "She absorbed Sophie's power!"

Caine stopped, but had a handful of Donovan's shirt.

While Donovan ensured Caine kept his head, Joelly let out a wild growl and clawed at her eyes. She squirmed to her knees and tried to look at me through black make-up streaked tears. Judging by Donovan's expression, he had no clue what happened, but I did. Memories of the first time my Soul Seer ability made itself known came to mind. Joelly stole my power and she couldn't handle it.

In blurred speed only a Magic could manage, Joelly rushed forward and wrapped a hand around Donovan's ankle beneath the cuff of his dark jeans. Before he could shake her loose, a strike of pain in my right ankle mirrored Donovan's. The dull ache dug deeper into my leg and lanced the bone like ants gnawing with sharp serrated-teeth were chewing their way to the marrow center.

Donovan and I screamed. Kim rushed to check my leg. When she pried my hand away, the skin was spotted with grey and spread like inky fingers towards my foot and up my shin.

"What's happening?" Caine's shouting was drowned out by my cry in pain and Donovan's growl as he used his hands to tourniquet his flesh in desperation to stop the climbing blackness.

My leg gave out when I tried to stand to get to Donovan and Joelly. They were close, a few body lengths away. I pulled myself along the grass as Kim and Caine tried to get me to stay put. In my objective to save Donovan, Caine tried to help me walk, but a thrumming alarm inside me pushed away his hovering hands with a warning to stay away.

With strained unsteadiness and awareness on my side, I threw my weight into a tightened fist and punched Joelly in the face. The force knocked Joelly's head back. Her eyes opened. The searing white and green of my soul glow with her unaccustomed sight overwhelmed her. She wailed and clawed at her burning eyes.

Before I give Joelly a dose of the magic eating at Donavan and me, she found her feet and blurred out of sight. She disappeared over the fence and into the night, leaving us to deal with the fallout of her inexperience at being me.

A retching cramp through my calf had me falling back again, Donovan doing the same as the gnawing travelled up our bodies, damaging tissue inch by inch. Both Donovan and I had the disintegrating power, the dark sister to our healing ability. No power came to us now. I couldn't concentrate fast enough to get a hold of it, and it had already taken over. If Donovan could heal, he already would have.

"This is—Andy saw it," I said as Caine, Kim, and even Bosco, moved around us robotically without a prayer of helping. Neither had the healing gift.

Not even Caine's influencing power worked. Either he couldn't focus, or my power was blocking his, but he tried. The slump in his shoulders was evidence of his last hope of fixing this.

Andy said the spots were 'all over'. As the creeping blackness took over more of our bodies, I knew this had to be what he meant. When I wasn't gritting my teeth against the pain, I was looking around for Death or anything resembling the cold end, fearing this was also the moment of Aunt Lacey's premonition. I didn't see anything but the others and none of them saw anything but me and Donovan frantic for the agony to stop.

When I couldn't feel anything below my waist, The Reds in Pario came to mind. Donovan and I would soon be nothing but twin piles of ash.

"Sophie." Caine sobbed my name, now holding my face in his hands. "What do I do? Tell me. Tell me what to do!" He said this over and over. I failed to find an answer.

"Get her to Donovan." Kim pulled at Caine to listen to her.

Did I say Donavan's name out loud? I didn't know, but I worried he was alone as Kim and Caine fretted over me. The feeling of despair was consuming. His. Mine. It didn't matter.

Floating black flakes caught my attention as they hoisted me up and shifted me so that I was lying next to Donovan. I didn't understand the black thing next to me until I realized it was my arm, Nya's ring on my charred finger the only thing recognizable. The gothic confetti around us was parts of me disturbed by the move. I was breaking apart.

"Put their hands together." Kim touched my face. I didn't feel it, but flakes fell and tickled my nose. My cheek. My face. It was falling apart.

Caine cradled my skin like handling a premature infant, moving my hand into Donovan's. When Caine's hand brushed Donovan's, Donovan took a shocking breath in as his vision flooded with images. His base power still worked and blinded him with whatever he glimpsed from Caine. The degradation of my power working through Donovan's body also degraded his ability to regulate his own. I didn't see the vision of Caine, but I felt its emotion, and whatever Donovan saw was no better than what we were experiencing in real time. Our hands must have come together, because the sensation of dread changed, morphing into one of bliss and contentment. The newfound emotion now possessed a greater strength of a different sort. Bliss so strong it enveloped me, melding the two lives into one.

"They need to heal." Kim's voice was raspier than normal in her desperation, but I couldn't see her. I experienced what Donovan had, in the lifetime we shared as soulmates. The aroma of an open flame and cooking food overshadowed the scent of grass beneath us and something else I knew was the scent of decayed human flesh.

"I'll try and find a guard," Kim said.

"Sophie? Sophie?" Caine tried as the sound of Donovan's infectious laugh echoed through the opaque vision. "Evoke your power, Sophie. Use your healing power." He could have repeated himself until he was speaking through thrashed vocal cords. I was too captivated by our surroundings and the hue of a red sky as the dawn bled through small windows.

"She's not hearing me!" His voice and the clang of something rang through my happy moment. I wanted nothing to do with it. I wanted the vision. I wanted the pleasure of Donovan's laugh.

"There's no one out there." Kim confirmed what we feared. We were alone.

"Fucking Christ. Of all times to flake out on us."

"Look at him," Kim said, and I wished I could.

Not whatever she saw in the backyard, but in the vision. I was hearing him, but I could only see through his eyes, so I saw myself and saw love reflected in the dark eyes of the woman I used to be. I wanted a flash of dimples, something before I died to remind me of the one who made me smile so bright.

Would I find him again? I hoped so.

10

MIXED SIGNALS

Caine

Mere minutes passed since Donovan was fighting Joelly, and now both Donovan and Sophie were being chewed into grit by their power. Time was moving both too fast and too slow. It was devastating to watch her fall apart without being able to fix her. She wouldn't listen to my Persuasion. I couldn't make her. If only I was stronger.

This was Donovan's fault. He knew his sister's power. He knew Sophie would get involved. Now she was dying, and the fucker couldn't even fix his own bullshit. He was getting what he wanted. Their death. Now they could be together again in another life. He robbed me of her, and I couldn't even be with her in death. Kim was right to put their hands together. Donovan couldn't heal Sophie, but whatever they saw left smiles on their faces. I lost her the moment they touched. I couldn't even have the pleasure of being the last person she saw. I wanted her to see me, not him or whatever they saw, but I didn't want her in pain.

She came from a family of strong Magics and was Nya's vessel.

She was alive in a previous life, for fuck's sakes, and she was going to die now? Here? No. It was too easy.

Her smile fell as they became weaker, but no sign of pain hung around as everything, including the whites of her eyes, went black. Her breathing calmed, her chest barely rising until I wasn't sure it was rising at all. A moment passed when the calm was too calm, and I knew.

Sophie was dead.

"Ohmygod." Kim sobbed into her hands.

"It can't be." I swayed back onto my heels. Sophie's face was obscured by the blackness and was now turned grey as ash, as was Donovan's. "How? It can't—"

The sight of the two of them would have been peaceful if featured in some shitty movie, but this was Sophie. She couldn't be dead. This couldn't be it.

"She can't die." I fought reality in a small voice. "She saved me. She's a vessel."

Kim's sobs pained me. She was part of this world before I was. She knew more about this stuff. If she was hopeless to fix this, then I had no fucking chance.

I broke down, hating every tear obscuring my view of her. I wanted to do something. Anything. Call someone. I didn't know who. I couldn't speak at this point and hated sitting here helpless because I would be without her for the rest of my life. How could I get through this without her?

Kim put her arm around me. I didn't want to take her comfort, but I needed someone to hold onto. Someone who knew Sophie in a way others didn't. Someone who saw the horror along with me and could attest to what happened. How could we tell Sophie's family?

A low sound broke through our sobs. Bosco. I never heard him growl before. The odd sound rolled deep within his chest before grumbling through his mouth. It was unmistakable when he began full-out barking. Short hackles on Bosco's back stood up all the way from his neck to his curly tail as he lunged side to side by the glass sliding doors.

We shot to our feet as a shimmer of motion was spotted by the glass. No discernable shape formed, though I thought the translucent outline distorted by the background behind it was human-sized. The form or entity remained a translucent film, invisible to us besides its distortion of the background seen through it.

"What the fuck? Kim—?"

She shook her head but didn't speak as she stared at whatever we saw.

"Sophie?" Was it her spirit? "Sophie!" I ran toward the shimmer. As soon I got close, the form dissipated, and I was left standing alone, a now silent Bosco at my feet. "No." My voice a whisper.

The shimmer was gone. She was gone.

That was my goodbye? How—? But I—.

I covered my face as more tears fell.

Power swelled from somewhere deep within, pulsing with every breath. I looked down at my hands. Tears puddled in my palms now itching with energy. Now? Now my power wants to do something? I couldn't do anything for Sophie when it mattered. I was fucking useless and she died because of it. Now it wanted to come out?

I closed my eyes and clenched my fists until they shook. Power continued to build in my chest and surge through me as I saw images of Sophie. Her sitting in the tree in the park, wet hair, dark eyes gleaming. The creases beside those eyes when she laughed. The feel of her pressed against me in blissful satisfaction. Her pale skin turned to ash as I reached for her, reality infecting my memory. They would all be memories, tainted by the fact that she was gone, and I would never get to hold her again.

The power in my chest turned to pain as the energy in my hands vibrated. I opened my eyes to my reflection in the glass doors and saw the person who couldn't save her. I drove my fist through the glass. A blast of shards flew back at me and threw me to the ground onto my back.

I rolled over when I could pull in a breath, my hands were in a puddle beneath me. It was water, not blood.

"What the fuck?" Kim was half-soaked, looking down at herself and then to Bosco who shook his wet coat off in a spray of water.

The ends of my hair fell in my face, water dripping into the puddles. I turned over to see the empty pane of glass and the surrounding area drenched.

"Don't!"

The warning in Kim's voice brought me back to her. Bosco was trying to get to Sophie. She and Donovan's ash piles now dappled with dark water spots. It seemed like he didn't understand why he couldn't go to his owner and would never know why she didn't come back.

"Come on." Kim grabbed hold of Bosco as he fought her.

I sat and looked at my hands and the door frame. I don't know what happened, but I managed to make more of a mess of things. I've lost people, but since Sophie saved me from the park, she became my life. I dropped my head into my hands again. My power subsided, leaving me hollow and aching.

"Caine." I didn't respond to Kim. I couldn't. "Caine!" She pushed my shoulder. My head snapped around to look at her. "Look!" She pointed at Sophie.

Light-headed and praying Kim wasn't calling me over to watch the love of my life crumble to dust, I followed where she looked at Sophie and Donovan and didn't understand what I was seeing. No, I understood, but I didn't believe it.

Sophie wasn't flaking away into non-existence, she was regaining her rigidity. Bosco nosed at Donovan's hand. A flesh-toned limb no longer akin to a burned-out campfire and then Sophie's which mirrored Donovan's. I leaned down a bit to make sure I was seeing what I thought I was and not what I wanted to see.

Black bled away from their arms and then face and worked its way down their bodies in an impossible miracle as the crawling black ash rewound, restoring their flesh as swiftly as it destroyed them.

Most of Sophie's body was already hers again, but she wasn't breathing. Her fingers lifelessly entwined with Donovan's, but they were her fingers. The ones I remembered holding and kissing and wishing I would never have to let go.

We hadn't moved since the transformation began. I held my breath and waited for Sophie to regain hers.

Sophie and Donovan's lips parted with a sharp expansion of their lungs, eyes opening wide and staring at the night sky.

"Sophie!" I grabbed her shoulders.

She blinked and looked at me with subtle recognition. A few seconds passed where neither Sophie or Donovan did anything but lay there.

"Are we okay?" she finally asked. She didn't look to Donovan herself to verify, maybe too scared to in case she made the trip back without him, but I understood what she meant.

I never imagined a sound so sweet than that of her voice. I managed to answer her with a nod. Her dark eyes glittered with tears and I rushed to grab and kiss her, fighting to pucker my lips against an overjoyed smile.

"I'm sorry," she said against my lips and I kissed her hard again, thrilled when her arms went around me and held me close.

"Still here cowboy." Donovan ensured his presence was not forgotten. "Wanna lay off a bit?"

"Donovan!" Sophie gasped as I pulled away from her. She sat up to embrace him, as did Donovan with her.

"Oh, babe." His voice was breathy as he buried his face in her hair. I don't know how they avoided making skin contact, but I didn't see either of them flinch. "I can't believe you did it. I knew you'd find a way."

She sat back. "I didn't do anything."

"You scared the hell out of me, bitch." Kim jumped in between them, gripping Sophie in a tight hug. Sophie laughed, and Kim's hug tightened as she rocked them. "Shit! Should I be squeezing you? How do you feel?"

"I'm fine." She turned to Donovan. "You?"

"Yup." He accentuated the "p" by popping his lips and flashed Sophie his dimples. "You fixed me up good, babe."

I wanted to punch him. The guy survived being turned to ash moments ago, but I still wanted to punch him.

"Stop saying that," she said to Donovan. "I didn't do anything."

"Let's get inside in case Joelly comes back." I stood and helped Sophie to her feet. She seemed fine, but I wasn't taking any chances.

"Why are you wet?" I led her through the glassless entrance instead of answering her.

Donovan was last inside and stood in the threshold. "And where's my door?"

"Ask him." Kim went for paper towels and dabbed her skin.

"I've never punched glass and had it morph into water, so I don't know. We'll have to fix it right away in case Joelly or someone else tries to get in."

"Joelly's in the wind."

"You sure about that?" Kim questioned him and then passed me the paper towels. I was too wet for them to make a difference.

Donovan made a throaty, dismissive noise. "Believe me." He opened the fridge, grabbed a bottle of water, and held it up in a silent offer to Sophie. She nodded. He threw it to her and grabbed his own, sucking back half the bottle.

"How do you know?" I pushed. "A nonchalant 'believe me' isn't gonna cut it."

Donovan closed the fridge and turned to me. "Joelly thinks we're dead." He shrugged. "So, we chill."

Chill? My jaw ached from clenching my teeth so hard.

"Why was she here?" Sophie asked. "I doubt she showed her face so you could choke her out."

"She liked it more than she let on," Donovan responded in a mischievous tone.

"And the actual reason?" Kim saved me the backlash by snapping at him herself.

"No clue," he answered. "She wasn't saying much. Hence my hands-on approach."

The fact that he was so comfortable strangling someone was off-putting and yet another noted reason not to trust him.

"Who's the Puppeteer?" Sophie asked him. Donovan shrugged. She looked to an equally confused Kim.

"Why?" I asked.

"When we were struggling, I overheard Joelly's thoughts. She was terrified of someone called the Puppeteer."

"Hmm." Donovan took another sip of water. "She said something about becoming 'his Puppet.' I assumed she was talking more bullshit about Loring."

"I asked you what she wanted!" Kim's rage echoed off the kitchen walls. "You think mentioning that first might have been helpful? What if because of what happened, Sophie didn't remember what she overheard?"

"Then I wouldn't have remembered what Joelly said either. How was I supposed to know she was being literal?"

Donovan's impassive glare before the cocky bastard left down the hall to the basement invoked her wrath. Kim had to know he was doing it on purpose, but she wouldn't let it go, and went after him. Sophie rolled her eyes and I reluctantly trailed her as she headed downstairs.

"Your twat sister is the link here, asshole." Kim words hit fast and hard as we got to the bottom of the basement stairs. "You can't tell us what you want and save the rest for later. You owe us—"

"Kim!" Donovan spun on his heel a foot from Kim making her skid to a stop. "How could I have known Joelly's bullshit was actually a clue? No!" He yelled, stopping her from attempting to answer. "I'm going to weld your mouth shut in a hot second if you don't stop your incessant bitching. I owe you jackshit. Sophie and I just died. You have no idea what that was like or what it's like now that we're back. I don't get to handle it the way I'd like, so neither do you." He picked his cell up off the table. "Now, is it okay that I call Ranlyn and see if he knows who this Puppeteer is and what we're dealing with? That good with you? Or would you rather drone on about how I hurt your feelings?"

"Prick. You might not owe me, but you owe Sophie. And since it's her life we actually give a shit about, I suggest you let us in on everything your hell-beast of a sister let slip."

"Savage," Sophie said under her breath.

"Honest," I muttered back.

"I'm surprised at you, Kim," Donovan said without looking at her. He redialled Ranlyn's number as the Elder hadn't answered. "You forget I can feel that Sophie thinks your shit-talking overreaction is out of bounds."

"Hey—" Sophie complained, though most days Kim's bluster was more bark than bite.

Donovan continued. "Not to mention likely because you were upset at watching us die." Kim looked at Sophie who remained impassive. "That part I don't need her to confirm. I'm not a moron, I get it, but I refuse to stand around and obsess about it. I'm working to solve this so it doesn't happen again, for keeps, because I'm not ready to give up this life yet."

"Never said you were," Kim shot back at him.

"Plus, you're deluding yourself if you think I give a shit about what Caine cares about."

"Never thought you did." I went ignored except for Sophie's sigh next to me.

Donovan relayed the incident and the "Puppet/Puppeteer" slip to Ranlyn's answering machine and swiftly left the room once he hung-up, leaving Kim to huff and puff.

"I hate it when he pulls that crap." Kim looked to Sophie and me. "That wanker spouts off BS than disappears like it ends the conversation. He's lucky I don't turn his bones into gelatine."

Sophie's laughed bubbled to the surface. "Can you do that?"

Kim didn't answer, instead, she gave us a look that said, "Maybe I can, maybe I can't." I doubted she could, but she was making strides in her Kitchen Witch role and I wasn't about to push her to the point of testing it out.

"It's Donovan, Kim." I pressed the heel of my palms into my pounding temples as I sat on the couch. "He exemplifies abject narcissism. What'd you expect? It amazes me anyone sees anything deeper than that."

The peak in Kim's brow said she agreed with me, but she looked at Sophie instead of saying anything. I've seen that calcified glare enough to know I'd pissed her off. When I replayed what I said in my head, I realized I fucked up, but she was already heading upstairs. Not fleeing. Probably going to him. Fuck my life. That's the last thing I wanted.

"I'm surprised she didn't shoot you the finger." Kim tried to laugh, but it came out awkward.

"Fuck. I'd have deserved it."

Kim shrugged and sat on the end of the couch. "Meh. Insulting him won't make her hate him or I'd have converted her the day they met."

"Can I be happy she's alive before it all goes to shit again? No, I have to walk on Donovan-shaped eggshells."

"Tap dance on them if you want but know she's under your foot as much as he is."

I groaned and dropped my head onto the back of the couch.

11

OPENING UP

The only thing that helped smooth my hackles from Caine's Freudian slip of, basically, calling me stupid—since I was honest about how I felt about Donovan, including the guilt surrounding the confusing emotions—was the sound of clanging metal and the smell of the gas burners of the stove heating up when I entered the kitchen. Donovan's back was to me as he moved from the stainless-steel appliance to the fridge and back. I sat on the island stool with Bosco in my lap, gaining a face full of kisses.

"You want one?" he said without turning. I sensed him wade through his emotions with silent questions. That not being one I expected.

"Depends on what you're offering."

"Right now? Grilled cheese."

"In that case, definitely." I didn't realize how hungry I was until the smell of melting cheese made my stomach growl. Was it because of what happened? I didn't know what lasting effects dying would have on us, but the offer of food was far better than whatever Donovan could have said.

He turned, his expression guarded. "I don't know what happened in the basement to piss you off, if it was me or Caine, but I know I'm standing here because of you."

"I already told you, I didn't do anything."

"Sophie." Using my real name changed the tone of the conversation. "I was flooded with more visions than normal when they put our hands together as we died." When the sizzling of melted cheese crackled in the pan, he broke his intense stare and turned back to flip the sandwiches. "The years we spent together in our past were spent in magic. It shouldn't surprise me your power transcended lifespans."

When he turned back to me, I focused on Bosco. Donovan proceeded as if I had warned him to tread lightly. "You were a powerful Magic then, but by this age you were already well-versed in your craft." He leaned forward. I looked up at him. "I watched you create, play, and bend your power to your will. And when you were satisfied, and I was, frankly, awe-struck, you encased us within your energy. Cooled electricity hit me square in the chest, equal parts pain and ecstasy. Then I was breathing again and back in the backyard." He looked saddened to make the return.

His yearning had me fighting against reaching out for him and I busied my hands with petting Bosco.

He shook his head. "And although it was excruciating until your touch brought me those images, once I saw you wield power like a servant biding your command with reverence and loyalty, I had no reservations about living." He gave a single-shoulder shrug. "Blind faith in you is an easy one for me. Now? I look forward to when the you of our past finds the you in our present, because when you find her, you'll be fucking unstoppable."

Donovan turned back to our food as I sat on the edge of tears. I wasn't sad. I wasn't angry. I wasn't even recycling emotions from him. No, his were steady and self-assured while I fell short of explaining what buzzed around inside me. Listening to him speak about the person I was in our past was inspiring. The added pressure piggybacking this inspiration was a dose of reality that weighed on me.

What if I couldn't live up to who I was? What if I did and I lost who I am now? Who would I be then?

No way Donovan missed my growing insecurity as I spiralled into overanalyzing something that may never happen, but he didn't ask for details. Instead, he served sandwiches onto square white plates.

He took a few bites before saying, "Maybe it's because you didn't see it yourself." He fished ketchup from the fridge. "You should really consider what I said and get training. By what I saw, I can only take you so far."

"And how far is that?"

He took another bite of his sandwich and moved it to his cheek. "You think I can't train you?"

I dipped a corner of my grilled cheese into a red blob of ketchup. "Well, what else can you do besides the Psychometry trick?"

He laughed through a mouthful of fused bread and cheese. "Trick? I don't pull a rabbit out of my ass."

"Can you? 'Cuz bestiality isn't my thing."

"Please. Plus, you've seen me grow things, heal, fight. Not badass enough for you?"

"Meh. Mid-level badass. You weren't fighting all-out against Loring." A rush of anger and regret twanged the thread of connection. "I didn't mean it like that. I would never accuse you of not doing everything possible to save her." The unnamed "her" being Aunt Lacey. "I meant, by what I sometimes feel from you, your power is far more potent than you've displayed in my presence. Including there." The uncomfortable vibration between us levelled out. "I don't get why you've dampened down your abilities."

"Why do you want to know?"

"Because. I want to understand you." I was further confused by the surprise this sparked in him.

"Okay. Well, when I was spanked by Loring and his goons, you faced the same punishment for my impulsive reaction. I've had time to think about it, and if I would've gone full metal jacket on his ass, we'd be dead. Staying low-key kept Loring conducting his own mindfuck circus instead of focusing on ways to torture us. The two of us would have been a dream science experiment for him and his devotees, the next Reds for him to control. He won't hold back next time."

I nodded, believing the same. "So, what would you have done, given freedom from me?"

His brows stitched in a grimace. "I'd rather be your conjoined twin then have freedom from you."

"As awkward as that would be, it's far from the point, Mr. Year's Best Staller." He raised an innocent eyebrow. "Either you don't want me to know or you're not the magic ninja you claim to be."

"I don't remember saying I was a Ninja Turtle."

"Fine, Donatello." I put Bosco on the ground and headed toward the basement. "I'll find Ranlyn. Or maybe Hinapouri can turn me into a badass tribal warrior."

My head cranked to the side. A tooth speared my tongue. The crunch of nose cartilage and the tang of blood in the back of my throat was nothing compared to the dizziness that made my knees buckle. I blinked and reached out for the invisible wall I smashed into and was now leaning against. My fingers hit a smooth, hard surface. I massaged the bridge of my nose as my equilibrium fought to right itself.

"What the fizz, asshole?"

"Fuck. Ugh, balls. Worth it." Donovan's laugh was a punch in the quiet kitchen.

"Are you kidding me?" He raised his hand to ward me off when I turned on him. The crunch of my kneecap against something immovable stung half as much as when my whole upper body smacked another invisible wall.

Donovan swore and laughed. Bosco jumped up toward me, his feet landing on the invisible wall. He backed off, looking suspicious. I hit the wall again. This time, a familiar ripple effect warbled the surface.

"No tricks, eh? Kim did that in Pario. How about you fix the glass door?"

"I don't need a Kitchen Witch spell to pull off a barrier like that and the door is an easy one. Well, maybe not as easy since the glass is now water thanks to Caine. I'll figure it out." He raised the intensity of his magic and crossed his arms. "Sexiest snow globe I've ever seen. Do you own a tutu?" The quirk of his mischievous brow told me I was sunk.

"Crapnoodles." A two-foot buffer contained me within the glass-like barrier. The most impressive result was the hysterical laugh it caused him. "Point made, asshat. Let me go. Now."

Kicking the barrier did nothing but hurt my toe—and Donovan's —only making him laugh harder. Words weren't working, so I grabbed and pinched the tender skin on the inside of my upper arm. He yelped and the barrier dropped.

"Worth it." I stole a half of his grilled cheese off his plate while he was too busy rubbing his arm of the sting of my pinch.

"That it?" My words contorted around my cheeks full of cheesy goodness.

"Really? I can hold it forever with minimal concentration."

"Humble." The edge of sarcasm was a guise. As far as I could tell, he was.

"Point is, I can train you. When you've outgrown my teachings, then you can let Hinapouri turn you into a spear-wielding warrior princess if you want. Loring is coming. If you want to be effective, we need to start soon."

"If we rush it, I'm gonna forget something and end up healing him instead of killing him."

He crossed his arms. "Is murder a newfound hobby?"

"It's Loring. You're not going to kill him if given the opportunity?"

"Oh, I'll decapitate the bastard with dental floss if needed, but causing death changes people. Remember how you felt when you killed The Reds? And that was by accident."

"I'm pretty sure it'll be in self-defence, so between Loring and myself, I'm keen on walking away with a heartbeat."

I rounded the island to put my plate in the sink. He stepped in close and said, "Don't take it lightly, is all," and moved a piece of my hair behind my ear. He managed to avoid skin contact, but what came next, I didn't understand. A stir of emotions hit me in response. Not Donovan's, my own, and I didn't know what to do with them.

He straightened at my inner reaction. "Sorry."

"No, I'm sorry. I don't...Umm...."

"Are you all right?" Pressure on my shoulder had me pulling away. The same whirl of emotions hit me again, becoming urgent before I was on the other side of the kitchen, away from him as far as I could.

"Whoa." His hands were splayed and awkward at his sides. "Babe—"

"I'm fine." The shake in my voice called me a liar.

"Why are you scared of me?"

"I'm not."

"You're scared of something."

"It's nothing. I'm going to let Bosco out."

Bosco recognized the words enough to whine and race towards the missing glass door, hesitating before realizing nothing was stopping him from going out on his own. He went straight for his favourite rosebush, now wilting from the high concentration of dog urine. I relished the hit of cool air washing over me. August was muggy-hot in southern Ontario, but tonight came with a chill. I left him to do his business.

"I'll start coffee and then we can get to training," I told Donovan.

"Fine." He wasn't fine, but he didn't push. "And you shouldn't leave him alone. He's not an animal to you. Anyone keeping moderate surveillance knows that. I wouldn't take the chance."

"Fuckers. I'd kill just for that."

The quirk of his eyebrow showed he believed me and I was

relieved he was content to move on from my mild freak out. Whatever it was.

"Here." He held out a red hoodie that had been slung over the top of a chair. I was going to refuse until I saw Bosco's circling routine. He sniffed a spot, decided it wasn't right and searched for another. I would likely be out there a bit.

My hair snapped with static as I pulled the hoodie on, now surrounded in Donovan's smell. While bolder than Caine's, it was tantalizing enough for me to contemplate an exit strategy and give it back. We were alone and if an emotional loop trapped us we were sunk. I couldn't put Caine through that on top of everything that he was already dealing with. This fear and chilled outside air doused the scent and spicy thoughts. Until Donovan joined me outside in a t-shirt, looking unaffected by the weather.

I pulled my attention to the blanket of stars above. Being further from the city had its advantages. Quiet was another. Niagara-on-the-Lake was different. Even the insects were finding quiet places to nestle in instead of buzzing around our heads.

I hugged my knees. "Do you like it here?"

"Not used to it being mine."

"Still hers?"

He nodded. Most of the house was unchanged. Removing Aunt Lacey's mark was impossible, and I got the sense he didn't want to erase her in any way.

"What would you be doing if you weren't holed up here like a hamster?" A quick change in topic was needed when I felt my throat clench, a borrowed sensation as I had tread on sensitive ground.

"Not in some ditch-pig watering hole." I laughed. "Depends. I might be at a bar, chillin' with people." He looked my way. "And up until you came along, prowling ditch-pig watering holes for some play." He flashed a vulgar smirk, I shook my head at. "Actually, I know a back-alley pool hall with great chicken fingers and home fries I bet you'd love."

"I'm sure I would." While frank, the pang of excitement this caused Donovan made me regret the casual answer. "So, is this place an old high school hang-out?"

"I never went to high school."

"As in, you never graduated?"

"As in, I never attended an organized establishment full of pimple-popping hormonal cesspools."

"Really?" He nodded. "You're so well-read, I assumed you had an extensive education."

"Not like the traditional educational system you would've experienced. Magics in my father's coven taught us everything we needed to know to navigate both Magic and Blind universes depending on where we lived. My Coven name, Wend, means wanderer. My family's a bunch of nomads. Would Taint ground until they exhausted local resources and then moved on. I was born in the Netherlands. We moved to the States for a few years. Now, the Coven's close by."

Details about him were scarce, and I didn't want to scare him off. Seconds passed when he skewed his chair toward mine.

"You have to understand. I was bred for a world I wanted no part of, but I didn't know any different until I grew up and was introduced to hotel porn and the news and realized how different other people lived." Feigned humour was lost in a limp smile. "People who didn't recognize the sabbaths or practice rituals, besides working nine-to-five and attending weekly mass. The dynamics of most families was much more," he sat back a moment, "complete than mine. My father is the Coven Master, well-respected for his cold approach to everything Blind. The type who believes people untouched by magic are weak and useless when considering the Coven's true creed to enlighten the Blind or let them suffer a sightless death. Many failed escape attempts since I was eight or nine meant I was dragged back by my father's followers."

"Devotees?"

He nodded. "He was grooming me to be his go-to-guy and heir. Made it his mission to toughen me up by making me front and center of every and all examples he could. Trained me to kill without remorse, had me teach others to do the same, and then punished me every day I refused. Sacrifice being his favourite method."

"Sacrifice? As in, killing you?"

He took a breath before saying, "Death is different for healers. I've been stabbed, sliced up like a Halloween pumpkin, crucified, eviscerated. Never a shortage of proficient healers to keep me inches from true death." His voice caught on the last word. "Which is how I know how impossible it was that you brought us back. We should be worm food."

It was my turn to nod. "Did he stop searching for you?"

"Yes and no. Before I could leave, I was subjected to a part of my father's deeper plans. Once they were complete, he didn't need me anymore. At least not yet."

"What about your mother?"

"Most never know who their biological parents are, though I knew my father was my father. He made it clear. While women were still powerful, their roles were much different than what you're used to. My father wanted no question that he was the leader and the only one to be truly feared."

"Where does Aunt Lacey fit in?"

His smile was the opposite reaction I expected. "When I left, I survived off pick-pocketing and fixing pool games, stuff like that. Bars and clubs are the best hunting grounds since guys usually carry money clips or wallets in their back pockets. Women, well, once I went back to their place, everything was easy access."

"Wow."

"Not proud, just how it went."

"So, Aunt Lacey?"

"Yes, well, I swore off magic altogether, but a simple binding won't supersede Psychometry, which came in handy for palm readings. Aunt Lacey came in as a first-time client and I was near knocked out but the visions. Few have given me a chance. She was one of them. I didn't know we were related until much later, and I don't know how she found me, but she knows—knew—more than most and knew I would never steal from or fuck any of her Coveners. She made sure I didn't go without, but she refused to put up with any drama. Once you came along, she didn't try and stop anything. She knew you were a deal breaker."

"Right. A hall pass on the cockblock. And now, after spending your life as a free agent, you're throwing in a grand bachelor lifestyle, now equipped with a mansion and plush bank account, to promise something you've never put into practice. I'm a serial monogamist. I almost wish I wasn't, but I always have been."

A yawn from Bosco at my feet reminded me of the coffee percolating. We went inside and I searched for a big coffee mug for Kim who was probably back to research. While I wanted to know Donovan, every scratch into the person he was drew me into his orbit and we were already too involved. It was a dangerous game and I was shit at keeping things on the level.

Donovan trailed me inside. "Does your past gauge your future?"

"Not always, but human behaviours don't change overnight. They take time and motive and practice. Especially if the person still seeks certain coping mechanisms due to unresolved trauma."

"Coping mechanisms?"

"Yes. The kind that involves a lot of alcohol and sex."

"I don't know about that, but I do know you've made lousy decisions and ended up with an ex-fiancé who was too weak to handle life and probably spent more time in other bitches than he did you."

I froze mid-reach into a top shelf. Donovan's stirring regret made me heady. Anger kept me from facing him. "Lashing out because I struck a nerve is understandable, but we both know you're not sorry."

"You're right, I meant what I said in a factual context. However, the way it came out was a shithead thing to do. For that, I am sorry. Yes, I've never held onto anyone long-term, but I'm not your ex, which was my original point. I've been through some fucked-up shit that's resulted in lingering issues, but I would never do what he did to you. Don't lump me in the same category as him so you can justify setting me aside."

As I turned, he was closer than I expected. "Maybe that's what I'm doing. I'll give you that. You're not him, but you missed my entire point by making it about my uncanny ability to fall in love with damaged men."

"I just don't get you and Caine."

I clicked my tongue. "Well, Donovan, when two people like each other, they spend time together."

"Cut the smartass bullshit. I need to understand. You risked your life to save his. You let him stay in your apartment. You've opened yourself up after the shit you faced with your ex. Clearly, you believe he's worth it and a safer choice than me." He exhaled. "I can't be another Covener, another friend. I don't want to become a part of your scenery. And since you're not able to take a chance on me, yet, can you promise me one thing?"

"What?"

He hesitated. "Keep asking questions."

"Questions?"

"About me. About my past. About what I see for us, if you really want to know. Anything. Keep my answers in mind for whenever you're ready to move on. I don't care if it's in three years or three hundred."

Of all the times he tried to convince me we were meant to be together, this was the most rational. I was curious about him, but it didn't mean my inner turmoil lessened with this understanding. If anything, it worsened. Caine might be my present and my future, but no matter what, Donovan and I shared a past and it meant too much to me to pretend it didn't exist.

His frustration regarding the situation was replaced with fear of my answer. Pressure in my diaphragm told me he was holding his breath in anticipation.

"I can promise that."

12

ADVERSE SIDE-EFFECTS

Kim was pacing the basement floor as I came down from the kitchen, cell to her ear and a worried crease in her forehead. Donovan hung back to fix the glass door. I wasn't sure how, but he had the same healing ability I did and far more creativity. I served Kim coffee in the largest mug I could find. One depicting a rosy-cheeked Santa reading to engrossed children was the last I expected to find. Confusing and questionable since the Coven didn't celebrate a traditional Christmas. Kim didn't seem to care as she mouthed an unmistakable 'Thank you!' and took the mug before going back to her conversation.

Frog wasn't happy.

He may have been Caine's best friend since they were daring each other to eat worms, but he and Kim were in the throws of the honeymoon phase. By the sounds of her one-sided conversation, he wasn't happy he was excluded from our camp out. Not to mention confused since she openly bad-mouthed Donovan and Caine hadn't told him what was going on.

Caine was more of a pop drinker, so I skipped the java and brought him a can of the dark and fizzy stuff. Relief hit me and then turned to dread as the smile on the edge of his lips disappeared when he looked me over. Fuck weasel. I was still wearing Donovan's sweater.

"Something to wet your whistle?"

He hesitated before taking the can of pop I held out for him and then set it on the floor before resuming his research. A sweater shouldn't make the difference between a good or shit-caked mood, but I got why in this case it did. While I didn't intend to test him, that didn't mean I was about to remove it. All that would do is draw attention to the minefield we tap-danced through from hour-to-hour while stuck under the same roof.

When the call ended, Kim groaned, gulped down some coffee, and plopped down next to Bosco on the couch. "Remind me again why Frog has to stay as blind as a mole rat. You guys are lucky not to have to stay stuffed in the broom closet."

"Sulk somewhere else, Kim." Donovan came downstairs with a note of happiness across the connection, so I assumed he got the door fixed. "I'd say our situation is far more complicated than you and some Frog."

"He's one of my best friends, dude." The fact that Caine addressed Donovan at all had me on immediate alert mode.

The sense of caution I sent over the connection earned me a glare instead of whatever mouthy retort Donovan primed to antagonize Caine.

"He'll probably call you, then you'll be in the hot seat," Kim said to Caine.

Caine exchanged a book for another one. "Sophie just died. Loring's on our heels. Not to mention whoever the Puppeteer is. I don't give a fuck about what Frog or my other friends think I'm up to. They've been without me almost four years, they can deal a little while longer."

Kim crossed her arms. "So much for my ally."

Caine shrugged. "Frog will either deal with the fact you can't tell him all aspects of your life, or he won't. Just because he doesn't know how talented you are, doesn't mean you should settle."

"Damn straight." Kim's posture straightened with new-found confidence.

Donovan set his empty coffee mug down with a clunk on the table. "Stick it out. Maybe he'll turn into a prince. Or you'll become a fairy-tale villain. Either is likely."

Kim responded with something snarky, but I couldn't hear her. The turn of Donovan's lips and squint of his eye evoked the same reaction as it had in the kitchen. My power buzzed in my ears and I panicked. Trying to stuff it back down from wherever the fuck it came from overwhelmed and discombobulated me. I stood up as if to escape to the bathroom and then forgot where I was going. I popped my eyes open when Caine called my name, not remembering when I closed them.

"Are you okay?" Caine asked.

"I'm good."

"You're lying," Donovan said. "Same thing happened in the kitchen."

"Sellout." My glare was off as I still attempted to right myself. They waited for more. "Ugh. Fine. I don't know why, because new and weird-flavoured shit is on the menu every day, but, twice now, I've got these—" I paused and had to force myself to continue. "—déjà vu moments."

"About what?" Kim asked.

"Like I said, déjà vu. You know, repeats of familiar things. About Donovan." Cue the discomfort from everyone in the room but Donovan. The zing of intrigue across the connection was intense.

"Like a vision?" he asked without a hint of his inner celebration.

I looked at Caine and saw patience in his impassive expression as he waited for an explanation. Or fearing one, which was more likely. I hated doing this to him.

"No, no," I said. "More like a thin layer of tracing paper between now and a snapshot of our past. A couple things triggered certain memories and scrambled my wiring for a split-second." I picked up the book I was reading. "Episode past and moving on to more scintillating research since the bad guys won't be content holding their dicks without making a move for long."

"Lame." Kim sat cross-legged and leaned back on her hands. "Compared to daily events, it's weak."

"Yeah, well, it doesn't feel weak." I looked at Donovan. "Though I do. You're fuelled up now. Let's get started."

"What are you guys doing, anyways?" Kim asked.

"Training, apparently."

"Ooooh, can I join?"

"Course," I said as Donovan snipped a definite, "No."

Donovan rolled his eyes. "You can't evoke power, Kim. Shouldn't you be memorizing spells and taking inventory on our stock?"

The cross of Kim's arms tipped me off to a headache of a conversation. "Your body has already experienced power, Kim." Her brow creased. "In the Woodland of Energies when the Elders passed on their gift of agelessness to Ranlyn and the others."

Her arms dropped to her sides. "It can't be. That was power sent from the Elders in death. You can't tell me every time you get a flutter of aggression or whatever it is with you two, that your body goes through that type of strain. I thought I was going to explode."

"Without the distraction of Donovan's visions, we would have crumbled, but it hit us differently than most because it was twofold due to the connection. Get a handle on the bursting in the beginning and you're golden."

"It doesn't usually happen that way," Donovan said.

"No? 'Cuz no one raised any alarms when it happened to me or Caine. Seemed pretty damned peachy about it, actually."

"Aunt Lacey had her reasons to celebrate considering you're backpacking her family's power around, but for most of us, it grows naturally. Yours was like a car flooded with NOS. You went from Sophie the girl-next-door with only her pug and a bar full of drunks to keep her company, to Sophie the stabbing victim who was pushed into the desperation of her power to keep her alive. Your body acclimatized too abruptly."

Donovan made a throaty sound of irritation I had no clue how to interpret before adding, "You can practice all you want, Kim. I'm sure you know the ratio of Kitchen Witches who cross into true power like Nya. Give yourself a stroke forcing it to happen if you want, but we've got work to do."

"Dick," Kim said.

Whether he was right or not, Kim could take care of herself, so I didn't intervene, but it did surprise me Donovan was so negative. Maybe it was reverse psychology as we both knew Kim would never give up, but he was still rude.

"So, what's first, babe? The wall?"

"Nah, thanks. Blocking Loring would be nice, but I'd rather beat the shit out of him."

Donovan's dimples caved as something close to pride tickled the connection. Seated on the floor with the intention of establishing a baseline first, Donovan had me rouse my power, then hold it steady to better control any resulting attack. Unsatisfied with my flabby results, Donovan surprised the fuck out of me by leading me through a meditation technique.

The fact that it worked surprised the fuck out of me more.

Once I established a steady dose of power, we worked on testing my senses to see which ones I was attuned to the most. Sight was my biggest tool. As a Soul Seer the souls of others were no mystery to me. After an hour of testing, I found that souls were tangible if I ran my hands over the light they emit. I wanted to walk up to Caine and give it a test, as doing so with Donovan felt too intimate, but Caine was still nose deep in a book, ignoring us. Kim was a safe option due to her low-wattage soul glow and easy prey while seated in her own meditative peace trying to evoke some true power. Wisps of energy brushed my palm when I hovered my hand close to her, surveying the dim light of her soul.

"Yo." Kim was wide-eyed at the invasion of her personal bubble.

"Let her try." Donovan crouched behind me supervising.

"Try what?"

A boost of my own power thickened the energy I felt, but the vibration from my power confused the sensation I was trying to feel out.

"Touch her already." Donovan's impatience was another hurdle.

"If this is your attempt at lesbian porn directing, you've missed the point," Kim said.

"Shut up and let her do it. I'll take your expert opinion on lesbian porn later."

"Wait." Kim sat back a few inches. "I'm all for consensual human testing, though that entails the subject is in on the particulars of adverse side-effects. Either of you want to let me in on what you're trying to do? I want to be ready if my skin starts growing moss or peeling off."

"No skin moss. Just hold up." I pressed my hand onto Kim's chest below her throat and focused on finding the root of whatever was in the energy I sensed.

I concentrated on the niggling sensation I found if I pushed. A sense of floating took over and dipped me into a place with no friction. The room fell away as did the hum of the basement's ventilation system, Caine shifting through page after page, and Kim's guarded breathing. A tingle flourished like my power in its initial stages. Instead of it threatening to take me over, this tingle drew me deeper and beckoned me to follow. My curiosity let it pull me along.

Nondescript flashes of people I never met were a blur, then focused. Places I never visited or could even discern their location accompanied them. Memories. Good and bad. Kim's first kiss with a pimply-faced grade schooler. The sheen of sweat on the back of her mother's neck as she was bent over a bucket full of vomit. Everything Kim experienced came with the same low radiance of soul glow. I pushed beyond the memories to focus on this light and to find its source. The light itself was proof Kim contained magic. Maybe a

Witch lacking the long-line of blood fuelling her power, but she found it on her own.

I tracked the light to a place deep within her. Either blocked or held back by something I couldn't detect, it hunkered down in a pocket surrounded by the movie reel of Kim's life. Shouldering through the memories to get to her power source meant facing a gauntlet of overwhelming information beyond my ability to absorb or fend off.

The intrigue had worn off. The steady draw of curiosity that piqued my interest now brought me to a place inside Kim that strove to be heard. All the things people hold inside, all their secrets, all the lessons they're too scared to learn, was pouring out of Kim and into me like a cleansing sob. I was under siege with no way to separate feeling from thought, hatred from need, or anxiousness from exhilaration, and no way to get a grip on any particular sensation to match it up with its appropriate memory.

Without feet in this place, I had nowhere to run and no escape route. Panic roared as the barrage of all things Kim pelted me like a horde of crazed locusts. Sucked back with g-force strength, I opened my eyes to find myself back in the basement, nauseous and shaking before recognizing the safety of my surroundings.

Pain stabbed my side with every pant. I went to press my hand into my ribs and a strong grip stopped me. Donovan's wide-eyes cast over my shoulder. I was in his lap. A mask of concern and confusion I seldom saw him wear sparked guilt within me I didn't understand. Not until I saw Kim across from me with Caine holding her by the shoulders, both with an accusatory gaze pinned on me.

Bosco stood with his chest out, on alert, while everyone tried to catch a breath.

"What happened?"

Kim didn't answer me. Neither did Caine.

My ribs ached when I turned back to Donovan. "Tell me."

"We couldn't get you off her." Donovan loosened his hold but remained where we sat. He took a deep breath and his calm fought to combat whatever he was being injected with through the connection.

"I came over when Kim started screaming. You didn't hear her?"

Both Kim and Caine's glares had softened, but the implication behind them hurt. I would never knowingly inflict harm on Kim.

"I w-was just trying to see what I could find out. I didn't hear anything."

"Find out? I don't ever want to feel that again. Not as painful as I imagine the epic *Braveheart* eviscerating torture scene, but close to. Felt like you were trying to wring out my insides like a wet towel."

Disappointment hit when I extracted myself from Donovan's lap and sunk into the couch cushions. If only they would swallow me for good. "I saw and felt so much while inside, so many memories, but I have no idea what any of it means. I connected with your spirit or soul. You have power, but I don't know what's stopping it from surfacing."

Kim stood. "You saw it?"

"I can see it right now. Your soul glows to me."

"Not what I meant." She sat next to me. "Real power? Not my Kitchen Witch, self-taught, non-blood born power. You mean actual power like what you guys have or like Nya ended up having? That type of power?"

"Well, yeah."

Kim squealed and hugged me.

"Calm your tits, girl. I don't want to get your hopes up. For all I know, it's like that for everyone, lying dormant until something triggers it."

"No guarantees. Got it." She squealed in my ear and pulled back.

The weight of Caine's arm draped around my shoulders. When I looked at him next to me on the couch, he planted a kiss on my forehead. Apparently, he wasn't mad at me anymore. "Why hasn't your family mentioned they could do this?"

Suspicion and jealousy from Donovan crossed the connection and made me inwardly question Caine's motive as Donovan did the same. I pushed his emotions aside and tried to answer Caine. Of course, I had no clue what I was dealing with and thought maybe the others didn't know. Kim threw in a theory or two while Donovan stewed and then busied himself with research.

———

We agreed not to sleep at the same time but didn't work out a watch system. Kim was the first to pass out during a read through of a book called 'Safeguarding Wights: Carry out & Conjure', lightly snoring in a curled heap on the couch with Bosco tucked in behind her knees. I fell victim next. Donovan lay out on his belly on the floor again, unable to fight my exhaustion from taking him over.

Music blared and shocked everyone awake. Including Caine, who succumbed to the Sandman at some point, head slumped back as he sat in front of the couch where I slept at the opposite end from Kim. An angsty voice screamed as Donovan groaned, rolled onto his back, and fished into his pocket without opening his eyes.

New to the scream-alarm, I sprung up into a seated position with a sucking breath, consequently booting Kim in the shin, and pushing Bosco off the couch. When I reflexively moved to catch him, I elbowed Caine in the skull and hit my funny bone. Donovan swore as the zing of pain tingled up and down the nerve of my elbow. He hit his speaker phone button as he rubbed his arm.

"You should be ant bait," a quiet voice said above our groans.

"Are you selling pesticides?" Donovan asked.

"How are you still breathing?"

"Been a pro since birth. Can I help you or are you calling 'cuz you like being a punch-line?"

He looked at me with the silent question of if I was okay. I nodded and curled my arms and hands back into the sleeves of his red sweater.

"You're such a fucking idiot!"

"Joelly?" Anger flared from everyone in the room. Donovan

picked up the phone. His fury so great my hands shook. "The fuckin' balls on you."

"Can you stop pulling your pubes for two seconds and get your shit together? Why haven't you left town? Gone into hiding? Reached out? Something other than the orgy you've got going on in your sugar mama's pad."

Donovan's nostrils flared. "You turn us to dust and then call in with survival tips? We managed on our own, thanks. Shit. You should have a psychiatrist on retainer."

"Oh!" Kim said in the end of a gasp. She was bursting from excitement about something but covered her mouth so she didn't interrupt Donovan.

"That's what you get for attacking me," Joelly said.

Donovan let out a humorless laugh. "Attacking you? Playing your victim role, I see." Donovan's tone was so restrained he was a rabid dog waiting to snap at a helping hand.

"We can't all be daddy's favourite."

"Get to the fucking point."

She sucked her teeth. "You have eyes all over your sugar mama's mansion. He's holding back but won't follow orders forever. So, I repeat, get your shit together!"

Silence of an ended call had Donovan's nails biting into his palms, giving me the impression if he were alone he may have punched something.

"She's clearly still in deep with Loring if she knows we're alive," Caine said.

"Clearly," Donovan shot back with heavy sarcasm, still battling his rage. "Though I'd rather endure a tortuous, bloody death by burrowing rats than call her back for a chat."

"You wanna share with the class, Kim," I said as she still held her mouth shut.

"Yes! Death will be brief. We forgot to tell them," she said to Caine.

"I'm pretty sure they know they're alive," Caine said.

"But the thing we saw? Come on, Caine, I know you saw it too. While they were crispy—"

I scoffed. "Who you callin' crispy?"

"You've been called worse," Donovan said.

"Denise's opinions don't count."

"The shimmer?" Caine finally said.

"Yes, the shimmer."

Kim sat on the edge of the couch next to me. "When you stopped breathing, Bosco started freaking out at the back doors."

"I thought it was your spirit." The grief in Caine's voice bitch-slapped the humour right out of me. I couldn't imagine what it was like to watch someone you love die, especially the way it went down. Talk about traumatic.

Kim's hand on my arm recaptured my attention. "After it took off, Bosco chilled out and you were both healing. Maybe it's why you survived."

"No, it's not." Donovan was firm.

"I was dead, too. I didn't see anything. You're a Psychometrist, not a dream interpreter."

"The dead don't dream. I know what I saw."

"You saw her spirit, too?" Kim asked.

"I have no clue what you saw, but it wasn't what saved us."

"Either way," Caine's voice was edged with frustration, "it was the outline of a person. Not ghostly, but still person-like. Transparent."

"Exactly. What if it was Death like the premonition mentioned?"

"We don't know anything for sure," Caine said.

"We know the shimmer wasn't Sophie's spirit if it didn't return to her body." Donovan was right. Not to mention I didn't remember leaving my body.

Playing referee was my least favourite game. "Unless it doubles-back and drops the Casper act to introduce itself, our best bet is to keep researching. Add transparent death voyeur to the list of shit we don't know. At least we're back good as new."

"Better than new. Your scar is gone." Kim grabbed my left arm and twisted it to display my forearm.

Before we knew Loring had bound our powers, I sliced my arm open and was left with a jagged reminder that meant Aunt Lacey couldn't heal me. Up on my feet with my shirt up and over my pierced belly button, I noticed the titanium ring was gone and so was the hideous reminder of my near-death experience by my knife-happy and vengeful drunk neighbour.

"Sweetfuckbeans! There's nothing." Smooth skin was left where my fingers kneaded the once disfigured area. A lusty vibration across the thread of connection had me pulling my shirt back in place and sitting down. "I didn't want to cart around those memories anyway. Though I guess I'll have to get my navel re-pierced."

"And your ears," Kim said.

When I pinched them, the balls of scar tissue in my lobes were missing. "Shitballs. I knew I should've been a smoker. My lungs would be fresh-from-the-womb now."

Kim relaxed back into the couch. "And all it took was excruciating disintegration with mysterious resurrection. Beauty's a bitch."

"I could market this. Make me a pretty penny."

"Hell, if I was dying of cancer, I'd consider it," Donovan said.

"Way to bring down the room, Negative Neil." I had no clue how much Donovan knew about Kim's mother and how she died of breast cancer, but it was a sore subject.

"Your tattoo's gone," Kim said instead of commenting on the cancer topic.

Donovan pushed up his t-shirt sleeves and found both shoulders bare of the intricate tattoos. "Fuck!"

His tantrum threw Kim and I into a fit of laughter.

13

IN THE LOOP

After a shower and clean clothing, I found Kim and Caine around the kitchen table. Not only had they changed venues but so had the pile of books now scattered on the kitchen table and floor.

"What are you guys doing?"

Kim didn't glance up from her book. "Knitting a pair of mittens."

"Nice. Don't forget the matching scarf and toque, Granny."

Caine met me where I stood, wrapped me in a tight hug, and kissed my wet crown. "Good shower?"

"Yup. Nice and steamy." I drank in the contact, missing his affection. While Caine's general attitude bordered on bastardly was understandable while exposed to Donovan for longer than a coven meeting, I still wished I could enjoy this part of him more often.

The sound of soft footsteps came up behind me. I didn't need to look to confirm it was Donovan. Besides being the only other one in the house, since Bosco was snoozing under the kitchen table, the pinch of dread across the connection and Caine's sourpuss expression, spelled it out. Still in his sleepwear of baggy black jogging pants and a plain white t-shirt, he headed for the fridge.

"Find out anything new?" I asked the room, focusing back on the danger causing our arrangement. Donovan didn't answer, too busy drinking straight from an orange juice jug, neither did Kim. Caine sat at the table again and picked up the book he was reading. "We're beyond actual words now. Super positive. Thanks guys."

"Serena called." Caine's deadpan tone followed his increasing negativity.

"Shitkebabs. Was she pissed?"

"Ask Kim."

"You're lucky she's family." Kim looked at me for the first time since I entered the kitchen.

Yikes. I loved them both for their strong personalities but pit them against each other and the blood would fly.

"My bad. I should've called her."

"Mhmm." Kim left it at that, but her tense shoulders as she turned back to her book told me she had a mouthful she kept to herself.

Caine handed me his phone. I dialled Serena and then reached into the fridge for water as it rang. Donovan's head perked up from where it laid on his arms as he sat on a stool around the kitchen island. Eddies of want floated through our bond, devoid of sexual craving. He wanted the orange juice again but didn't want to get up. I passed him the jug, gaining a smile in gratitude.

"Lazy ass," I muttered as he gulped his prize.

"You think you can freeze me out?" Serena yelled into the receiver in place of a hello.

"It's a bit complicated, cuz." I walked into the living room for some privacy.

"When is it not complicated with you? I don't have power, so you boot me from the club? You could've at least let me in on what the hell was so over my head I had to hear it from Olive."

"You're in the Ballard Family Coven club."

"Then why'd you tell Olive?"

"I would've preferred no one knew."

"What? Did they fix you with a doormat spell?"

"Yes. Now I have a permanent boot print on my ass. Bathing suit season will never be the same." Before she hung up on me, I moved on. "I get you feel snubbed. I'm sorry, no one likes that, but I didn't want to get more people involved in this. Shit is real dangerous, and I refuse to be responsible for getting you killed to save your feelings."

"How about vaguely informed? Olive says whatever this is, it's payback for the stuff that went down in the Creation thing, but now there's a premonition in the mix?"

Guilt flushed from my under-eye circles to my hyper-extended knees. Before the magic stuff took over every aspect of my life, Serena and I shared an effortless understanding. You have a secret, you have me to tell and to trust to keep it. Now, Serena was Blind with an unshielded mind and enough knowledge to bury herself without knowing why. Loring or whoever the Puppeteer was would enjoy her confusion and inability to fight back and I would never forgive myself.

"This is serious, Serena. We're not talking about some bitch who swiped your favourite shirt or hit your car with a shopping cart and bounced without leaving a note. They're powerful and pissed off and bent on guaranteeing we pay the price for making him look like novices in magic diapers." I took a steadying breath and said, "I died yesterday." Devoid of emotion for someone directly involved in the loss, I ignored my detachment as silence on the end of the line lasted longer than I liked.

"Where are you?"

———

Over an hour and a half passed since the phone call with Serena and, with her insistence on involvement, I was pissed she took her time getting to Donovan's. When the doorbell rang, I answered and found Serena wasn't alone. The time delay made sense when factoring in a trip to and from Dunnville to pick up Olive. More intriguing then the two of them being on Donovan's doorstep, was opening the door to their backs.

"Who is that, Firefly?"

Behind the cars parked in the driveway, stood Donovan's middle-aged neighbour who walked her Frenchie around the block in her best dressed like she was on camera 24/7. Her equally well-groomed substitute offspring groaned and pulled on the leash without a flicker of acknowledgment as she stared at us with rapt attention. My blood felt like it drained from my head and didn't clot until it soaked through my socks.

"Inside. Now." One hundred percent protected or not, at least inside they wouldn't be stared at by Mrs. Suzy Homemaker of the Year. Both moved quickly, but so did Serena's questions and I wanted them inside before letting them know what the staring was all about.

"What happened?" Donovan sprinted into the room, the others right behind him.

"Just your Frenchie-walking-attention-whore neighbour, staring at them."

He nodded stiffly.

I started at the beginning so Serena wouldn't have a reason to stop me with more questions, though Olive knew chunks of events already. Serena was a bundle of energy as I talked, her expressions shifting from curiosity to anger and even sympathy. I expected far worse and was happy to get through it without interruption. What I didn't expect was the shakes. During the whole recall of what we knew, what we hoped to learn, and what we endured, a steady vibration had me talking too fast and pacing the kitchen as I talked. Regurgitating some of the worst times of my life was cleansing, in theory. In reality, it made me feel like shit. Olive's tear-filled eyes and Serena's pursed lips didn't help.

"So yeah, that's it. Fun times all over." Humour did nothing to counteract my adrenalized reaction.

Olive shook her head, hand to chest in silence. "Ego fuels evil and corrupts the innocent with such ease. My heart goes out to you, Firefly. Not all magic brings such sadness."

"I sure as hell hope not."

"You've had so little time to find your power. This man has no idea the army gathered to fight this war for you."

"*Pfft.* What army? Swiss Army? 'Cuz I don't carry a knife. Though having one is a good idea."

"The Coven Aunt Lacey has left behind is legend. Are they not involved?"

"Well—"

"The Elders have been out of reach," Caine said, to which Olive responded with an incredulous glare. "When it comes down to it, they'll fight."

"This is family, blood or otherwise. Seedlings with wet wings against a seasoned brute? This can't be allowed."

"I don't have the juice, Soph, not yet, but I'll help with what I can." Serena paused. "And sorry for coming down so hard on the phone. I didn't realize how big a clusterfuck this was."

"I should've called."

"Hmm." Serena squinted her bright blue eyes and regrouped. "Yes, you should have."

"I'm proud to see my nieces can be mature enough women to make up for their grievances, but there's much work to be had. Where is your flock, Firefly?"

"Not my flock. Ask my leaders." I chinned in Donovan and Kim's direction. Olive's gaze shifted to them sitting on either side of the kitchen island with Caine.

"Of course it's your flock, babe," Donovan said. "She wouldn't have left the Coven to us without thinking of you, too."

"Babe?" Serena said to Donovan, her brow knitted, then looked to Caine's deadpan veneer.

"You're the only one I hear complaining," Donovan said.

"I shouldn't be." Her glare slid from Caine to me.

"The flock is living their lives," I told Olive instead of getting into it with Serena. "Not all of them are open about the Coven and they work and have family."

"And you think scooping ice cream for minimum wage or selling cars is worth your life? You need to access all available resources. Your immediate Sect should be first to come to another Covenmates aide."

"They're not all exactly useful," Donovan said.

"Then Elsa was smart not to leave you as their sole guardian." Olive was right, though Donovan was beyond seeing her logic while his anger surged. "Any one of them can read a book, gather ingredients for spellwork, or contact others of your Mother Coven for advice. It takes much more than power to make a Sect."

Olive turned to me in question. "What of his skills? Were you able to glimpse the concentration of Loring's power?"

"He spoke smoother than an evangelical egomaniac and has the creative flare of Hannibal Lecter, but his soul was too Tainted for colour so I couldn't see if he has a specialty gift."

"He's been referred to as the Puppeteer, though it's possible that's someone else entirely," Donovan said with only a hint of frustration.

Olive straightened. Her dark eyes unfocused and wondering in thought before saying, "You're sure he was called the Puppeteer?"

"Not technically. Sophie telepathically overheard the name from Joelly before she took us out."

"Telepathically?" Serena's eyebrows couldn't have reached any higher.

"In Joelly's rabid panic it's all I heard, but given the name, it doesn't take a Rocket Scientist to interpret they can make people do things."

"As outlined within our family tome, a Puppeteer's soul, if able to be read beneath any potential Taint, would glow much like yours." Olive looked at Caine who went rigid with the comparison. "Being a Puppeteer is a position of persuasion. Much like you, Caine, a Puppeteer can strip an individual of free will. And while you may be able to make them to do something or tell you something they would not normally let go of, not only can a Puppeteer accomplish this easier, but to a much higher degree." Olive shook her head. "I should have realized as soon as it happened."

"Realized what?" I asked.

"The neighbour. The way she stared, not like she knew us or was trying to place us, no suspicion or derision. If this Loring is the Puppeteer, then it was he looking through the eyes of the neighbour."

"He can take over someone's body?" Caine was taken aback by the possibility.

Olive nodded. "Different than possession but amounts to the same result."

Donovan leaned against the counter. "So why doesn't he slip Sophie on like a Halloween costume and have her walk into traffic if he wants her dead?"

"Eww," I blurted.

"Maybe he can't," Olive said. "You're all within the fold of a highly powerful Coven. Maybe Loring cannot overtake you. Or maybe his goal doesn't include killing you."

Kim gave a humourless laugh.

"We don't have that kind of luck," Caine said, and I had to agree with them both.

"Now there's the true future to fear, slavery by the Puppeteer sounds far worse than machines or zombies."

"Let's not think that far ahead, Firefly. For now, we need to learn more, and we need help." Taking charge of the game plan, Olive ordered us to hit the phones and explain everything to each Covener, insisting they do their duty to the Sect and show up immediately and ignore anyone who stares at them. Kim had a list, so everyone took a number and got dialling, even Olive who surprised the shit out of me by taking a cell phone from her bag. I didn't even own a cell phone.

Blake and Jared were down for anything, as always. No hesitation, no questions asked. Not everyone could drop everything, but by two in the afternoon, we received either promises of "I'll be there as soon as I can" from most members, "Absolutely impossible" from only a few, and "What the hell is going on?" from far too many before they would agree to anything.

Not only had the Coveners shown up to lend their power, they also brought good eats for the whole night. I assumed having a life or death crisis would dampen everyone's spirits, but when the group showed up, it shifted into a party.

"Let's bring these pieces of shit down!" Blake's exuberance was super fuelled by a tall boy energy drink taken from the case carried on his hip. The plastic was torn away with two cans already missing. His hazel eyes were bright with battle ready anticipation, buzzing in caffeine overload, his gelled, dirty-blond curls were in more disarray than usual as Jared followed close behind his best friend.

"Can I get one of those?" Serena asked. I assumed she engaged with the hyper ball of energy, but she was checking out Jared, not Blake. His tanned skin mirrored the colour of his eyes. Not black or even dark-brown, but delightfully caramel. Jared set down the two cases he carried like they weighed less than his wallet, smiled, and ripped open the case to pass her one. A second later he side-eyed her and then looked at me.

"Oh right, this is Olive, my great-aunt and Soul Seer. And my cousin Serena, Kitchen Witch in training."

Olive gave a soft smile and a nod.

"I'm Blake." He shook Olive's hand with far too much vibrancy for a woman her age. "Goredema's my Coven name. And my giant friend is Jared or Molan."

"Will we get Coven names?" Serena asked Olive.

"Call yourself whatever you want, dear." She was being polite, but something in her tight expression told me she thought the concept was silly and far from a Ballard Coven tradition.

"I'll get the rest." Blake beat Jared on the shoulders as he bounded out the door, speeding around Gwen coming in with her hands full.

"So, why the last-minute invite?" Jared asked. "Last resort?"

Kim shrugged. "We hoped we wouldn't need you."

"I doubt that. Thanks for the inclusion, regardless of the reason. Aunt Lacey meant something to all of us. Loring comes down on one of us, he gets the wrath of all of us. That hasn't changed."

"Yes, he does," Donovan said.

Olive's discreet smile went unnoticed by the others, but she was right to put some fire under our new Sect Leader's asses.

"Help?" Gwen raced into the room with fruit and veggie trays stacked across her forearms and a reusable cloth bag full of food options, both clutched and cutting into her skin. We took the stuff she carried, and I made quick introductions of Olive and Serena. "Why aren't there any safeguards on this place?" she asked Donovan.

"The Theban Heart and Home carvings were enough for Loring to avoid coming inside during the Coven gathering."

"Because it was Aunt Lacey's spell and attached to her power. With her gone, the spell would be untethered and broken."

I didn't have to look at Donovan to confirm he didn't know anything about this.

"And you think a simple ward will save the day?" Donovan's bite was a bit much.

"No." Gwen pushed a wayward strand of thick, orange-red curly hair behind her ear. "But it might warn us if someone Tainted or with evil intent breaches our defences, so you're not caught on the toilet."

"Can you perform a warding spell?" I asked, ignoring Donovan's doubt.

Gwen's mouth opened and closed. "Not the one Aunt Lacey did. I've got the tools for a different one. Luckily, only the basement entrance would need to be secured as it contained no other access points and no windows, but this is a big place. It'll take many of us working simultaneously to give it strength anywhere close to fend off Loring. Your gift can gauge who would be the strongest and best to perform the spell."

My stomach sunk an inch. "Oh, goodie. How many do we need?"

"At least eight."

"Ready to disappoint all but 8 people?" I asked Olive. She displayed the same amount of thrill for the task as I had.

———

Coveners arrived without knowing Olive and I were being judgey-pants of their soul glows. No one was told, but Jared was present for the conversation with Gwen, so, naturally, everyone knew. Stolen glances my way by smokers in the backyard were heavy with intrigue. Each one was ignored as Serena and I stood outside with Bosco so he could get some fresh air before we locked him in the safety of the basement for the duration of the spell.

"This is totally awesome," Serena said with sudden giddiness.

I snort-laughed without sharing her enthusiasm. Serena had only a taste of magic without the danger of its reality. In her place, I would be riding an adrenaline high too, but I had no illusions of how fucked we were. Loring and whoever else were working on a plan and they were sitting back and smiling as they watched us freak out and scratch for a sense of safety. I thought it possible they pulled some supernatural block to keep out messages from reaching Ranlyn. Would make sense. Cut your enemy off from their salvation. But then why let us call the Coveners? They enjoy the show and know how weak they are in comparison to the Elders? Nah, wherever Ranlyn was, he was out of touch, busy with Elder duties, or—I didn't want to think of how the last Elders ended up, but the image of Aunt Lacey's barbed-wire-wrapped naked body sprung to mind, along with the heap of ripped up and blood-seeping bodies in the barn.

To think of Ranlyn ending up that way constricted my throat and had my head swimming. The wave of headiness intensified and distracted me from the blood and gore of my memories. This wasn't anxiety, but something else. Too familiar to go unnoticed. "I could kill him."

"Dog's dig. Chillax yourself."

"What?" Bosco had finished and was covering his business as if he hoped to preserve it for future generations. "Not Boss." I called his name so he would stop before he emptied a hole big enough to lose himself in. "Donovan's dipped into his alcohol stash." Everyone was nervous, but the spell was important. He had to know he would be a part of the group strong enough to perform it.

"Hmm. Hate to drop it on you, but I'm not a Donovan fan."

"Don't blame you. When he's not busy scowling at people he's a decent guy. One of those hard-shelled kinds who forgets to use his genius because he doesn't give a fuck about how others feel about him."

"Unless he's a Ninja Turtle, I don't care how hard his shell is. And genius? The guy got you both ashed up by his sister. Real genius. If this connection thing is real—"

"It is."

"—you're about to ruin everything with Caine."

"Thanks."

"He's not my type, but I get it. Donovan's stereotypically hot in all the fun and most dangerous ways and, no surprise, you're defending him. Classic you. Don't lose your panties under his bed."

"My panties are securely in place."

"Yup. Securely wrapped around Donovan's wrist."

"Shut up."

"For reals, Soph. Don't let him weasel his way in. Caine's a good guy."

"I didn't say he wasn't."

"You don't have to. You're letting Donovan treat you like he's already won you. Calling you babe in front of your boyfriend. Seriously? Would you want someone talking to Caine like that?" I didn't answer her. "It's not about ownership. Who cares if he was your past life ball and chain? He isn't now. How about basic respect?"

Everyone else in the backyard was too busy in conversation to hear her, but I still looked around to check since her lecture was equipped with a louder than normal speaking voice.

Serena snapped in front of my face to regain my attention.

"You're not arguing back, which means you agree, but not enough to change anything." We stood and stared at each other a moment. Serena let go a heavy exhale. "Which means you're legit into this guy, even if you don't want to be."

Again, I didn't argue.

"Shit, Soph. You really know how to complicate a good thing." Serena bent and picked up Bosco. "Go deal with your alcoholic next boyfriend. I've got this little man." She walked away, leaving me behind to chew over what she said.

When I didn't feel like standing in the middle of the backyard alone, I found Donovan in the kitchen. He downed the whisky in his glass then dropped it into the sink, winking at me through the crowd. He was a habitual line-crosser, but as Serena pointed out, I wasn't forcing him to stop. Did I contain a breaking point when it came to him? I was resigned to the fact he was who he was, but I shouldn't be entertaining his blatant disregard for—for what? He didn't care about Caine and he has been upfront about his intentions. Yelling at him was wasted energy since I doubted he would alter his behaviour.

A part of me questioned if I didn't stop him because I liked it. Maybe the part who used to be his wife? Another part of me was ecstatic to avoid the brewing shitstorm and focus on the spell.

———

Olive and I compiled a mental list of names for who would participate in the spell. Donovan offered to make the announcement. Technically it was his Sect, so it was appropriate. Perhaps a more dominating reason for him making the announcement was that he would do so without feeling bad for those left unchosen. He stood in front of the group and read off the list.

"We will also be joined by Olive. She may not be a member of this Coven, but she is Sophie's family and amongst a long line of powerful Magics who can be verified by Salix's power. Anyone insinuating Salix is lying can leave, because I assure you she's more honest and dedicated to the success of this Sect than most of you."

Pure overkill, but as I looked over the crowd, it seemed only Denise was insulted.

"Also," he continued, "those chosen are done so as the first line in defence of our lives. So set aside your ego. If you want to whine about it, you can speak to Kim."

Serena set herself next to Jared on the couch and gave me a pursed smile. No one called Donovan out, but the side-eyed stares the Coveners gave each other spelled it out for them.

"Besides the main group, we'll have the extras in the front room and the kitchen to hold a constant flow of energy to complete the process. That will be done by Deidra and Blake. Myself and Sophie will take the front lawn, while Caine and Olive take the backyard. Louise, you'll be upstairs with Henry and Gwen. Kim will show you which rooms to use. You'll need to begin in the attic, so hopefully you're not freaked by tight spaces."

No one protested.

"The spell itself," Gwen said, "is called The Shield of Aegis. When complete, it will create a safe zone where the Blind, or those knee-deep on the wrong side of things, will not *want* to come anywhere near this house. It's like a bubble that will encapsulate the property. Although it is a powerful spell, it might not be enough to stop Loring once he realizes what's happening. If he does cross the boundary, the people who are a part of the spell will be instantly alarmed and will warn the rest. I'm assuming falling back to the basement would be smart in that case since they would have to bottleneck their efforts to try and get down to us."

"More like burn us alive within it," Donovan said.

This jostled the group. No one agreed on what the best course of action was if a retreat was eminent, but some refused to be trapped in a windowless hole. Myself among them.

Everyone who wasn't directly involved in the Shield of Aegis spell was to perform a different ritual as a separate group in the basement, away from the others. Kim's idea. Donovan thought she was trying to give those without power something to do so they wouldn't feel left out, but he was clear—if only to me—he believed their ritual was useless and would do nothing to increase the outcome of the main spell. Everyone else figured it wouldn't hurt, so Kim explained their part, while the others readied themselves to perform The Shield of Aegis.

14

SAFEGUARDS

Gwen unrolled a leather pouch that sectioned off bunches of herbs and other unlabeled containers and fabrics. "Blessed Athame?" she asked Donovan.

Blake moved first, searching his duffle bag and holding up two options. She chose a black horn-handled knife with a damask pattern along the blade and began slicing up a piece of stiff fabric. "The spell is called The Shield of Aegis because it refers to mythology in a time where Zeus ruled. Goatskin, which is what this is," —she referred to the caramel hide in her hand— "was what Zeus's breastplate was made of and called The Shield of Aegis."

Everyone watched her pick through herbs and small bones and sprinkle them into the center of the cut-up sections. No one questioned where, who, or what the bones came from, though what was more off-putting was how she handled the bones without trepidation. Donovan smirked at my uneasiness.

"The goatskin shield represented the God's invulnerability for when Zeus would become the mortal manifestation of his immortal form. Later, the head of Medusa was added to stone all who dared forge an attack against him." Everyone was impressed by Gwen's knowledge. Clearly, she wasn't a simple Tarot card reader.

"Will the spell turn people to stone?" Rachel asked.

Gwen smiled. "No, but once someone is within proximity of the spell, they'll be hit with the undeniable need to flee. With the addition of alarming us to their presence. We'd need Medusa's head to turn them to stone, and that gem was lost many years ago by greedy treasure hunters."

"Like Lara Croft needed Medusa's head to make her enemies hard," I muttered. Donovan's laugh had heads turning with more surprise than Gwen sprinkling bones like decorating a cupcake.

The basement filled with the remaining Coveners, plus Serena who was jacked to be involved in her first "Witchy" deed and, again, situated herself strategically next to Jared as they readied for a protection spell Kim found the day before. This spell would protect the ten Magics working the spell and act as an accelerant to heighten the potency of the shield. Or so we hoped.

Donovan memorized the spell as I pretended not to be impressed while holding my cue card with the spell jotted down in my almost illegible scrawl. First step, dig a hole and place the goatskin pouch full of bones and goodies inside. For those in the house, it included punching a hole in drywall. Donovan could fix it, but I was a tad jealous they got to wield a hammer while I was equipped with a serving spoon.

Kim set the pace by directing the others by cell. A mass text would confirm when each team was ready and then another would trigger the beginning. Less complicated than working out a conference call and less conspicuous than yelling for all the neighbourhood and Loring's goons to hear.

Donovan and I waited in the threshold of the front door to spend the least amount of time outside exposed, while the others moved into position.

"Can you still feel it?" he asked.

"Feel what?"

"The whisky."

I huffed as he flashed a dimpled, sly, grin. "Not really."

"Figured as much. Thought you needed to loosen up a little."

"Bullshit. You just wanted a drink."

"And that's so bad?"

"No but doing it without warning me or doing it and claiming you did it for me, is a load of steaming yak piss and you know it."

He laughed. "Love it when you call me on my shit."

"Next time you decide to do something you know will piss me off because you want my attention or are bored, I won't say a thing. I'll let you dangle yourself by your short and curlies instead. You want me bitter and resentful? That's how you do it."

His dimples faded. "Noted."

Donovan's cell chimed, a group text from Kim to let us and the others know everyone was in place. I had no idea how large the attic was but was glad I was outside and not covered in itchy insulation or spider webs. A flutter of power tickled my ribcage. Donovan closed his eyes, lips moving in a whisper, then he blinked out of sight.

"What the fizz?"

"Oops. One sec." His disconnected voice came from where I last saw him. Ten seconds later, he was visible again. "Wrong spell. I'll tweak it so only the Blind can't see us."

He vanished again and then recited the spell line-for-line. Nothing happened. "How do you know it worked?"

He motioned to the car window at the curb and lead the way. "See?" He leaned towards the window.

The top of the house and a clouded night sky reflected back, but not us.

"Sweetbeans." Our footprints compressed our path across the grass. "I bet people think they see ghosts when really it's one of us being sneaky."

"Maybe. Though spirits do exist."

"Really?"

"I may be a shit disturber, but I'm not a liar." I stared at him. "Not to you."

Of course.

We checked the street for the Blind or others and got started on the first part of the spell, digging holes at the corners of the front property for the goat pouches to be buried in. I dropped the goatskin pouch into the hole and pushed the grass plug back into place, padding it down so a pesky squirrel or raccoon wouldn't go looking for whatever smelled so good to their mischievous noses.

"Regrow the grass to seal it in," Donovan said across the yard.

The prickle of his power grew in my chest and itched my palm before I could summon my own. I stopped when green blades of grass sprouted higher than the surrounding lawn, then tugged the blades to confirm the plug re-rooted. No matter how many times I used my magic, it awed me to the fullest. I was a notorious black thumb and now I could grow a lush forest from the roof of my building if I wanted, which reminded me to get a greenhouse if I ever bought a house one day.

Donovan gave a hearty chuckle. A sense of enjoyment stronger than my giddiness crossed our connection. "You ready, babe? You can tend my gardens day and night." I looked over at him and smirked. He raised his hands. "Not a euphemism. Promise."

"Ready, Freddy. Let's do it." He smirked at me. "That's not what she said, Sir Pervs-a-lot."

He laughed and took out his phone from his back pocket. "Bring the power," he spoke his text aloud, sent it, and then nodded my way to begin.

When my power engaged, so did Donovan's. It rushed down my spine, arching my back. The yard and houses around me fell away as my eyes rolled back. Power wrapped me in a cocoon of safety as energy raged through me with chaotic freedom. My skin blazed with a dizzying heat. A euphoric sensory overload had me close to passing out as I struggled to hold onto the high and pull more from it to keep it going.

The front yard whiplashed back into view. No! Fuck. What happened?

Reality filtered through when a car drove by. I looked over at Donovan. He looked down, and then hesitantly at me. We overshot and used too much. If he hadn't found a modicum of restraint and regulated our power to a manageable level, I would have been lost in the blissful high forever, trapping him as well.

Talk about a dangerous and addictive adventure I didn't want to walk away from. The embarrassment of that thought gave me neck sweat. Guarded shock filtered across the connection and then fear as if Donovan expected me to freak out or take off.

I couldn't look at him. He didn't comment or question the experience. Instead, he moved on and recited the spell, his focus prompting me to follow along, reading the cue card in my shaky hand.

"Within the soil doth offering stay,
To rid this land of those who strayed.
Evil forbade to walk along,
This place the pure Wight's worship upon.
From earth to sky bind this sanctum sealed,
For all who pass within, the corrupted and Blind must yield.
Draw from the Gods the affinity to ward.
To thwart our enemies without use of a sword.
Protect us within The Shield of Aegis.
The mighty warrior called upon to conceive this."

I channelled the ache for more power into the spell, hearing Donovan's voice steadfast and fearless to my left as we faced the house helped. As we concluded the recitation, he said a quick goodbye to his power. I didn't get the chance.

The world spun. After a breathless second, I looked up into honey-brown eyes inches from mine. Pressure on my shoulders kept me down, then dug into my collarbones, before a hand gripped my throat.

"I look forward to meeting you in person." The woman sneered. The stench of tea and Caesar salad diluted by mint-flavoured gum stung my eyes.

Her vehement stare seeing beyond the cover spell told me this was a Puppet. Sickening panic wrenched my guts and stole all sense of action. A growl, a blur, a loud crack, and all pressure on top of me released as the woman flew across the lawn. A lighting clash of pain zinged through my right fist up to my shoulder.

Donovan stood between me and a woman with light-brown hair while I moaned and rolled onto my side to cradle my hand. A neighbour. She raced backward into a parked car at the curb, slumped over, and then blinked back into her surroundings. She looked around in confusion.

"Donovan—" I said.

"Shhh."

"Who said that?" The woman questioned and scrambled to stand up.

She couldn't see us anymore.

Deciding she wasn't waiting around for an answer, the woman took off across the street and back into her house.

Donovan pulled me to my feet by my good hand, the other broken or containing a dislocated knuckle, and hurried me toward the house. I dug my heels in, skidding in the grass. The stone facing of the house glowed. A bright aura like a second skin stretched over the property and under our feet.

"I know." Donovan pushed me forward against my protest.

The Coveners had converged in the kitchen in excitement. Caine's head peeked above the crowd. Donovan waved a bloody hand for his attention, receiving a rather stern glance in return. Donovan pulled me into the first-floor main bathroom, sitting me down on the side of the white and sandy coloured mosaic-tiled edge surrounding the bathtub.

He kicked the toilet seat closed with a bang that made me jump, then grabbed a towel off a tall silver rack, knocking bathroom items over on their small shelves. The white towel soaked with blood.

"Jesusfuck!" The pressure moved something beneath my flesh, and he held his injured fist limply at his side as he tried to work with his less dominant hand. "Heal. Worry about the blood after."

Donovan cradled my towel-covered hand, his injured one shaky and held slightly open. With a rise in power, the pain in my hand increased as the magic took its toll. A choked scream threatened to rip from my throat. A low whimper escaped as something clicked back into place and the skin closed itself, erasing all signs of the wound. We exchanged an exhausted look. He squeezed my hand through the towel and I squeezed his back, grateful he jumped in against the Puppet when he did.

Caine burst into the bathroom, looked down at us, and a flash of anger clouded his eyes. Kim followed behind him.

"Close the door," Donovan said.

"What the hell? Where are you?" Kim looked around the room without seeing us.

"Fuck sakes." Donovan murmured another spell. Since the cover spell shielded us from the Blind, it meant Kim's power was too low to count her in. "Better?"

She pulled a face. "Yes. What's with all the blood?"

I turned on the tub facet, using a bottle of shower gel to wash away the blood, turning it to pink bubbles. "She came out of nowhere. I was a useless tit. Again. So much for progress. I didn't see her until she had me pinned."

"Joelly?" Caine asked.

"No, a woman from across the street turned Puppet. This time, she talked."

"What'd she say?" Kim asked.

"'Looking forward to meeting you in person'." I turned the water off after all the bloody bubbles were washed down.

"So why the blood?" Caine asked.

"Donovan punched her."

"You couldn't find another way? You knew the pain it would cause Sophie."

Donovan looked up at Caine from his seat on the toilet. "Did you expect me to let the chick kill her?"

"It was a warning. By the sounds of it, the woman or Loring or the Puppeteer or whoever, had the jump on Sophie and could have killed her, but didn't."

Donovan's jaw worked. "I wasn't taking the chance."

"Better than letting your other Blind neighbours see you using your powers, I guess," Kim said.

"Or inadvertently hurting Sophie in the same attack," Donovan said. "A broken knuckle is nothing compared to what I could have done to her."

"More importantly—" I dried my hands on an unsoiled part of the towel Donovan had used "—why don't we focus on what the woman said to me?" Caine straightened as Donovan looked down at his still bloodied hands. I handed him back the towel. "She said, 'I look forward to meeting you in person.' The Puppet-bitch was straddling me like a mechanical bull, so she wasn't speaking for herself and I've already met Loring."

"Maybe he flubbed his wording," Kim said.

Donovan threw the bloodied towel into the tub. "After days of surrounding my house with Puppets and passive observation, you think once the opportunity was taken he wouldn't have had exactly what he wanted to say down pat?" Kim's lips twisted in some form of agreement with Donovan. "If those were the words that were spoken, those were the words Sophie was meant to hear. Loring's a master at this cat and mouse bullshit, and he, or whoever that was, now knows her curiosity will be driving her nuts over the exact interpretations of that one tiny sentence. That's the way she works, and somehow, they know that, too."

If he wasn't completely right, I would be insulted.

Donovan did as I had and turned on the bathroom tap to wash his hands. The sound of the water covered the sound of the door opening.

Matt looked at the four of us beneath the low brim of his NY ball cap twisted to the side. "Private party?"

"Just ended." Caine left the bathroom, the rest of us soon after.

Only members with heightened powers could glimpse the sheen of magic protecting the house, not that anyone cared. They were too thrilled to be involved in something bigger than themselves, something that carried substantial weight and importance. We could have kept the incident with the neighbour under wraps, even for a bit to let them bask in their post-spell glow, but they needed to know. With a healthy dose of reality to dampen their spirits, they absorbed the danger and returned to their conversations, which no doubt changed in tone.

"You *need* to contact your Coven Elders, Firefly," Olive said. "You'll need their help against Loring. If he is the Puppeteer, he's very powerful."

"I tried to make Ranlyn wear a bell, but it clashed with his soul glow."

"Firefly—"

"We've tried. I don't know where to start looking. He could be anywhere."

Kim chimed in. "They could be in a Creation like Diluculo or Pario and we'd have no way to contact them if that's the case."

"I don't accept that." Olive turned to Kim. "Where can I find your house ingredients?"

"For what?"

"Locator spell?"

"Oooh. I like the way you think."

———

The locater spell was a bust. Chances were the Elders had spells to block us from those brands of snooping or they were in a Creation.

The alternative meant they were dead and that wasn't a theory we were willing to accept. The trial and error gave Kim the idea to cover all the Coveners thoughts since we all lacked the power to do it ourselves. If they didn't know already, the enemy didn't need to read our minds and find out we were out of touch with the only Magics who could potentially save our asses.

Olive was right to call the Sect in. With so many hands on deck, the only issue now was sifting through which spells and tactics were best out of all the ones we found in Aunt Lacey's collection—which was much harder to recognize than we thought.

15

DELVING DEEPER

"**W**hat's with all the death talk?" Serena overheard the end of a conversation with Olive about Aunt Lacey's premonition. Finding a room big enough to fit us away from prying ears wasn't easy, so we squirrelled away in Donovan's room.

"If you haven't noticed, that's the reason you're here." Donovan tone had bite. "It's a blast to play Witch in a Sect you're not a part of, but if you're done bitching we're trying to save your cousin's life here."

"News flash, you empty toolbag, Sophie has a boyfriend."

He scoffed. "Please."

"Reschedule the battle royale. I'm done playing ring-girl." I sat on the edge of Donovan's unmade bed, then regretted it when Donovan's intrigue crossed the connection. "Death is a buzzkill, but the fact that it keeps being talked about like it has legs and a heartbeat is what I really care about. We thought Joelly taking us down was what the premonition talked about. If not, we've got bigger issues." I looked at Caine. "If we could borrow Andy's gift for a tic and see if I'm still condemned in the death spots, without the guilt of making him look at me again, I totes would."

"For real. I won't pretend I haven't thought about heading over there. Not sure Eli would appreciate the drop in to use the kid's gift. If the spots came with a solution, we would've been there already."

"You can read someone's soul now, and I know what I saw from our past," Donovan said. "The power you accessed fighting Loring is nothing compared to what you can do, so instead of talking about this until I cut my own tongue out with a jailhouse toothbrush, why don't we get to training?"

"You're such a dick," Serena mumbled and went ignored.

"Read a soul?" Olive asked.

I shrugged. "Best way to describe delving into the soul and seeing someone's memories and source or hinderance of their inner magic, though I tortured Kim in the process. Why didn't you tell me we could do that?"

"I'm not sure we can, Firefly, though I intend to find out. If it's an evolution of our Soul Seeing than it must be documented somewhere in the estate's files." Olive stood and pulled me up with her. "You get to training. You'll need it. I'm returning to the estate to see what I can find out about this reading souls business, and of a Puppeteer's capabilities. Maybe I can uncover something useful." She pecked me on the cheek and called after Serena when she was already out of sight.

"Dammit," Serena muttered, shoulders sagged. She gave me a lingering hug with a warning. "Watch yourself with him." No need to guess at who she meant. "And get my number to Mr. Caramel." She trundled off through the French doors like she was being pulled from her favourite swing. I would have felt worse, but chances were she was going to lose herself in the Ballard Family Estates attic treasures anyway.

"She's a peach," Donovan said.

"And you're a scabby ass pimple. Let's go."

Halfway down the stairs to the main floor, I was hit with a sense of urgency so strong I was running before I knew I had taken the rest of the stairs two at a time, the others fast on my tail. Coveners were crowded at the front windows as others came from the kitchen.

"Olive and Serena tripped the Shield of Aegis spell when they left," Gwen said. "Now you know what it feels like."

"About as fun as being shocked awake by zombie nightmares." I had my fair share.

We didn't realize someone leaving the house would be tagged as a threat since they had already been within the bubble of protection, but the spell didn't discriminate.

"Look—" Deidra pointed through the window.

Two young men in shorts and t-shirts were on the sidewalk. One guy held a basketball tucked under his arm. They paused and then moved across the street away from the house with casts of paranoia. As the meandering guys reached the edge of the barrier created by the spell, a feathering of warning rang through each of us, letting those involved in the spell know someone was flirting with the mansion's defence. Nothing close to the urgency as when Olive and Serena left, but was a helpful comparison.

"Are they Blind?" Rachel asked me.

"Yup. Not sure if it'll be as effective on the Tainted, but it's something."

Practice was what we needed and although having all the Coveners around was handy, with so many of them, it clogged up the available space to stretch our abilities. Ever the project manager, Kim set up with a group doing spell work and meditation, re-enforcing her goal to have every Coven member's soul glow by the New Year. Ambitious, but a goal nonetheless. Gwen was given a group to read. Their focus on obstacles and identifying them within persons to better overcome whatever it was holding them back from further enlightenment. Another group continued with research and Elder harassment, including calling others on Aunt Lacey's connections list to see what they may know or to see if they had seen the Elders.

Once Kim had the groups settled into their tasks, she joined us in the backyard. "Each of us has something to work on. I'm obviously trying to uncover true power."

"I guess I'm developing my Soul Reading, though I can't say I'm psyched about it."

"I've had my soul read. Dibs on not being your next torture victim."

"I need to see past my visions of Sophie." Donovan crossed his arms. "The connection won't fade, but we're ineffective if it blinds us both."

"Well, then I need to work on that too. You're not the only one that can lessen the intensity."

"But you also need help magically in general," Caine said to me. "Plus, what about Nya's power?"

"What about it?"

"If it's her power that drove off Loring the first time, then you need to find a way to access it on cue."

"Meaning Gareth's power is waiting to be unlocked too. We've had a peak at Nya's. We have no clue what Gareth's packing."

"We don't know his power is there. Other than finding you from the park, even while fighting Loring, Gareth made no cameo."

"Fine, let me read you first. I'll try to find evidence of Gareth. It'll be a part of both our training."

Caine smiled larger than I had seen in too long.

We sat at the patio set. Bosco wanted to sit in my lap, no doubt feeling neglected over the past few days, so Kim took him in hers and scratched his head until he calmed.

Caine and I sat facing each other, knees touching, reminding me of the Awakening Ritual. Except this time, without the pressure of failure concluding in a life stuck in a sleeping curse with Caine until our bodies gave out on this side of reality. We may not be surrounded by the lush, rain-filled park, and Caine now had the addition of his blue soul glow, but it still hit me all the same.

Minimal effort had my power buzzing. I reached out, eyes closed, until I touched Caine's shirt with my fingertips. He took a deep breath when his chest met my palm. A memory of Caine beneath me in a different setting gave a rise in my libido and was smacked down by a dose of Donovan's jealousy.

Caine's soul glow tickled my hand. Before I could gain my bearings, I was hauled through flashes of nonsensical memories. Slowing them down was like pulling back on the reins of a scared horse. Too much power behind them meant the tug of war was on. Most of the time, I lost.

I put the brakes on and won when I saw a conversation between Caine and his mom. He later confessed he accidently used his persuasion power and influenced her to tell him where to find his father. The replay not only came as a movie from Caine's perspective, but with his attached emotions. Disappointment seeped into every part of him.

I allowed myself to be pushed further, stopping again when I saw my face. Yikes. My expression was stiff. Guarded. I wanted to hold me. No, Caine wanted to. His desire to reach out and kiss me so great I was frustrated by the fact that I couldn't move to do it for him. I had kissed another man, had a past with this man, but he knew, with no wavering doubt, that he loved me. When I said yes, his happiness washed over me, shocked me from the re-enactment, and spiralled me past other events and images in a kaleidoscope of colour.

Raging wind and rain from the park was a replay I didn't need. I had zero desire to piggyback that memory or the memory of him killing his father. The hi-def. reality was enough for me. The experiences were peripherally torturous enough. Seeing it through his eyes would be debilitating.

Looking into his childhood would have been interesting. Maybe even peeking at the one other serious relationship his friend Dom mentioned, but I resisted and focused on what I came for. A sign of Gareth's power was all I needed.

Colour.

A flicker at first, one I mistook for deeper memories. The colour became brighter and bluer and filtered out the reel of his lifetime until I saw only his soul glow. His power. Controlling others was never something he asked for, but like his unique eyes, it was passed down from his father and genetic history full of evil assholes. Caine was terrified by the possibility of becoming one of them. I knew this, not only because he said so, but because the closer I waded into the shower of near blinding light, the clearer I saw the intricate work of evil.

This wasn't like any Tainted soul glow I saw in the past, more like the illusion of evil. Caine was so constricted by his fear of losing himself to the Berisford legacy, he stopped himself from growing his power into anything substantial. If he wanted to experience power greater than his current ability, he would have to take the risk.

Now, where was Gareth's power?

I waded deeper into the blue, weaving myself around Caine's illusion of darkness in search of something more. The blue of his soul glow became diluted and washed with white. I thought I saw something within the light, but as I tried to explore it, I hit the end of my leash. I resisted and got a few inches closer, seeing the haze of something more. A memory? Angered voices echoed too far away to hear what they said. Blurred movements flitted in front of me as I struggled to see more. I gained one tiny movement after another, until the emotions surrounding the memory became clearer than the memory itself.

Disgust. Anguish. Disappointment. Fear.

I fought for more. I needed to know more.

The resistance I met gave way and propelled me into the memory. The clarity jarred me into the firsthand look of the twisted faces of my townsfolk screaming to burn me—the Witch—alive. To cleanse the town and my soul. The stench of soiled hay and wood burned my nostrils. The fire was building fast. I looked to my left and found the stoic face of my love. How Nya could retain composure under such conditions was a mystery, but her soft lips moved in a whisper, her eyes closed, focusing on the spell we spoke of. If it worked, we would meet again, but the end would be grim.

Pain lanced my feet, the smoke growing thicker. "Nya!" I needed to see her eyes one last time. My pant legs caught fire, as did Nya's shift. The pain grew, greater than expected. I called out for her as she kept up the spell, now fighting against her own pain as it grew deeper into her skin. My screams were drowned out by the townsfolk's damning words.

Beyond the crowd, at the edge of the stables, through the smoke, I saw Mother. Tears shone on her cheeks, devoid of the anger she expressed when she first learned of our plan through her second sight. She promised she would leave before the burning. That she wouldn't watch the end and only remember the beginning. Goodbyes were already extended. I couldn't bear for her to carry this memory. With no power to do anything but scream, I looked away from my mother to my bride.

Nya's scream roared above the rest, above my own. Her pain so great I panicked to get free. Finally, I caught the eye of my love as we screamed for the mercy of death's embrace. Instead of death, power grew within, power so great it added to the pain. Had I not been strapped to the pyre, I would have collapsed. My breath was stolen, sucked from my lungs in a gasp so loud it silenced the townsfolk. Power burst from my body and took with it my suffering.

"Open your eyes!" Someone yelled. Their voice a tiny demand as the relief was as great as my pain.

The voice became louder and screamed for me to listen, to breathe. How could I? I was nothing but an empty husk, basking in the nothingness.

A shock awakened the empty parts of my body, refilling them with pain. I lashed out in the darkness, my arms moving through mud without catching anything.

"Sophie!" A voice called. "Sophie, can you hear me?"

My chest hurt. I tried to push on the parts that hurt and felt my arms being restrained. This was enough to pull me out of it. I looked into blue, narrowed eyes with crow's feet dusting the edges. They deepened with a smile when I blinked and tried to sit up.

"Slow down, my girl."

Henry? The Coven physician was in my personal bubble like never before.

"What's happening?" I looked down to see my shirt and bra had been cut down the middle displaying my tits and whatever was stuck to my chest.

Henry peeled a sticky pad off my skin as I tried to cover myself. He continued as if he hadn't seen anything. As a doctor he likely had seen so many he was unaffected. "You're lucky I carry an AED in my trunk. I'll get you one for the house in case of another emergency, but I don't recommend you do that again."

"Sophie," Donovan called out for me in a raspy voice.

"You okay?" I asked him, clutching my shirt closed tighter before he could see me.

"Are you?"

"After four shocks of about three thousand volts, she's good," Henry said then patted me on the shoulder. "Your healing ability should do the rest now that you're breathing."

The horrified faces of the Conveners were at the glass doors trying to rubberneck at what was going on. Or maybe they wanted a glimpse at my tits. Wonderful. Henry and Caine helped me up and into my chair, which wasn't far as I was on the ground next to it, though every muscle screamed. Donovan sucked in air as he attempted to get up. No one tried to help him. He would have waved them off, but I still wished someone would have tried. He fell into the chair and put his hand to his head, it came away bloody. Whatever happened, it happened quick, and we hit the ground hard.

Breathing was a chore and caused us to cough when I tried to inhale too deeply too quickly. Henry was talking. Saying something I wasn't tracking as my mind went back to what I read from inside of Caine. I ached for Nya and Gareth's pain as much as for my own and when I took in an involuntary gulp of oxygen Henry seemed to notice I was about to lose it and told everyone the show was over and to give me some space. He joined them inside.

The Coveners could still see me through the glass doors, but my back was to them as I curled into myself and covered my face against my sobs. I couldn't stop myself. I kept flashing back to Gareth, watching Nya, craving her one last time, seeing his mother in the distance, his life coming to an end in the worst possible way. Aunt Lacey had lived with the memory of her son and daughter-in-law burning to death and then learned the truth of how Loring convinced Nya to die by the pyre. Then, Aunt Lacey had died by his hands as well.

Despair shifted into anger and I composed myself enough to sit straight. Kim's cheeks were streaked with tears. She handed me a tissue and I did what I could with it, needing a roll more to take care of the mess that was my face.

Donovan had got up and wandered further into the dark yard, away from the others. He was sobbing along with me. He wandered back now and used his sleeve to clear his eyes.

"Guess I need to learn to stop being so pushy," I finally said. They looked like they didn't know what to say and didn't want to ask if I was okay when clearly I wasn't.

"Is that what happened?" Caine's voice was soft and hesitant.

"Basically. I wanted to know more, I got more, and now I know what it's like to be burned at the stake. Yay me." A rush of goosebumps covered me.

"Oh my god. Who?" Kim asked.

"Gareth and Nya." I tried to explain to them what I saw, starting with the venture through Caine since I needed a moment to gather myself. I tried and failed to keep the tears at bay when I got back to Gareth and Nya burning, but Donovan was doing his best to level us both out, losing against his own set of overwhelming emotions. He wouldn't have seen what I saw, but he would have felt everything.

"I can't even imagine." Kim sat back in her chair and wiped away another tear.

"I'm guessing I stuck to you like an octopus like I did with Kim?" I said to Caine.

"Yeah. Until you went into a seizure and stopped breathing."

"Hence the AED and nakedness."

Caine nodded, and I did what I could not to look at Donovan.

"Good to have a doctor in the Coven."

"Care to doctor us?" Donovan asked. "Or are you wanting to retain this pain as a healthy reminder of being too pushy? I feel like I lost a fight with a yeti."

The psychological pain of living out Gareth's last moments was greater than my sore body, and my healing power had no impact on my emotional well-being. I nodded at him and he worked quickly to raise his power to heal us. As it always did, the pain grew worse before it got better. My head fell back, body tensed, as power charged every part of us and fixed the damage of being shocked back to life, the seizure, the head wound, and anything else my careless adventure caused us.

When I opened my eyes, Donovan was doing the same, and Kim was giving me the side-eye. "You two need a smoke?"

"Shut it," I told her and then remembered me throwing my head back in pain and then ecstasy, the visual made more pornographic considering my shirt and bra was slit down the middle, though I managed to keep my shirt draped enough to avoid a nip slip.

"You can fix that," Kim's pointed at my shirt, "but I recommend tossing it. Not your colour."

"I might keep it like this. Start a trend."

"Can I vote against that?" Caine asked.

"Nope." I stood up. "Freeing the tatas is in full effect. Actually, I probably will fix this. I only brought so many clothes."

"Practicality wins out," Kim said.

"Nine times out of ten. When we get back to the real world, freeing the tatas will re-enter the ballot."

"Here, here!"

After what happened, even our attempts at humour were limp, but remaining in the pit with Gareth and Nya was too powerful. I needed everything to pull me out of it. A trip to the bathroom where I could fix my makeup and my clothes gave me a few minutes alone, but even then, I had to compartmentalize and get out before thoughts of Gareth and Nya dragged me back down again.

Bosco waited for me outside the door. I picked him up and nuzzled his soft fur and he lapped at my forehead. Puppy kisses had the most healing magic.

The Coveners were in the kitchen snacking and talking. I told myself they weren't waiting for me, but after seeing Denise's gauging stare, I figured at least some of them were hovering in the hopes I might tell them what I saw. I had no intentions of sharing anything and moved the subject to something other than me.

"How was practice?" A general inquiry with hopes someone would bite at talking about themselves to pull the attention away from me.

"Awesome!" Blake was quick to answer. "I felt it."

Jared added a low, "That's what she said." Matt and a few others laughed.

"I assume you hit puberty years ago and aren't referring to your unit," I said, happy to joke around.

"Nah, me and my gear are well acquainted," Blake quipped without hesitating. Denise rolled her eyes, which meant I thought it was much funnier for offending her.

"You mean you felt your power?"

"Hells yeah, I did." He high-fived Jared, who looked like he'd been high-fived to death since it happened. "Am I brighter?"

"Umm, you're all one big blur to me right now." Not everyone glowed, but the one's that did made up for the ones that didn't. "Come here a sec."

Still a smile on his lightly freckled face, Blake stepped aside so I could see him clearly. "You do, actually. You also have colour."

"No way! What colour?"

"Purple." A few laughed at this. "A bit watered down right now, but definitely purple." His expression soured. I laughed. "It's a great colour. Means you have the power of Elemental Influencing. It's actually quite rare as far as I've seen."

"Nice." He changed his mind. "Which element?"

"No clue. I only see the colour, not the power."

Blake was ecstatic and gave Jared another exuberant high-five, Jared raising his hand for Blake to hit, but not making the effort to move his own. I headed down the hall to the basement, assuming Caine and the others were down there since they weren't in the kitchen or outside, I heard Denise's snotty-edged voice speak about Blake's name and the "obvious" element he could influence. The rest was lost as I kept on walking, glad to be out of range of her attitude.

When I reached the bottom stair, the urgent alarm of someone crossing the spell onto the property sent me flying back up the stairs. The others tied to the spell came running too. The doorbell rang before we made it to the living room. The flush of warning continued as Donovan raced to the door. He murmured a spell and the door went see-through.

"Frog?" Kim said aloud. Not only Frog, but Dom, Teddy, Lee, and Reid. The whole gang stood on the porch, waiting for someone to answer, looking up at the house and around them.

"Who's Frog?" Gwen asked.

"You invited your boyfriend here?" When Donovan questioned Kim, the spell he put on the door fell.

"No."

"Please tell me you don't role play as a princess," Matt joked, though everyone was too edgy to find the humour.

Donovan looked at Caine.

"Fuck no."

The doorbell rang again.

"Let them in," Kim said.

"With a house full of Coveners?" Donovan crossed his arms and stood in front of the door. "Do I have to spell out in crayon what a bad idea that is? I'd have thought it'd be clear, but I can break out the Crayola if it'll get through to you faster."

The doorbell rang again.

"Donovan!" Kim glared at him.

Caine took a few quick steps towards the door. Donovan didn't move. A tense moment passed. I thought I might have to jump in, but Donovan ended the stalemate. "Everyone, remember, they're Blind, but probably not stupid, so retain your manners. Anyone who talks about Coven business or uses in front of them will find themselves looking for a new Coven." No one would mistake him for joking and no one challenged him, not even Denise.

Donovan moved, and Caine opened the door to his friends. They got inside so quick you'd think someone was chasing them. Caine gave them hugs and started introducing them to people.

"This could be a total disaster. You realize that, right? We don't even know why they're here," I said to Kim, making sure to do my best-friend duties by warning her with honesty.

"Oooh, yeah," she said, then adopted a huge grin and met Frog with an exuberant embrace.

16

CONTAGIOUS OVERREACTIONS

"How'ya doin', girl?" Dom picked me up off the floor, his arms digging into my ribs.

"Great!" I injected a dose of enthusiasm. "Did Kim or Caine tell you about the party?"

"Nah. Frog did."

Didn't answer my question, so hopefully Kim could get it out of Frog.

"Celebrating anything or just a reason to get drunk in a huge fucking house?"

"Who needs an excuse, right?"

Dom laughed. "Damn right. Oh, and we brought you your stuff. Reid—" He called over to the ball of energy in the group who looked to be already checking out his female prospects. He looked over. Dom pointed at me. Reid nodded, excused himself from Denise – no surprise – and brought over a bag.

"Your faves." He handed me the bag. Inside was a bottle of Kraken Rum, a six-pack of Dr. Pepper, and Doritos Ketchup Chips.

"Holy shit."

"You're weird. Enjoy." Delivered, Reid rejoined Denise and a few others and jumped back into conversation as if he hadn't left.

"How'd you know?"

"Frog said we had to pick up your favourites. Figured Caine told him. Reid's right, though. You're fuckin' weird."

"Well, thanks, man. I'm going to get a glass. Want one?"

His expressed screwed up. "The beers I brought are good, thanks."

I doctored a drink, making sure nothing was pre-opened, in full paranoia mode, trying to keep an eye out for anything else off with Caine's friends. Caine and Kim were too wrapped up in talking with the others, so I couldn't ask either about who invited who or how they knew about my drink and snack preferences.

I found Dom where I left him, now with a can of beer in his hand.

"Hey man, what's up?" Dom chinned over my shoulder as I approached.

Donovan was behind me all stone-like, jaw clenched, and arms crossed. I shot him a 'play-nice' look which was more a 'play your part until we find out what the fuck is going on' look. "Dom, this is Donovan. He owns this place."

"Awesome. Thanks man," Dom said.

"No problem." Because of the intensity of his power, Donovan avoids handshakes, but now, he thrust his hand out first, Dom following suit and shaking his hand. Whatever Donovan expected, he didn't get, evident in the confusion flickering along the connection while keeping his expression neutral and dropping Dom's hand.

"How do you know Caine? Or are you Sophie's friend?" Dom asked.

"I know Sophie," he said without a hint of warmth.

"Cool." Dom took a few pulls of his drink.

Donovan walked off without a word. Dom watched him leave, then turned back to me. "How do you know that guy? He's Norman Bates weird."

"Nah, I seriously doubt he has his mother's corpse in her best-dressed in one of these rooms. Though it's a big house so you never know."

Dom made a throaty sound I interpreted as a sign I wasn't making him feel any better. "Donovan's great," I insisted. "Sort of awkward around new people."

He gave a half-smile. "So was Norman Bates."

I laughed, happy to have skirted answering his initial question since I didn't have an answer I could give without flat-out lying.

Hoping I could glean some useful information, I kept Dom talking while surveying the other guys as best I could without looking disinterested with what Dom was talking about. Reid and Lee stuck with the Coveners, mingling with the women and trying to snag themselves a date. Teddy stuck with Caine, Kim, and Frog so it was easy to keep tabs on everyone. Donovan had disappeared.

I suggested we go over to Caine's group and see what was up. This was more comfortable as I didn't have to keep up the questions, but Dom stayed close enough I couldn't say anything private to Caine.

"Shoot." I looked up at Caine. "Can you help me give Bosco those drops? I forgot and you're better at holding him."

He looked at me, his lips moving as if to ask me what the fuck I was talking about. I had my arm around his and gave the underside a light pinch.

"Ah, sure. Do you know where he is?"

"I think I saw him on the couch."

I pulled him towards the living room, scooted into the bathroom, and closed the door.

"Umm—"

"Calm your boner, it's not for sex."

"What's the matter?"

"Wha—? Are you kidding me?"

"What?"

"Did you tell any of your friends about my favourite alcohol and snacks?"

His eyebrows arched. "You have favourites?"

"Currently, yes, and Dom said you asked Frog to bring them for me."

"What are your favourites?"

"It doesn't matter what my favourites are. That's not the fucking point."

"Yo. Now you're getting pissed at me?"

"I'm sorry but think about it. Something isn't right."

"Like what? They got inside without getting killed by the door spell thing. They're acting normal."

"How did they get through the spell outside? And how would they know we were all here?"

"I have no idea. Are their souls Tainted?"

"No. They don't have soul glows."

"Okay, well, maybe it's an issue with the spell. They seem normal to me, but we can keep them talking and wait and see if they do anything suspicious." He leaned forward and kissed my crown. "It's easy to get paranoid with all this Loring stuff. They're not dangerous, so try and have a bit of fun. You deserve it."

Donovan rushed into the bathroom moments after Caine left. "What'd he say?"

"Nothing. He thinks they're being normal and to keep an eye out for anything suspicious. Could the spell fritzed out and let them in by accident?"

"Not a chance. Plus, they show up uninvited when we have the Sect here? That's not suspicious enough?"

"Agreed, but it's not proof. Plus, devotees can't get in here."

"No, I know. They have no soul glows, right?"

"Nope."

"They have no pasts either. I made a point to shake all their hands and picked up nothing. That's never happened to me before."

"Nothing?" He nodded. "Shitcrackers."

We rejoined the party, doing as Caine said—keeping an eye out for anything extra weird, besides them showing up. The Coveners played their roles and went on with the fake party. I did what I could to pretend while feeling like I was under potential surveillance.

I sat next to Caine in the basement, where he, his friends, and a few Coveners hung out. Frog and Kim sat on the floor, Kim perched on his lap. She looked to be having fun. I didn't know the reason she gave him for why she was staying at Donovan's, especially since none of their interactions in front of Frog were friendly, but he seemed content to spend time with her. Nothing Puppet-like about him, I noted, while trying not to listen in too closely to what they talked about.

At one point, Teddy thought the closet in the basement might have been the bathroom. Books were easy to explain when the guy was too booze-addled and blurry-eyed to catch the titles, but the ritual knives were a dead giveaway. Didn't help that when he opened the door, Caine, Kim, and I all jumped to stop him, the freak out alone enough to make even the drunkest person suspicious.

I offered to show him where the washroom was on the main floor. Finding it occupied, with Jared not leaving anytime soon, we went to the top floor to use one up there. Empty and sans nasal destruction, Teddy thanked me. I went in search of Donovan. He wasn't in the basement or kitchen, so the easy assumption was his bedroom.

The glass panel of the doors were still decorated with Aunt Lacey's doily-like curtains. I peeked inside when my knock went unanswered. Donovan sprung up, slamming a foot to the floor as if to rush the door. Blasting music came from ear buds in his ears and a book dangled in one hand. Recognizing it was me, he relaxed and removed his ear buds.

"Sorry, I was showing someone to the bathroom and figured you'd be holed up in here."

He answered with a hitch in his brow. "Easier than putting on a show for Caine's friends." He used his book's dust jacket as a bookmark and shifted himself to the corner of the bed with his legs on either side of mine. "I'd much rather hang out in here with you."

"I'm sure you would. Though hiding isn't helpful when the others might need you."

"Please. As much as I thought there was, there's nothing going on. Something must have happened with the spell or maybe the purpose was to get them inside and that was it. I'm better off up here so everyone can have fun with Caine's friends. They've been corrupted by worse than frat boys, babe."

"True. They did see my boobs earlier."

"Wait, what?"

"Is the party in here now?" Dom's booming voice entered the room before he did.

Donovan was instantly on his feet. "Party's still downstairs."

"I'll go down with you." I moved towards the door. Dom didn't follow.

"But you guys were having such a pleasant conversation about frat boys and boobs. My kind of convo. I was just making sure I shouldn't get my friend Caine up here to join in...babe." The looked he gave me was damning.

"Not so interested in Caine's boobs, thanks." Donovan regained Dom's attention. "But you, Caine, and all your pals can steal a room. Got plenty vacant. Wash the sheets after your circle-jerk. I'm not a hotel maid." Donovan took a half-step closer thwarting Dom's opportunity to counter. "And watch how you speak to her." Power spilled from him.

"Donovan." I brushed his hand with mine.

This action caused his visions to blind him, as I meant for them to. Without the warning, Donovan had zero opportunity to protect himself and was flooded with an overload of images. He gasped, his head and shoulders slumped before I backed off. I took a huge risk. Dom would have questions, and I hoped those questions would distract him from asking questions about our conversation.

Donovan collected himself and told Dom to rejoin the party in a flat voice devoid of the aggression it held before.

Dom nodded, spun on his heel, and left us alone.

"Fucknuggets." I rubbed my face like I could wash the last few minutes away. I shut the door, wishing I had in the first place.

"So much for discretion." Donovan smiled with deep dimples. "At least it wasn't my fault." I glared at him. "What? That was all you, babe."

"Why'd you have to get all territorial?"

"Please, that wasn't territorial. It was holding him accountable for his disrespect."

"Where does a circle-jerk fall into the pie chart of respectable behaviour?"

"I wasn't going to stand by while he threatened you."

"He wasn't threatening my life. He was doing right by Caine. If you overheard whatever he did, you would've too. He doesn't realize Caine wouldn't be surprised."

"Hmm, nice to know." Donovan smirked and sat on the edge of his bed.

"Knowing about you calling me babe or the Coveners seeing my tits is completely different than having his friends know about it."

"Again, when did they see your tits?"

I scoffed and turned to leave.

"What are you doing?"

"Damage assessment." I kept going, hearing him follow. "You don't need to come."

"I'm not letting that asshat hang you out to dry. Plus, it's my house. I can go where I want."

When we reached the bottom of the stairs, Caine was in the kitchen, Dom telling him something that had him crossing his arms and arching his eyebrows into a familiar angry expression. Caine looked over Dom's shoulder at us and I froze. Of course Dom would tell him what he overheard. Of course the house had to be full of people when it happened.

Dom followed Caine's glare and saw me standing there with Donovan. His expression smoothed as he reached into his pocket and pulled out a knife.

I gasped but couldn't say anything.

"What the fuck, man!" Matt was in the living room to our right where Teddy was holding a knife and wearing the same expression Dom did.

A rise in voices and a thud had me spinning back to Caine, who was now on the ground on his side, blood on his lips as Frog stood over him, fist still clenched as if he had punched him.

"Frog!" Kim pushed him. He grabbed her shoulder and shoved her to the side. She stumbled into Gwen who helped her gather her footing.

Reid and Lee all stood with knives in their hands, positioning themselves around the Coveners, keeping the ones in the kitchen in a tight group so they wouldn't run off or intervene. Their faces were blank, no anger or adrenaline present, not even intoxication, staring as if they were doing as they were told.

"Puppets," I muttered.

"Yup," Donovan muttered back.

Caine's resentful gaze met mine before he refocused on his friends.

"What do you want?" Donovan asked.

Puppet Dom turned to us. "Nothing at present. Only to make a point."

Donovan exhaled. "We're not safe in here or anywhere. That it?"

"Yes. With your training and prodigious bloodline, expectations of your conduct have been disappointing." Donovan didn't respond. "I'm inclined to allow you to resume your soiree since it fits my current needs." He looked around and then at me. "However, I find those you surround yourself with, those you call Coveners, to be much like yourself. Of inferior stock perpetuating a diluted bloodline."

"Uterus is spic and span and I don't intend on perpetuating anything. Worry about your own bloodline."

Puppet Dom's expression twisted. "An odd comment given our relation."

"Relation? As in related?"

Puppet Dom straightened and folded his hands in front of him, knife still in hand. "You have yet to ascertain my identity." I didn't respond. "Hmm. More evidence to prove your unworthiness."

Donovan stepped towards Dom. "Get to your point or leave. You got in, you can let yourself out."

"Yes, I can. Though I suspect you'll have an issue with the Blind since they will not remember having arrived. They would, had I gifted them the sanity of mind, but efforts to conceal this world is not my concern. You have five minutes."

Puppet Dom, and the rest of Caine's Puppeted friends, collapsed to the floor unconscious.

I sprang forward and grabbed the knife from Dom's hand.

The Coveners voices raised in panicked questions. Ones we all had, valid ones, but they weren't helping.

"Shut up!" Donovan roared over them. "Get those guys in here with these ones." No one moved. "Now!" They jumped to move them, others being sure to take away the knives.

"Caine," Donovan said as Caine was checking his friend's pulses, "Can you persuade them to believe they came here for a party and forget the rest?"

"We have five minutes. They'll wake up at the same time, I can't take them all on."

"If we can contain the others while you persuade them, can you do it?"

"I have no clue."

Donovan came at me and grabbed my shoulders. I tensed a moment, then he backed off. Caine was suddenly at his side when he asked me, "Do you remember?"

"Remember what?"

"Perfect." Donovan clapped his hands and turned to Caine who looked more pissed off than when Dom initially confronted him. "As soon as they wake up, you make them forget. Make them think they attended an awesome party and they were just on their way out."

"Wait, remember what?" No one answered me. Not even Caine who shook his head.

"They're on the floor, idiot, how do you explain that? They'll freak out as soon as they wake up." Kim had a point.

"Can you make the ones you want to fall back to sleep until you can focus on them?" Gwen asked.

"What?" Caine was still shaking his head.

"Try me." Gwen laid down on the floor. He hesitated. "Come on, come on."

Caine stepped over her. His power rose, and her expression went blank. "Gwen, sleep now and don't wake up until I tell you to."

Gwen closed her eyes. Rachel bent and shook her, but she didn't wake.

"Gwen," Caine called, "wake up."

Gwen opened her eyes and sat up. "Did it work?"

The Coveners laughed and clapped.

"Shut up." Donovan held up a hand. "Celebrate when we're done."

"Maybe thirty seconds left," Jared said looking at his watch.

"Okay," Donovan said. "Caine will get them situated. While he does, not a fucking word from anyone. Afterwards, you raise a glass and say goodbye so we can get them the fuck out of here."

"What do we do if Caine can't get them to forget?" Deidra asked.

"We'll worry about Plan B when we get there." He looked at Caine. "You won't like Plan B, so I suggest you make Plan A count."

Frog's leg twitched. Kim jumped and stood back. Everyone went quiet.

Caine knelt at their feet with his power enacted. Reid woke up first. As soon as his eyes opened, Caine put him to sleep. Lee too.

"What the fuck?" Frog woke up as he was putting Lee to sleep.

Caine answered by taking his will and giving the sleep command, but Dom and Teddy were too awake and saw what he did.

"What are you doing?" Teddy scrambled to his feet.

"Jared—" Donovan pointed at Teddy. Jared rushed forward and grabbed the guy.

"What the fuck?" Dom moved to attack Jared. Donovan was quick and used his power to telekinetically grab Dom and throw him down. Dom grunted in pain as Donovan held him in place.

"Hey!" Caine yelled.

"Keep going!" Donovan yelled back.

"Caine? What's going on?" Teddy struggled, looking over his shoulder at Jared and around the room. Caine put him to sleep.

Dom struggled as Caine approached him. "I don't know what the fuck's got into you, man, but I'm going to make sure you regret it."

Caine hesitated then got to work. His sigh of relief for them all being out was short-lived. He needed to move on to the next step.

One by one, he woke them up, snatched their will, and fabricated a story about them attending the party, having fun, and about to head home. Then he told them to put their shoes on and stand by the door and wait. Each complied. Once the five of them were equipped with new memories, Caine rolled his shoulders, looked around, and then got some to hide so it looked like the party was basically over and most had gone home.

"Show time, people." Donovan turned to those left in the living room. Coveners sat on the couches and started fake conversations.

Caine clapped his hands and said, "Good seeing you, guys."

His friends returned the sentiment and either shook hands or hugged. Kim jumped on the chance to give Frog a big hug and kiss goodbye before the guys left, running out to their cars at the curb as the shield reacted and sent a sense of urgency through everyone who did the spell.

"I can't believe that fucking worked." Blake laughed and clapped Jared on the shoulder. The Coveners celebrated with more drinks and conversation about Donovan's plan and Caine's execution, while

Caine, Donovan, Kim, and I thanked our lucky stars it worked and worried about what it meant.

The Puppeteer got inside. He knew about us. He's seen the inside of the place, including the closet of magical items. What if he could somehow remotely view through someone without fully taking them over?

And not to forget, he said he was related to me. How was that possible?

More and more questions went unanswered until the party dwindled and the four of us were left alone. The Coveners knew they could contact us at any time if they encountered more issues with any Tainted jackholes, but they had lives to get back to, so hiding out at Donovan's wasn't an option. I worried, even after all they saw tonight, that they didn't understand the full dangers. The thought crossed my mind that we should lock them up in the basement for their own safety, but they saw the difference in Caine's friends as Puppets. If anything, they knew what to look for.

"Since my boyfriend had to run out of here after being used to terrify everyone, I'm going to bed." Kim had had a few drinks, and a few more as we sat and theorized, but looked like she would rather have left with Frog.

"Me too, I guess." Donovan walked away without saying goodnight.

It wasn't until we got into the room we used that Caine finally asked for an explanation. I recalled Dom walking into Donovan's room, what he may have heard, and what assumptions it led to. Caine turned into something akin to a wax figure and sat there, probably comparing what I said against what Dom told him before turning into a Puppet.

"We got past the Puppeteer turning my best friends into Puppets. I achieved something I didn't know was possible and saved my friends in the process. Donovan managed to take advantage of the situation, as he always does."

"How?"

"By making you forget he kissed you."

I sat on the bed. "Oh."

"Yeah."

"Makes sense why you looked so pissed off afterwards."

He nodded slowly. "Not that I could compel the rest of the Coveners to forget, so they watched me get played like a fool. And yet, he still manages to look like the hero."

"Hero is a bit much."

"Even if I didn't care what the Coveners thought, you should. He took advantage of you and you don't even care."

"Wha—? I just found out. I'll talk to him about it later, but I realize the situation called for rash action."

"And now you defend him, like you always do. And in trying to defend him in front of Dom, I, again, was made to look like a fool as I stood there with my best friend telling me how my girlfriend is up in a room with some guy calling her babe and talking about spells before she did something weird to him."

"He doesn't know what he saw or what he heard."

"Talking about spells isn't normal."

"No, not for him. I get—"

"I worked hard to shield my friends from finding out about all of this stuff."

"I know. I didn't—"

"You thought it was okay to risk my friends, so you could stop, what? A fistfight?"

Caine got into bed, slid down into the blanket, and rolled over onto his side away from me.

"What are you doing?"

"Going to sleep. Nothing I say makes a difference anyway. You'll do what you want and expect me to be okay with it, so why bother?"

"What you say always matters to me. I know this isn't easy, but I don't know what else to do. Do you want to go home? Or my place?"

"I want to go to sleep."

I didn't answer him. I wasn't sad or trying to think of a rational retort. I was pissed. Pissed that he thought this was an appropriate way to leave this conversation. Our situation wasn't easy on any of us, and while Donovan made it his job to make things more difficult, Caine knew what this was about from the beginning. Now I was painted into a corner. If I said anything, I was saying so in defense of Donovan and saying nothing looked like I didn't care. Either way, Caine was no longer listening.

Against every Relationship Counsellor's advice, we went to sleep angry.

———

Waking up with a headache in an empty bed didn't surprise me. Well, the empty bed part didn't, anyways. The skull-banger was annoying, yet more manageable than finding solutions to my Caine drama. The issue from last night ran deeper than the conversation with Dom and what that might do to their friendship. Caine couldn't cope with being cooped-up under Donovan's roof and dealing with his bullshit in close quarters. Only a couple of nights, and already he was dangling from the end of his rope.

I readied for the day, making no attempt to cover the dark circles under my eyes. Caine lay next to me all night, rigid with his back to me. It made for a restless sleep. Mad or not, it was a sickening feeling. I wanted to be content with leaving it alone, but I wasn't. So, the night had consisted of an endless reel of what I could say to him, how he may respond, how I might react. Over and over and over.

We were stuck here whether either of us liked it or not, and until someone broke down the door and snuffed us out, this would continue. I reminded myself living was more important. Happiness didn't matter if you were dead, so the priority was staying alive long enough for happiness to become a priority.

Mindset in check, I went to find Bosco. The tension between Caine and I last night was so great, my usual bed buddy found somewhere else to stay the night. I didn't blame him. Though I found him, all paws on the kitchen table, finding his breakfast in the form of a neglected plate of leftovers.

"Hey!" I clapped my hands loud enough to make my head ring and cause Bosco to drop the food and scamper off the table.

The problem with getting a pet with the cutest face ever was over-sized dark eyes that poured into your soul and a punched-in nose you couldn't help kissing. The whole cuteness package made it difficult to be mad, especially once the charm was turned on. Bosco had his own supernatural arsenal. Plus, I went all night without a hint of comfort and I wasn't about to punish him for doing something any animal would.

"Why are you yelling?" Kim came into the kitchen fixing the bottom hem of her shirt.

"Is that your food?"

"No, I just got up."

I gave her a double-take. Long, deep-red hair to her waist, no flyaways, clear skin with no signs of sleep deprivation or stress, and a light green eye shadow I could never get away with but looked amazing on her. "What the tits?"

"What?" Kim looked down at herself.

"Is waking up flawless a spell too? I can barely see past the bags under my eyes and you're ready for the catwalk."

"Try sleeping for a change. I slept deeper than I have in weeks. Even after all the shit from yesterday. No idea why, but I'll take it."

"Good to hear," I said, instead of complaining further before I couldn't stop. Kim's minimal soul glow made her look majestic, though it was still straining my eyes.

"Have you seen the guys?" I asked, as Kim poured herself some coffee.

Swallowing before answering, Kim said, "I'm assuming Donovan is getting up if you just did. Maybe Caine's in the basement."

I checked downstairs hoping to gauge Caine's mood and maybe have a few words before the others joined us, but the basement was empty. Moving past Kim, cradling her coffee mug in the kitchen, to look out the front windows answered why. The Shield of Aegis was still intact, shrink-wrapping the front lawn in the sun of the day and making it twice as hard for me to see.

Caine's car was missing.

"He's gone," I said. Kim paused while breaking an egg into a frying pan. "His car's gone. The fucker actually left without telling me."

"He's probably at the store. How you can get so uptight about small things, like him not telling you he left—while you were sleeping —and then stand idly by as worse shit goes down, is beyond me. I don't get you, girl."

I plunked my ass onto the stool. "No. He's gone. I know it. I can feel his hatred from here." Not in a connection sort of way, but in an I-know-it-to-the-fullest-without-evidence kind of way. "We had an argument last night and I'm sure he's still boiling from it."

"You did?"

"Yeah. He refused to talk about it and now he's gone. Can I borrow your phone?"

"If you're right, do you think bugging him is the best way to handle it?"

"No, but his car being gone doesn't mean he's not in trouble. I'd rather confirm he's pissed and not dead." Or that's what I was telling myself.

She handed over her phone.

An automatic answering machine meant I didn't get to hear his voice. I texted him, hoping he would respond. Fifteen minutes later, I got my answer.

The text read: Alive. At Eli's. Need a break.

And that was it. No, "Don't worry," or "I love you but hate Dono-van" like usual. His whereabouts and a firm statement meant to stop me from contacting him further, all without a hint of emotion. Texts were easily misunderstood, but it was still possible to freeze someone out digitally.

How was I supposed to feel? Should I be mad at him? Mad at

myself for causing his anger? Mad at Donovan for being the cause of the division between us? All I knew was that I was upset. Maybe he needed some time away from Donovan's, but if that was the case, I was certain he would have asked me to join him. It wasn't a Donovan issue. It was me and I had no one to blame but myself.

"Everything okay?" Kim asked.

If I knew how to navigate the phone I would have erased the message, but I couldn't manage it, so I handed it back, knowing Kim would read it.

"Oh. Okay. He probably needs a break for the day, not a relationship break."

I didn't respond. I sat with my racing, damaged, and self-conscious thoughts. What if he did mean a relationship break? Was he done with me? Maybe he realized I wasn't worth the effort after all? Was reassurance all he needed? Even if I gave it, was it realistic? Caine said nothing he ever said mattered. Everything he says matters to me, but did it make a difference? Would I have been able to deal if Caine had a female version of Donovan? Someone with a past far greater than our potential future?

Shit. I didn't—Did I mean that? Was my future with Donovan far greater than any prospect of one with Caine?

Did someone call my name? Would Caine ever say my name again with anything less than disdain? What did he tell his family? They knew about Donovan and our past.

What could I do? Should I go there? Should I harass him until he talked to me? I knew that was a no-go, but it was exactly what I wanted to do. Should I insist we hide out somewhere else? What if I was separated from Donovan and it made things worse? Clearly, I die if he dies.

My name, being called again, niggled at the edges of my attention. Different tone. Deeper.

Maybe I could hide out at the estate? Olive wouldn't mind. Though we would hit the same wall if Donovan had to come with us.

My name again. Donovan's voice. Cautious. Worried. No. I

didn't want to talk to him. Not yet. I needed to think. Needed to figure this out. My skull pounded. Donovan's confusion grew as I closed my eyes. His emotions invading mine. No. I needed to think without his influence. I pushed back, but the intrusion of his emotions doubled.

A hand on my shoulder snapped me out of my head and had me on my feet. I needed space. I needed distance. My power awakened and got me up and moving outside into the backyard. I needed space. More space. Alone. I needed to be alone.

17

TALKING IT OUT

Donovan

Her thoughts were a snarling mass of brambles that couldn't untangle themselves, catching her skin with serrated thorns, and drawing blood that drowned out her rationalization. Nothing Kim said got through to Sophie. A tear trickled down her cheek as she closed her eyes. I tried to figure out what she was feeling. I wanted to help her, but I didn't understand what had happened.

I touched her shoulder, hoping it would bring her out of her head enough to speak to us, but when I made contact, she shot up off the stool onto her feet, took off towards the backyard, and erected a milky white shield across the door.

"Holy shit!" Kim stumbled back from the island, sloshing coffee to the floor.

She's shutting me out? What did I do?

Adrenaline, anger, guilt, confusion, sadness. Mine? Hers? I wasn't sure at this point. No matter what, all of it was too much for her. We heard the door slam like she was throwing it shut but couldn't see through the clouded wall.

"God dammit!" I grabbed the back of a chair and tossed it to the side. It hit the wall with a crash and I heard the scramble of Bosco nails on the floor as he took off. I turned on Kim. "What the fuck happened?"

"H-how did she do that?" Her voice quiet and disjointed.

"Kim!" I stepped in front of her so she would stop staring at the shield Sophie still had up. "Tell me what the fuck I missed. Start talking!"

Kim huffed. "I don't know exactly what happened last night. I only know what she told me this morning."

"And?"

Kim recounted what she knew, including the text message from Caine, and her comments made to Sophie about a potential relationship break.

"That pussy-ass piece of shit!" Rage added to the pot of Sophie's emotions, threatening to boil over. I wanted to punch the wall. I wanted to punch Caine. "How could he do that to her, knowing what he does about her ex?"

"Be more concerned with her right now. How the hell did she do that?"

"I showed her. Once. As a joke. I didn't even tell her how to do it and mine was transparent, so I have no clue."

A show of great strength didn't surprise me. I knew she was capable of more, but she was able to perform a rather difficult spell for someone so new to the craft with only a hint of power. No warble of energy occurred either, so she was holding it up with no other effort than wanting it to be there. Or maybe she didn't know she was doing it. That was most likely the case, that her power manifested the barrier out of desperate need and would remain as such until the need dissipated. If I wasn't so worried, I'd be impressed.

An hour later and I was still pacing. "It's not subsiding." I tried beating my fists against the solid shield, thinking I could break through it or maybe the pain would snap her out of it. I even tried concentrating on our connection and funnelling calming emotions to her. She blocked it out, as if the shield extended to the connection as well.

"You can't beat it down." Kim's irritation irritated me more. "She needs to process."

"She's out there thinking about how another douche-bag she loved screwed off on her again. Caine knows her history and he still left." From the look on Kim's face, she had no idea about Sophie's ex and what he put her through by taking off whenever he needed a fix and then leaving all together. I wasn't about to tell her Sophie's story, though I was surprised Sophie hadn't told Kim herself. Not that she told me. My Psychometry did that for her.

"We don't know he left-left. He could come back."

"Besides the point." The remnants of my patience were lost. "Fuck this."

The backyard didn't have an entrance besides through the house, but I was more than capable of climbing a fence. Around the back of the house, through a small space between the neighbouring lot, I was left enough room for me to pop up onto the ten-foot fence, wedging my shoes between the vertical slats to keep me steady.

"What are you doing?" A neighbour kid holding an action figure in his hand asked.

When I turned to him, my expression must have still been in 'fuck off' setting because the towheaded boy went from curious to frightened and turned to race inside. Before the kid reached his door, he stopped dead in his tracks, turned towards me, and stared. Fucking Christ. That's all we needed. Sophie to be in a mental health crisis and have the Puppeteer waltz in.

"Sophie." She stood against the house looking out into nothing, her expression unchanged from when I entered the kitchen. "Come on, babe. You need to get inside."

The shield erected inside raised itself to surround the entire backyard and blocked me out. She didn't move. I didn't notice a rise of power. Her need evolved and so did the shield.

I dropped to the ground and spied the staring kid between the slats of the wooden fence, his gaze followed my movements until I was out of sight. If the shield kept me out, I could only hope it would keep the Puppeteer out too. Not that he had tried to turn Sophie into a Puppet before, but in her vulnerable state, I didn't know if that would change things.

"She covered the whole yard. Didn't even look at me," I told Kim as I re-entered the kitchen. "You have to talk to her."

Kim tilted her head. "Not only would it not work, Sophie's not a typical person with a traumatic relationship history. She has self-awareness on her side, with full understanding of how I'd come at her. She knows damn well this" —she pointed at the shield— "isn't a normal reaction, but she's stubborn and hurt and she needs her space. With your connection, that's more than a little difficult to accomplish."

"How do you know that?"

"Because she's educated on this exact thing and has put herself in a fishbowl to keep us out while she tries to unravel her thoughts. When Sophie sets her mind to something, she's immovable. It's like cow-tipping an elephant. Not going to happen. You want to help her? Back the fuck off. Give her the time to figure this out without you and the connection stuff clouding her every thought."

"You're not even going to try and help her work it out? You're her best friend. Maybe she needs a soundboard."

"If she did, she would've asked for one. And I'm performing my best friend duties by doing exactly what I believe she needs. I'll be available to support her when she's ready for it." She sipped her coffee as if illustrating her intentions.

I was choked with the helplessness of seeing someone I loved hurt and being unable to do anything about it. This wasn't right. This wasn't healthy. I knew what it was like to be stuck in a darkness so alluring you could remain in it for eternity. How could I leave her there without trying to pull her out?

The heat of the sun beating down on Sophie heated my cheeks and had me sweating. I slid down the shield in defeat onto my ass and waited. Seconds flowed with the sensations of Sophie's inner turmoil forced me to endure fluctuations of emotional content I could only guess at. If I thought it would help, I would have raced to Caine's family's house and dragged him back, but I couldn't make myself leave her and resolved to wait it out.

———

CLUNK. "Fuck me!"

Hours into the freeze out of the century, I fell backwards, my head thwacking off the glass of the sliding doors. My eyes had been closed, undergoing the emotions of a tattered woman, when the wall she constructed to keep the world out came down. I jumped up and raced to open the door.

"You have to force yourself on her, don't you?" Kim said. "Can't you give her one second to make the decision to come inside herself? No wonder she's going insane."

"If she didn't want me out there, the barrier would still be up."

"Maybe she couldn't hold it up anymore. Did you think about that? No, you thought of yourself. Sit your ass down and give her a second."

Against every instinct I had, I waited. Another ten minutes passed, and I couldn't wait any longer. I wanted to test the waters. Best ice breaker and Sophie's greatest weakness? Bosco. So, I sent him out.

"Hey, buddy," I heard her say as he whined and barked, the life in her mood unmistakable.

I peeked my head out around the corner. "Safe to come out?" I took her small smile as permission and then panicked at what I might say to her now that I could speak to her.

18

BAGGAGE

The sun had changed places in the sky at some point, beating on me from every direction and leaving a coating of sweat on my skin. My stamina was exhausted from the marathon of thoughts. Like a battery no longer able to hold its charge, I gave out and slid down the side of the house. A nudge beneath my arm was Bosco shoving himself onto my lap, then whining and barking when I responded.

"Hey, buddy."

He rubbed his body into me, commanding love and attention. Scratching at the pit above his tail had his nose in the air and wriggling on my lap.

"Safe to come out?" I heard Donovan ask.

Verbal permission was unneeded when acceptance skittered across the connection instead. He knew the coast was clear. Plus, saying "yes" gave the impression I wanted him out here with me. I didn't want him here, but I didn't oppose it either. Though he sat so close our shoulders touched, I didn't mind his presence as I thought I might, which may have been more to do with Bosco's expert buffering skills. His need for affection provided easy distraction as Donovan scratched his back and saved me from uncomfortable eye contact.

The hesitance within Donovan told me how out of his element he was, yet his relief said more. He wanted me to be okay and saw this interaction as a good sign. Tragedy and pain were more comfortable for him, something he waged and won many times over. My current brand of emotions was off his radar, and since they came from interactions with Caine, the eggshells he trod on were delicate and razor sharp. I had to give him credit for trying. Points for being present.

"I don't know what to say," I told him. Partial lie. I knew what I could have said, but I didn't want to.

"Good, 'cuz I don't either." His response made me laugh. "You did a new spell. Kept it up for a long time too." He meant it as a compliment, but it evoked the opposite.

"How long?"

He shrugged. "Few hours."

"Wow."

"Obviously you needed it."

Our buffer decided he needed the rose bush more than an ear scratch and left us buffer-less. I found myself on the brink of losing it. All the time I stood in the backyard I never shed a tear, never felt the need. But now, reflecting on how I had spent my day, and why, it was all I wanted to do. Catching his breath as I caught mine, I rested my head against the house. A wash of calm leveled me out. Donovan's head was back against the house too, his eyes closed. He turned my way and peeked at me through a narrowed lid. We laughed. The break in tension eased the knot in my stomach.

He was far better at accomplishing that than I was. My cheeks heated with embarrassment because I needed more help than he did.

Donovan turned to face me. "What happened? Was it because of the stuff at the party last night or because he left?"

"No, it's none of that." I looked up at a cloudless sky. "Actually, it's probably all of it. Stress. Baggage. We haven't been fair to Caine and I don't know how to change it."

"We?"

"Yes we. This isn't easy for him."

"It's not easy for me either. Watching you and him together isn't right, but I fight through it because you need to be safe."

"Caine and I don't shove it in your face. If we did things like you do, we'd be fucking like wild horses every night regardless of the connection. For starters. You don't hold anything back."

"You can't imagine how much I'm holding back, but I see what you're getting at. I don't want to make this easy for him because it's not easy for me. Pushed it a bit too far, I guess. But it still doesn't mean he should've left without telling you. Not after the shit with Brock."

I sighed. I partially agreed but didn't want me agreeing with him to make it seem like his behaviour was justified. I hated that Caine leaving made me project feelings about Brock onto this situation, but it did. My time alone was spent trying to stop myself from doing so and facing inward at all my fucked-up-ness.

He leaned back on his hands in the grass. "Did you know you were doing it? The shield?"

"No." I laughed humourlessly. "I didn't focus on anything or realize I'd been out here so long."

"Did you stand the whole time?"

I nodded, lifting an eyebrow in my own disbelief.

"At least you know a bit more of what you're capable of while emotionally driven."

"Would be peaches and cream if I could re-enact them on command."

"Hmmm. Hey Kim," he yelled then said, "Try it."

"What? No."

"Just try."

Kim came outside, and Donovan waved her over. I raised my power, it ached in my bones from being used so soon again, like I had spent the afternoon working out. Kim bounced into something unseen, the warble of the flexible shield I erected protecting her from actual harm. I dropped the wall immediately as Donovan busted out in a childlike, uninhibited laugh I found too infectious to fight.

"What the hell?" Kim started into a rant but dissolved into the giggles along with us. "You guys are assholes."

"Love you," I called when she turned to go back inside, shooting us a well-earned middle finger.

———

After showering the afternoon sweat away, I emerged from the washroom feeling lighter, yet raw. The smell of food had my stomach growling. "Please tell me there's lots."

Kim laughed. "Yes, there is." She and Donovan sat in front of plates of rotini and meatballs with thick meaty sauce. "Save me some to bring to Frog's."

"You're going to Frog's?" I asked as I loaded a plate.

"For the night. And I'm not feeling bad about it, so don't try. Donovan already lost that argument."

"I'm not arguing with the one who keeps my stomach happy." I ate a mouthful and talked around it. "The other night must have been a total tease. Get what you can." I twirled another fork full. "There is the Puppet issue, though."

"Told you." Donovan popped a meatball into his mouth.

"Stop complaining," Kim said. "Letting the Puppeteer trap us in here is another way he wins. I have a life. I would like to live a portion of it semi-normal."

"You're horny and risking your life to get dick. Not exactly a rebellion."

Kim scoffed at Donovan.

I held up my hand. "Get the 'D', girl, and have an extra 'O' for me."

She returned my high-five. "This will end at some point, and I may not have a relationship left if I don't take some risks. If the Puppeteer end us, I'd like to enjoy some of him—"

"Some small part of him."

"—while I can." Kim sneered at Donovan. "My thoughts are shielded. I'll set up a small barrier spell the best I can when I get there, and I'll be back early since he has to work in the morning. It's happening, and I refuse to feel guilty about it. Oh—" She got up from her chair and started filling a container of food for Frog. "Olive called while you were in the shower reminding you about the party and said something about the attic directory being finished and poised for action. I have no idea what that means, but she was all bubbly about it. Have you told her about the Puppeteer being related to you? I'm assuming it's through the Ballards."

"Ugh. No, I haven't. Who wants to think they're related to such a piece of shit? Maybe the attic directory or the family tome has a family tree or something."

"Are you going to the party at the estate?" Kim asked.

"May as well. It's a risk, but I want to go."

"Way safer," Donovan's said. "No way the property isn't shielded. And you said the attic is huge and full of craft items. I'd think the Ballards would be smart enough to protect their own and everything that entails. Probably safer than here."

"It's more of an issue of putting the others in danger. Here we're away from them and everything Olive worked so hard to get back. She wouldn't care if the Puppeteer knew the estate existed. If the Puppeteer really is blood, they probably already know."

"Bet he does." Kim scooped up Bosco, laying a peck on his head before putting him back down.

"They'll be plenty of people there, and you guys are welcome to come, of course. Though you'll need evening wear. Olive has planned an upscale, pinkies-raised kind of shindig."

"Not a problem," Donovan said.

Kim and I exchanged a look that said we doubted his version of evening wear was what I had in mind, but it didn't matter. He didn't need to impress my family or the Dunnville Historical Society who would be there to check out the restoration to a local historical building. He would be there to ensure I was safe. My expectations of anything more was limbo-bar low.

Kim's cell rang. "Caine," she told me and passed me the phone. I went into the living room to talk privately.

"Hello?"

"Hey." Caine's voice was all wrong, his deadpanned tone telling me nothing had changed.

"Hi. So, you're at Eli's?"

"Yeah."

"When are you coming back?"

"Not tonight."

"Come on, Caine. I know things are messed up and clearly my fault, but I can't fix anything if you're not here or willing to work it out."

"I'm not coming back."

"We can go somewhere else."

"No."

"Why not?"

He exhaled into the receiver. "Because things shouldn't have gotten to where they did in the first place, and I don't want to talk about it. I need time to work it out on my own."

I nodded to myself, at first saying nothing. Caine might not have been able to see me, but there was no mistaking my subdued anger. "So, you called to tell me you weren't coming back and didn't want to talk to me?"

"Figured you'd want to know."

"Yeah, I'd want to know. I'd want to know why you left, too. And what made you feel okay about leaving. I'd have wanted to know when you were coming back. I'd want to know lots of things. Shame you didn't stick around for us to have a conversation about it."

"You didn't have to ask. You already knew."

"Oh, how nice. Your mind reading ability came in."

"Sophie—"

"Or seeing the future like Aunt Lacey, did that suddenly develop? I'd like to think not considering how I spent my day." He huffed into the receiver again. My voice shook, but I forced it to steady. "You know, I never expected you to enjoy this anymore than you would a hefty dick-punch, but you could have at least waited long enough for me to wake up before disappearing so I knew you weren't kidnapped or turned into a Puppet or so that we knew we had one less person to protect ourselves with."

"I couldn't. And with Kim, the Coveners, and Donovan, I'm assuming you'll be fine."

"Huh, I guess you'll find out eventually if your assumptions are wrong."

"Don't make me feel guilty about this. I had to—"

"No, you didn't. Not the way it went down, and not with how cold you're acting now. Your point was to make me feel guilty. Well, mission accomplished. I feel horribly guilty for what you have to go through because of my connection with Donovan, but the connection won't disappear because you want it to. We're a package deal. You knew that from the beginning.

"However, what I don't feel guilty for is being upset that you left. I'm doing everything possible to keep the important people in my life safe and breathing. I get that for you, that doesn't include Donovan, but for me it does. And that's fine. I even get that. But you can't expect me to coddle you through this or agree with you, when me living depends on him living."

"I know that."

"You know that?"

The other end of the line was silent.

"Okay. Well, I'm super happy we've had this talk."

I hung-up.

After the line went dead, I realized I had never hung up on someone before and immediately felt the tug of war between justified anger and a bucket full of more guilt. Kim was alone in the kitchen. I returned her phone and told her what happened, relaying the gist, but I didn't want to shit talk him only to later regret it as I knew I would.

"Do you want me to cancel my plans?"

"And cockblock my bestie? I don't think so. Enjoy yourself."

"But you'll be alone with Donovan all night. Bet Caine doesn't know that."

"Nope."

"Honeymoon over, huh?"

"We never had time for a honeymoon period. We went straight to battle ready formations and dealing with Donovan and I's ever shifting connection."

She hiked an overnight bag over her shoulder and gave me a hug. "You'll be okay here tonight though, right? I've got a bad feeling about this."

"Don't worry. I won't burn down the house or let in any strangers or order any pay-per-view porn. Scratch that last one. No promises."

"Okay, okay. Call me if you need me."

"I definitely won't call you. Don't forget the condoms. Unless you have a spell for that too."

Kim laughed. "Science has that one covered."

"Hail to Bill Nye the Science Guy."

All joking aside, once Kim was gone, I was indeed left alone with Donovan. With the way I was feeling, combined with my life and death being rolled around in a game of rock, paper, scissors—With the addition of an enemy I didn't know but was possibly related to—I wasn't in the mood to create any wet spots with anyone.

I found Donovan in the basement.

"You want to practice your Soul Reading thing?"

"*Pfft.* Not into having a seizure again so soon after my last one. I like to space them out or they start to drag me down."

"Sarcasm. Nice." He sat on the floor next to me, leaning back against the couch and grabbing a book.

"Sorry, a little edgy."

"Mhmm. When's Caine due back?" I looked at him. "He's likely the reason for your edginess. I'm surprised he's left you to your own devices this long." He gave a laugh as he flipped through half the book he'd already read, when the emotion in the air significantly changed. "What?" When I failed to comment, he knew Caine had no intention of returning. "That son of a bitch."

"Well, his mom doesn't like me, but she didn't start out a bitch."

"After all his talk, Mr. Self-Righteous bails." He shook his head.

"He's trying to figure things out his own way. Not only am I uninterested in how or why he can't do that here, I'm definitely not into talking about it with you right now."

"For the record, I called this from the jump." I gave him a stern look of irritation. "Fine, I get it. Not my fault he can't hack it."

"Wonderful. Now can it." I disengaged from the conversation and opened a book.

Donovan played music for us through his phone. After twenty minutes of distracted research, he asked, "Do you not want to read my soul?"

"No, actually. I don't."

"Oh. Okay."

"I've had a glimpse into your nightmares through that dream in Diluculo, and heard some things from yourself about your upbringing. The trauma of your past sounds terrifying. Satisfying my curiosity, when clearly my power is still weak enough to take us both over, and with no one here to save us, isn't smart. Caine's background isn't nearly as dark as yours and his soul sent my body into extreme overload and then complete shutdown."

"That was Gareth's personal history, not Caine's."

"Still. What if I end up being sent back into our past? I don't know what that looks like, and we can't risk it right now."

"I can see how that would suck."

I nudged him with my shoulder. "When I'm stronger, okay?"

He smiled and nodded, but his disappointment made me guilty for not possessing the strength.

We sat and read for a long time, flipping pages, Bosco in quiet snores on the end of the couch. No interruptions, no meaningless conversation to fill the emptiness, just sitting and reading. After a couple of hours, Donovan went up to the kitchen to grab us some drinks and a snack, with Bosco quick on his heels. He returned with two large bowls of snack options in one hand and two cans of pop stacked in the other. It surprised me that the drinks were non-alcoholic.

Bosco was still at his heels, this time jumping up into Donovan's legs begging for him to drop what he was carrying, making his way across the basement. "There's your ketchup Doritos or party mix." I grabbed the bowls from him. "Plus, caffeine to keep us going. Oh, and Bosco went outside, too."

My pug buddy jumped on the couch again and used his advantageous position to lick my face, water dripping down my cheek to my shoulder. "Nice, thanks buddy."

Donovan's expression twisted as I swiped my face only for Bosco to sneeze a snotty spray across both of us. "Gross."

A few minutes passed, and Donovan's inner thoughts were stealing my concentration. "Out with it already."

"Are you sure you can trust these Berisford's Caine's with?"

"They saved my life. That's good enough for me."

"No. The kid saved your life by telling you what he saw. Actually, you saved your own life as well as mine."

"Whatever. I trust them."

"And what if Caine follows in his father's footsteps?"

"He won't. Or if he does, he's nowhere close to that now, and Eli and Bernie aren't going to guide him there. That I believe."

"And if he does, where does that put you?"

"We should all be scared of turning, no?"

"You'd have a better chance of turning into a unicorn."

"I'm sure they all have their reasons. Would I follow Caine if he did? Probably not, but it depends on the circumstances. No one goes full-on Tainted soul overnight. I'm assuming it's a gradual thing. I'd at least try to save him."

He nodded. "You'd be foolish to think you could drag him away from it."

"Sounds like you're building to something here."

"I am. No matter where you end up, I can handle it. Even if that means you joining Loring or remaining as you are and sticking with Caine, because I get it's not about me, no matter how pissy I seem. I have the knowledge of this world and can help you where you won't know I'm helping. Caine's already needing a break. That annoys me to no end. We're in the first round and he's already showing signs of crumbling."

"Donovan—"

"You wanted to know where my head was at, that's where."

"Yes, I did, but you allowing yourself to be drawn into it or coming up with potential 'what ifs' isn't helping. Plus, you should be more scared of flipping sides than of Caine in any capacity. You already have the blueprints. Plus-plus, you can't tell the future. Every person doing evil believes they're doing something right. Whether it's right for the world or the people in it, for their race, country, religion, whatever it is, they all believe in a cause."

"I could say that's accurate when referring to humans."

"We are human."

"Not the same. Evil Magics know they're superior to the Blind and they still enjoy bringing them down. It's like sport-hunting big game by people who have bigger guns than courage. It's not thought of as murder. It's a pleasure retreat with bloodied, gutted, and beheaded deer carcasses to stick on your wall like trophies while the town newspaper takes photos you can stick to your fridge. Forget about the sanctity of the animal or needing the meat for survival. The perspective is far different because we're not simple humans. Whether you want to admit it or not, you do not fall within the lines of normal society anymore." He poked my shoulder. "We're above it. Flipping occurs when you not only recognize that but use humans as your weekend getaway in a game of predator and prey. And, like I said, you don't have it in you. However, a healthy dose of fear towards it is perfectly fine."

Okay then. Must be nice to be so certain of anything.

Thoughts purged, we went back to research. Donovan found reference to a Burattinaio in the text of the Italian tome.

Donovan moved his finger along the script. "It says a Burattinaio can not only use those as slaves but could tell them to throw themselves over a cliff and the affected would obey. Burattinaios can turn a righteous man into a murderer and a loyal wife into a prostitu'ire," Donovan laughed. "I'm sure even you could figure that one out."

"Why would they make a woman have sex?"

"The book leads us to believe that this would be to disgrace the woman practicing infidelity so her spouse could leave with cause, which also shows that it's not uncommon for a Puppeteer to make money from their power. Plus, there's speculation the Puppeteer would have the woman sleep with them to create children that may bear his power. Then, once the child is born, the woman would be disposed of and the child stolen."

"That sounds made up."

His rested the book on the knee of his bended leg. "See? You can't even imagine the evil things Magics do, let alone repeat them. Securing an heir is number one for any Coven Master. Since immortality isn't guaranteed, it's the only way to ensure the bloodline remains strong and their legacy prevails. Wouldn't surprise me if the chicks he impregnates are Magics themselves. The process of finding the perfect uterus was probably longer than the pregnancy."

This made me think of how Donovan spoke of his own parentage. Before taking off, he was to be the heir of his father's Coven, or at least a valuable aspect of it. Maybe his mother was another well-chosen uterus.

"Why does it always refer to the Puppeteer as male? I doubt the power would discriminate against gender."

"I doubt it, but with a male-dominated world wielding the pen, everything greedy or powerful was male and everything weak or subservient was female. Tons of strong female Magics are out there, you included, but while hiding from the general population they had to fall into their Blind roles, so many men were still looked at as evil while women were usually taken over by evil because of their weaknesses."

Since many women were still killed in the name of it, I understood what he meant.

"What are we supposed to do if Loring or the Puppeteer sends the Blind after us?"

"He already has. Forget your broken hand or the erasing minds dance Caine did on his friends?"

"That's my point. What if we couldn't stop them and it came down to having to kill a Puppet? Could you, even though they were innocent?"

"Yup."

"It wouldn't be their fault."

"Wouldn't be our fault either. Dying to save a stranger isn't an option."

"Still messed up."

"Purposely so. Recruiting is easier that way." I looked at him in question. "Make an honest person do something below their moral flexibility, and they're more likely to repeat the act and assume it was a part of their base nature. Most think once you've crossed the line there's no going back."

"Hmm. True."

"Don't worry, babe." He put his arm loosely around my shoulders again. "Whether it's Loring or someone he uses as his creepy little doll, they won't get close enough to force the choice."

Always so many promises. I gave an appreciative smile, grateful for his optimism without thinking it was warranted. Loring was coming, and by the looks of it, would rather do so head-on then through a Puppet.

19

THE SHIFT

Pages began to blur. Hours of reading can do that. I had no concept of time in the windowless basement and was confused when the scenery around me surged and ebbed, disorientating me. My vision blurred, stomach roiling, as I became desperate for traction. A jarring halt splashed bile on my tongue, the world around me reeling into near pass-out spins. Moments passed before I found stability, the nausea taking longer to recede.

I opened my eyes to see a young girl no older than ten or eleven being led into a small room by a man I thought I recognized. Standing in the middle of an unfamiliar space, smoothing stray wisps of her light brown hair behind her ears and fiddling with the strap of her forest green overalls, all I could focus on was the girl's red-rimmed, puffy eyes cast to the floor as if fearing to look up. Her sadness was a striking contradiction to the Mickey Mouse smiling on her shirt.

Rage filled me at the sight of the man with the girl. The girl didn't matter. She was unimportant as anger for this farce-of-a-being waltzed in, his wavy dark hair pulled back in a ponytail at the nape of his neck, like he was in costume. Not like a cape or gory zombie, but that of a man of virtue. Light khakis and a long-sleeved teal cashmere sweater completed the costume. His professionally-creased exterior and wax smile expressed dad-of-the-year, and although I didn't understand why, my gut recognized the beast in tanned loafers.

"Meet Joelly. She's yours now, son," he said thoroughly confusing me. "You will be a power pair, Donovan. Acquaint yourself. The union will follow this night."

As the man left, I understood as Donovan understood. This scared girl had been taken and brought to him as his bride. He had seen it done before with his brother and the girl brought to him the year before.

When the door closed, the unmistakable sound of a lock closed them in. "Stay a slave like the others or follow me." He motioned to the window.

The girl's eyes went wide, and she looked at the door behind her. "How do I know it's not a trick?"

"You don't."

Instead of waiting for her to change her mind, he forced the window open, leapt out, and sprinted as fast as he could with no destination in mind.

Darkness and numbness enveloped me until my entire body shivered and the darkness cleared, bringing with it a cramp deep in my gut. On the streets for days, eating at soup kitchens, and dumpster diving wasn't enough to stave off hunger. For what he did get, Donovan was grateful, but starvation was preferred to returning to where he had escaped.

He sheared off his long hair—a replication of his father's—with stolen scissors from a mall and changed his clothes to a heavy toque and an old jacket from a church donation to disguise his identity. His father's men found him anyway and dragged him back. When the men Donovan spotted, apparently watching him for days, used a Binding Spell to ensure he came quietly, fighting was beyond his power. The flock did everything to attempt to cut through his stubborn refusal to accept his expectations as heir, but not even public humiliation or torture swayed him.

———

When I could no longer endure the crying boy that hardened and rebelled against duty through blood and degradation, I closed myself to it. And when the sound of the broken boy faded away, I opened my eyes to dirty hands. I stared at those hands, not soiled by dirt, but caked in flour and sticky dough.

What am I doing? I thought, immediately remembering the bread. I had been kneading dough, adding flour so it wouldn't stick as my mother taught me, the combination creating a necessary mess.

As I rolled a smooth, floured stick over the dough, the front door scuffed along uneven wood floors, the sound of heavy boots creaked under heavy weight. I didn't investigate my guest, choosing to ignore his advance. That was until he entered the kitchen. The thud of dropping buckets of water to the floor with a splash was familiar and, though my back was to him, I couldn't help but smile.

My companion, Isaac, came to my side, seating himself on the edge of the butcher block he made, staring at me as I held my gaze on my task. I didn't acknowledge him until he reached out and tucked a piece of long hair behind my ear. The feeling of this small movement caused my heart to swell with undeniable affection, stopping my hands in mid-movement, eyes closing as it riddled my bones with a wash of adoration.

Sucked away from the kitchen, I watched moments of Isaac and Millicent's life together. Escaping into their own world, they ran through the forest amongst nature away from the townspeople. Practicing nature's magic was their little secret. They had even wedded in secret. No family, no witnesses or clergy present, only the birds and the life amongst the long grass and nearby stream. They declared heartfelt vows wearing their best clothes, and small white flowers Millicent had woven through her hair. They cleansed their pasts away within the stream to begin anew and then made love beneath the trees.

A blissful existence remained beneath the attentions of the others, until one day when Isaac was injured while cutting wood. Millicent was with a townswoman when it happened, she witnessed a wound appear out of nowhere on Millicent's arm, blood dripping down her skin and onto her frock as the woman gasped in fright. Isaac healed his wound in the privacy of the trees, leaving Millicent on stage for the woman to watch as her wound miraculously disappeared. The townswoman screamed the word "Witch" and everything unravelled.

They fled the home they built and everything they knew. The forest became their sanctuary, the only place to offer protection. Not even the trees could save them. Discovered in their sleep, worn by the cold and nights of restlessness, they thought it enough to take magical precautions, but in their exhaustion, both physical and emotional, their defences were down, and they were found. Hogtied, gagged, bound, and even hooded, the townsfolk took every preventative measure to thwart an escape or usage of power.

Their hearing still viable despite the hoods, they listened to the townspeople debate the best possible form of execution. Burn at the stake, hung until dead, behead with a blessed axe, or drown in the troughs of holy water. They were as creative as they were ruthless. Beheading with a blessed axe became their final decision. A quick death to avoid escape. Burning their bodies would follow to ensure reattaching their own heads would be impossible, their ashes to be disintegrated in a mixture of holy water for good measure.

Screaming did nothing, struggling earned them beatings, but Isaac insisted on trying, stopping when Millicent suffered the blows. His muffled protests were all Millicent heard, her tears lining the hood in disparaging sadness that her last moments would be spent away from him.

When the plan was set, the blade blessed, and the townspeople set to fulfill their duty to the lord, Millicent was granted a glimpse of Isaac's face. Instead of seeing her good-hearted companion, she found the twisted mask of a tortured man. Memories of happy times were too far away for her to transform the tears and sweat-clogged cheeks back to the bright eyes and jovial dimples she fell in love with.

Other able-bodied men dragged them to a designated area and dropped them to their knees. Stones and fallen branches dug into their bones, but these men had no concern of their captors, as they bent them over tree stumps. Fluids ran from their lips and noses, and tear-stained faces as they remained gagged. Positioned to amplify pain, Millicent was to watch Isaac die first. She was the one accused of being the Witch, nevertheless Isaac was now stained by evil. Refusal to repent called for his death first, so Millicent would witness the death of her cohort and live long enough to be soured by pain for her treachery.

Isaac screamed for her around the soiled fabric stuffed between his teeth and cutting into the edges of his lips. In desperation for each other, their eyes remained locked, minds racing in fear for their coming fate. They prayed to go back to days in the forest, practicing that which made them happiest.

As the audience spat foul names and damning curses, the axe was lifted and Isaac was held tighter, pressed in place so he wouldn't evade the axe-man's strike. She wanted to look away yet was unable to break her lock with his eyes and leave him alone in his last moment. His last breath.

He didn't blink. Isaac stayed brave until the end with an affixed stare, so she too wasn't alone for as long as it was the last thing within his control. Millicent watched as the unforgiving blade was brought down upon him. Millicent screamed against the gag as her lover's severed head fell from his strong shoulders, his blood spilt, soiling the earth below him. In that moment, nothing remained to steal from her. The instant Isaac's head left his body, Millicent was dead too, and the townspeople watched as her head fell without the aid of the axe-man's blade.

I awoke in the midst of a choking scream. Beside me, my love was alive and looking at me in panic. "I thought I lost you." I grabbed onto him, squeezing him to me as I sobbed.

"It's okay. You're okay." Donovan tried, but I was inconsolable.

"They killed you!" I cried out.

"No, babe—" My lips were on his before he could say anything else.

He pulled me in close and entangled his fingers in my hair. I wrapped my arms around him. He was alive, we were safe, and nothing else mattered.

————

"Ow!" I shot upright reaching for a pain in my leg. I saw Bosco through blurry eyes, digging at my calf to get me to move it so he could snuggle in. I shooed him, and he moved further down and snuggled against the couch arm instead.

Bare legs. Four of them. One pair distinctly males. I pulled away from—Donovan?

No. Not possible.

A shirt the same colour as the one I was wearing was now a crumpled mess on the floor. Others belonged to Donovan. Was that a bruise on my arm? I shifted to look closer. A bite mark?

The movement behind me meant Donovan was awake. Shit. As soon as I broke skin contact he would be back in the real world and seeing me instead of our past. Okay. Remove it like a Band-Aid.

I pulled away and scrambled for my clothes. The connection became alive as he did, then confusion strummed it like a drunk guitarist.

"Don't freak out," he said.

"Are you fucking kidding me?" I yanked up my underwear to find it torn and fit for the garbage. Commando it is.

"Sophie—" He was seated on the couch now, still naked. Far too naked.

"Turn around!"

"I've already seen everything."

"Do it!"

He shook his head and reached for his jeans instead. "Babe, please—"

"Stop. I can't hear your voice right now."

Memories of the previous night filtered through, blocking my mission to find my clothing. Puzzle pieces of fear and passion didn't make sense and I couldn't figure anything out while standing in front of him with no underwear under my jeans and cupping my tits. Focus. Commando. Bra? Where the fuck—? Fuck it. Shirt on. Go home.

"Wait. Sophie."

Shoes. I need shoes. I took two steps at a time to get upstairs and find my shoes. I grabbed them and pulled open the door. The sun was low. Early morning dew on the grass was cold on my bare feet, the chill reminding me of Bosco and his morning walks. I spun and ran back in the house as Donovan was catching up. He was still in only jeans and had deep scratch marks on his chest and shoulder. If I could get my head in order I would heal off the evidence, but I couldn't. I needed Bosco.

"Sophie, please. Let me get my bearings first."

I pushed past him to find Bosco's leash, thankful he had followed us upstairs and was now in the kitchen, so I didn't have to search for him.

"Not like this. Don't walk out on me. Please, Sophie." I picked Bosco up and headed back towards the door, Donovan following. "Let me drive you home, at least."

I couldn't answer him, bent on getting as far from him as possible. From his voice, his skin, his pleas. Begging made me want to run. His desperation for me to stay fuelled my desperation to flee. My fight or flight response screamed for distance without a destination, anywhere to get my head straight. What happened? Something happened. Research doesn't end with sex. Maybe we didn't, I told myself, but I knew different.

When I reached the street, I let Bosco walk on his own, clipping on his harness, his stumpy legs pumping to keep up as I left Donovan and his pleas behind me. He yelled something I blocked out. The connection made his intent loud and clear without the words and propelled me to walk faster. As did memories which refused to remain buried.

Isaac? Isaac and Millicent. Fuck. It was them. Not us.

Without my purse, cab fare was out of question. Not that a pay phone would be anywhere in Niagara-on-the-Lake since they were damn near extinct. The street was going to end and, since I was directionally challenged and too freaked to guess which way was the right way, chances were I would choose the wrong way and walk until my feet bled. All I wanted was to be in my own space. I needed to be alone and nothing I did would accomplish that. Donovan was always there, the connection unbearable.

The early morning air chilled my skin, heated under the sweat of my braless escape, yet thankfully chasing away the echoed heat radiating from the previous night. Walking faster had me coughing and my temples pounding. A rock stabbed into the bottom of my foot and buckled my knee. Sitting to put on my shoes was wasting time, but I had to get the rock out of my foot. Blood welled when I removed it, sparking a memory of Isaac losing his—Fuck. No. I couldn't think about it. I shoved my feet into my shoes with a chorus of cursing the bitch-ass street and its bitch-ass rocks and fuck it all and your bitch-ass mother too.

Trying to organize my thoughts to think up a plan became harder and harder as Donovan's rage spun out of control and influenced my emotions. I didn't have it in me to consider his feelings right now, couldn't manage thinking of him without making things worse, but I had no choice to feel them along with him. Another spiral pulling us in and mixing us up which only pissed me off, and then pissed him off more.

In a dead stare ahead, the road became obscured by flashes of the previous night. Slick skin, moans turned screams. I dissociated from the emotion coupled with these memories to focus on how it all started, hoping the answers would bring clarity and an explanation that didn't result in Donovan and I having sex.

Was I dreaming? Joelly. She was a girl. No purple streaks or panda-eyed make-up with a caustic attitude, but it was her. Isaac and Millicent. He moved her hair behind the ear. It was the déjà vu moment I remembered in Donovan's kitchen. Nothing overtly special, a simple interaction and the sense of how Isaac made Millicent feel loved that had the moment stamped on my soul.

And then Isaac died.

An ache in my chest brought tears to my eyes. My head fell back as grief for their end hit me, followed by disgust for what was done to them.

But still, why would I sleep with Donovan? Not that I had never considered the possibility of being with him, but how could I? I cheated on Caine and I didn't understand why. I had full knowledge of how it felt to find out someone you loved fucked someone else. How could I do that to him? How would I tell him?

A horn blared and had me grabbing my chest in a full body cringe. A car idled next to me with the frantically worried face of Kim behind the wheel. "What in the holy fuck are you doing out here?"

I didn't want to look at her, as if everything I did was written across my face, bare to be judged. My chin quivered, and I looked away from her. Bosco's panting reminded me we had taken off at a clip and he wasn't the fittest animal. When she called my name again, I got into her car.

"Are you crazy, walking down the street by yourself? What if Loring or the Puppeteer found you?" Kim moved to pull a U-turn.

"Stop!"

She stomped on the breaks. "What?"

"You have to drive me home."

"What do you—?"

"Please, Kim."

"It's not safe there."

I grabbed for the door handle and fumbled my escape since Bosco was on my lap. The locks shot into place.

"Sophie. Talk to me."

I spun and stared at her. "Unlock the door or let me go home."

Something in my eyes or maybe my deadpan demand had her nodding and heading back towards St. Catharines.

When we arrived at our building, Kim parked and helped get me and Bosco upstairs. Thankfully, she had an extra key for my apartment since I didn't have my purse. When she followed me inside, I didn't complain, but as if expecting me to kick her out, said, "I'm not leaving until I make sure you're okay."

We sat on my couch. I curled my knees to my chest and started crying. Donovan's anger and worry pushed at the connection for me to acknowledge. My refusal caused more anger I chose to ignore. Arms wrapped around me and had me jumping. Kim backed off and I apologized but asked not to be touched. She gave me space and was quiet a moment until I found some control.

"What happened?"

Another twenty seconds passed before I could make myself say it. "I slept with Donovan."

I expected a ranting outburst of denial and guilt-rending blame but was met with a stern unchanging gaze. "That little shit."

"No. I think it was me." I used my sleeve to dry my face. Kim remained impassive as I recounted the dream of us as Millicent and Isaac, working out the truth as I spoke. "They made me watch him die, but because of the connection, we both died. I can't put into words of how elated I was to open my eyes and find him alive." My voice cracked. "It felt so real. Like I watched people murder my husband for something they blamed me for. And then—I think—It just happened. I know it's a lame excuse. I don't know how else to explain it."

"It was a connection thing. That's not—"

"At some point, I had to know it was him. I didn't realize until I woke up, but it was Donovan and not Isaac. I had to know."

"What do you mean?"

"I remember thinking about where we were, knowing it wasn't the forest or the old place Isaac and Millicent built, but also still thinking he was my husband who somehow escaped death. Like the two lives overlapped."

"Were you touching him while you were sleeping? You could have read his soul without trying."

"Does it matter? Why did I pass out so close to him in the first place?"

"Sophie...."

I shook my head, tears falling, pissed at myself for putting us in the position to end up naked. I knew better. I knew Donovan would keep things cozy unless I pushed him away. I didn't force distance like I should have.

"This wasn't some planned hookup at a pay-per-hour hotel, Soph. By the sounds of it, you were trapped in an emotional loop with no one to intervene."

"Caine won't see it so black and white, especially since we're already fighting—about Donovan no less."

"Stop thinking about Caine for a sec. After the traumatic reliving of you and your husband's execution, you're entitled to think about yourself for a hot minute. As much as Donovan rides my patience, and as much as I'd like to put him in the hot seat for this, it sounds like he didn't plan it either. Which means he's probably freaking out and messing with your emotions even more. I don't know how it works but try and put all that aside and concentrate on how you feel about it."

"Taking off like a pack of zombies were after my spleen is probably a hint about how I feel."

Kim made a face at me and I sat back into the arm of the couch.

"You know what makes it worse? Being with Donovan, even if it was in the mind of Millicent and Isaac, was the best sex I've ever had." Kim's brows arched. "And I don't mean he hit the right spots—though he did and because of the connection knew exactly what I wanted like a reflexive vagina magician—but in an emotional sense. Being with him felt right and organic and fulfilling. And no, I don't need dick jokes right now, though you have permission to store them for later."

She smiled at my poor attempt at diversionary humour. "Best sex of your life and you feel guilty because—?"

"Caine! How could I do that to him?"

"I got that, but not guilt or regret for the simple fact that you had sex with Donovan?"

I groaned and dropped my head back onto the couch. "Was it really us having sex, though? Even if I subconsciously realized it was Donovan and not Isaac, he would've been blinded by his visions the whole time and thinking he was dicking a previous-life me instead of the present me. I wasn't even truly with him and it's still going to fuck up my life."

"Look Soph, all you can do is explain and take your lumps. If Caine forgives you, great. But you should figure out whether you want to be with Caine at all, because you didn't seem too positive about it before this happened."

"That had nothing to do with this!"

Kim gave me a face that said, "You take that tone with me and you'll regret it."

"Fuck. Sorry. Donovan's pissed and hurt and it's coming at me in waves."

"I bet. You're allowed to like the Donovan of today. And whether he saw you or past you last night, that guy is love-drunk over you."

"I'm not single. Well, I probably am now, but I wasn't. I'm not that cock-hungry chick who screws with men whether they deserve it or not because they have no self-worth and a love-hungry vagina. Caine doesn't deserve this." I gasped. "We didn't use protection. Shit. I'm definitely not a bare-back on the first go kind of chick either."

"Hmm. Well, if he had something contagious from some scag-ho, death by disintegration probably took care of that. Though babies are a different story."

"Oh, kill me now."

Kim suppressed a giggle. "Relax. You're on the pill. And if one slipped through, the kid will be absolutely gorgeous."

"That's not comforting."

She laughed a bit harder. While the situation was serious, I appreciated her attempt to make me laugh. What happened, happened. I couldn't change it now, but the full revelation of consequences had yet to be seen.

"We even talked about this in Diluculo," I said after a quiet moment.

"About babies?"

"God no. Donovan said he didn't want us getting together during some stupid emotional loop. He wanted it to be me and him making the decision to be a couple in this life. He doesn't deserve this either."

The phone rang. I jumped at the sound.

Kim checked the caller ID. "It's the front door." The phone kept ringing. "Should I get it?"

The phone rang again before I found the courage to nod.

20

BLIND-SIDED

"Hello?" Kim asked the caller.

"Let us in," I overheard my brother yell into the downstairs intercom.

"Now? He comes now?"

Kim shot me a sympathetic look then suggested I head to the bathroom to fix myself up while she let in whoever "us" was.

While I washed my face, I heard my brother and mom's voices down the hall. There wasn't much I could do besides press a cold cloth against the red blotches on my face. I didn't even have my makeup bag with me, so I salvaged what I could and got out of there.

When I entered the room, my mom looked at me, her smile disappearing. "What's wrong?"

"I'm fine. Shitty night."

Adam stretched out on the couch with Bosco and flipped through channels.

"Would you like some tea, Lu?" Kim asked my mom.

"Sure. Thank you."

I whispered a thank you to Kim. She nodded and gave us some space. The apartment was so small she only had to walk ten paces away, but I appreciated her hanging around. I didn't want my mom to stay too long and Kim and her positive attitude was always an effective conversation buffer.

"What's happening here?" Mom asked.

"What do you mean?"

"I called the bar yesterday, hoping to get a hold of you since you haven't returned any of my messages, and some woman told me you were on a leave of absence. Is that true?"

"Woman? Was her name Danielle?" I wondered if Joelly was still there and had a brief flash of her as a child being told she had to marry a stranger.

"I didn't ask."

I nodded. "Sorry I didn't call."

"Is it true?" she persisted.

"Yeah, unfortunately. No, I can't explain why. Yes, it pains me to my core to leave you out of the loop, but right now isn't the best time to talk about it."

"Is that guy here?" Adam asked.

"No," I said, trying not to spontaneously burst into tears.

"Is this a guy thing?" Mom asked. "You can't let it get to you like this."

"Mom, it's not—That's not why I'm not working." It was true, work had been stalled for a far greater reason and me being here was only putting myself and my family in danger. I needed to get a hold of Ranlyn.

"Crap," I heard Kim mutter.

My mom was going on about me needing to keep myself busy, when Kim brought in her tea and then handed me her cell.

"Sorry, I turned it off last night and just turned it back on."

Missed texts from Caine saying to tell me he's sorry and that he would see me back at the house. The time stamp was over an hour ago. Shit. He would be showing up at Donovan's, if he wasn't already there.

"Everything okay?" Mom asked and went ignored.

"What should I do?" I asked Kim with panic in my voice.

"Call Donovan?" She shrugged. "No, I'll call him." Kim took the phone and headed toward my bedroom.

My mom put her mug down on the table. "I don't like this. Is there something I can do? Is it a legal thing? You know I have contacts."

"Not a legal thing. Save the favours. Adam will probably need them."

"Eat it, hooker," he deadpanned, the majority of his attention still glued to the TV as old hockey game highlights paraded across the screen.

"Hey!" Mom shot at Adam, though it was what he normally said. I wasn't in the mood to throw it back at him. "Come out with it, Sophie. What is it?"

Pounding in my chest was evidence of Donovan's blood pressure rising. Frustration followed, along with regret, anger, and then shock.

"He's not answering," Kim said as she entered the room.

"Sophie—" My mother called as I tracked Donovan's emotions.

"He's there," I said.

Kim swore under her breath.

"Who? Who's where?" Mom's tone rose.

Donovan's shock reverted to anger. I sprung to my feet. "I have to—"

Pain spiked through the left side of my face, throwing my head to the side with a spray of blood. Mom shrieked. As soon as I tried to talk, another blow hit me in the same spot, laying me out and knocking the small coffee table over and sending my mom's tea in a hot splash across my arm and ribcage.

"What the fuck?" My brother was perched on the couch with Bosco.

"What's happening?" Mom rushed to help me up.

"Move!" I got to my feet in time to be thrown into a small shelf. Every movie, book, and knickknack crashed to the floor as the cheap wooden rack split into pieces. I was pulled up off my feet and back into the wall, my toes off the ground and held there before being thrown back down again.

"No!" I heard Kim yell.

"Move!" Adam argued.

"You can't call the police," Kim said.

"Adam—" I couldn't say more before a hoof to the gut left me sucking in air in gaping breaths. I writhed and pulled myself into the fetal position. Relief washed through me, Donovan's relief, and I knew it was over.

I looked up and found the horrified stares of my mom and brother. "I'm okay." Kim helped me get to all-fours, but vertigo and cramping stomach spasms stopped me from getting vertical.

"We have to get to the hospital." Mom grabbed her purse. "Adam, help her."

"What? No." He looked scared to touch me regardless of how hurt I was. Not that I blamed him. Facial bones were broken and leaking fluids—my nose judging by the faucet of blood spilling out of my face and back into my sinuses, though possibly a cheek bone or ocular bone and a couple of ribs—and he watched it all happen when no one touched me. He was justifiably terrified.

"Come on." My mom tried to grab my arm and pull me to my feet.

"No," I garbled through an aching jaw with lose teeth. "This is part of what I need to tell you."

Kim ran to my kitchen and returned with a hand towel. I moaned in pain as I swiped at my face to remove as much blood as I could, so she could see.

"Watch." Kim stood behind me between them and the door. I didn't think they would run, but they might.

I called upon my power and forced it to my face, so I would heal it the quickly for the purposes of my impromptu demonstration. They stood and watched as split skin knitted, blood clotted, bones reset, and all evidence of a beating disappeared. Fear in my mother's eyes had her putting enough distance between us to sting.

"No way," Adam said. "Nah—you didn't—"

I didn't respond to his reaction as I was more concerned with my mom's. Once I knew I was healed, I wiped the rest of blood the best I could, hoping my mom could look beyond the gore and shock of the moment to see me and what I did.

"You were attacked," Mom said in a weak voice.

"I know. Please, let me explain. I'm not—"

"Possessed?"

"No! I promise, I'm not."

After a moment of consideration, Mom sat on the couch with Adam, leaving no room for me as it was clear neither wanted me near them. I sat on the cedar chest. The knocked over coffee table and tea seeping into the carpet between us and took a moment to gather myself. Donovan's adrenaline was still pumping. I didn't know what he was doing, but he was in overdrive and made concentrating on the room around me exhausting.

I didn't know how much to tell them. Could I explain the phantom beating without starting from the beginning? I looked to Kim who sat on the floor and returned a compassionate glance of encouragement. Including the fact that Kim was the one who got the ball rolling by introducing me to Aunt Lacey's Coven would only have my mom thinking Kim corrupted me. Plus, Aunt Lacey's Coven wasn't the beginning. It started with my mom's bloodline, so I started there.

"Seriously?" Adam said when I finished. His lack of sarcasm surprised me.

"Olive is really a Witch?" Mom asked. "But she—mom said—"

"Your mother lied, and because of her own jealous bullshit, she had Olive institutionalized. Planned for her to die there and now hates the sight of me for being like Olive and so many others in our family."

"Guess a few things make more sense now," she said in a quiet voice.

"You think?" Adam's sarcasm was back. "Because I'm still stuck on the fact Witches are a thing."

Many other things were brought to light, but Mom became increasingly restless, contributing a nod and minimal comments to the conversation.

"So, what does all that have to do with what just happened, Soul Seer?" Adam asked.

I exhaled and pushed through an explanation. Some parts were harder than others to repeat. Mom let out a few "ohmygods". Once I unsuccessfully suppressed my tears through accidently mentioning Aunt Lacey's death—without explaining Diluculo—I moved right along to last night. I skipped the nitty-gritty details, though Adam added his brand of commentary to colour the story.

"Caine must have showed up at Donovan's, found out what happened, and what you saw was them fighting."

"I can't believe I'm even entertaining the possibility, but how dare they fight knowing it would hurt you?" Mom said.

"I know everything you do. I have no idea who started it, maybe it wasn't Caine who hit Donovan, though I doubt it considering we know Caine was headed there."

"Okay, so, let me get this straight." Adam sat forward in his seat. "Olive's party is at a family estate, that one day might be yours and has a complete magical Batman-style hideout in the attic, but you won't tell us how to get up there? My band's supposed to be playing at the party, with other Magics, but you won't tell us who they are either?"

"If you prove you want to join the Coven, then you'll meet them, but you have to be serious about it, not just curious about the cool shit people can do."

"How do I even know this is real? You could be screwing with us and we wouldn't know the difference?"

"Seeing me get my ass handed to me by an invisible force wasn't enough proof for you?"

Adam's expression showed it wasn't.

I huffed and erected a shield around him, it white so he couldn't see through it.

"Whoa." Adam knocked on the wall.

This was too much for my mom who shot up from her seat. "What'd you do?"

I altered the shield and made it see-through. "See, he's fine. Now it's easier to pin him down."

Mom reached out to touch the shield like it was going to grow arms and grab her, but when she got to it, Adam stood and mooned us. Before we could react, the door crashed open and the shield dropped. Donovan stumbled over Adam's shoes left in front of the door.

"You can't be here." Kim was first to her feet, stepping in front of him when he came in my direction.

"Babe, please. He came at me. I couldn't stop him."

"Shut up. Come here." I stepped over the debris on my floor and headed towards my computer room. My mom called after me. Kim responded in some way, but I couldn't hear what as I closed the door behind Donovan and me.

"I'm so sorry." Donovan moved in close and quick, his hands in my hair before I could stop him.

"Stop." I shrugged his hands away. "It's my fault, but I can't worry about that now. My mom and brother were here when the fight happened."

"Not fight. Caine attacked me. You know I can't lie to you. I did nothing to instigate him. I thought you would have called him, but then I could tell he didn't know what I was talking about. I trashed the place, so he knew something was up and he couldn't find you. Then, I accidently let slip what happened."

"I get it, I get it. Shit hit the fan quick. My concern is my mom and my brother who watched me get the shit kicked out of me by an invisible attacker and they know everything. Your Sect, the Ballard Coven, my grandmother, you, Caine. I can't even stress the importance of these next few minutes. Please, let me talk to them like this is normal so they don't see the shitshow it's become."

"I won't say anything." He attempted to move closer to me, but I couldn't take it.

"Please, Donovan." I raised my hands between us. "This is my fault and I'll deal, but please, I can't."

When I reached for the door handle he didn't move to make room for the door to open. "Promise you won't leave."

"This is my place."

He shook his head and lowered his voice. "Promise me you won't leave the Coven or take off like that again." The ache in his voice was palpable. "I couldn't stand it."

The desperation in his eyes was new to me. "I promise." I was smart enough to know my problems wouldn't disappear with an extended vacation and I had a lot of damage control to work out.

Kim was trying to keep Mom and Adam calm when we returned to the living room, the three of them standing amongst the wreckage of my apartment. When Adam saw us, he glared at Donovan, who didn't challenge him or call him out. Donovan didn't say anything but crossed his arms and managed to look small as I introduced him.

"Donovan assures me that, unfortunately, Caine's attack was unprovoked, but with cause."

"Sophie—" Mom said.

"No, it's not okay. Caine should have thought of me first, but even Donovan could attest to the fact that Caine's reaction was immediate and not premeditated."

"Temporary insanity?" Kim asked.

"Looked like it," Donovan responded.

"And you believe him?" My mom crossed her arms and glared at Donovan. "Why? Because his character is oh-so-noble?"

"No," I said as I felt the spur hit Donovan. "I told you, our connection makes it so that he can't lie to me."

She looked down and pursed her lips as if refraining from arguing.

"I get this is ridiculously absurd, mom, and not what you expected out of coming here today." I swallowed through a constricted throat. "It's my life now and I can't be okay without you in it."

Mom was quiet for half a minute and sat down. Every second was brutal.

"Can you stop?" she asked.

A flare of anger from Donovan crossed the connection, though he remained impassive.

"Technically, yes. I could stop and my power may dissipate, but this isn't a condition, mom. This is in my blood—and yours—reaching back generations. To be honest, I don't want to stop."

"Someone killed your mentor. You're in danger."

"It's not a choice to fight. I'm shackled to this life, but I won't be taken down without trying my all. I might not be as strong as some—"

"Yet," Donovan said.

"Yet." I looked at him in warning. "But I still have some tricks up my sleeve and I can heal."

"You did that?" Adam asked, as if he wasn't there to witness it himself.

"Yup. Healing, growing, bits of telepathy, Soul Seeing, and now Soul Reading. It's a progression, and right now it's mostly emotionally driven."

"You don't see anything around me, do you?" Mom asked.

When I shook my head no, the relief in my mom's expression was like a haymaker to the skull. She didn't want to be what I was. Ouch.

"You don't either," I told Adam before he could ask. "Though it may be waiting to be released."

"How was yours released?"

Adam's question opened a new can of worms. I insisted they didn't want to know, but my mom pushed, so I told her how Jack tried to kill me. "I would have died without the Coven."

"Without Donovan," Kim said, surprising both Donovan and myself. She rarely stuck up for him.

Donovan was quiet while the rest of everything I had skimmed over poured out of me. No point in stopping now. If she couldn't accept who I was, then at least I knew I gave it my all by giving her every piece of information I had and giving her a choice. By the end of it, I was exhausted.

"Hating this power would sour my soul," I said. "Grandma's is suffering. I know how that sounds, but I can't do that, and although this scares the crap out of you, this is me. I wish it didn't have to come out this way."

Mom nodded. I didn't know if it was an acknowledgement that she heard what I said or an understanding of who I was now, but it stung that she had to think more than twice whether or not we wanted the same things.

"And Serena?" Mom asked leaving the last item unfinished.

"She's in the newly reassembled Ballard Family Coven, but no, she doesn't have any power yet. No doubt she'll try anything to make sure she does."

"Nice one, broom rider," Adam said. "You'll rat out Serena, but won't tell us about anyone else?"

I ignored the semi-amusing slur. "Serena wants the entire world to know, so yes, I ratted because she wouldn't have cared. Before you say anything to anyone, you can't."

"Can't what?"

"Tell anyone. No offence. I love you both, but not the whole family knows. I wouldn't have told you at all if you weren't here to witness that throwdown," I said to Adam specifically, then looked to my mom. "Sorry for wanting to tell you. I was hoping to make it gradual."

"I wish you had."

I expected as much, but Donovan was fuming.

My mom stood up. "I think I will call it a day and take the afternoon off." When she stepped towards me and opened her arms for a hug, I wanted to collapse into them, though resisted and held on tight.

"I'm still me, mom." When we pulled apart she nodded, eyes glossy.

"I suppose I should thank you." Mom extended a cordial hand to Donovan to shake.

He shifted on his feet and she dropped her hand. "It's unfortunate we met this way, but my ability would allow me to learn things about you with a mere handshake. Unless you're comfortable parting with some personal history, it's probably best we leave it for now."

"Oh," Mom said. "I don't think I'll ever look at a handshake the same way."

Donovan gave a small smile as my mom called for Adam to get going.

Mom and Adam would still be attending the party at the estate, our parting words were to see each other at the estate soon, but it didn't seem like something they would be looking forward to. Why Olive hired Adam's band to play at the event was concerning. They were far from the conventional music option for that type of party.

Once the door was closed and locked behind them, I collapsed onto the couch in a heap of blended nerves.

Kim sat as well and put my legs on her lap. "Think she'll be okay?"

I shrugged.

"And now? You gonna call Caine? Sleep? Or do you two have more to talk about?" She didn't look at Donovan when she asked, and he didn't jump in to answer.

"Definitely not calling Caine. He needs time to cool off and figure out what he wants."

"You too," Kim reminded me—a tad embarrassing since Donovan stood looking around like he was afraid we would notice him and kick him out.

I held my best friend's meddling gaze. "I guess." Then I looked to Donovan. "Kim thinks I accidently read your soul, or mine."

He sat on the cedar chest, leaning back against the wall. "You know more than I do."

"Got a fresh glimpse at standard old-world fear at its best." I ran my hands over my face and through my hair, then filled him in on the details before I woke up and things got steamy. When I was done, he nodded. I tried not to analyze his shifting emotions too closely.

"I think I made you a Magic," I told him.

"Why?" Kim beat him to asking.

"Overwhelming guilt hit me in the end. Guilt for bringing Isaac into my world and how it led to his paying the ultimate price for loving me."

"That makes sense, too," Donovan said looking off in an unfocused stare.

"To whom?" Kim said. "You can help someone practice, but you can't make a Witch like the Queen knighting someone."

"Yes, you can." I sat forward. "There's a story in the Ballard Family Tome that states the Ballards became Magics when they were given the power as a gift in gratitude. An act of bravery against an evil Sorcerer to save the life of another Sorcerer. He gave my ancestor part of his power and made her the first Soul Seer. Eventually they married and carried on their gifts."

"Could be a family fable," Kim said.

"No," Donovan said. "I told you what I saw while we were dying. You showered us in immense energy and light and I remember feeling like it was such a gift. Maybe it was a memory of you giving me power. The visions I get don't come with a timestamp and we were in the forest so there wasn't any landmarks or clues to how long ago it was. They could be from anytime we were together, which means you could have repeated the spell in different lifetimes."

"I doubt it's easy to give power away. If I did do it, you think someone would've had to teach me and it felt like we didn't have a Coven or any allies who could have back then."

"Probably not. But maybe the Coven was too scared to help." Kim was right. Millicent and Isaac were careless. Innocent, but careless. A Coven may have thought they risked too much to save them.

"Though it's more interesting that you said a Sorcerer gave your family the power. Means you're a Sorcerer, not a Witch."

"What's the difference?"

"Some say Sorcerers are stronger," Donovan said, "but only another Sorcerer. If it's true, it's probably why your power can sometimes seem effortless. Sorcerers are known to run off their emotions. That type of absent inhibition and precarious strength are also why half of Tainted Magics are Sorcerers. Think of it like the difference between a mountain lion and a panther." He shrugged. "They're both felines, both strong and predatory animals, but at a deeper level, they are different."

"You can just say you have no clue," I said with a hint of a smile as Kim laughed.

He mirrored my smirk. "Either way, you're powerful, so I wouldn't worry about the distinction. Though if the Puppeteer is a relative, then it's possible they're a Sorcerer too."

"Wonderful."

"Speaking of your family, when's Olive's party?"

"Ugh." I deflated into the couch cushions. "If it wasn't so important, I wouldn't bother."

"Could be the fun you need," Kim said.

"I've seen movies and teen dramas. Parties always end in mayhem. It's like a neon sign for wasting money on a swank set-up."

"I'll leave the vat of pig's blood at home."

"Bring it. With that crowd, we may actually need it." My spellwork was still rather non-existent, but I didn't doubt pig's blood could be a useful ingredient.

Donovan sat back and crossed his legs at his ankles. The chill of an internal defence skittered down my spine before he said, "Is Caine in the Ballard Coven?" I sensed him steel himself for the answer.

"No. I have to thank my Uncle Lewis for that. Though Caine was supposed to attend the party." Kim gave me a sympathetic look. "It's fine. I'm used to going stag and once Serena knows what happened, she'll be pissed and wouldn't keep it to herself." I looked at Kim.

"Maybe don't give her the vat of pig's blood." I was happy to see her sympathy dissolve.

Donovan's steely defences remained. "Loring, his devotees, the Puppeteer, and probably Joelly, are still after us." The hesitation before he continued was brutally apparent. "Are you returning to my house?"

Good question, one that had even Kim looking at me in side-eyed discomfort.

21

DISAPPEARING ACT

Would I rather stick around in my shitty apartment in the sinkhole of the city to stand on principle and risk my life? Or could I handle slinking back to a place safeguarded by magic? I promised Donovan I wouldn't take off again. I didn't plan on taking off the first time, but I reacted impulsively. Justifiably impulsive, but still impulsive. It cut him deeper than I imagined it would. No doubt a deep-seated need to hold onto someone considering how much he has lost. As much as I wanted to dissect the reasoning behind this with a psychologically glittered comb, I pushed it aside and focused instead on avoiding the question.

"Sure, I'll return to the scene of the crime." Donovan smiled enough to hit me with a flash of dimples, his elation overshadowing his opinion on my perspective of what we did. "We have a Coven accessible to us there and I don't want to bring danger to Olive any more than I have to. Exposing her tonight is more than enough. At least until we get a hold of Ranlyn."

He nodded. I detected a passive inner sigh and then something else. As if the wheels were turning or fixating on his next move once

Ranlyn showed up, and what that might mean for our temporary living arrangement.

A hot shower helped distract me from thoughts about the previous night and the spectacle of my reveal to my mother. Hot water couldn't slough off the memories to put me in full party mode, but it helped—having Kim pick my evening wear, even more so. She chose my only dress that didn't look like a high school prom dress or fit for a funeral. A silk, little black dress with a low, square neckline, and inch-thick shoulder straps. The smooth fabric clung and landed above the knee. My one caveat was simple jewellery. Nya's ring, the triquetra necklace from Aunt Lacey, and sleek, calf-height black boots which laced up the back instead of the strappy sandals Kim had no hope in convincing me to wear.

Straightening my hair wasn't enough for Kim, so she sat me in front of an antique mirror and ten minutes later had my hair in a low, loose bun resting behind my left ear, with a swoopy bang. The designer-do was backed by Kim's assurance it was dance floor boogey and arm wrestling contest proof, though I insisted I wouldn't need to test it out.

I let Bosco out one last time before the hour drive to Dunnville. Leaving him behind wasn't an option and Olive insisted I bring him.

Introspection took over as I waited for Kim and Donovan to finish getting ready. Caine was still radio silent. I expected as much. Calling him was a mature option, but I couldn't both compartmentalize enough to get into party mode and face my problems like a big girl. I didn't let Kim take an hour to get me ready to only cry off my makeup. Plus, I needed to find that place of resilience again. The cozy and empty home where functioning is possible, yet still allows for an amiable outward appearance. Me and that place knew each other well and I called upon it now to get me through.

Donovan's resistance to my tactic hit me before I fell comfortably in that place. Maybe he hated it, maybe he feared it, but he didn't fight it like he could have.

Kim emerged in a knee-length, deep-navy number reminiscent of a 1940s swing dress, belted with a white ribbon, accentuating the best parts of her figure. From the peek-a-boo manicured toes to the high bun with silk flower, Kim radiated confidence. True confidence, unlike my carefully constructed semblance of what passed for confidence. She didn't dress up like a little girl in her mother's clothing, she owned that shit and commanded attention. I was instantly proud and jealous.

Restrained desire hit me. It threw me off as I was about seventy-five percent certain it wasn't directed from me to Kim. Movement in my periphery caught my eye and Kim and I turned to see Donovan standing in the living room, hands in the pockets of his black dress pants. His black single-button suit jacket was left open, his black tie over white shirt combo was simple and gorgeous. Far from his daily forte, but with his hair left in his usual controlled disarray he retained his air of cockiness like a badge of honour.

"Well shit, kid," Kim said. "Are those cufflinks? Could've beat me with a stick of butter before I'd believed you were capable of looking like a gentleman."

"Wow. A genuine compliment. You're looking good yourself." He looked at me. "And you. As always."

My tongue may have flopped out of my mouth like a German shepherd if I tried to speak. My restraint and contained demeanour were slipping.

"All right, you two. None of that." Kim handed me a teal scarf for me to wear as a shawl. She held a white one for herself. "You'll wrinkle your suit and there's no time for stain removal."

Donovan pulled a face. Kim smirked at him while I did everything to shake off the change in mood. So focused, I forget Bosco and had to turn back for him, then noticed he was in his best-dressed as well—in what looked like a satin collar, with a dapper black and white polka-dotted bowtie.

"I had extra," Donovan said and made his way out to the car.

———

The sun was already starting to hide behind the horizon and would be gone by the time we reached Dunnville. Kim insisted on sitting in the back, stating she would sit with Bosco so he wouldn't get fur all over my black dress. Hers was apparently more pug proof, though I sensed her meddling again and assumed she wanted me to sit in the passenger's seat of Donovan's car. Whatever sparked her sudden interest in Team Donovan, she picked the worst time to jump on the bandwagon.

Donovan's music pumped at conversation level while allowing us to sit quietly as he drove at high speeds around thin one-car bridges and shoulder-free semi-paved roads. The fight against reflection came in waves of numb success and overwhelming failure. An indulgent memory of being in Aunt Lacey's backyard with Donovan was a reminder at how the impulse to be with him felt painfully right. I shut down the memory as quick as a social media creeper when my body responded—it was a treasonous, dick-hungry body that I wished would make up its mind. Other thoughts broke through my resistance. Each would capture an ignored internal reaction from Donovan, and a loss of time. No doubt he drove on autopilot when this occurred, so I did my best to focus so he wouldn't wrap his Z24 around a tree and burn us to death in our best-dressed.

Sudden light from behind us lit up the entire car, someone relying on their high beams to get them through the country roads.

"Asshole." I squinted as the light bounced off the front windshield into my eyes.

"What'd I do now?" Donovan looked from the road to me with a stitch in his brow.

"Not you, the dickhead driver behind us with a fetish for blinding us." I looked behind us, then spun back in my seat as it was too bright to withstand.

"Right now?" Kim asked, craning her neck to see.

"No. I've got delayed complaint syndrome."

"Babe, there's no—"

Kim screamed. Donovan swore. The car swerved, tossing my body into the door with a jarring smack. I looked back at Kim still screaming and saw a man with eyes like a husky, a bald head, and thin-bridged nose. Bosco was squished in Kim's arms as she tried to get as far from the man as possible while trapped in her seatbelt.

Donovan slammed on the brakes. The tires squealed and filled the air with the stink of burnt rubber. Before the car came to a complete stop, the husky-eyed hitchhiker slapped a long, thin-fingered hand down on Donovan's shoulder and both men disappeared. The driverless car barrelled toward the ditch.

"Emergency brake!" Kim yelled.

I grabbed the emergency brake with both hands and wretched it back, digging my booted feet into the floor. Kim sprung forward, somehow getting out of her seat belt in time to grab the wheel and keep us on the road. The car finally came to a complete stop.

"He okay?" I looked back to Kim holding Bosco again. He was panting, and no doubt confused, but otherwise fine.

"Where'd he go?" Kim asked, green-blue eyes wide with shock looking out the windows.

An adrenaline fuelled heartbeat hammered my chest. Not only from the near miss as the Z24's engine popped and hissed, but the panicked beats were borrowed from Donovan. "He's scared." Pressure squeezed all around my wrists to the point of pain and throbbing to my fingertips. I hissed and rubbed them together. "Now he's pissed."

"What's happening?"

"His wrists are being bound."

The longer we stayed in the car, the longer we were sitting ducks if Husky-Eyes returned. Slipping over into the driver's seat in a dress meant an awkward pull, clench, and wriggle with a helping of scrambled obscenities. Kim did her own shuffle and squeeze to get through the seats into the passenger seat, clasping Bosco to her chest. I didn't bother trying to find the seat adjuster or put on my belt. Donovan's adrenaline had me hyper-focused and more in control than I would have thought possible.

We reached the estate in less than ten minutes. Cars lined the street, eager partygoers arriving before the invitation's arrival time, forcing me to drive onto the grass. We slid, the tires grinding up gravel, dirt, and grass. I could fix it later. Right now, I needed to get inside.

A pitch in anger and something else—resentment? —had me dizzy and grabbing for Kim's arm to steady me. I still wasn't right when we got to the arched front doors and found a Magic playing the role of Bouncer. His muscled shoulders barely squeezed into his black on black suit, his posture military straight, clipboard in hand. Both our names were on the list. He lifted his brow and gave a friendlier nod then he had to those in front of us as if recognizing us as one of his kind and sharing a greater respect.

We entered the estate and stopped dead, captured by the scene in front of us. Thinking back to our first visit to the estate, lost in the dark with inadequate light to guide us through dust-covered spider-webbed rooms, the newfound life was extraordinary. Trill laughter and conversation gave a lift to the ambiance as caterers meandered the floors with serving trays of hors d'oeuvres and beautiful crystal glasses of red or white wine and something golden and bubbly. The liveliness of Olive's guests in their best dressed on their best behaviour—and in a genuinely good mood—revitalized the spirit of the estate as if the walls themselves were bloated with newfound joy.

Dizziness and pressure in my chest from Donovan's panic continued and was made worse when the sensation of the estate personally welcoming me had me kneeling before I passed out. The pretense of fretting over something with Bosco covered my near collapse. While the estate's exciting greeting evoked the warmth of my own magic in my belly, Donovan's panic eased as if the sensation were a balm for both of us. I took in a deep breath and managed to stand.

Enamoured by the estate's beauty all over again, I was overwhelmed by the opulence. The large oval chandelier glistened, the fireplace burned with something mixed in the hearth to create an earthly aroma. I forced a steady inhale and exhale as my cheeks still burned with the rise in blood pressure, hoping whatever that scent was would get into my lungs, overtake me, and give me strength.

"It's incredible," Kim said, her tone one of awe.

"Yes. It is."

I gasped and clawed for Kim's arm.

"What's wrong?"

As I had panned over the splendor of the Ballard Family Estate, everything disappeared. Heat gathered in front of my nose and mouth, stifling my breath as if I was wearing a face mask.

"I can't see." I tried to whisper. "They hooded him."

Nightmares of Isaac and Millicent suffering the same hooded fear flooded me. As within the dream or reading of mine or Donovan's soul, I was overcome by Donovan's terror, rage, and concern for me. He couldn't see, couldn't move. As his anxiety rose so did the ache of my wrists and now ankles. Sweat broke through my brow and between my shoulder blades.

"Hello!" came a boisterous greeting I recognized as Marilyn, a lifelong friend of my mom's. Loved liked a true-blooded aunt all my life, Marilyn's unforgettable gravel of a jazz singer was lubricated with something alcoholic, amplifying her natural exuberance. Arms grabbed hold of me and pulled me in. Marilyn's black natural curls tickled my cheek. I screwed in a desperate smile and hugged her back, then consciously adjusted my line of sight to hopefully match Marilyn's five-foot-three. Elated when she noticed Bosco in his bowtie, she greeted him as enthusiastically as she had us.

Rescuing me from what would have been a long-winded bout of, "How 'ya doing?" "How's work?" "Did I hear you have a man?" "Are you thinking of school again?" and every other conceivable question Marilyn could ask to bring us up to date on current life events was difficult yet accomplished by Kim who whisked me off to show her to the washroom with promises to find Marilyn again later.

Kim led me by the elbow, taking Bosco's leash, and navigating around bodies, furniture, and hired staff. We rushed into a first-floor powder room where Kim left me for safekeeping while she went to find Olive. I drank cold water from the tap, then sat on the closed toilet lid hyperaware of Donovan's ebbing emotions. Now I knew how it felt to be away from him when he needed me. He had been through it with me during a few incidences, and I was mostly annoyed at the time. Never again.

Bosco whined and rubbed against my leather-covered legs. I stroked his back and tried to concentrate on the softness of his fur, his slowed breathing, and use those to mimic a sense of calm within myself, though my eyesight was still a blank sheet of darkness.

Alcohol-heavy bladders brought knocks to the door by a handful of people, some impatiently pacing. I imagined a line forming and dreaded what they assumed was going on inside. This wasn't the only washroom in the house, so I was annoyed they insisted on waiting at all.

I refocused on Bosco, who was now sitting on my feet, lounging against me. I fought to help Donovan. Awareness and the space to find calmness was on my side. Deep, rhythmic breathing and stroking Bosco's back helped ground myself and Donovan with help of a simple mantra. *I am not in danger. I am safe and unharmed.* The plan was to trick my body and Donovan's into believing the threat was clear. If I could manage that for him, then it was possible his rational mind could reengage and help him escape whatever he was facing.

After a few minutes of dedicated focus, I opened my eyes. Mussed guest hand towels hung on a brass towel rack near the sink. Fresh soap and a bottle of hand sanitizer were on the counter. I hoped Donovan realized what I was attempting to achieve and sensed my relief at having my sight back. I was somewhere safe trying to help him.

Having no other reason for holding up the wine-soaked bladders lined up outside the door, I exited, receiving a slew of colourful under-her-breath comments from Kassie, a cousin I didn't like much anyway.

"Are you okay?" Kim asked in a high-pitched voice pulling Olive behind her.

"Firefly?" Olive looked me over. "You appear perfectly well to me. I little piqued, but okay. Absolutely beautiful in fact." She looked at Kim. "I thought you said—"

"I fought through it for now. You're looking magnificent as well, Olive." My aunt's swoop neck dress with pale colours in a simple abstract design, paired with a matching jacket and a string of pearls was far from her daily wear in the institution. It was the first time since her release that she had cause to dress up, and she was radiant.

"Can we talk elsewhere?" I looked up to imply the attic. "Too many ears."

The purpose of the party was for the family to equate themselves with the unknown Ballard Family Estate, so there were plenty of people exploring upstairs rooms, making it difficult to access the attic unnoticed. Since the process took some finesse, we would only do it once. I protested with a quick recount of the trouble Donovan was in, but we needed a collective mind to fix the issue anyway, so I gathered the Ballard Family Coven members. We needed to have the meeting, and keep suspicions low, as Kim continued to try and get a hold of the Elders by phone.

No surprise. She hit the answering machine every time.

Olive and my Soul Seeing caught the glow of potential family with minute powers unknown to them. With Kim's lacking sight, I pointed out a few and Kim confidently pressed through the crowds to reel them in, telling them Olive needed them ASAP. Once I found Serena with her mom and brother, I was ecstatic to go from room to room to seek them out.

In the original meeting, we agreed Mason was too young to recruit without his parents' consultation, so he was left to play with the other kids, using olives on their fingers and trying to touch each other's faces. This decision was an easy one when I saw how happy he was, then transposed Caine's little cousin Andy's sullen pout while wrestling with a power he was too young to comprehend.

The kid deserved to be a kid.

Ten potentials stood or paced in the upstairs hallway. Two had already voted a big fat no—Gloria and Iris—though came anyway, and eight others looked to each other in confusion of what they were pulled away from the party for. While Gloria and Iris grumbled beneath their breath about interrupting the fun for such "trivial matters", I looked about the group at the faces I didn't expect.

Not everyone attended the family reunion where the first glimpses of hopefuls were surveyed, but this event had drawn a larger crowd. Now added to the few I anticipated—Gloria, Iris, Lewis, Priscilla, Serena, Ronny, and Dwayne, who was being torn from the open bar—were a mix of highly interesting candidates.

An older couple I recognized from pictures Olive kept at The Royal must have been Leon and Tapi—survivors of the old Coven. Leon was a short man in his sixties with a bad comb-over he'd slicked for the occasion, wearing an older style brown suit and polyester dress shirt. Tapi's hair was uncoloured, streaked white with age, eyes bright and excited behind her thick glasses, relics from a past generation. The dress she wore fell loosely around her thin features and was peppered with a small flowered design on a polyester burgundy background. Both looked like they were straight from a seventy's hippie protest. Add some painted peace signs to their cheeks and they were set to go.

I was willing to bet they were the nicest people of the bunch. Something about them radiated kindness. You would think Tapi shared the Ballard DNA, with her reedy form that towered her husband, but it was Leon. Despite the fact they were related by marriage alone must have not been their only thing in common, for Leon and Tapi shared the same enlightened Soul Colour. Sunny yellow. A few moments of mentally chewing over the Soul Colours list reminded me they were Transmutators. The possibilities of what type of animals both could conceivably turn into ran through my mind. As far as I knew, it could be anything.

Another hopeful consisted of the not-so-loved cousin Kassie. She and I never had direct issues, though never found a reason to like each other. Kassie had long, professionally-streaked hair, with an ass and hips that fit too perfectly in her off the shoulder evening dress. She was in her late twenties, and I got the idea that her life didn't turn out the way she had dreamed and was now pissed at the world she thought would open their thighs with glee at the prospect of her cozying up to it. Hollywood was her goal, but the Canadian border and few local commercials was the extent of her celebrity.

Shannon, however, was a beloved cousin and the daughter of the hilarious Uncle Roger. Shannon's blue eyes were striking against her dark hair, with a curvy body and a sense of humour like her fathers. She was the type of woman of the mid-thirties that fit in anywhere, because she didn't look at people to size them up, like Kassie. She fit into a crowd by being a part of it instead of thinking she was above it, and I was a tickled pink unicorn to see her soul glow peek out like a curious groundhog.

The last two were Kevin and Chelsea. Brother and sister, Chelsea was older by two years and shorter. Not short in comparison to my five-foot-ten, but short as in a whole foot shy of my height. She shared Shannon's dark hair and blue eyes, though she had a mane of flowing curls past her shoulders, looking far too much to hold up on top of her petit frame. Kevin shared my dark hair and eyes and had something his sister somewhat lacked. Charisma. Kevin was in school for Radio Broadcasting and was excelling, which came as no surprise to those who knew him.

Wrangling the last member of the group, Dwayne, in his dress cowboy hat and matching outfit—down to the boots—included prying a drink from his hand and a reminder it was an open bar.

"I've already been up here," he complained, confused as to why Serena muscled him up the stairs.

"Not where we're going, cowpoke," she added without elaboration. A huge feat considering her ear-to-ear smile.

I gave Olive an encouraging smirk that masked my impatience at the time it took to amass the group. She wrapped her arm around my elbow and set to begin. Unfortunately, it didn't solve the problem of how we were going to get into the attic left unseen, as kids and their parents still roamed the upper floor.

"Seedlings." Gloria huffed and turned her back to the crowd. "As bad as the Blind," Iris added to her sister's supplementary complaints.

I heard a clipped murmur escape her lips before she turned back to us, adjusting her large maroon hat, fit with lively embellishments including feathers and some type of nestled bird. Garish and ridiculous, but not compared to her sister's as it rivalled for the title of superfluous. The two were an example of dramatic pretence and bitter drama and, if Donovan wasn't in danger, I would find them entertaining. They too wanted this over and done with. A plan I could get behind.

Gloria's pursed lips and bored expression, as well as what she said, confused the newcomers. She surprised me by rolling her eyes. "The Blind see the door as it is and nothing else, including any noise we make. Even from him." She looked down at Bosco. "Proceed."

For most present, Gloria was showing her age. Her comment was left unaddressed, except for a couple snickers from Ronny. Those in-the-know understood Gloria had fixed a spell much like the one Donovan used outside Aunt Lacey's during the Shield of Aegis spell. I didn't know how long the spell would last and tried to imprint on my mind to suggest to Olive we add a permanent fixture or boundary spell for members accessing the attic.

I stopped Olive from proceeding and thought to include a rejection clause. "You're about to be shown a part of the house others won't be lucky enough to see. This family comes with some secrets that we're all a part of for a reason that will be explained, but the point is, if you want to be in-the-know, then you don't talk about it with anyone else, even your immediate family."

"Is this like Fight Club?" Kevin mocked. "'Cuz I can kick all-y'all's asses."

"Yes, Kev. It's like Fight Club. You first in the pit? Because you can't take me."

Kevin laughed and anyone over sixty had no idea what we were talking about.

22

ACCUSED

Olive called upon Lewis to access the attic instead of climbing onto the sturdy chair herself while in her beautiful dress. He pulled out the corners of the door frame, turned them, and tucked them in tight, unlocking the attic to the tune of clicks and clanks within the wall and watched as the door slid itself into the pocket of the wall.

I spotted my mom and her sister—Serena's mom—Karen, both stopped in the hall, scanned the people wandering about. I assumed they were looking for Serena and me, or possibly Olive, but the spell Gloria performed hid us from them. They gave up and returned downstairs as the potentials were herded into the small sewing room. Tension grew. In Kevin's case, he got punchy. In Kassie's, she got mouthy, her tone lacking the humour as she made no attempt to mask her opinions.

With the frustration and increase in body heat in the claustrophobic room, my vision began to spot and wane with the throb of my wrists and dull ache I was becoming accustomed to. I was losing it again. I needed to regain composure since Donovan didn't have the luxury. I tried to tell Olive to hurry up, but the room blinked away and when I could see again she was mid-explanation of the antique sewing machine working as a combination lock.

As their attentions were glued to Olive, Kim helped calm me by grabbing Bosco and pushing to the outskirts of the group to gain some room in a corner, stealing deep breaths clogged with the collective cologne and perfume. We caught Serena's confused attention, but Kim waved her off for now. She would know soon enough.

I climbed the metal winding stairs by feel alone, as my unreliable sight blinked in and out like someone fingering a dimmer switch inside my brain. My cheeks and ears were on fire. Kim was behind me, not that she could catch me with Bosco in her arms if I fainted, though the thought of killing him if I fell kept me moving forward. Fresh air filtered through my sinuses and I knew I reached the top of the stairs without being able to see any of it, but I tripped, and someone caught my arm before I polished the floor with my sweaty face.

"Can I speak with you a moment, Olive?" I spoke over the crowd, cutting my great-aunt off mid-sentence as she introduced the family to the attic.

Lewis took over and Olive was at my side, her soft hands grasping for mine.

"Firefly?" Olive said.

"What's going on?" Serena asked.

"I can't see." I braced my hands on my knees as a wave of nausea hit me. "Donovan was taken." The panic I shoved aside was now drowning me, as tears threatened to spill over. Acting tough when the blubbering started wasn't an option, so I refused to let it happen.

Kim skimmed the details of the husky-eyed man who appeared and then disappeared in the Z24, taking Donovan along with him.

"He's hooded. That's why I can't see."

"And bound by the looks of it," Kim added and held out my arm.

They must have looked bad because although I couldn't see her expression, Olive and Serena caught their breath loud enough to paint a grim picture. In trying to keep my focus on rounding up the recruits, I avoided thinking of what tortures Donovan faced as compared to his past as Isaac. I had forgotten to check myself and wondered if the colour only ravished my skin when Donovan took me over, and then disappeared when I regained control of myself.

"Could the guy have been a Teleporter?" Kim asked.

"Possibly," Olive said. "Though they're known as Apporters or Apportation for the act itself."

"I thought the term Apport referred to the movement of ghosts?"

"Think of what it must have looked like to some." Olive rubbed at my wrist, the movement and pressure soothing.

"So, a Teleporter or Apporter or whatever the bald taint-picker is called, has Donovan. How do we figure out where he took him?" Sweat trickled down the back of my neck. I tried to pace it off and shake out my hands, but I was too unsteady and had to sit down. Judging by the way it hugged my ass, it was Olive's desk chair.

She placed an icy hand on my cheek and then my forehead. The coolness had me giving a grateful moan as I pressed into her palm. "You're burning up, Firefly. The potency of this connection is astonishing."

"Let me try and fight it again. Go. Help Lewis. Most are going to need convincing and I can't help like this."

Lewis was a talker. Always a wizard with words, this is what made him such a good Mayor. He was a man of the people, understanding the way they think, their expectations, and a knack for twisting a person's perspective to match his own. None of this related to his otherworldly gifts. It was all Lewis, and many of the potentials were quiet, so I assumed he or the attic itself captivated their attention.

A good ten minutes of Lewis talking, and the potentials gawking, was allotted before Lewis called for them to join him in the research and meditation area where he unveiled the full extent of the Ballard Family secret.

"Nah. No way, man," I recognized my cousin Ronny, the eighteen-year-old skater kid. I wondered if he had switched out his DCs with dress shoes for once.

"You expect us to believe that?" Kevin asked with a humourless laugh as I heard shuffling from the others as if they were getting up in a threat to leave.

"Look around you," Lewis said. "Peruse the family tome. It outlines the Ballards' history."

While Lewis tried to convince the inconvincible without scaring them, I struggled to balance myself and help Donovan.

Kim started fanning something in front of me to create a cool breeze. "Think of you and Donovan having sex."

"What?" Serena gasped. "You fucked that asshole?"

"If you were after details, you could have asked, Kim."

"Hmmm, nice to know," she said. "I meant that maybe thinking of you and Donovan having the best sex of your life could help both of you. Find a happy place so you can control this."

"I can't believe you fucked him and didn't tell me," Serena complained.

"Relax, Serena. It wasn't a planned hotel stay and a romp in a heart-shaped soaker tub surrounded by candles and a foreshadowing UTI. It just happened. I figured my mom or Adam would've told you."

Serena gasped louder. "They knew before me?"

I ignored her. "Envisioning nakedness will only compound the problem considering I'm sweatin' balls already."

"Use the concept, then. Something happy about you two or Millicent and Isaac."

"Right." Serena's tone was weighed with snark. "Think of something other than the fact you've messed up something perfect with Caine by screwing that dickhole. And who are Millicent and Isaac?"

"Again, you don't know what happened. And you can't physically screw a dick hole. Not with my parts."

"Well, apparently you can, dickhole screwer," Serena shot back.

"Okay children. Concentrate, Soph." Kim continued to fan me, but it didn't amount to much.

I was raw and drawn in too easily. Serena was fanning the flames instead of dousing them and the nausea was building, constricting my throat.

With my face in my hands and the ground beneath my boots feeling like a good place to stretch out, I was moments from puking or passing out. *Where is he?* I thought desperately. In the hands of some Apporter, and here I was, exchanging schoolyard spitballs amid a recruitment campaign. *Why am I trying to convince people to get themselves into this hot mess?*

Thinking about sex of any capacity was an instant fail. As splendid a specimen as he was, the flashes of tight, sweat-slick skin only raised my blood pressure, adding to my headiness. I settled on the man himself, anything about Donovan in times when he wasn't either acting like an ass, riddled with pain, or pissed off.

The first time we met.

The first time he kissed me.

The understanding we shared in Diluculo.

Every time he insisted on calling me 'babe'.

Goosebumps raised on my arms as my body registered the pulse of air Kim made by fanning me. Happy with the result, I pushed ahead with the tactic.

The connected past we shared that contributed to our current mess.

The full smile and dimples I was gifted while few others were.

Isaac and Millicent's marriage: so simple, so full of love and genuine devotion.

I wished I could steal that memory and recreate the ambience whenever I needed my own personal wonder drug. Before Isaac and Millicent lost their heads, they lived a life worth emulating. They enjoyed each other, their secrets, their craft. They wanted nothing more than to have a life of happiness. The thought of such ease and contentment melted my tension. So much so that I swallowed without the sense of choking.

I straightened in Olive's chair and opened my eyes to test out the result. Finally. Soft lighting glinted off the plank wood flooring and sparkled in Kim's eyeshadow as she strained to keep fanning me.

"You can stop that."

"Oh, good." Kim plunked a large book on the table with a loud thud and massaged her arms. The sound reverberated off the attic walls gaining the attention of the rest of the group. "She can see again."

I stood without wanting to pass out and gained the weight of mixed expressions from the Ballard Coven potentials. Instead of explaining what Kim referred to, I got to the point Lewis and Olive were trying to make. "Look, the history and the power of the Ballards' bloodline is real, whether you want any part of it or not. Foster the history and you'll become what you were meant to be. You'll access a history that was hidden from you. Your life will change. Not all for the better, depending on a few things, but you're all already displaying soul glows which means you already have released power in its infancy."

"I've never felt a damn thing." Kassie's scowl was deep as she stood like she couldn't get out of the room fast enough. She muttered something under her breath I didn't quite catch. The indignant smirk she gave had me on the edge of my patience.

Fine. No more hand-holding.

I evoked my power, forcing it out of me and into the open space. Experienced Magics present knew what I was doing, but as I amped up the intensity, I watched the group of potentials and tracked their reactions. Most looked around the room, shifted with suspicious glares, adjusted their clothing, scratched an invisible itch. They didn't know what the sensation was, but they felt it.

"No way in hell can you deny what you feel right now. Others with abilities, like this family, including all of you, can feel it when another Magic uses their power. What you're feeling is a taste of my power. If you don't want to fulfill your potential, that's your business. Pretending you have no idea what I'm talking about is insulting. Be a deluded asshole if you want, but don't be a lying asshole."

"You're some super special magic chick and all you can do is make us uncomfortable?" Ronny said. "I've had jock itch with more force."

Serena stepped forward. "Has your jock itch disintegrated people?"

Kassie crossed her arms and screwed up her pretty little nose. "Disintegrated? Right."

"In my defence, that was an accident. But they were trying to kill me and my friends."

"Present friend included," Kim said.

Kassie rolled her eyes.

I approached Ronny, who opted to wear dark jeans and a t-shirt tux and forgo a brush through his long, light-brown hair. "Our power isn't all gnarly." I grabbed his forearm.

"Hey!" He tried to pull away. I gripped him tighter and ignored his protests. He gasped. His shoulders shot up towards his ears. I watched as my power pushed its way through him and healed all the swollen and red zits on his teenage mug. The picking scars from previous years of raging hormones would be a lifelong reminder, but for tonight, he was whitehead free.

"Holy shit." Kevin spun Ronny toward him and took a hard look.

"What? What'd you do?" Ronny was freaked until Chelsea took out a makeup mirror from her purse. Then he was stoked and couldn't stop touching his face. "Wicked show and tell. I'm sold."

"Now hold up," Dwayne said. "You do whatever you did to the kid, but you can't heal your wrists? Something's not right."

"Boyfriend get a little too kinky?" Kassie said with so much snark, I would be proud if it wasn't directed at myself.

The angry red chafing around my wrists brought me back to thoughts of Donovan. "I could heal them, but with the cause still an issue, it would come right back."

When I withdrew into thoughts of what Donovan might be going through, essentially bowing out of the sales pitch, Lewis stepped back in and took up the cause. Instead of inviting them to read the Ballard Family Tome, he paraphrased the story of our family genesis as he learned it recently. Then he spoke directly to Dwayne regarding Mason. "We wouldn't include him without your say so, but we thought you should know."

Dwayne was as sober as a cow and looking like he might topple over. Whether he believed passing on the power to his son was a gift or a curse, he landed on consulting his wife before deciding on what to do about it. He was then reminded about the family secret and the drive to keep it that way. Expecting him not to tell his wife was naïve, so I volunteered to make a demonstration for her if she insisted, but she wouldn't be permitted into the attic and neither would Dwayne unless they chose to join the Coven.

An ache in my ankle had me restless and rubbing at the unmistakable rope impressions in my wrist. Was it getting worse? Tightness clamped around my skin as if wherever Donovan was, he was struggling to escape. Shitpickles. Did he feel me using my power and think I was in trouble? I tried to send the impression of safety across the connection, but he fought harder.

The urgency to flee became overwhelming. The raw skin broke open and dripped with blood. Shock stole my focus as I stood staring at my shaking arms and seeping, bloodied wrists. Was this it? Was whatever the bald man kidnapped Donovan for happening? Fear spilled into the well of Donovan's fury and overboiled. A scream type growl was muffled behind my gritted teeth, loud enough to tip off Kim and Serena, their mirroring gasps and echo of worry. They spoke, but no words made it to my ears, nor did the moment they helped me sit. I was standing and then I wasn't.

Bosco looked up at me from my feet, Kim still had a hold of his leash. I couldn't reach down to comfort him. I didn't know what to do and none of this was helping.

Clanking metal in rapid succession quieted the group and pulled a fraction of my attention away from siphoning emotions from someone I couldn't see. A few silent seconds passed before others had entered the attic via the metal winding staircase. Lewis rushed to intercept whoever it may be from seeing the attic, though not fast enough.

"Leave here this inst—" Lewis's efforts were cut short.

Thinking another threat had presented itself, I stood and turned to protect myself, finding a severe expression from someone only Kim and I had the somewhat pleasure of meeting before. A lifted hand was what stopped Lewis. A simple action with instant results. Magic was responsible, but anyone looking at the person who walked in would feel obligated.

Hinapouri's tattooed face and exotic presence quieted my great-uncle. She led the Elders into the attic as if she had been given express permission to come as she pleased. She had dark cascading hair that fell to her waist, tanned animal-hide boots, and an outfit that could only be described as some type of handmade armour—her Maori warrior tattoos covered the left side of her body and spanned across her exposed stomach. The epitome of intimidation.

The expression surveying the attic was one on a mission, and the dually imposing figure coming into the room behind her, Miklos, with his dark Hungarian features, equalled her in its imposing nature, stern and expectant. Of what, we didn't know, but I was elated when Ranlyn and Veata followed with friendlier auras.

More complaints from the Ballards arose when Lewis was cut short. Ranlyn spoke up to quiet them, gaining Hinapouri's baneful glare, but she conceded the lead.

A tactic no doubt discussed beforehand.

"Our apologies for interrupting your meeting." Genuine remorse shone through the dirty-blond Elder's green eyes as they met mine. "Our business here will hopefully move along smoothly."

"If the princess will allow." The quiet sardonic comment came from Veata. Her wiry white hair fell around her as her clouded eyes scanned her surroundings. I loved her honesty. She looked unimpressed at being dragged along and ruining her plans.

Was this Hinapouri's idea?

"What business?" I asked Ranlyn.

He took a few cautious strides towards me and reached out to tenderly hold my forearms to checkout my wrists. His brows creased with sympathy, followed by gasps from a few of my family members as they hadn't seen my arms.

"You know where he is." I ripped my arms out of his hands, not without the consequence of more pain, but I couldn't stand him touching me once I realized his look of sympathy was actually one of guilt.

Before he could answer, we heard pounding. More like someone was booting the entrance to the attic with steel toes. After some more pounding, I ran down the steps hoping to see Donovan on the other side and knowing this was stupid. My mom's voice demanding someone let her in solidified my disappointment.

For fuck's sake. All I could think of was the attention Mom must have been drawing. Over a hundred or so people milled around the estate and could be behind her waiting and wondering what she was doing.

"Out of the way, Firefly."

This wasn't the gentle usage of the nickname I came to love. Gloria pushed past me, knocking me aside in my short-heeled boots. Gloria adjusted her hat back and lifted a hand to the door. After whispering a low incantation, the wooden door of the sewing room lost its wood facing and ran clear as glass. I swore as I became face to face with my mom and my brother, Adam the one offering his heavy boot.

"You and that mouth, girl," Gloria said, then speaking low with thin lips covered in soft pink lipstick. Gloria then forced me into a quick decision, as she recast the spell concealing Adam and Lu from the eyes of anyone that may have been passing in the hallway: To decide if they should be given access to the attic. I hesitated but opened the door.

Mom and Adam knew about the family's power, now this would be the test of whether they could handle it. Gloria gave a disagreeable grunt, then proceeded upstairs to the others while I closed the door and stopped them from speaking.

"Something big is going down up there. You'll see the potentials for the Ballard Coven and the Elders from my Mother Coven. You both need to shut your mouths and listen. Don't say a goddamned thing. I'm not fucking around, and neither are they."

Mom tried grabbing at my bloodied arms and asking what happened. I waved her off and repeated myself. Without offering further explanation, I led them upstairs.

Serena and Kim gave me cautious looks after my mom and brother followed me back into the room. They knew how difficult this was for me and now was the worst time for them to become involved. Serena waved over mom who pulled along Adam when he had stopped to admire Hinapouri. I, too, pushed him along thinking another second of his leers and Hinapouri would remove his eyes with her fingernails.

Having my mom present was freaking my shit and spotting my vision. Refocusing to stop Donovan's panicked state from taking over took effort, and I forced myself to see Ranlyn and his silvery immortal glow until the spots subsided, leaving me with my normal eye strain from the strength of his Magic.

"Where is he? I know you know," I said to Ranlyn, as he was my closest ally in the bunch.

When Ranlyn's response hovered in silence, my suspicions were confirmed. "I'm sorry, Sophie. This was unavoidable."

"That's a piss-poor apology for someone who knows they're doing something wrong. Did you get that bald fuck to kidnap him?"

"The attacks leading the last Elders to their deaths would not have been possible without the assistance of someone scheming within our ranks." Hinapouri's passive-aggressive insinuation sent my anger into hyper drive.

"Donovan fought to save Aunt Lacey. You have no right to accuse him!"

Refraining from wilting under the weight of Hinapouri's intimidation as she took deliberate steps toward me was a chore, but I stood strong.

"Fighting ants makes you no more than a Blind child with a magnified glass, Hinapouri," Veata judged from her standing position on the outskirts of the group.

"Quiet, old woman," Hinapouri hissed, her attention fixed on me.

Without returning a witty retort as per her usual, Veata's eyes narrowed to snake-like slits and sent the beautifully frightening warrior to her knees at my feet. Hinapouri cried out in a wild shrill of pain. Whatever Veata did, it was effective. Once the freaked-out Ballard Coven members and potentials quieted, Veata allowed Hinapouri to rise. "If acting like a child is how you insist on conducting yourself, then you will find yourself bowed at the feet of them time and again, warrior."

I wasn't insulted by her comparisons. A child, a Seeding, an ant was all accurate when pit against the Elders in the attic. They could squash me without notice and pick me out from between their toes a week later, but I still enjoyed the hit to Hinapouri's pride. Being a bully in a Blind world or a magic one still made you bully, and those like Veata wouldn't stand for it.

Olive stepped towards Ranlyn. "I understand you have a point in disrupting my family in our sacred place. Get to it without violence or leave."

"Again, accept my apologies on behalf of my Coven. Any more violence from one of mine and they will find themselves reaping the consequences."

"I made no threat." Miklos looked either half-bored or half-resentful to be looped in with the others, though it was difficult to read his expression below his facial hair.

"We're all responsible for imposing our presence on the Ballard Coven," Ranlyn told him.

Hinapouri spun to Ranlyn. "The treachery that caused the deaths of our immortal leaders has brought us here through no fault of our own."

Shifting in my peripheral was the potentials who caught the 'immortal' comment. The revelation was much more than was intended for the Ballard hopefuls.

"Stop flicking your dick and tell me where Donovan is." I regained the weight of Hinapouri's baneful attention.

Ranlyn's softened green eyes didn't have the persuasion effect Caine possessed. "In order to resolve this, we need to permit another member of the Coven into the estate." He turned to Olive. "The wards around the attic are preventing him from entering."

"That would only happen if he was Tainted."

"He's not evil, but under the circumstances he cannot enter through the front door."

"Please, Olive," I said to my great-aunt when she hesitated. If it meant we got Donovan back, we had to try.

Olive nodded.

With permission granted, Miklos removed a pouch from his pocket and found open space in the middle of the floor. Silence reigned as he knelt and poured out a powder onto the hardwoods. While he did this, Ranlyn came up behind me to speak over my shoulder. "It's brackish water."

"It's not a liquid."

"Part fresh water, part salt water, this particular sample has been put through a process turning it to a dust-like state for these such occasions."

Miklos ran his hands through the powder to craft a symbol.

"I don't care if it's Gold Bond, I just want whatever this is over with."

Mom was already looking at me from across the room when I snuck a peek her way. I noted the silent concern in her pursed lips and clutched hands as she discreetly pressed a pressure point on her hand, seeking some calm in sudden chaos. The glance didn't last long. Looking at the dark-haired man kneeling on the floor was easier than looking at the daughter you hardly knew anymore, or at least that's what I told myself. I had no clue what was going on in her head and hoped whatever came next didn't wear out the remainder of her tolerance.

Miklos created a complicated sigil in the brackish water, comprising of multi-point shapes, and then took a step back. Foreign words left his lips with silky confidence as everyone waited, crypt-quiet for something to happen. The powder changed form, solidifying the particles into a liquid that seeped into the floorboards in a flare of bright light. When the light subsided, the wood plank flooring was seared with a blackened brand.

More light, a different light, swelled and flooded the attic from the spot of the sigil. Lewis and Olive squinted and turned their heads to the side and I realized we Soul Seers were the only ones affected.

"What's that?" Kassie asked.

While Ballard potentials may have assumed she meant the sigil itself, when I saw Kassie squinting, I knew better. I looked at Kassie and then Olive and Lewis. Kassie lied about feeling anything when I raised my power before the Elders crashed the party. Kassie was a Soul Seer too, and the kind of light coming from the sigil wasn't easily ignored.

The bald, husky-eyed man appeared at the spot of the sigil radiating light, and he wasn't alone. The tux was a dead giveaway, but the hood and tied hands behind his back was verification.

"Donovan!" I surged forward. Ranlyn wrapped his arms around me and held me in a tight grip. The true reason he stood so close.

"Hey!" Adam's brotherly instincts took over when he saw Ranlyn grab me. He was shut down after a mere step. Not by our mom's outstretched hand, she wasn't fast enough, but by Hinapouri showcasing more of her power, this time sending Adam to his knees as

Veata had done to her. Adam cried out and crumbled. Shocked gasps and raised voices echoed through the attic in protest.

"Please don't make it worse." Ranlyn held me tighter to his chest, pinning my arms at my sides as he pleaded for my understanding.

"Are you fucking kidding me? You're Elders. My Elders. This is how you treat one of your own?" Struggling got me nowhere, but I sure as fuck wasn't making it easy for him. The vibration of his power tingled my arms and hitched in intensity anytime I got too wily.

A spike in his power had me inhaling deep and stopping my kicking and screaming. Ranlyn was trying to wrangle me and deal with Hinapouri overstepping her bounds by taking down my brother, as well as calm the crowd about to turn on them. I couldn't hear what he was saying, but Ranlyn's tone called for trust in their methods, which went over as much as trusting a stranger would be expected to go.

A groan from Donovan brought my attention back to him, his captor, and something I hadn't noticed in the dim light of the Z24.

"You're working with a Tainted Apporter?"

"He sides with the light. His position forces him to cross boundaries into darker ventures."

"Bullshit. You've put Donovan in evil hands and you did it on purpose." My vison blotted with my anger, the connection impeding on the fragile control as my anger shifted into panic at the betrayal.

"You have my word this is necessary," Ranlyn offered with sombre sincerity.

"Keep your fucking word. It's useless and reeks like donkey shit covered fish guts."

"Please, Sophie," he pleaded again as I thrashed in his grasp.

"How dare you do this to him!" Knowing nothing would have happened without Ranlyn's say so, I knew where to lay blame. The other Elders didn't always listen, but Ranlyn was the voice of reason, the leader of leaders.

My power flared, reacting to the threat as my sight blinked out, sending my head in a whirl, but not before I saw my mother being held back by Kim and Serena taking control of Adam.

My vision may have escaped me before, but the gag now pressed against my tongue and had me choking. Donovan and I coughed in the same phlegmy grotesque manner. Millicent and Isaac, and what the intolerant townspeople did to them flashed before my eyes, swapping out one hopeless scene with another had me hyperventilating.

"Take it off!" Ranlyn's voice rang above the flurry of concern from the crowd as I doubled-over in his grasp.

The attic whipped back into view, the pressure on my mouth and tongue lifted. Blinking through tears, Donovan was trying to see me as well. His hair was matted with sweat, his face reddened, but he was unharmed. Exhaustion and gratitude crossed the connection. He stood and was forced back to his knees. Pain shot through my bones.

"Enough!" Ranlyn ordered the Apporter as he still had a hold of me while I writhed in pain in my evening dress.

I looked up at Ranlyn. He was angry at the chaos he created. Angry he lost control when he was the one who barged in uninvited with an agenda, without care for what pain it might cause.

"Sophie?" The question in his expression pissed me off even more. He had no clue how wrong this was.

"You're as bad as the Witchburners."

23

HARD TRUTHS

Ranlyn let me go in a moment of shock. We stared at each other, stuck in that moment together as I filtered fury to him through the anarchy he created around us. He blinked and looked up at the others and then back down at me as if judging the room with new eyes. He picked me up and held me to him until I regained my footing. Any bruising caused by Donovan's binding or excessive force by the Apporter would be taken care of by my thrumming power, though the impotent rage at what the Elders were doing left me feeling helpless.

"You don't get to be indecisive," I told Ranlyn. "Either you're duty-bound to your Coven or to your Elders. You're following a warmonger like Hinapouri? If you're so sure Donovan's guilty, why's he still alive?" When I tried shrugging him off, he let me go and stared at me and then at the floor. "Save your guilt and get on with it."

He gave a commanding nod to the Apporter, who disappeared and reappeared in-between blinks, returning with another bound and hooded captive, this one in skinny jeans and boots, her cleavage not easy to miss in her opened leather jacket. The Apporter forced her to her knees and whipped off her hood.

I gave a humourless laugh. "Congrats. You caught a spongy bartender. Did you cover her hands when you bound them? Doesn't look like it. You're lucky she didn't absorb your Apporter power and zip out of here, baldy."

"She is a Loring devotee," Hinapouri said.

Joelly started to struggle at this, her protest lost against the gag in her mouth.

"Besides being raised by the same fucked up family, Donovan has nothing to do with her." I didn't know why Donovan wasn't speaking up for himself, but the absence of guilt running through him told me I was right.

"That's not how she tells it," Hinapouri replied.

Joelly wouldn't meet my glare.

"You festering twat. You show up out of nowhere pretending to want to help, and then you turn his Elders against him? Ripe fucking job. Try absorbing a conscience from the next dick you grope."

"As you pointed out," Miklos said in a gruff voice, "She has the ability to breach our defences by disguising her essence. Planning an attack with your companion would prove rather simple for two of the Sorrel flock. Especially with deep ties to Loring created centuries ago. Your personal connection clouds your judgment, Soul Seer."

"Our connection allows me to detect his lies, asshat. If you think I would swallow the lie at the expense of the whole Coven, and now my family, then I should be bound alongside them." I turned to Ranlyn and thrust out my healed, but still bloodied arms. "Go ahead, oh great leader. You know everything, right?"

"You wouldn't—" Ranlyn began.

"No, he wouldn't! He folded the Sorrel lifestyle. Aunt Lacey saw enough good in him to accept him into the Mother Coven—to bring him into our Creation where he could do the most damage if he was sucking Loring's tip. Do you doubt her judgment too?" I looked at all the Elders and got nothing back. "If she was alive, you would have been fit with a muzzle before snatching someone. From a moving car no less."

Ranlyn looked to the Apporter, whose jaw flexed in response. Putting others in danger to get Donovan didn't seem to be part of the Elders' plan, but that's what happens when you outsourced to a Tainted Magic.

"No one doubts Aunt Lacey," Ranlyn said slowly. "Now that she's gone, we need to bring her death justice."

"Justice?" Olive said. "You're no caped crusaders. This isn't about justice. This is an old-time Witch hunt in its purest form. And believe me, I know how this ends. I won't let you do this to these Seedlings. I know nothing of this Joelly, and little of Donovan, but my Firefly won't be called a liar, especially not here."

"Donovan and I weren't the only ones to see Daniel Berisford, Loring, and Loring's current sidearm Malina, kill Aunt Lacey that day. Suspect me all you want, but neither Kim or Caine would ever lie to protect Donovan." The comment may have been true, but I felt like an ass for saying it out loud and refrained from looking Kim's way to see what reaction it caused in her.

"Joelly works all sides with Loring, the Puppeteer, and the Raddies," Hinapouri said. "The Elders are killed and suddenly she reunites with a member of the dead Elders Coven? This is no coincidence."

"The Raddies? Do you mean the Eradicators?" Olive asked.

Hinapouri gave a curt nod.

"Who are they?" I asked.

"Humans," Miklos deadpanned.

"More than humans." The Apporter spoke for the first time in a deep monotone voice that matched his darkened soul and spoke of a Norse background.

"They are a faction of humans," Ranlyn said, "created in a time of hatred and corruption. Living long before the Witchburners, but giving those like the Witchburners the encouragement they needed in the name of saving humanity from the beasts of magic sent by the devil." He shook his head. "The problem is that over the years their creed has become more violent in nature. They're called the Eradicators for a reason. Their sole purpose is to eradicate all forms of magic. Be it innocents like many of you—" he motioned to the Ballard potentials "—or those who know nothing of it but have the bloodline of possibility within them. Not even a child is out of reach of extinction."

This unsettled the group. History outlined the heinous destruction caused by such people, but we were led to believe it was a wayward sanction of the church or dealt with on a smaller town by town basis by jealous wives pointing at their husband's mistresses. To think an actual group of people out there wanted them dead didn't sway the potential newcomers to join the Ballard Family's Coven.

"So, you're saying Joelly has something to do with this group?" I wanted to get back to why Donovan was still considered a target.

"Yes," Hinapouri answered sharply, but Ranlyn took over with a softer approach. "According to sources, Joelly works with the Raddies. Fink for hire, providing information and spell work against both sides."

Joelly attempted to speak through the gag as her eyes glared into slits, her dark makeup smeared from sweat and tears.

"None of that surprises me, but you still only have her family tie to Donovan to show any involvement on his part. She's not even a blood Sorrel. She was taken as a child and brought into their Coven." The side-glances the Elders gave each other said they didn't know this. "I know the Sorrels fought with Loring and his Coven, but Donovan left them as a kid."

"Too risky to chance," Hinapouri said. "The Raddies are everywhere the Puppeteer can't reach. With Loring as his servant, the Puppeteer has brought upon this entire Coven a danger we have not sought to contest for centuries. The deaths of the Elders are but the beginning of our strife."

"We've had our share of the Puppeteer already, but we weren't certain it wasn't Loring," I said.

"You have?" Ranlyn asked, the craze of his fingers on my arm pulling my attention.

I crossed my arms. "So much for checking your messages. We've been calling you nonstop with updates on everything."

"Sophie and Donovan nearly died. Correction. They did die," Kim spat out. "The Puppeteers Puppets are everywhere. We can't even go home, and we've been grasping at straws trying to protect Donovan's long enough to hear back from you, and you had no clue?"

"You died?" Ranlyn asked me with genuine astonishment.

"Sophie?" I heard my mother call from across the room, but I couldn't talk to her about it now. I would never have told her if Kim hadn't blurted it out, but a part of me was happy she put Ranlyn in his place.

"Catch up, buddy." Kim snapped her fingers at Ranlyn. "That trussed up bitch over there absorbed their power and used it against Donovan, which obviously works equally against Sophie. So, yes, Caine and I watched them turn to ash. She wanted Donovan dead, she's not working with him. Check my memories if you don't believe my word."

Kim stood stalk straight, prepared for him to check whatever he had to. I don't know if he did or if Kim's thoughts were still hidden by the herb we all took, but something in his expression said he knew all he needed to.

"These Seedlings within your Coven fought for their lives while you left them unprotected," Olive said. "Now you're here making accusations based on suspect truths made by a self-professed traitor."

I needed to end this. "You need a guarantee, I get it. Did you come here for Caine's power?"

"It would certainly help," Ranlyn said. "Others possess persuasion, but we believed Caine was easiest to access."

"He's a Berisford," Miklos stated coolly. "A breed as bad as the Sorrel."

"Berisford or not, Caine is a Persuader. By the time he leaves, you'll be ashamed at how shitty your investigative tactics are." I turned to Kim. "Call Caine and get him here. He won't listen to me."

Having Kim call was not an act of fear on my part. If it meant saving Donovan from Joelly's fate, I would call non-stop like an obsessed stalker until Caine picked up and screamed at me. When Caine answered, Kim didn't give him a chance to hang-up before she explained the situation in a verbal projectile fashion. When she gave the thumbs up that he agreed to help, my knees tingled with relief. The Apporter disappeared to pick him up and left Donovan and Joelly in the eager hands of Hinapouri and Miklos.

"You sure about this?" Kim asked me in a low voice.

"Nope. As much as Caine probably imagined ripping Donovan and me apart in a bloody *Braveheart*-like death scene, I don't think he would actually let it happen." I paused. "He wouldn't, right?"

She shrugged. "He agreed to help. We'll see what that means soon."

The attic filled with the frustrated voices of the Ballard potentials. They wanted to rejoin the party—many to pretend this never happened. My mother never attempted to come over to Kim and I on the other side of the room. It stung, but I could hardly worry about that right now. The Apporter returned through the sigil like he was beamed from the mother ship, and the room went quiet.

Not only had Caine appeared, so did Eli, Bernie, Jet, and even Andy. Apparently, they wouldn't allow Caine to go alone.

"Sophie!" Andy called and ran to me. I pulled Andy into a tight hug, smelling peanut butter and the rubbery stench of play-dough as his short arms strangled my neck.

"Hey buddy." I squeezed him tighter before putting him back on his feet.

"You're alive." He laughed, showing off his baby teeth.

"I sure am."

"You're the only that hasn't gone away after the spots. You're pretty without them."

Tears swelled as I gave a small laugh. "You saved me, little man."

"Can we get this over with?"

Caine's voice was so full of contempt I was too shocked to hide my expression. The rest of the room's attention was on me as well.

Most didn't know this little boy or what he referred to when mentioning the spots. Most also didn't give a shit and were as impatient as Caine to get on with it. I gave Andy another tight hug, lingering an extra second, pained to think I may never get to see him again. He may forget me and what he did to save my life, but I never would. He hugged me back and then ran back to his mom. Jet locked eyes with mine, extending a passive hello. No doubt Caine told them what happened, but the hate I expected to find was nowhere in her stare. Instead, I found a sense of understanding. Something she kept from her cousin and remained where she stood as a show of compassion for Caine's hurt.

I wiped my eyes, doing my best not to break down as Donovan's features crumpled with mine. Ranlyn explained to Caine his expectations. Kim put a reassuring hand on my arm, her quiet support doing little to settle my shaking, but meant everything when I saw the betrayal etched on Caine's features. I deserved it. I knew I did, but it didn't make it easier to take.

"If I'm doing this as a favour to him. I have my own questions to ask first." Caine said this as if saying Donovan's name was too much of a stretch for him.

"What?" Ranlyn asked.

"You heard me." Caine stood firm.

Ranlyn looked to me, brows stitched in confusion. "If your motive is to either humiliate Sophie or Donovan, then no, you cannot."

Caine turned and looked directly at me. I held his stainless-steel gaze, expecting nothing less, but would be lying if I said I didn't hope for something softer instead of the jolt of jagged ice that ran through me. He knew how powerful the connection was, but it was too soon for him to see beyond his hurt and now we wanted him to make life easier for Donovan.

"Go ahead," I finally said. "You could've asked me anything. You know that." Caine crossed his arms, his thrashed knuckles from beating Donovan an angry red. "I hope you get the answers you want." This was said with disdain, but I was willing to bet whatever

Donovan said would hurt Caine as much as he wanted them to hurt me.

Donovan was seated in a chair adjacent to where Caine sat, half a body's length between them, tensions so high I expected another brawl to break out. I too took a seat before I fell. Donovan broke first and looked my way. With his glance came an apology that skittered across the connection. No one knew what Caine was going to ask, but Donovan feared his answers, which instantly had me regretting giving Caine free rein.

Caine brought forth his power. The potentials in attendance shifted in unease as they felt the rise of his strength. Donovan's hesitance was a reflex, a survival instinct which gripped the thread of connection before he forced himself to freely forfeit his will. What I didn't think of beforehand was what it would do to me. My will remained intact, but a part of me felt as Donovan did, as I had in Aunt Lacey's backyard when Caine gripped my will in order to save me from pain. The urge to listen to Caine and only Caine was overwhelming, but I knew I could look away or leave the room if I wanted to.

Caine leaned forward, elbows to knees, as he looked at Donovan. The hint of a predator with his pray in his grasp was undeniable and his power grew stronger, his grip tightening on Donovan, his numbing effect causing my focus to slip into disconnection with the room around me.

"Caine." Eli called in some type of warning.

The slight ebb of Caine's power released the tight grip on me while retaining his hold on Donovan as he sat back in his chair. Whatever Eli's warning, Caine listened, but none of us knew what would have happened if Eli hadn't stepped in. Caine took a moment, sanded his hands together, and pushed his long hair behind his ears.

"Are you in love with Sophie?" Caine asked, then swiftly amended by adding, "Not the past Sophie you were married to, but the Sophie in the present?"

I dropped my face in my hands and then leaned into a fist on the arm of my chair. I wasn't sure if Kim's light chuckle was at how dumb a question it was or what, but I didn't enjoy publicly bleeding my business. I knew it could be a worse question, but fuck, I wanted him to get it over with and thankfully didn't have to wait long.

"Yes," Donovan answered in a calm, robotic voice.

Surprise wasn't what I expected to feel, but it was. Donovan was open about how he felt about me, but I wasn't so sure if he could separate his love from the past with that of today. The peak in Caine's thick brows told me he too was surprised by Donovan's answer. The smugness Caine began with eased, but he wasn't done.

"Did you plan to have sex with Sophie while I was away?"

Oh, forfuck'ssake! Kim wore a withering expression as I looked over at her in a chair next to me.

"No. She initiated it," Donovan answered.

"Is this necessary?" Adam blurted from the crowd and muttered. "Jesus Christ," under his breath. No one answered him, but it was what everyone wanted to say, including me.

"One more," Caine said and moved on. "Did you plan to come between Sophie and me since I awoke from the sleeping curse?"

This should have been easy, but I was surprised when Donovan answered, "No," then that surprise turned into an exhausted exhalation as Donovan added, "It was my plan before you were awakened."

Caine nodded and sat there as if absorbing the truth he had uncovered.

Veata spoke for the first time. "Now that the soapbox drama has concluded, can we accomplish what we're here for?"

It came as no surprise to most of them that, as I had claimed, Donovan was innocent. He admitted to seeing his sister on a few occasions, but someone was always present whenever she would randomly pop up. And, in at least one case, the whole Sect was present. Though they did speak alone, Donovan confirmed the warning Joelly gave as well as the uncomfortable attempt to get in his pants. With all the Elders' questions asked, and no further loopholes for the truth to possibly hide in, Donovan was freed from his bindings.

He immediately came over to me, closed the distance in a few steps, and I sprung up from my chair and wrapped my arms around him as he rocked us back and forth. Donovan was no longer captive. No matter who held him prisoner or what danger he truly faced, I was ecstatic he was free.

"I remember what he asked me. Are you okay?"

I gave a noncommittal noise and offered nothing more. With my emotions all over the place and his ability to siphon them across the connection, I wouldn't need to say much anyway.

"Now question Joelly," we heard Ranlyn give Caine his next directive.

When Donovan and I pulled apart, the hardness of Caine's expression was back. Probably because of our hug, but regardless of what happened between us, I would have hugged Donovan. He stared down the barrel and came out on top. Being alive deserved an embrace. While Caine didn't look like he had it in him to proceed, he cracked his neck when the Apporter forcibly plunked Joelly into the chair Donovan vacated, and focused ahead on the true reason we were all here.

Joelly's hands stayed bound, the gag removed, but Baldy remained close in case she made a desperate attempt to cast.

"Suck it, shithead!" Joelly spat a stream of mucus at Caine. He wiped at his arm, as that was the only place she managed to hit. His jaw flexed, his retaliation a hitch in his power with intent to take her will. As soon as Joelly sensed it, she clamped her eyes shut.

"Doesn't work if she won't look at me."

The Apporter hit Joelly open-handed in the back of the head. The crowd didn't like that, but not only did it not work, it had everyone on their feet in protest for a girl they didn't know.

"Calm yourselves," Ranlyn said in a commanding voice. It did its job, but if he was launching a recruiting campaign, he would be losing his audience. "Now, Joelly, you have a chance to absolve yourself this very moment. I advise you to take the opportunity."

"Fuck you too, crotch-grabber. You think I haven't had worse. Ask my darling brother. Whatever you can give, I can handle. I heal with the best of them, so try cutting my eyelids off. I ain't saying shit."

Joelly kept her eyes snapped shut, but they could hear the fear and empty posturing in her voice. Whether true or not, they kept trying to persuade her without the use of force.

"Olive—" Ranlyn turned where she was standing, next to Lewis and the rest of the Ballard family. "I am not unfamiliar with this estate, having been within this sanctum before." This came as news to me, but it did explain how the Elders entered without aide. "I happen to know the estate was equipped with a rather operational cellar that would be quite helpful in this situation. Is that not still the case?"

Olive remained stoic as the stares of the others landed on her. "This is true." Judging by her brother's expression, Lewis knew nothing about it.

"Excellent," Ranlyn said with clap of his hands and then motioned for the Apporter to gather up Joelly. "The mechanism is beneath the timepiece, correct?" Ranlyn confirmed walking towards the door near the hourglass without waiting for Olive's response.

The enormous hourglass was stationed at the corner outside a door covered by an old tapestry. When we first explored the attic, I insisted Caine help me turn it over, but we never noticed any type of mechanism. Olive did state it went to the cellar but said nothing about what it was used for. Now we knew why. My imagination was running wild at what ugliness the beautiful estate held in some secret cellar.

Everyone looked at each other as if questioning if they were allowing something like this to happen, but no one on either side spoke up. As Joelly was gagged again against a slew of obscenities, I couldn't stay quiet.

"Wait!" I moved into the Apporter's pathway, but he pushed by me. I grabbed his arm and sent a hit of power through my hand. He gasped, and his grip released Joelly. Hinapouri surged towards me and I raised my hands. "Hold up!" She did, but only because Ranlyn rushed to stop her.

"You dare—" Hinapouri started.

"She's right," I interrupted her. "If what Joelly's experienced is anything like what Donovan went through, she's not cracking. She won't spill answers because you tear her apart. She'll talk shit and goad you on until you kill her or turn her half-insane, but she won't talk."

"And you have the skills of a seasoned interrogator, Soul Seer?" Miklos's voice dripped with sarcasm.

"No. But I know we're in an attic full of herbs and shit that are probably better for getting into her mind. I'd read her soul if I thought it wouldn't kill me. I say we dose her and then sic Caine on her. Less bloody and quicker. We've got a party to get back to."

Using Olive's attic directory, we searched the attic for something that would alter her mind without breaking it so we could trust the information we gathered. Anything hallucinogenic would create information rather than divulge it so it had to be specific to our needs. Olive knew of a spell and the directory pointed us to the ingredients. Once it was broken down and mixed with a marble mortar and pestle, we realized we had another problem. Joelly wouldn't open her trap to get it down.

"Here." I handed the bowl to Caine.

"What are you doing?" Caine questioned.

"Sit and trust I know what I'm doing."

"Trust you?" Caine said with a throaty sound of disdain.

That pained me more than I was willing to dwell on right now. "Unless you want them to take her to the cellar to torture her, there's a better method. Though don't touch her. I said somewhat safe, not totally safe. When you see your chance, stick the pestle handle between her teeth." He glared with such hate I had to look away.

Joelly struggled against her bindings. The gag was removed and the Apporter bore down on her shoulder to keep her still.

"Open your mouth," I said to Joelly. She clamped her teeth down, as expected.

I brought my power to the surface and laid my hand on Joelly's other shoulder. As with the flower during the Make It Grow test, I had many missteps. After Diluculo, I saw what I did to The Reds and experienced it firsthand in Aunt Lacey's backyard. I didn't want to push it that far and hoped for control when I sent my disintegration power to work on her shoulder.

A creeping black snaked up Joelly's shoulder to her neck. A gasp from the crowd made me hesitate and stopped the decay eating her skin.

Joelly groaned.

"Not so fun when it's used against you, is it?" I whispered and retracted the creeping disintegration, but Joelly still refused to open up her eyes or her mouth.

I gave Joelly another dose, sensing Donovan's passive encouragement. This time, I hit her with a pulse of it and Joelly's own healing ability arm-wrestled against me. She groaned louder as she fought me, and I knew I was onto something. Before giving her a chance to recover, I hit Joelly with a deeper and longer dose of my power. She collapsed a bit to the side and the Apporter grabbed her forehead and wrenched her head back, her mouth agape. Caine seized the opportunity and shoved the pestle in between her teeth as the Apporter held her in place. Not standing on ceremony, I dumped the mixture between her teeth around the pestle. When I got it all in, Caine removed the pestle and the Apporter clamped her mouth closed and held it there. She struggled, but eventually she swallowed. She had no choice. Then the gag was replaced while we waited for the ingredients to take effect. When the muffled swearing stopped, we knew the spell had done its job.

"Looks like your way was effective," Ranlyn said as I went back to my seat next to Kim, and Caine got ready to overpower what was left of Joelly's will.

Now that she was tamed, Joelly would answer anything Caine

needed her to. With her defenses down, the Elders could read her mind to see what she saw and not only hear her retelling. Effective was right, but I still didn't feel good about my part in making it happen.

Kim gave a hearty "good job" that I gave a twisted smile at and Donovan reached down from where he stood behind my chair to hug me and land a kiss on the top of my head.

"She deserved more, babe. Don't worry," he whispered knowing my success was overshadowed by guilt.

24

THE BALLARD FAMILY COVEN

Boredom wasn't how I would characterize being ringside for an interrogation of the magical sort, though it was slow going. Caine hammered Joelly with question after question. The mixture we gave her turned her answers into a languid song. Caine's impatience of Joelly's snail speed and for the Elders to rifle her brain once Caine's questions prompted answers, was evident in the constant shake of his knee. The guy couldn't sit still.

Side-eye glances were aimed in my direction if Donovan or I moved and accidently caught his attention. This seemed to frustrate Caine further, but he stayed the course.

"Working with Loring is necessary." Joelly spoke without attitude or facial expressions of any kind. Relaxed shoulders and straight-forward answers without her regular condescension was weird. Everything that made Joelly the vision of her I remembered was gone while trapped under Caine's persuasion.

"Why is working with Loring necessary?"

"Loring is everywhere. Orchestrates everything. I needed his contacts and his political reach in the Coven and with the Blind."

Caine's knee stopped bouncing as he started getting the answers he needed.

"Do you work directly with Loring?"

"Yes."

Ranlyn prompted Caine on the next question.

"Are you a devotee?"

"I'm devoted to myself."

No one was surprised. Not even Donovan whose emotions remained steady as she responded.

"What are you trying to gain?"

"Power, money, prestige, safety."

The last one was a bit of a heartbreaker. The lengths people go to feel safe were sometimes devastating.

"Have you killed to gain these things?"

"Yes."

I thought as much. Hearing her say it while under Caine's command made her sound cold, though I doubted she would show remorse had she control over her will.

"Does Loring consider you a close confidant?" This question was, again, prompted by Ranlyn.

"No."

"Why not?"

"Because I refused to fuck him." Snickers came from a couple of the Ballard Family Coven potentials as she continued without notice. "Those who refused to service him at his request don't get pulled into the inner circle, regardless of strength, influence, or loyalty."

A part of me was proud. She had boundaries and her quest for power didn't include giving parts of herself over that she didn't want to give. She paid the price, but she still found a way to get what she wanted without compromise. Not all of what she wanted, or I doubted she would have come back into Donovan's life.

"What's your involvement with the Eradicators?" This question came from Miklos and Caine repeated it to Joelly.

"They approached me with an offer of twenty-five hundred dollars for any verifiable information."

"What did you tell them?"

"I told them about Loring's plans to retake the Creation outside of the Puppeteer orders. That a civil war was imminent and would work in their favour. That Donovan and other Mother Coven members escaped Loring. How he planned to kill them, but was ordered not to by the Puppeteer. I told them where to find the mansion where Elsa's Sect meets and their scheduled Coven Meeting night. I told them what they wanted to hear. I told them lies when they trusted me enough to stop verifying my information."

"How did you hide this from Loring?"

"I absorbed the ability from another magic a long time ago. Loring couldn't get into my head."

"Have you met the Puppeteer?"

"Not in person. Only when channelled through a Puppet."

"After all this time in hiding," Hinapouri said. "Why?" Caine relayed the question.

"The Lughnasadh murders were never sanctioned, neither was entering their Creation. Loring was spared punishment due to bringing pride to the Master for the deaths he caused and for the information of those who escaped. Many bragged about the deaths of the Elders like a psychotic bedtime story. Nothing remains a secret from the Puppeteer. Not even my argument with Loring to save Sophie for myself to kill."

This piqued my interest tenfold.

Caine's stare was the first time he looked at me with curiosity.

"I hadn't met her yet." I earned more confused stares from others.

"Why would you want to kill Sophie?"

"To take Nya's power back."

Caine looked over at me again. I shook my head, mouth agape, hoping he understand I had no idea what she was talking about. He refocused on Joelly. "What do you mean by take back Nya's power?"

"Malina told me I was Nya in a past life. The rightful vessel and owner of her soul. Elsa held onto Nya's essence to transplant within Sophie. Nya's power should be mine."

"She's lying." The growl in Donovan's voice vibrated down my spine, but I knew better.

"Caine's power won't allow her to."

The Elders directed Caine to move onto figuring out what Joelly knew about the future plans of her various allies. I was too stuck in my head to hear a word. Could what Joelly said be true? Could Aunt Lacey have mixed her own proprietary blend and gifted me Nya's power instead of it finding me after spending centuries lost and searching for a vessel? How different would my life be now without Nya's influence? Why would she pick me? I didn't even know her.

I worried my ring. Nya's ring. The weight of its gold far heavier than a moment ago.

"Hey." Donovan bent down in front of me and held my hands, stopping me from sanding my finger raw. "Please don't do that. This is yours. Aunt Lacey wouldn't have lied, you know that. She said Malina told her—"

"Loring had to have told Malina."

"Oooh," he drew out. "I forgot about how trustworthy Loring is." I groaned. "No really, he should be a scout leader." His sarcasm forced me to crack a superficial smile. "There's no more reason to believe Loring than Malina. Please, remember what Aunt Lacey told you."

"I seriously doubt Aunt Lacey lied." Caine, standing behind a crouched Donovan, alone, arms crossed, was a surprise. Joelly was being re-gagged as she began mouthing off in a sloth-like protest with her will intact. I stood, as did Donovan and Kim.

"Thank you." I managed not to stutter or break down.

Caine didn't acknowledge my thanks. "You said yourself Aunt Lacey's soul was pure in death. Manipulating you to believe you're Nya's vessel wouldn't leave her soul untouched. Either she was certain, or she thought she was, but was wrong. I don't think she was wrong."

I nodded. The clench in my throat was caused in part by the reminder of Aunt Lacey's soul in death and partly by Caine reaching out to make sure I knew his thoughts in the matter.

Without another word, he rejoined his family. I wanted to run after him, wanted to talk to him, wanted to let him yell the rafters down around me. But, in the end, doing so was my own selfish need to feel some type of punishment for what I did. He deserved the chance to let me have it, but that time wasn't now.

"He's only across the room. I doubt he'd brush you off," Donovan said quietly at my side.

I gave a small pathetic laugh. "Not here."

He didn't push it.

Ranlyn approached. "I want to officially apologize for the Coven's absence in your time of need."

I actually giggled. "Officially? Is that something you're required to do?"

"I deserve that."

"You deserve worse," Donovan said.

Ranlyn could have argued, of course. Explained where he was all this time, but he didn't. He took the hit without a hint of defensiveness.

"What now? What will happen with Joelly?" Kim asked.

"She'll be released."

"Ex-squeeze me?" My amazement was echoed in the others protests. "Why the hell would you release her knowing she's trying to kill me? Do you hate me that much?"

Ranlyn's brows dropped to shadow his light eyes. "Not in the least. For Joelly to steal the power she believes is hers, she needs you alive."

"She already tried using her absorbing power on me, probably to try and get Nya's power. Instead, she got an eye full of my Soul Seeing ability and freaked out. Her big plan to absorb her rightful power didn't work. A devious, criminal mind like Joelly's would never result in her carving me up like a Thanksgiving turkey while trying to steal my power the old-fashioned way." I huffed. "I best get a body wax before she can pluck me to death."

"A plan is in place. She won't roam free without us knowing where."

"Says you," Donovan said. "You underestimate her survival instincts."

"We'll take her history into consideration."

"Right," Donovan muttered.

Ranlyn took a breath before focusing on me. "I wanted to thank you for your self-sacrifice. It's what I wanted to say originally."

"Oh?"

"You brought in Caine although you've had what I'm assuming to be a recent and ugly fall-out, to help the Coven and, more importantly, the other person who was apparently the reason for the fall-out." I nodded, refusing the look at Donovan as my skin crawled. "Someone lesser would have jumped through layers of Hell before putting themselves in the position you did, in front of your family and Coven Elders no less."

"Yeah, well, I think my brother about had an aneurysm imagining me having sex with anyone, let alone having it outted publicly by an ex."

Ex. Ugh. Caine was my ex. The title was a straight jab to the heart.

"You have a lot of work to do with the resurrection of the Ballard Coven. With some damage control, most will follow your lead."

"Oh, they're better off following a herd of cattle. If the last few months have proved anything, they're safer staying far away from me."

He tilted his head. "Not your fault. Now that we're back, expect greater security."

"Great. You can call me Whitney, Jeeves." He would have to earn my trust as far as that went.

———

The Elders' exited after they accomplished their objective, without an apology for Donovan's capture. He said he expected nothing less, though I would have thought a simple acknowledgment for what they put him through would have been appropriate. The Apporter gave them a quick exit, returning them and Joelly to wherever they came from. The husky-eyed Norseman returned soon after to return Caine and his family to the farmhouse.

"Sophie?" I turned to see Jet and Andy. "He wanted to say goodbye."

I knelt in front of him and was wrapped in strong, skinny arms.

"Can you visit soon?"

The question shot tears to my eyes. It took everything I had to stop them. "Um, I don't think I can, buddy."

"Yes, you can. Caine said you were with that guy now, but you can still visit me." I saw Caine over Andy's shoulder standing next to his aunt and uncle, speaking to each other as Caine stared blankly at the floor. "Pinky promise you'll come." Andy shoved his crooked little finger in front of my nose, forcing my attention away from Caine.

Cue the tears. I clenched my teeth and willed myself to keep it together. "How 'bout this? I'll pinky promise that if I can, I will see you again, but I can't promise when."

He took my pinky in his. "It's not the same, but okay." His smile wasn't as big, but he hugged me again anyway.

Jet surprised me more by pulling me into an embrace when I flexed to my feet. She held tightly and let go. "Can't say what happened was right but knowing about the whole freaky link and past life thing, I told Caine I'm not surprised." She leaned in to say, "At least he's hot," before heading back to her parents, who made no attempt to address me.

Even with a small portion of Caine's family's understanding, it wasn't what I needed to hear. I appreciated Andy and Jet's undeserved good wishes and hoped I might cross paths with them at some point in the future.

"Cute kid." Kim stepped up to my side.

"He's the kid that sees the spots."

"Wow, really? He's so little."

"Where I come from," Donovan said, "kids younger than him have already discovered their powers and are pressured to excel."

Kim laughed. "No wonder you're an asshole."

Andy waved as he stood with his family. I waved back and caught eyes with Caine before the Apporter whisked them away, seeing a mixture of softened hate and solid disillusionment. He would never look at me the way he had since the park, and I despised myself for being the cause. I knew the pain of such betrayal from my not too distant past.

Lewis was mid-debrief. A wildly ill-conceived account since he didn't know the background of events leading to the Elders display of power. I stepped in and received his muttered thanks.

"First, let me formally introduce two people. As you have obviously gathered, this is Donovan—"

"And you're nailing my sister," Adam rudely finished as a few others barely stifled their laughs. Donovan stood unflappable as Adam bared a pompous smile.

I ignored my brother's ridiculousness. "And this is Kim. Both Donovan and Kim are my Sect Leaders. The others were the Elders of what's called the Mother Coven who includes a much larger group of Magics and is older than—Fuck, I don't know, it's super old. Sorry you had to sit through all that, but it was important and will probably never happen again."

"Probably," Ronny said with a sneer.

"Now," I shot a shut-your-fucking-mouth glare at my mouthy cousin, "this isn't normal as far as Coven life goes, so don't expect meetings to be such chaos. It's more training and discovering your abilities and histories and such. It's not the same for everyone, but I assure you, rebuilding the Ballard Family Coven with Olive as the true heir, is important. This is in our bl—"

"I'll join," Kevin announced, leaning against a shelf.

"What?"

"I'll join." He shrugged and checked his posture. "I'd rather lose a nut than get into that drama, but having powers is badass."

"You'll have powers whether you join or not," Olive said.

"Even better. Until now, I didn't even know I had them. So, basically, it's a good day. You find out you come from a family of Witch-people who want you in some secret division of the family where we get to use this wicked space. It's like hitting puberty, losing my virginity, and rolling my first car all in one."

"Nice," Donovan said under his breath at the same time as Adam and Ronny.

"Okie dokie. Titsgold. Welcome aboard, Kevin."

"Me too." Chelsea raised her hand like a school kid.

Most everyone in one form or another agreed to be a part of the family Coven. Gloria and Iris threw in their hats—figuratively—with reluctance and wouldn't stop grumbling about it. Kassie was the only hold out until Shannon told her to "jump off your high horse and get over yourself, Soul Seer." Kassie couldn't deny what she saw while looking at those of us with released powers, but like Gloria and Iris, she wasn't happy about it.

Shannon gave a wink my way and I responded with a smile.

Olive thanked the group, unable to hide tears of happiness, and had them sign their names into the Ballard Family Coven ledger, an old book whose last entry was made decades ago. Olive and Lewis let them know they would be contacted soon about the next steps, and took this opportunity to remind them about the secret remaining a secret.

Mom and Adam's vote to join wasn't taken because they weren't brought in as potentials. They beat their way in the door. Tension in my chest tightened as I stopped them from rejoining the party with the others. Mom practically skidded in her heels she stopped so abruptly, then flat out retreated a step to create distance between us.

I crossed my arms. Not for being pissed off, but so I could still my hands. "I would never hurt you." The deadpanned statement didn't help, but my mom readjusted her stance as if she could erase the last fifteen seconds and pretend she didn't refrain from scurrying away from her daughter.

Mom adopted a new trajectory to try and get around me to leave. I sidestepped into her path. "Really?" Mom's jaw clenched as she huffed and glared at me. "Come on, Mom. After what you just saw, I need you to talk. Anything and everything you could possibly yell at me for, warn me about, flat out refuse to see me again, anything. Please."

A few tense seconds passed before Mom looked at Adam with a narrowed gaze, a significant exchange common to our mother. One that said, "Go find something else to do." Both of us had experienced the look on many occasions growing up. This was a relief, except "find something else to do" resulted in Adam bee-lining for Donovan and Kim. As far as I was concerned, that wasn't a good thing.

"Sophie...." Mom started and paused as if choosing her words. "I understand this is something you cannot walk away from. However, I am not sure I can be a part of it." I nodded, expecting as much. "The display I just—I never thought my daughter was capable of something so barbaric. Torture, Sophie? Really? This is where these new powers have brought you? To the belief that torturing a girl for information was justified? I've helped put people in prison for much less."

"That girl you're worried about killed me only days ago. Not tried to kill me or planned to kill me, but actually killed me dead and ran off without giving a shit as me and Donovan slowly turned to ash."

"I know. You didn't need to hammer in the visual. I was listening the first time. What scares me is the eye-for-an-eye mentality these people have regarding their affairs. No policing, no order. Torture and release like you've trapped a pesky raccoon and left it to relocate in the forest. By the sounds of it, they've had long enough to secure a ruling establishment, and yet, revenge is their fallback. Yet you have faith in them enough to stand here and defend their actions."

"Not because I was having a hoot. I'm not Tainted. Olive or Lewis would tell me if my soul darkened." Mom didn't roll her eyes, but she may as well have. "Can you at least understand how everyday police and judges can't handle something like this?"

"Granted. Yet a fact that scares me no less considering your involvement."

"If you were me and had gone through some of the things you've heard about—"

"God, is there more I haven't heard?"

"Mom, listen. In my shoes, without the responsibility of kids, at my age, given the opportunity to explore something powerful already within you, would you have taken it?"

She looked up as if the answers were on the ceiling, though her eyes shone with tears for already knowing them. Her nod brought me immense relief until she said, "Now, about this guy situation."

"Ohmygod. I can't even with that one. You saw where it's ended up. I have no clue where it's going." My sex life was the lesser evil at present, one my mother wasn't shunning me for, and was a closer subject to something halfway normal for us.

"You sure you're not with him now?" She nodded toward Donovan, still standing with Kim and Adam.

Seconds after we looked his way, Donovan's dark eyes panned in our direction and then he graced us with a full set of dimples. Mom gasped and looked away, as did I and we both discreetly laughed.

"Could he tell we were looking at him?" she asked.

"Yup."

"What? Now you've cornered the market on the tall, dark, and handsomely creepy?"

In his tailored suit, hands comfortably in his pockets, even with his hair not in top shape, though it never was, Donovan had an undeniable attraction about him.

"Okay, stop. He can tell we're staring."

"He didn't look that time."

"That's because he happens to enjoy it."

"Cocky bugger, is he?"

"Yes. Very much so."

"That could be an issue, though I'm sure you can handle him. About this touching thing—he can learn things about me through a handshake?"

"By touching any part of you. As long as there's skin contact."

"Hmmm."

"Yes, even during that. Though it only happened once and there's no promise of a repeat," I was quick to add. "With me, it blinds him, but he'd be lying if he said he hasn't been doing it on purpose since he realized he would see our past together."

"Not the most flattering attribute, though he did say he loved you. Or at least he was persuaded to admit he loved you."

"I already knew he did." This earned me a raised eyebrow. "He's told me before. That was Caine's way of proving it. Probably for himself. Not like that made what he did okay."

"What did you say back?"

"Mom."

"What? You want things to be normal, asking my daughter what she said to a guy who told her he loved her is very normal, as far as we go."

"Now who's being manipulative?"

"You said it back, didn't you? While you were with Caine? That's not like you."

"We can't lie to each other. I had to be honest."

"Oh, Dolly." She reached out and smoothed my hair and I thought I might melt. She didn't flinch or pull away. "You both care for each other, it's obvious. Although, it was obvious with Caine, too." I gave my mother a see-what-I'm-dealing-with-here look. "You're too young for this forever talk anyway."

"Not just forever from this point on, even though it's too soon after Caine to even consider. A few centuries and a few lifetimes ago."

"Bit late for that but thinking things through is good. Might as well be sure before either of you gets hurt." I knew he'd stick around but was still undecided on how I felt about it. "He seems to be getting along with your brother."

"You say that like it's a good thing."

Mom hooked her arm with mine and we walked back to the small group that included my brother. The warmth and lacking reservation in her touch was divine. She may not be on board with Team Magic, but she was making a considerable effort to try and separate the things she fears from someone she loves.

Olive gave a full demonstration of her cataloguing system. A way to find things on the dusty shelves of the attic instead of sifting through them. A hand on the book and a call-out of what she needed was all it took, and everyone watched as the book flipped its own pages and stopped at the thing she had called for, complete with how many there were and where they could be found. It was simple and since another spell shifted everything back into its place, it made everything simple to find.

"That'd be great for client files," Mom said remarkably casual.

"Not all aspects of our power are for the defence of our race," Olive said. "They're merely an extension of everyday abilities— making tasks simpler, or in some cases, more fun." She closed the book. "I'll make it official and ask you, Lu, are you joining?"

"Oh, I-I don't—"

"If you decide to be honest with the path of your blood, then these doors are open for you to explore. Unfortunately, you cannot be permitted free access to the attic if you are not willing to accept that which you are."

"I am," Adam answered.

"Really?" I said. "You can't use it to vamp up your chick quotient or to get your band signed without consequence."

He shrugged. "Why not?"

Donovan gave a throaty sound, not quite a laugh. "I'm pretty sure Sophie's thinking tonight's freak show would be sufficient to cover the 'why not' question."

"Yeah, but you run a coven."

"A Sect."

"What-the-shit-ever. A Sect. That's badass. Saying no's plain stupid."

Olive wore a proud smile as she passed the Coven ledger for Adam to sign, officially making him a Ballard Family Coven member.

"Lu?" Olive asked for my mother's answer.

"I need time."

I wasn't so sure a decade of time would be enough judging by the look of restrained horror on her face as my brother scratched his name down in the old book.

"You can join when you're ready. No matter when you make the decision, you will always be welcome."

Mom nodded her thanks, but I wasn't so sure an answer would come.

———

Back at the party, everything moved on smoothly, as if the others in the attic hadn't been missed. Not surprising, considering the amount of faces bloating the estate walls. Amazing how easily we could leave the attic and the events that occurred within it behind. Olive fought for this night with years of her life she will never get back. She earned it and I wanted every moment to be perfect. The fact that a trial-by-Elder jury, semi-torture, and forced admission of treason occurred in the attic only solidified how the estate operated on both sides of the Blind and Magic realms.

Adam and his band were commissioned to perform and had been waiting for Adam. They set up in a large, long room that could easily hold a wedding reception of over two hundred guests. Their instruments stood beneath a decorative plaster ceiling and crystal chandeliers to rival the one in the sitting room, creating the perfect amount of elegant ambiance. Knowing their music—and thinking the screaming routine would be too much for the present crowd—I was floored when they played acoustically and altered the heavy screaming into melodic singing so people could hear thought-provoking lyrics.

"Wanna dance?" Donovan asked me with surprising nonchalance. I blinked at him, and my gaze swept to Kim. She gave the same leer of uncertainty. Not a hint of nervousness across the connection coloured his request. "Come on. I promise I won't scuff your boots." He leaned in closer. "Which are totally hot, by the way." This made me laugh and I accepted.

Kim smiled as we left the table, keeping it at a low voltage as Frog, who had finally showed after work, had been staring at us with confusion and suspicion since he arrived.

Donovan had skill. Nothing fancy, but he knew how to lead and, as promised, never scuffed my boots once.

"What'd you and my brother talk about back up in the attic?" Adam's band moved to the next song. I glimpsed my mom over Donovan's shoulder dancing with Brian. She gave a light smile and refocused on her date.

"Music."

"Of course." I laughed. "Probably a test to see how cool you were."

"Apparently we have similar tastes. And they're not bad." He tilted his head toward the stage.

I looked to my brother sitting on a stool of the makeshift stage with his bandmates. He was now in the Ballard Coven and would have to hide it from everyone he knew, including the guys next to him who he spent most of his time with. I hoped he could carry the burden with minimal angst. Though his music would be a good outlet.

"Soooo, what were you and your mom talking about?" He flashed the full deviousness of his dimples without missing a step of our causal swaying.

"*Pfft*. Like you don't know."

"Not exactly. Naturally, I assume me, but details work better for conversational value."

"Nice theory on getting your way." I took a breath before answering. "Yes, we talked about you. Caine too." He nodded. "And about the asylum that is the Coven and how the Magic world operates. She's afraid I'll get hurt."

"Does that stand regarding me too?"

"In a mother's eyes? Always. Caine's questioning made her more at ease, but still."

"You're not convinced."

"It's not that."

"Too soon after Caine." I nodded. "That's okay."

"Is that so?"

"I know how this ends. I can wait."

"No guarantees." I looked up at him, my arms still clasped behind his suited shoulders.

"I know." His smile didn't convince me he actually believed what I said, but there was nothing else I could say and nothing that would change his mind, so I left it alone and enjoyed the dancing I hadn't remembered doing since high school.

"Did I tell you how beautiful you look tonight?"

"Shut up."

He just laughed.

25

SURREAL

"When did you become such a hooker?" Adam said as he grabbed a toothpick with some type of cubed meat and cheese, added it to his plate, and then pushed in front of me to steal the tooth-picked sweet pickle I had been reaching for.

A punch in the kidneys moved him out of my way.

"Ow! I'm just saying." He popped the pickle into his mouth and talked around it. "Single forever, then you're double-dipping? Not like you."

"What? Only you get to stick it in everything that walks?" I got a side-eyed look from someone outside the family filling a plate with finger foods. They continued when I didn't apologize or bother to address them. "Plus, I'm not double-dipping."

"Oooh, Caine not gettin' any?"

I scoffed. "Not like it's any of your business."

"Okay, fine, I won't recap your sudden sex life."

"You say it as if you knew anything about it in the first place."

"Whatever. Fine, you're the cockmaster of your generation.

Congratulations. Hope the crown comes with a cream for the rash you're probably hiding."

I shook my head and started to head back to our table. Adam followed, then stopped me.

"Seriously though, go for Donovan. That guy's decent."

"Are you high?"

His face screwed up. "Obviously." He held up his plate full of food fit for satiating the munchies. "But for reals. He's more your type."

"Since when was Caine not my type?" I remembered Kim making the same point, like it was a fact and wondered why this was easily seen when I didn't think I possessed a type.

"Since when was he? Caine's more like Brock, which isn't something to brag about. Frat boy. All I gotta say."

Brock and Caine were nothing alike, though I couldn't fault Adam, he knew nothing about the real Brock and what he did to me. "He's not a frat boy." The label fit the version of Caine before the sleeping curse, but not at all the Caine he became since he was awakened. "Serena's not a Donovan fan."

"*Pfft*. Who cares? She liked Brock, too. In the beginning, at least. Look how that turned out. Plus, this Donovan kid is attached to you or whatever. How big is that? No matter what guy you meet, they'll never top it. And come on, from a chick perspective, being able to tell if your man's lying is like a bitch's jackpot."

"Classy, Adam. You really know how to drive your point home."

"'Kay, but from a brother's perspective, you could do a helluva lot worse than someone who's not only cool, but willing to lick your boots for the rest of your life. Don't screw it up."

Wow. Usually I was the one telling him not to screw up a good thing. Super surreal.

Including finger foods and cocktails wasn't enough, Olive made certain the night included a catered dinner. Pulled pork, steak, seafood, vegetarian, and allergy friendly options had them salivating, plus baked or roasted potatoes and steamed veggies gave the plate some colour. Bottles of red and white table wine were emptied—plus Champagne or anything else that could have been asked for, from the cheapest beer to the fanciest scotch. I imagined the kitchen was a madhouse with oven mitts. By the beaming look radiating from Olive from across the round table, unless the kitchen was burning down, she was in bliss.

The large table was topped with cream-coloured satin tablecloths and a tall, glass centerpiece of exotic-looking flowers. The table was comfortable and alive with conversation between myself, Donovan, Lu, Brian, Serena, Adam, Kim, and Frog. When Frog asked why Caine wasn't present, my comfort bloomed tension and I hesitated on an answer. Clearly Caine hadn't spoken to his friends about our split, and dwelling on it would only spoil Kim's special night.

I told them Caine came by earlier, with no elaboration. He nodded but didn't look to have bought it. When Donovan left the table to use the washroom, he commented to Kim that Donovan seemed "far too comfortable" next to me. Kim waved it off and shot me a look I had no clue what to do about. I wasn't about to get into it now, and it wasn't my fault Caine didn't update his buddies, though it was odd that he hadn't.

Exultant voices and unadulterated laughter erupted from party goers, all seeming to be having a wonderful time. No uncomfortable silences among family, and a much better turnout than the reunion. As I scanned the room, I caught sight of an unexpected attendee. My grandmother, Elizabeth.

"Who's that?" Donovan questioned retaking his seat with a fresh drink in hand.

I leaned in to explain that she was the formally loved and now detested "Grandma Lizzie", as well as her role in the saturation of the Ballard bloodline, sustained family breakdown, and Olive's unjust institutionalization. My grandmother's soul glow had resumed its sickly state. After glimpsing the slight enlightenment after releasing Olive from the spell holding her prisoner within The Royal, I was hopeful she would no longer shun her heritage, but her soul was still suffering as it had been the first time my power took it in.

I knew Olive would invite her, but I never expected her to RSVP with any amount of pleasure. The estate was the physical representation of every blasphemous notion my grandmother had. Being within the mouth of the epicentre of evil should have left her beyond enraged, but as Donovan and I looked to the aging woman in her sleek sea-foam pant suit and newly set perm, she showed no hint of this hatred. Genuine happiness radiated through her with no need for theatrics, enjoying conversation with my Uncle Roger, his wife, Yvette, and their five children, Shannon being one of them.

Movement at our table was Frog nudging Kim, his head bowed, blond brows stitched while his baby blues read a text message. I watched it play out, reading him like a thought bubble popped above his head. I would bet my boots Frog had decided to text Caine about where he was and that now the cat was out of the bag.

Dread had my stomach in knots, though mostly for Kim.

She leaned over to read the text Frog showed her and her expression tightened. No way to hide it now. Whispering in his ear, what looked like part explanation part apology, Frog went from confused to pissed as Kim begged for discretion until they could talk more later.

When Kim's gaze flashed my way, I mouthed an apology, but before anything more could be done, Lewis was on his feet. He raised his glass and clinked it with a knife to quiet the room for Olive to make a toast. Her heartfelt thanks came with stifled tears. She blurred in and out of view a few times, especially when she called out myself and Serena for bringing her back to the family, but only lost a tear or two and stood with most others in applause—or a whistle in Roger's case, as if it had been a bikini contest—when she finished. The family and their guests shared a drink under the roof of a place long neglected, and now overflowing with celebration and love. Then, I lost another tear when Olive made her way through the crowd to wrap me in a tight embrace, while ruffling Bosco's fur as he sat gladly taking all the table scraps people threw him.

No one could have asked for a grander event. Except for the kidnapping, interrogation, and abysmal act of humiliation that should have been avoided, everything turned out beautifully. The Ballard Family Coven was bursting its seams to make room for many more. Plus, no one got fall-down hammered, and Adam's band was booked for gigs past Christmas.

Smiles all around.

Anyone needing or wanting to stay the night were put up in a room. I could have stayed, but I decided to return to Donovan's and reconvene with the Elders since they were back in the picture. Communicating with them from Donovan's still seemed like the safer choice. They had imposed themselves on Olive long enough. Adding this wasn't an option in my mind.

Kim wasn't so sure about her plan yet, so we hung back as she and Frog talked in the front sitting room. My mom hugged me goodbye and left with Brian. She was too enamoured by the night after the incident in the attic to hold onto anger, at least for the moment. Adam punched me in the arm and then laughed after remembering his hit was also against Donovan. Serena was sticking around for the night but was making herself busy so she could sneak back up into the attic.

All extended a goodbye to Donovan. The reception he received was an amazing surprise to me. What I expected was what he and I received from my grandmother, a sizing up resulting in disgust layered beneath her sweet, grandmotherly disguise. His soul glow was no doubt greater than mine and not something she could miss, but he remained confident and aloof, refusing to wilt under her scrutiny.

We moved outside at a snail's pace behind Kim and Frog, as they still hashed out whatever they were talking about. Donovan stopped and talked to the Bouncer, who he apparently knew and didn't see since he entered though the attic. I decided I had waited long enough. Frog was either going to come to terms with Caine and me no longer being together or he wasn't. If our drama wasn't the topic of their conversation, then talking about it surrounded by strangers wasn't going to help.

"Such a great party, Soph," Kim said as I approached, painting on a smile.

"Is it balls or stupidity that made you think you could walk up to me?" I thought Frog was talking to me, but he was looking over my shoulder as Donovan had approached.

"Frog—" Kim's shock matched my own.

Donovan gave a curt laugh. "Is it a birth defect or are you always a douche?"

"Come on." I grabbed Donovan's arm to eject him from the situation, but he didn't budge and Kim's efforts to stop Frog went equally unheard as he stepped closer into Donovan's personal bubble.

"Sleeping with my boy's girl, huh? How's it feel to get his sloppy-seconds?"

Donovan gave a bugger laugh. "Not my fault your boy didn't know what to do once he got in there."

"Yo!" I shot back at him and sensed a hint of regret across the connection before it was erased by a blur and blinding pain across my jaw.

The gasp of others still hanging around outside was heard before my vision cleared. A zing of blood washed over my tongue as a gruff voice joined us and then was waved off by Donovan. The Bouncer was doing what he was paid for, but we didn't need his type of power against Frog. When I could see Frog again, his eyes were wide, and he was pointing at Donovan. He hadn't punched me, not directly, but he saw it impacted me anyway and was freaking his shit. Talk about worst-case scenario.

"We're fine," I managed, holding my face and smiling at a few people around us so they wouldn't get involved.

Kim hauled Frog away and toward where I assumed his truck was, but even in the dark under imposing oaks, denying what he saw was impossible. Whatever Kim was going to tell him, it would either end or solidify their relationship. She talked about wanting to bring him into the fold. Now was her chance.

"Asshole," Donovan muttered and spat blood into the grass and healed the damage.

"*You're* the asshole. How about we go one week where I'm not left bloody?" I swiped my face and wiped it on the grass.

"You're gonna blame that jock-licker's hissy-fit on me?"

"Considering he has no clue what's going on—plus you made his best friend seem like a limp chump—You're damn right I am." I stalked away.

"Where are you going?"

"Your car, dickcheese." I headed towards the Z24 still parked askew in the grass, full of dust and mud.

"What did you do to her?"

"To her? Seriously? Sheee didn't exactly slow to a soft stop when Baldy snatched you. I was a tad rushed to get to Olive's and off the road. And, since I hate fighting, drop it, and think about what's actually important."

"Being?" He checked his blind spots and pulled off the grass.

"Stop." I passed him Bosco and jumped out to use a dose of power to fix the grass, disguising this as me trying to fix my boot and assuming no one could see in the dim light.

"Really?"

"Yes really," I shot back at him.

I jumped back in the car and took Bosco. "Frog knows nothing about us, but I doubt he would have hit you knowing the damage it could do. Obviously, he found out about me and Caine, and was sticking up for his friend—"

"No. His 'boy'. *Pfft*. Such a tool."

"Still. He was being an immature sock-humper and you took the bait and gave him ammo to shut your smug mouth."

The car was quiet after that. He left his pissyness to ride the connection in silence as we sped down sky-lit roads back to the highway.

Returning to Donovan's was still quite the sight. The safeguard in place on the mansion glowed as bright as *National Lampoon's Christmas*. Opening the door was less than exciting. At least no one was hiding, ready to rush us as soon as we entered.

Bosco was given some water as I headed to the room Caine and I shared to change out of my dress. I had used the room twice now, and the blankets were still messed on Caine's side, contaminated with the memory of that stewing night sleeping with his back to me. I could change rooms, but then would have to admit why, and I didn't want to confess it bugged me as much as it did.

Kim arrived an hour later, finding us in the basement. I couldn't mind-meld Aunt Lacey's premonition to make sense, but it didn't mean I couldn't try. Donovan was busy trying to find more information about the Puppeteer, when we were hit with a sense of urgency of someone crossing the wards. Donovan sprinted in front of me and slid in his socked feet in the kitchen when he saw who it was.

"Oh, hey."

"Hey," Kim said, en route down the hall.

I followed and leaned against the threshold of the Victorian-style room Kim was using as her bedroom. "You don't look completely pissed. Is he?" Kim sat on a bench at the end of the bed and fought to get her strappy sandals off, throwing them into the corner. I took it as a yes. "What did he say?"

Kim clutched the edge of the bench, her head falling forward, and inhaling deep. "He's not sure what he saw. Actually, he knows exactly what he saw, but because I wouldn't confirm I saw it too or that I know what happened, he's pretty pissed. Plus, Caine told him what happened with you two, or close enough since it's easier to say, 'She fucked around' than get into the magical aspect that could possibly have triggered your libido, especially since Caine still doesn't know what happened. Thus, Frog knows very little and is pissed I defended you."

There's a best friend for you. Has your back even when they know you were dead wrong. "You would never, under normal circumstances, condone what happened. So, I'm guessing he's thinking if you thought it was okay, then you might do the same."

"Pretty much." Kim wrenched the bobby pins out of her bun. "What now?"

"Nothing concrete in the way of Splittsville, but I have a feeling the whole, 'I have things about my life you can't know' isn't going to hold up much longer."

I nodded. "Frog had every right to hit Donovan. Though Frog was an immature twat as well."

"Fucking right."

———

"I think we should call Ranlyn." Kim's voice reached us in the basement before she did. "Read him the premonition since he didn't get our messages."

"Go ahead," Donovan said without looking up from the book he read. "If he hadn't checked his messages before, after Olive's spanking, I bet he did when he left the attic."

"True."

"Don't pout, Kim," I said. "It won't get you out of research."

"Ugh. I hate research." Kim plunked onto the couch Donovan and I utilized for a much unintended purpose. I couldn't sit on it yet without invading images of him, opting to sit on the floor instead.

"We'll probably figure it out before him, anyway," Donovan said, again without giving his full attention.

Kim took the premonition to review. "Part of it has already come true, so at least we know it has some validly. We know who's behind the eyes, even if we don't know who the Puppeteer is."

"And enemies coming in threes," I added. "That's gotta be Loring, the Puppeteer, and now the Raddies."

"And the Raddies have the strength of someone referred to as the Human Engineer," Donovan said.

"You memorized it?" Kim asked.

"Carrying it around isn't smart, so yes, I memorized it. The 'childish interference' part is clearly the kid with the spots."

"Andy," I said. "Though I'm not sure what ancient cost he paid. But he definitely didn't think I was going to survive, so I'm not sure the 'he' means him. And it's not on the same line, so maybe 'he' is someone entirely different."

"At least it's right about the death part being brief since you two weren't crispy for long."

I nodded gratefully, though was still confused as to how we came back. "And tonight, the estate became a place of bloodlines converging and torture. By my own hands, which was—"

"Justified," Donovan interrupted. "Woulda' been cool to see that cellar."

"Relax the devilish dimples, bro," Kim said. "Olive wouldn't have let it happen."

"Bro? Picking up vocabulary skills from your boyfriend?"

"What about the 'Trees of Heaven'?" I couldn't handle their bickering. "Apparently they bring answers and the Devil. Excellent."

After another forty minutes of fruitless research, Kim stretched out on the couch and groaned, while Donovan left for some caffeine.

"So, do I get details?" she asked me.

"Details?"

"You and Donovan? You haven't said anything except, 'It was the best ever.'" She spoke in a nauseating, romantic voice that was thick with mockery.

"I didn't have a measuring tape available if that's what you're asking."

Kim laughed. "Gotta be nice to know you christened his new bed. The conquests the last had seen are not something you want to mix with."

"If by bed you mean the couch you're lying on, then yeah, it's probably clean of slut-bag sludge." Kim popped up onto her feet. "Or where you're standing."

"Come on. We have Coven Meetings down here." She kicked my straightened legs.

My attention snapped to the stairs as Donovan's hyperactive brain registered while he was still upstairs. "What's up?" I asked loudly before he reached the top of the stairs.

"Damn, that's creepy," Kim muttered.

"Ranlyn called. They have a lead on the Trees of Heaven."

"And?" Kim egged on.

"They think it could be the Woodland of Energies."

The fact that we hadn't connected the dots before was embarrassing. "So, then, there's actually a Heaven?"

"Trees of Heaven come from the premonition as it was communicated to Aunt Lacey for her to understand," Kim said. "People associate death and the afterlife with Heaven or Hell these days, it's probably no more than that, but maybe."

"Seriously doubt it." Donovan pulled on a hoodie. "Either way, we have under ten minutes before the Apporter shows up."

"We're going tonight?"

"Would you rather wait until your schedule permits it, Kim?"

"Dick."

"Get your shoes on, he's meeting us in the car." No apology was attached to Donovan's command. He left the basement before we could ask why the Apporter would meet us in the car, of all places, and something about the emotions crossing the connection made me nervous.

Shoes and sweaters on, we piled into the car and Donovan backed out of the driveway and parked at the curb in front of the house.

"What are you doing?" I asked him.

"The wards stop the Apporter from coming onto the property and we don't have the stuff Miklos did to make the exception." He checked over his shoulders, me and Kim looking as well, fueled by his suspicion, then heard him murmur a spell.

"Can the Apporter see through a Cover spell?" Kim asked.

"Doesn't need to. He knows we're here."

The Apporter's soul glow filled the car a couple minutes later. I warned the others. When his form was added to the backseat, we were whisked away as Donovan had been the first time we met. I didn't know what I expected, but I didn't feel anything but the difference between the stillness of the inside air of Donovan's car and then the unrelenting wind across the open field outside of Diluculo. The Coven marker was already activated and shimmering with a silvery-blue cone shape above it. The Elders were waiting, Ranlyn standing with a stainless-steel container in his hand.

"Shitcakes!" A chunk of my wind-whipped hair in my mouth muffled my words. "We can't skip the horror movie cheese grater experience through the veil?"

"Only Elders and non-organic items can make the trip without aid. The consequence of bringing you and Donovan through together is not one I'm willing to risk." Ranlyn handed over a cup and filled it with orange, chunky fluid and I reminded myself not to smell it. "Until you're ready to be an Elder, you'll have to endure the pain."

"Who said I wanted to be an Elder? Don't get fancy ideas, Jeeves."

Ranlyn gave me a crooked smile and filled a glass for Donovan.

"Don't worry, babe. It'll only feel like death."

While we waited for the others to get their cups filled, I noticed the Apporter's liquid was darker than everyone else's. Without waiting, he drank his down, and I watched the Taint of his soul dissolve. Once his slate was clean, he stood over the Coven Marker within the wispy cone of colour and took the ride from hell into the Creation.

"Ranlyn." He turned and invaded my personal space by leaning in close to speak within inches of my ear.

"Keep your voice down," he told me.

With the high winds, it wasn't difficult. The hitch in tension and jealousy told me what Donovan thought about our huddle and that he wasn't trusting my response in a wordless "Calm your tits" sensation. "If there's a drink to un-Taint someone, then anyone could have come into the Creation to kill the Elders or get through our wards or pretend to be—"

"Only we have the recipe."

"Then why not look at the current Elders for corruption instead of its members?"

He pulled back enough for me to see regret in his eyes as he said, "I am." He then stood back and watched with the others as the Apporter disappeared in full as if he hadn't dropped a bomb on me.

I had so many questions. When did he start to suspect another Elder? Did he always suspect one? Could they have planned all this to get themselves a seat in power? Why were they granted immortality from the deceased Elders if they killed them? Did he know this before he allowed them in my family's attic? Could Ranlyn himself be a suspect? I trusted him over the others. Did I miss any signs to say I shouldn't have?

Kim, and especially Donovan, were looking at me with degrees of suspicious curiosity and I couldn't say a word.

Kim was next to take the spiralled rollercoaster from Hell through the veil. Her loose hair blew wildly around her face and then she crumbled to her knees and gouged her nails into the grass. The silvery magic covered her body in powerful symbols to guarantee her passage into the Creation. Nothing made the fight easier. The term "grin and bear it" came to mind, but there was no grinning.

Donovan opted to pass through before me, so I wouldn't be on the other side waiting for when he might come through. Gentlemanly in his own way, but no matter who went first, the result was the same.

I gave my drink to Ranlyn to hold onto since I dumped it the last time. Donovan swallowed down the *Tono di voce* to activate the ability to get through the veil. Both of us went down. Symbols of power and the pain of transitioning into something that could get into the Creation, had me writhing in the grass as Donovan was catapulted through to the other side.

Having your insides blended with a wood chipper and squeezed through a Play-Doh press wasn't a feeling you got used to.

Waiting only a minute, as not to prolong the agonizing wait for Donovan, Ranlyn handed me back my dose of 'fuck this sucks' and I downed the viscous fluid that stuck to the paper cup. The feeling of rusty pitchforks mincing my insides had me right back down in the grass in the fetal position gritting through the ride into Diluculo.

When pain subsided enough to open my eyes, I didn't see the Diluculo I left not so long ago. No vibrant autumn colours, no hum of running, laughing, and yelling children and families, or vendors pitching wares. Diluculo was a ghost town. Night had fallen on the semblance of perfection, and when Donovan and I managed to get to our feet, the look shared between us was a silent question to make sure we were okay. We survived the journey, but seeing Diluculo again, being in the place where Aunt Lacey was lost to us, meant we were far from okay.

26

WOODLAND OF ENERGIES

The sign welcoming us to Diluculo looked sallow as it hung above us. The Creation took on the likeliness of the outside world, minus the grating wind. No one spoke as we made our way past the square where Nitsa delivered her powerful speech. She was then cremated in the exact spot as another speech for a Crossing Ritual was spoken for her and the other Elders.

Walking by Aunt Lacey's cabin and the lapping waves off the white sand beach, it didn't take long for us to cross the Creation and come upon the outskirts of the trees where we watched Aunt Lacey and the dead Elders ashes grow to become beautiful trees amongst the others within the Woodland of Energies.

"Since we're not in the *Lord of the Rings*, how do we get the trees to talk?" Kim asked. I looked at her confused and she muttered, "Ex-boyfriend was a fan."

"We don't. A Summoner does." Ranlyn pointed within the trees.

When we followed his line of sight, we saw a person in the distance. As the willowy figure came closer, her short dark hair swopped over her forehead. Her reed thin frame seemed to float towards us as she bore an exulted smile and held her arms out to brush leaves and branches with her fingers as she passed them.

"So much life," the pixie of a woman sang as she met us.

"Jheri." Ranlyn snatched her attention from the greenery around her. "Thank you for making the trip. It was my understanding you were not readily available, so again, I thank you for coming on short notice."

Jheri waved him off with a throaty sound. "Bein' present for this is an honour, Elder Ranlyn. Clients can cool their pies," she insisted in a southern drawl.

Making quick introductions, Ranlyn stepped back, allowing Jheri room to begin. Jheri took a small metal object from her back pocket. Not until she held it out and rang it did I realize it was a tiny bell. I counted as Jheri rang the bell seven times before slipping it back into her pocket. She then rubbed her hands together and went still as power prickled at my skin.

"Impressive," Donovan said then leaned in closer. "Usually takes much more than that and a shit tonne of props. She's powerful."

"And in the first stage of immortality," I added looking over her rose-coloured, metallic soul glow like Ranlyn used to have. No doubt she's already slowed the aging process.

Jheri's lips began to move, the escaping whispers meant for the dead, as the atmosphere thickened with unseen presence. Light flared in random increments around us. Some close, others deep within the forest growth. After half an hour passed, the light became concentrated. The process of finding the soul needed was made more difficult since we stood in a graveyard. Every buried soul of a Magic begged for the opportunity to make itself known, Jheri having to shoo them off to get to the soul she sought.

Jheri moved her hands in a way that mimicked guiding fragile bubbles in the air, then held them out in front of her, her eyes still closed as if she found what she needed and was holding it in place.

Before us, what started as a flash of an indeterminate form, had morphed into a body. The energy within the air grew unsteady before snapping into view, leaving Jheri to stand in place with a gleaming satisfied smile stretched ear-to-ear.

Mouths were catching flies—primarily mine, Donovan, and Kim's. We watched in awe as Aunt Lacey come into focus. No blood, no gasps for breath she no longer needed, no fear, no goodbyes, no nothing but our mentor and Leader standing, yet not standing, in front of us.

Numbness washed over me. Something instinctual from Donovan, I guessed. He was processing everything in tiny increments, not quite trusting what he saw. I knew this wasn't a trick and knew Donovan knew this as well, but like me, he didn't prep for this and was knocked off guard. We thought we would never see her again. It took considerable effort to push aside his denial and focus on the rise in emotion her presence caused.

Aunt Lacey came through as vibrant as she had in life, looking at her audience with pleasure. "How joyous it is to see you all again." Her eyes landed on each of us and paused over Donovan for a lingering moment. Pressure in my eyes told me he was fighting tears with all his strength.

"Our apologies." Ranlyn bowed, as did the other Elders. "In this time of great stress, we call upon you and no other. Your guidance is greatly needed in a matter that has unfortunately persisted as you and the others have not."

Aunt Lacey nodded in grave understanding. "Loring lives on." Hinapouri straightened as if it took effort not to fold under disappointing a superior. "My premonition has taken some time to make it back to me." Her gaze shifted to me.

Tears trailed down my cheeks against my will, be it from Donovan or my own unconscious despair. I swiped at my face and worked to pull myself together. "I didn't understand it."

Instead of the dissatisfied leer I expected, Aunt Lacey giggled. "Of course not, Salix. That's what the aid of the Coven is for. My translations were primitive at best. Only in death could I see the truth of them."

A million questions begged to be asked. Maybe the anticipation was Donovan's. He said Aunt Lacey saved him, that she was family. I couldn't imagine what he wanted to say to her if given the privacy.

"Your premonition, as written to Salix, explains going to the 'Trees of Heaven' for answers," Ranlyn said. "Do you know anything that could assist us in fighting the Puppeteer and this Devil you state comes concurrently with this meeting?"

"You already know the evil you face. Loring, of course, but he is but a player in the plan to bring your world down. The Puppeteer is Loring's Coven Master, his involvement expected. Even the Eradicators have crossed your radar, as they too will soon make their move. The enemy, I fear, is not one that shows their ugliness by bearing arms. It is the one left unchecked behind the smile of a jackal—dangerous and much closer to home."

"I knew it," Hinapouri said with a growl. "Who is this traitor?"

With Ranlyn's suspicions in mind, I looked to the new Elders, wondering if Aunt Lacey was insinuating them.

"It is not simple treachery as you believe it to be, Hinapouri," Aunt Lacey said. "The Puppeteer is no match for some. Even some perceived as impervious can fall to his will."

"Meaning?" Miklos asked with thick irritation.

"Ask him."

Everyone looked to each other in confusion. Any face time they had with the Puppeteer would result in blood and gore, not a civilized conversation. He was happy fighting them through his Puppets instead of getting his hands dirty.

Aunt Lacey smiled and clasped her hands in front of her. "It has been a long time, Evaristus. Old tricks always were your forte."

More confusing than the name that she used was the fact that Aunt Lacey was speaking to Veata.

"Veata?" Hinapouri questioned as everyone faced the old woman.

"Not at the moment," Aunt Lacey said.

The aged features of the small Asian Elder changed into the

sinuous smile of the true bearer behind clouded eyes. "Shame I was not the one to end your life, Elsa." The Puppeteer spoke through Veata's discoloured teeth. Energy swelled as everyone tensed for battle. "You cannot kill me by ending your co-Elder's life. You will merely need to find another substitute for my Coven to strike down."

Anger seethed with every breath as the Elders were handcuffed against taking action.

"These games are fanciful, but I begin to tire," the Puppeteer said. "My presence in this body is proof of this Coven's fallibility."

"Then speak with your own tongue long enough for it to be cut out." Hinapouri had a long blade raised and looked more than capable of using it.

Veata's hostage eyes swept to Hinapouri with a smile all their own, meeting the challenge. She then looked away, and above us, cocking her ear to the sky as if listening. "You may get your opportunity yet." Slow movements had the Puppeteer looking back at Hinapouri. "If you possess the bravery, warrior, you must merely stand, and you shall have your wish."

What he meant became clear seconds later. Cracking, breaking, whining. Undiscernible sounds filled the air, growing louder as they drew closer.

"You must all leave. Now!" Aunt Lacey warned. Jheri struggled as Aunt Lacey's form wavered. She had a firm hold of Aunt Lacey's spirit, but as soon as Aunt Lacey broke with orders, Jheri's hands had whipped out in front of her again as she strained to hold Aunt Lacey to our world. "Your enemies have surfaced! Leave now!"

We broke into a run.

I looked back to where Aunt Lacey once stood, but she was gone. This time, there was no goodbye. Left in her place was Veata, her expression so twisted you could glimpse the monster inside of her. She ceased to be the kooky old immortal and took on a whole new perverse role as our prime tormentor.

"What about Veata?" I yelled to the others as I sprinted as fast as

I could, knowing I couldn't keep this pace up. "They'll kill her." Either no one heard, or they did and didn't care.

The crushing sound of pulverized wood blistered our eardrums and the ground trembled under our feet. The Trees of Heaven were ripped into toothpicks. While risking feverish glances over our shoulders, we couldn't see what destroyed Diluculo's resting place, but wood and foliage were tossed high in the air like sawdust.

Expecting a fleet of savage Tainted mystics with snarling grins and missing teeth—resembling the majority of every movie star villain I could imagine—I was shocked when I turned and saw people. Just people. If I couldn't see what I usually did, I would have assumed we were being chased down by an angry mob of political protestors. Most of them were Blind, with no soul glow at all. No billowing darkness escaping their souls.

Looking harder, as much as I could while running, I saw an ample amount of true Magics clearing the way for the Blind, hiding themselves in the back ranks for the addle-brained humans—or, most likely, Puppets. One of the shepherds leading the lambs to the slaughter had a formidable ability but hid within the mix of the Puppeteer's pawns and rained fire down on us.

No Molotov cocktails were needed when fireballs dropped from the sky in random pot-shots like mortar rounds—in sizes that ranged from golf balls to a bachelor's widescreen. Running towards the direction of the cabins, expecting safety, we only found building-sized infernos. Bursts of dirt and debris blew up in our faces as fire plunged into the earth like some box office war flick, knocking us off-balance.

Communal buildings that used to sell wares and host inspired mystic events now exploded, setting the sky above to a midday brightness, then a fierce black. Thick, toxic smoke blocked out the sheen of the moon amongst the clouds. The sting of fragmented rock pelted my skin as I looked behind me again, spotting the demented group in the distance.

Unseen Magics within the group treated this like a game, instead of an all-out lynching. A flash of light blazed somewhere in front of me and showcased a mob with no supernatural extras. No soul glows, no Tainted evil. Swords, axes, flails, and other crude weapons I had never seen beyond a History Channel special, were in the grips of the enemy now less than a football field away.

I was losing speed, surviving step-by-step on adrenaline alone. Donovan kept stride near me, but I knew he could have been yards out front by now if my years of asthma and laziness weren't holding him back. Miklos and Ranlyn held their own, as did the Summoner, Jheri, whose short legs moved so fast they were barely visible. Hinapouri trumped us all. Celerity was one of her gifts and her speed shot her out front of the pack so far ahead, she disappeared.

One-by-one, the Elders began to vanish, whisked away by the Apporter. He couldn't use his power to skip the barrier through the veil, but once inside the Creation, it was fair game. Since we were spread out along the width of the field, he couldn't scoop us all out in one swoop. The Apporter snatched who he could, the Elders his first priority.

In his haste to escape the encroaching Puppets, the Apporter made a grab for Kim after the Elders and Jheri were gone. He popped up next to her, scaring the shit out of her, and causing her to hit the ground in a wild skid. She careened headlong into a solid wood table. The grass beneath her did nothing to soften the blow as it flew into the air around her when her head bounced, and her body somersaulted off the wood. Legs and arms rag-dolled at all angles, consequently tripping the Apporter, both entangled in a knot of limbs.

The group was gaining on us. Donovan and I turned back for Kim. He was inundated with visions as he grabbed for Kim and made skin contact, his shock racing through me without the visions that blinded him. A gash in Kim's head wept blood and mixed with the red of her hair and ran across her face. I yelled for Donovan to hurry as he hoisted her limp body up by her armpits and heaved her up to her feet in one grunting, muscle-flexing movement. I took a side to try and drag her along as best I could. Her head flopped around. Her weight was unevenly distributed, threatening to pitch us forward with every step. Running was out of the question.

The sky around us was still bursting in fire. The horde gained considerable advantage as we struggled.

"They're coming!" Donovan yelled to the Apporter struggling to his feet. Effective, but as soon as the Apporter's husky-eyes widened in comprehension, he lunged forward, grabbing hold of Donovan, and disappeared.

Donovan's panic shot through the connection, rage on its heels. Kim's dead weight pulled us down and we landed hard.

The ground destabilized further, akin to walking on a grass-covered water bed. I pulled at Kim's arm, and then fell back on my ass as the ground hitched under my feet and threw me off-balance again. Kim rode the waves flat on her face. I pushed her onto her side to roll her over, and got her halfway, when a long reed of grass snatched her forearm and pulled her back down.

A high-pitched screech came out of me—one I'd never heard me make before—choking me as I fell back on my hands. The grass beneath me was sticky. When I shrunk away from it, the grass peeled off like little alien fingers. A lash of more grass struck out like the one now twisting its hold around Kim's arm and pulled me down into the sticky blades, trying to cover me.

I ripped the reeds off me and freed Kim's arm, only for the grass to lash out and replace its hold. I got up and attempted to drag Kim toward the Creation exit, trying to pull her all at once from the reeds instead of a blade at a time. She came loose, and I raced backwards, calling her name with no response. A ball of fire landed and threw sparks like fireworks, tossing us back down onto the greedy vines.

Reeds grabbed me around the throat. I scratched at them to get loose, the sting of my nails broke skin. No! Kim was covered. Her red hair stuck out in tangles from the grip of the reeds, the rest of her lost to the suffocating end-game of whoever's magic was bent on killing us.

I bucked my hips and flailed my feet like a pissed off donkey, shaking myself free enough to slide down into my sweater and slip out. I wrenched my head free and lost a chunk of my hair. Panic had me clawing at Kim's face, trying to stop the grass from smothering her. I pulled back with a hiss, finding my hands bloodied. The blades of grass had transformed into actual blades, piercing my skin as if protecting itself. With the wobbly ground and enemies closing in, I had no other choice but to persevere and ignore the fact that my calves were shackled to the ground where I knelt.

When the Apporter popped through with a flash of light, I threw myself onto Kim. "No! Take us both!"

The field blurred around me, the whiplash a gut-turner, but we didn't go anywhere. The grip of the grass on Kim was keeping us grounded. While the army closed in, vertigo had me rolling off Kim, yet flailing to keep hold of her so the Apporter wouldn't leave her behind.

A second attempt had the Apporter groaning, throwing my arms and rest of my body out of the way, and then ripping Kim from the reeds in one jarring pull.

The whirling world around me settled and brought clear the faces of our enemies. Adrenaline and raw fear surged through my aching veins. Another grunt had me turning to see the Apporter heave Kim's limp body over his shoulder. I pulled at the cutting blades to free myself and reached out for the Apporter's bloodied hand.

It worked. I felt myself falling to the grass near the entrance of the Creation. The rise of Puppets across the Creation was still a cry of fury, though now in the distance. Donovan was on his back, his bloodied hands mimicking my injuries, raging with raised fists at Miklos straddled atop him trying to force-feed the veil concoction into him.

"Sophie!" Donovan yelled as his terror rushed from him, Miklos allowing him to stand.

"Kim's out cold." I tried to push her hair away from her face and smeared blood from my fingers across her cheek. "How's she gonna get through the veil if she can't drink the concoction?"

"Force it," Hinapouri said.

"How 'bout I force something down your fucking throat?"

"We wouldn't get enough down before she chokes." Ranlyn stepped between us. "Take her through," he said to Miklos.

"You want me to sacrifice my life for a Kitchen Witch?"

"She's still—"

Ranlyn cut me off. "Safety is my concern. My homestead is best and we both know without my conscious presence, access is unachievable." Miklos huffed and looked at the others as if expecting them to volunteer in his place. "There's no viable alternative. Coven before self." This must have been a part of some Coven Elder oath I hadn't heard before. I didn't care, it worked. Miklos gave a curt nod, accepting his responsibility.

"Get back through the veil," Ranlyn ordered everyone.

Donovan took the concoction willingly this time, taking the plunge first. Dropping to all fours the instant the concoction hit his gut. Donovan fought the urge to projectile vomit, making the bile rise in my own throat. A zing of metallic ran over my tongue as the crunch of teeth bit through my cheek. Before he fully disappeared, I drank down the concoction, enduring the pain, hoping to someday return, and praying the Puppeteer's hostile takeover left something to return to.

As I clenched the grass in my fists, before the spell brought me through the veil, Veata appeared in front of Hinapouri, standing serenely as if present the entire time. Hinapouri materialized a long weapon, poised in the possessed Elder's direction. Veata flashed a wicked grin, neither impressed nor afraid. The impasse was intense. I closed my eyes. The quicker I got through the veil, the safer I would be.

27

BLOOD PLOT

Dropping onto the other side of the veil was supposed to bring freedom, not Donovan's high-volume curse. I struggled against the effects of the veil jump and a punishing wind to see what was happening. A figure flew twenty-feet in the air. He flailed with a squealing protest and grunt of oxygen-loss, as a blond smacked him into the ground in an awkward crash of limbs.

Donovan sprung protectively between myself and a wall of strangers when he registered my re-entry into the open field. A man from the group stepped closer with the cocky demeanour of a leader. His dirty blond hair was matted with sweat and tied at the nape of his neck. With a day or two's growth on his jaw, his chin was patched with a goatee. His strong shoulders gave him the look of a roofer, while hazel eyes feigned benevolence as a sheathed hunting knife and holstered gun hung from his belt, holding up his gear and roughed-up jeans.

"Don't worry, sweetheart," the man said, maintaining his attention on Donovan, whose power was vibrating at the ready. "We were waiting for you two to come through, and your boyfriend here just got a little spooked."

More humans? No Magics, no shining soul glows among the strangers, and no Puppets. The keen look of subdued hate told me their wills were intact. They had been waiting for us? How could they know we were here? Did they work for Loring?

I wasn't cool with lying on my back and taking whatever these pissed off Blind had planned, while Donovan acted like my personal bodyguard. I flexed to my feet, keeping my stance confident, while still behind Donovan. A strategic decision. Donovan's fighting experience was leaps ahead of mine and I wasn't about to fight my pride while sixty pairs of hungry-for-something eyes glared back at me.

We knew the Elders were coming. We needed to stave off attack until they arrived, but Donovan hadn't seen what I had before leaving Diluculo. The Elders would be tied up longer than comfortable.

"You Raddies don't spook me," Donovan said. "Move closer and you'll die bloody for your cause."

Raddies? You got to be fucking kidding me. These were vengeful, merciless crusaders, fighting for some private motive that fuelled their detestation of anything remotely magic—far more dangerous than the pawns we left behind in the Creation.

The blond man laughed enough for us to see his missing tooth as he stood with his hands on his hips, unafraid of us. "You see, boy, you're not the first demon I've faced. You won't be the last. I'd ask you to come quietly, but I've heard you're not the surrendering type."

He heard? Donovan's inner questioning was a niggling sense of unease that matched my own. How did this guy know about him? I remembered Joelly's confession in the attic and cursed her weakness. But a demon? I had no idea if there were true demons in existence, but I would never envision myself as one. How did they get like this?

"Then I'm sure you've heard more," Donovan said, his cocky smile coloured his tone. "I know enough about your band of reject misfits to be confident I can take a few down on our way out. Including yourself, hillbilly."

A few of the Raddies actually laughed. They trusted their leader could survive two lonely Magics.

The blond man took a few steps towards us. Donovan didn't flinch as the blond man spoke in a low steady voice. "Not if you're busy on your knees, begging for me to slit your throat to relieve your pain."

A piercing tone sawed into our heads. We doubled over at the feet of the cocky asshole, covering our ears to try and stop it. The noise didn't just pierce our eardrums, it invaded our bodies, reverberated through our bones, and dug deep. I had felt this before, though it was now magnified to the nth degree. Excluding the noise, it mirrored the first days of my power building, threatening to bust me into a million pieces.

The noise suddenly stopped. The pain dissipated. Exulted laughter of the onlookers was muffled by blood clogging my ears. I peered through red-stained eyes, sniffling more thick blood I could taste in the back of my throat.

The blond man knelt over Donovan, a slick, self-satisfied grin tugged at his lips at the gory result. "Nice little invention, don't 'cha think?" He straightened and looked down at us in disgust. "Keeps you demons in check. Pat myself on the back every time I watch one of you abominations writhe like the maggots you are."

On my back, still shaking off the pain, I remembered something from the prophecy. The Human Engineer. This man was definitely human with skills far beyond a bow and arrow. Whatever the device was, it was created by his own hands, and he didn't bother to stifle his gloating.

Another of the Raddies handed him something. "Effective, right?" He held a beat-up silver, 1990s rectangular boom-box with a mash of wires, like veins and arteries, escaping it. The makeshift atrocity looked like it could have caused accidental electrocution before it debilitated anyone. "Magnifies whatever devil mojo you got crawlin' 'round inside ya'."

Anger within Donovan shifted into action with a taut fist

punched into open air. A telekinetic hit flung the man above the heads of his followers. The Witch-torturing-devise fell to the ground before it could be reactivated. The man's fellow fanatics caught him before he too collapsed into the grass, coughing, clutching his chest as we gained our footing.

Another loyal co-anarchist, a slender woman with muscular, war-trained features, bounded towards us. The instinct to protect us had me raising my hands and erecting a wall, like the one I had used to keep the world out in Donovan's backyard. The woman hit the wall with a smash of blood from her nose and mouth, then bounced off and onto the ground. She held her face a moment and looked at her bloodied hand before staggering to her feet, ready for an offensive attack.

Instead of giving her what she wanted, I extended the wall to encapsulate us and run cloudy. I wasn't sure why, but I didn't want them looking at us.

"That won't keep them out forever," Donovan said.

"No, but the Elders are too busy with Veata, who popped her possessed ass up in front of them before I left the Creation. They're not saving our asses. Got a backup plan?"

"Fuck. They were my backup plan."

"Got a backup plan for your backup plan? 'Cuz holding this up while out of it in trance-mode is way easier than in fear-mode." I was already beginning to shake.

"My backup's backup involves killing them all. You down for that?"

I looked at him but didn't answer. The blond man found his voice as I lost mine. "Fight all you want or hide within your fake worlds." The blond man's timbre dropped, and I felt the pressure of his fingers drag across my wall. "In the end, whether you live a hundred or a thousand years, your enemies will find you, and boy will they have fun when they do."

This life brought with it true enemies. Not the schoolyard moron who thinks you want her boyfriend, but true enemies who hated you for what and who you stood for, what side of the line you fought for, even who you are. I never anticipated such deep-seated hatred from people who had never met me. The Raddies were fighting a war, while I was happy to fight for the right to exist. I understood their fear. If they were in league with Joelly, or even the Puppeteer in some way, then they knew about real dangers and would be quick to kill anyone with power. Like the blond man said, they would have fun doing it.

Sick fucks.

Donovan's gasp brought me out of my reflection, followed by a glimpse of our enemies who stood an arm's reach away as Donovan's hands shot up into my peripheral vision and his power enacted a wall of his own as mine had dropped without me realizing.

"Fuck, my bad. I wasn't—"

A lashing of pain through my skull had me clutching my head, my mouth wide open, vocal cords too stunned to scream. Neither of our walls were soundproof and the device had no trouble sending us to the ground again, leaving us shaking as we hugged our heads, choked, blinded, and deafened by oozing blood.

Rough hands yanked me to my feet. Jarring impact against my knuckles told me Donovan fought back, but I couldn't find the strength. A strike against Donovan was echoed in my already pounding skull, then mirrored in my knees as the Raddies forced him to the ground and wrenched his arm behind his back with the muscle-ripping finesse of a pissed off beat cop.

They dragged me away, the device still active. My head was pounding—my hands were restrained so I couldn't use them as a vice against the pain. Not even an unconscious Kim was immune to the damaging effects, her body a bloody mess on the ground next to an unconscious Miklos. Kitchen Witch or not, Kim had a semblance of true magic and the device sought out her power.

"What is this?" Hinapouri's powerful voice trickled through my bloodied ears.

The hands around my wrists and ankles tightened, those who

owned them stopping in the field, letting my body hang until my ass touched the grass.

"They're unaffected." I heard a deep voice say.

"I told you it wouldn't work on the old ones." A younger voice said, panic evident in their voice.

"Shut it," both were warned by a third.

"No!" One of my captors screamed and gravity took over. My left shoulder and side of my face hit the ground before the rest of my limbs. I curled into the fetal position as yelled protests around me were made distant. I struggled to concentrate through the throbbing in my skull. I got the impression that some of the Raddies saw the Elders arrival as an opportunity to kick some ass, while others knew it was a death sentence.

I blinked through a red haze to get a handle on the situation and saw Raddies running for the Elders. A couple Raddies remained near me, watching their comrades engage in an attack. As they got close to Ranlyn, he raised his hand and stopped multiple aggressors in place mid-stride. He turned his palm parallel to the ground, then slapped the earth in a blurred movement that made the ground undulate like ocean waves.

Anyone in front of Ranlyn was tossed into the air, then dropped back onto the now rigid ground, myself and Donovan included. Groans and shouts in pain filled the field and were swept away in the wind. An errant steel-toe crashed down on my torso, and I heard my own ribs crack. The other boot came down on my throat with a crunch. My panicked breathing was now wheezing through gargled blood.

Fear and confusion spread through the Raddies as they scrambled to their feet to collect their cohorts. Ranlyn's tactic shook up the enemy, but we weren't lucky enough for it to destroy the device. Again, the sound invaded my core. I cried out and scratched at my chest and skull, unable to reach deep enough to rip the pain out of me.

Numbness would have been a blessing, but the only thing numb was my strength to retaliate. I was useless. The pain was overwhelming. Every nanosecond brought excruciating agony as the device attached itself to our power like a parasite, threatening to dig its way out through our pores. Trapped in a foreign husk as convulsions took over, we were victims of our own magic.

It was the perfect weapon.

The Raddies were scared, angered, and confused. I was too debilitated to find out why.

I was wrenched to my feet again, my head lolling to the side as they forced me up. I peered through blood-streaked eyes to see Hinapouri approach a young man with a look that dared him to face her head-on. Entranced, or too stupid to see the danger, she got close and grabbed him by the scruff of his collar and let out a clarion battle cry that resounded through her young enemy and into the air beyond him. He struggled to get away, but it was too late for him.

She let out another cry of her Maori people, and the young man went limp. Her intimidating facial markers creased with her satisfied smile. Driven straight through his back were two spear-like weapons constructed of dark wood, long feathers covered in blood protruding from the gaping holes that appeared from nothing. The weight of the spears pulled him towards the ground. Chaos rang all around them, yet Hinapouri was deathly still as she discarded the skewered dead at her feet.

The veil entry reopened with a hitch in power in the field. Veata stepped through, raising the threat level as the Puppeteer still controlled her. "More trouble?" The Puppeteer's possessing influence spoke through Veata's thin lips in mock concern, her wrinkled hands folded on her cane with ease.

I didn't know if they would kill her and didn't care. The Raddies' leader was right. I would relish someone slitting my throat right now. Get it done already. Time crawled. I was losing the strength to hold on and suspected it was Donovan's strength doing the heavy lifting for the both of us. I vomited, my crushed throat closing in protest. Strings of blood and vomit hung from my lips as I choked into the wind and contemplated passing out before I suffocated on my own bodily fluids.

The Apporter resurfaced. His bald head and surprise presence had the enemy trying to drag me away, causing them to drop me again. Baldy scooped me up and suddenly we were next to Donovan, freaking out his captures who also dropped him and backed off. The Apporter took his chance to zip out of the field.

A wash of safety was the last sensation to cross the connection with Donovan, coupled with permission to let go and embrace the painless darkness.

———

Crust across my eyelashes glued my lids shut. A shift in position bloomed a deep ache in every muscle. Far worse than anything I had felt before. Maybe not the ride through the veil, but that was a quick, crushing blow. This ache lingered. I couldn't process anything else besides discomfort and a pounding headache, like my brain was trying to escape my skull to save itself from the agony. Squeezing my head like a vice in the fetal position, did fuck all to help. Neither did moaning and rocking. Softness and a rustle of fabric below me meant I was no longer on the grass in the field. A vague memory of the Apporter rescuing me came to mind.

I froze at movement beside me. I couldn't open my eyes to see if it was a friendly face or the semi-familiar guise of an enemy. More movement and my name was spoken, sounding distorted through my ears. The rustling next to me was more like a quick thrash. The pressure in my ear was odd, but it wasn't my ear. The pressure against my eyes wasn't my eyes. Fear was mine, and yet not mine. These sensations were making things worse for my pounding head, my stomach close to heaving again. Remembering how well that went over in the field, I refused to throw up, hoping to avoid choking on vomit for the second time today. Was it still today?

I rubbed my left eye and felt eyelashes pluck out with whatever crust kept them shut. Squinting through one eye that burned the moment I peeled it open, I peeked beside me and gasped before realizing I was looking at Donovan. Blood was caked all over his face, dried over from his eyes and nose, and streaked across his cheeks. He was shoving a finger into his ear canal to get the dried blood out.

Around us was a small, dark bedroom. Muted moonlight filtered through a small curtained window. Accessing any source of power was out of the question or I figured Donovan would have healed us by now. I reached to grab his arm, so he would stop jabbing his clogged ear and was hit with a hammer blow to the skull as a vision took him over. I pulled away, swooning with the pain, then decided it was our way out of this until we could heal.

I grabbed him again, this time holding on, even when my stomach wrenched and threatened to add to the problem. Whatever images attacked Donovan's scrambling brain were powerful, and his filter to take it in with control was obliterated. His anguish flowed from him into me and back again, accelerating as I refused to let go until it gave me what I needed. We fell back into the blissful, painless darkness.

———

Pressure dug at my eyelids. I couldn't get away from it. I flailed and pawed at whatever I could hit, feeling the weight of whoever straddled atop me. My limbs didn't have the energy to overpower whoever was now yelling at me. Muffled words were nonsense in my clogged ears, even when they moved close enough to my face to feel hot breath on my neck, followed by hands holding me down by my shoulders.

I fluttered my eyes open. Tickling debris fell onto my cheeks. I shook my head and Donovan sat up and away, letting go of my shoulders so I could rub my face. I dislodged more tickling debris, my face covered in what I assumed was blood, judging by the reddish-black streaks still all over Donovan's skin.

He rolled onto his back in the small bed we laid on. I scraped my hands over my face knowing I wasn't getting it all. Light filtered through the thin drapes on the window, hours later than the last time I had woken up. I could finally see the room around us in full. The bed we were on was old. Not in a steal from an unawares old-lady yard sale antique way, just old. The mattress sagging though the brass frame was rigid. The walls were layered with yellowed wallpaper, covered in illustrated horses and cowboys frozen in action poses. A small dresser with four drawers stood in the corner, a trunk on the opposite wall, again small, hiding its contents. From the look of things, we were in a kid's room. Dust covered every surface, obscuring faces in hung photos too thickly to identify which kid.

"Where are we?" My voice was still distorted. I stuck my finger in one ear and then the other, finding more dried blood to dislodge.

Donovan rolled his shoulders and cracked his neck, relief echoed in my bones. "No idea."

For all we knew we were in a place the Puppeteer commandeered and they were waiting downstairs for us to emerge. I remembered the Apporter snatching us away, but once we passed out, anything could have happened.

Donovan went for the door. I followed. He turned the knob as a test. We weren't locked in. He opened the door an inch to peer out. Before we could find out more, heavy footsteps on wooden floorboards, as well as a growing shadow, crossed towards the door. I stifled a gasp. Donovan closed the door back to the inch it was cracked, but we knew we had been caught.

"You can come out." Ranlyn's apathetic voice became distant with his footsteps.

Exhaling the tension, I was elated to be with someone safe. I didn't have the strength to execute an escape plan if trapped by our enemies. I would have tried, but the protests in my knees—and every other joint in my body—would have won out quickly. We still weren't fully healed.

We emerged from the small room into a thin hallway, scattered with a handful of closed doors leading from it. Reaching a stairway, the hallway continued ahead of us and passed an overlook railing that separated more doors on the other side of an identical hallway as the one we came from. The top of the stairs gave a view of the entire first floor. The home was much cleaner and modernized than the room we were left in led us to believe. Beige walls with white lower wainscoting and thin crown moulding bordered the ceilings. An open-concept kitchen was right off the entrance, while the centre held the living room. A fireplace crackling with lit logs, filling the place with a homey aroma. Plaid couches in front of the fire created the perfect place to relax on a chilly night. In between them, in place of a coffee table, lay Kim's and Miklos's inert bodies.

I bounded down the stairs two at a time, my aching body forgotten, Donovan running into me when I stopped at Kim's feet.

"What?" he asked.

"I—I—" I didn't know what I was seeing.

Ranlyn came up behind us. Hinapouri, seated on one of the couches, was uninterested in our presence. Instead, she sat braiding her hair. Something out of context, I hoped, not wanting to think she was so cold to the bodies lying before her.

"What do you see?" Ranlyn asked.

"Their soul glows are wrong. She's too bright, he's not bright enough. Maybe she accidently absorbed some of his power when going through the veil?"

"Wishful," Hinapouri said as her attention never left her hair as she braided over one shoulder.

Ranlyn sat on the couch facing Hinapouri. "Jumping the veil as we do is allowed due to our given right as Elders of the Mother Coven. Pulling through another, especially one in a grave condition, is tricky because it involves a level of shared existence. Your Soul Seeing proves what we've only previously speculated."

"The veil made them one," Hinapouri said. "Coming back, their souls did not return to their rightful bodies."

"He's inside of her?" I said, my voice too high.

Hinapouri actually chuckled. "Only particles. And she in him."

"Wooow," Donovan drew out the word. "Puts a whole new twist on gettin' it in." I spun in a reactionary strike, hitting Donovan in the chest with a hallow *thwump*. "Come on. He's inside her."

"Shut your face."

"This may seem worthy of humour, but I assure you, Donovan, their current dislocated state is serious."

"I'm aware, thanks."

"Now what? You can't leave my best friend's soul or power or whatever it is, fucked up and in someone else. I don't care that it's an Elder."

Ranlyn stood, paced a few steps. "I am not sure this can be undone."

I stared at Ranlyn, he reluctantly met my gaze.

Most aspects of my life were messed up. My love life was a joke, my family life subpar compared to before I was a Magic, my abilities were flimsy against the multiple enemies we faced, and both my Covens were in the process of pulling themselves together after a time of great loss. Kim was my lifeline in all the messed-up factors of life. She was there for everything, was my Sect Leader and my best friend. No. This had to be undone. I wouldn't let Ranlyn or anyone else tell me different. Kim had saved me enough times.

It was time to save her.

Sign-up and stay current on book cover reveals, sales, giveaways, and more with S.J.'s newsletter! http://www.sjcairns.com/newsletter-sign-up/

Read on for DISTRACTION, SOUL SEER CHRONICLES, BOOK 4 teaser.

DISTRACTION TEASER

Distraction, Soul Seer Chronicles, Book 4

Family is supposed to protect you, not hunt you down.

The Mother Coven isn't blood, but they've lost enough members to band together in the deadliest time for Magics in countless years since the Puppeteer decided he had unfinished business—hunting down every last remaining Magic in our bloodline.

But the Puppeteer isn't the only one trying to end us.

The pressures of war shift us all into combat mode. I'm an emotional wreck trying to process layers of family secrets, developing both sets of my powers, and trying to navigate what my heart truly wants.

Hiding out shut down any hope of preserving a normal life. My psych degree falls further away, as does maintaining non-magic friendships, or even a crappy job.

Sacrifices for victory are expected. No one asked for this, and nothing prepared us for what we still needed to lose in order to win.

ABOUT THE AUTHOR

S.J. Cairns creates paranormal romance fantasy from her hometown in Southern Ontario, Canada. When S.J is not plugging away at her laptop on her comfy couch, you can find her chasing around her two-year-old daughter alongside her husband of twenty-one years or working in true chaos at the local women and family's homeless shelters and an anti-human trafficking safe house.

Website: www.sjcairns.com
Facebook: www.facebook.com/SJCairnsauthor
Twitter: www.twitter.com/SamiJoCairns
Email: samijocairns@gmail.com

www.ingramcontent.com/pod-product-compliance
Lightning Source LLC
Chambersburg PA
CBHW051457030726

47592CB00006B/1975